Quest for the Lost Relic

Welcome to Quest for the Lost Relic, the third thrilling installment in the saga of Jedidiah Davenport and his ever-expanding world of adventure, ingenuity, and daring.

Our resilient protagonist, Jedidiah Davenport, is no stranger to challenges, but this time, the stakes are even higher than ever. From the treacherous depths of a ravine to the shadowy corners of Automaton Alley, Jedidiah and his companions face foes unlike anything they've encountered before. The quest for a mysterious artifact, the Chronomechanism, sets them on a journey greater than any they've experienced before. Along the way, alliances are tested, secrets are unearthed, and the very fabric of reality hangs by a thread.

Quest for the Lost Relic brings back beloved characters such as the eccentric genius Phineas B. Hargroves, the steadfast Matthew Colton, and the enigmatic Lady Seraphina Blackwood. New faces and fresh challenges add depth and intrigue, while steampunk marvels like airships, automatons, and futuristic weapons elevate the adventure to an epic scale. The vibrant world of the series expands further, transporting readers from the gritty alleys of Toronto to the windswept cliffs of Octopus Island.

At its heart, this novel explores the timeless struggle between ambition and morality, power and responsibility. As Jedidiah and his allies race against time to prevent reality from being reshaped to benefit personal greed. The narrative weaves a rich tapestry of action, emotion, and thought-provoking dilemmas, all set against a backdrop of breathtaking steampunk innovation.

Quest for the Lost Relic invites you to journey deeper into a world where the extraordinary becomes ordinary and the impossible feels tantalizingly within reach. With its fast-paced plot, richly drawn characters, and imaginative twists, this book promises an unforgettable ride.

Buckle up, dear reader. The quest awaits, and the adventure is just beginning.

The ancient relic protected for
centuries by a secret order.

Quest for the Lost Relic

A Jedidiah Davenport Adventure

BY PAUL EDWARD TURNER

Copyright Notice

Quest for the Lost Relic a novel by Paul Edward Turner

© 2025 Paul Edward Turner

ISBN 979-8-9924477-0-5 (paperback)

www.pauledwardturner.com

This is a work of fiction. Names, characters, businesses, places, events, and incidents are either the products of the author's imagination or used in a fictitious manner. Any resemblance to actual persons, living or dead, or actual events is purely coincidental.

Cover Design by: Paul Edward Turner

First Edition: March 2025

Contents

Chapter		Page

CHAPTER I

The Interrupted Journey

The rhythmic chugging and hiss of the steam engine filled the air, a soothing backdrop as Jedidiah Davenport studied the mysterious letter he had received over a week ago. In his other hand, he clutched the pocket watch that had accompanied it. Beside him, Phineas B. Hargroves fiddled with a small mechanical device, his fingers moving with practiced precision.

Across from them, Matthew Colton held a folded newspaper. He glanced up from the headlines to watch the countryside blur into a tapestry of green and gold.

Without warning, the D.&R.W. Railroad train lurched violently, its wheels screeching as it ground to a halt. Matthew's hand instinctively went to the revolver at his hip just as the car door burst open. Four masked men stormed in, brandishing glowing green weapons that looked unsettlingly futuristic.

"Hands up, and nobody gets hurt!" the leader barked, his voice rough and commanding.

Jedidiah exchanged a quick glance with Phineas. They raised their hands slowly, gauging their attackers.

As the men, their faces obscured by bandanas tied in classic outlaw fashion, moved leisurely down the aisle, Davenport's mind raced back to the events of the previous day, when everything had seemed so ordinary...

****

Twenty-four hours earlier, at Davenport Ranch, on the crisp morning of October 4th, 1881, Jedidiah, Phineas, and Matthew prepared for the opening ceremony of Spoon Fork's new train station. The conflict with Elijah Perkins, the railroad's disgraced former executive, was finally behind them, and this event marked a fresh start for both Jedidiah and the town.

Phineas was particularly grumpy as he packed his belongings. "I still can't believe I'm going on this trip," he grumbled to Agatha Porter, Jedidiah's stern but matronly housekeeper.

Agatha adjusted the bun on top of her head and asked, "Aren't you looking forward to the trip at all?"

Phineas shrugged. "If Jed hadn't insisted that I

come along, I'd be staying here, working on my experiments and continuing the repairs to the Phoenix."

Pat Bennington, hearing the conversation, chuckled and joined in. "Jed insisted? That's funny. The way I remember it was you who insisted on going with them!"

Phineas shot him a look. "That's not how I remember it!"

Pat laughed heartily. "Of course not, Hargy. But we all know you couldn't bear to miss out on the adventure."

"That's Hargroves..." Phineas squinted his eyes with frustration and said, "I know by now you're doing this on purpose!"

"Me?" Pat tried to act innocent. "Why, I have no idea what you mean!"

Agatha patted Hargroves on the shoulder. "Just enjoy the trip, Professor. It'll be good for you to get away for a while."

Phineas sighed but couldn't help but smile a little. "Fine, fine. But don't expect me to like it."

As he stepped toward the door, he paused to mutter, "At least this trip will give Pat time to finally deal with the mice issue in the barn like he's been promising for months. Although I could have invented a gadget that would've solved the problem weeks ago."

Pat grinned as he called over his shoulder, "No

need for your gizmos, Hargy. I've got it handled."

Phineas frowned, his voice rising slightly. "Handled? Ha! The only thing you've got handled is your knife and fork at dinner!"

Pat waved him off. "Trust me, you'll come back to a mouse-free barn, no gadgets required."

Shaking his head in irritation, Phineas muttered under his breath, "Luddite…" before walking out and joining Jedidiah and Matthew outside.

"Got everything we need?" Jedidiah asked, tossing his luggage into the rear of the wagon.

"All set," Phineas replied, as he carefully placed his bag in, it clinking with the weight of a few of his latest inventions.

Matthew checked his suitcases one last time. "Let's get going. We don't want to be late."

They rode into town, the air thick with anticipation for the day's grand events.

Spoon Fork was alive with excitement as the new train station stood proudly, a testament to progress and prosperity. Built from red brick and adorned with ornate wrought-iron details, the station's grand clock tower soared above the town, its polished face gleaming in the sunlight. A wide, wooden platform extended along the tracks, bustling with townsfolk eager to witness the inaugural ceremony.

Jedidiah dismounted and looked around, spotting familiar faces in the crowd. Railroad officials and local dignitaries took turns at the podium, extolling the virtues of the new rail line and its promise for the future.

The mayor of Spoon Fork then took the stage, his voice booming through the crowd. "Ladies and gentlemen, it is my great pleasure to introduce the president of the D.&R.W. Railroad, Mr. Samuel Harris!"

Samuel Harris, a distinguished-looking man with silver hair and a confident demeanor, stepped up to the podium. "Thank you, Mayor Carter. It's an honor to be here on this momentous occasion," he began. "Today marks the beginning of a new era for Spoon Fork and the surrounding areas. This railroad will bring prosperity, connect communities, and open up new opportunities for everyone."

He paused, his gaze sweeping over the crowd before continuing. "But before we move forward, we must acknowledge the past. I want to publicly apologize for the troubles caused by our former executive, Elijah Perkins. His actions, as many of you know, brought conflict and hardship, particularly to one of the valley's most esteemed citizens, Mr. Jedidiah Davenport."

Harris gestured for Jedidiah to join him at the podium. "Jedidiah, your perseverance and integrity through those trying times were commendable. For those of you who may not be familiar, Mr. Perkins engaged in some underhanded tactics and attempted to acquire Mr. Davenport's land by, shall we say, less than honest means. He sabotaged his operations and discredited his character in his ruthless pursuit of profit. However, Jedidiah stood firm, exposing Perkins' corruption and helping to bring him to justice."

The crowd murmured, some nodding in recognition, others hearing the story for the first time.

"We are truly sorry for the troubles you endured, and I am personally glad to see you here today as one of our first passengers on this maiden journey," Harris continued.

The crowd erupted in applause as Jedidiah shook Harris' hand. Among them, Luther Caldwell, the savvy owner of The Rusty Nail saloon, clapped enthusiastically. Jacob Harrington, the town's steadfast blacksmith, offered a firm nod of approval. Horace McKinley, the meticulous operator of the telegraph office, adjusted his spectacles with a small smile. Henry Porter, owner of the general store, exchanged a pleasant smile with Gideon Stewart, proprietor of the competing shop across town.

"Thank you, Mr. Harris," Jedidiah said with a wry smile. "It's good to see the railroad moving in the right direction." He paused for effect before adding, "Away from my property!"

The crowd erupted into hearty laughter.

Harris smiled warmly. "We're committed to ensuring the past mistakes are not repeated and that our railroad serves the community as it was always intended to."

With the formalities concluded, Harris stepped down, and the crowd's applause slowly died out.

After the speeches, Jedidiah began to mingle with the crowd. Matthew made his way toward the freight office to check in on Tom Miller, who was set to oversee operations for the next few days.

Meanwhile, Phineas engaged in an animated discussion with anyone who would listen about how airships would someday render railroads obsolete, gesturing dramatically as he expounded on the inefficiencies of ground-bound travel.

Jedidiah nodded along absentmindedly, his mind preoccupied with the enigmatic package he'd received from New York weeks ago and the unsettling silence that had followed its arrival.

Making his way through the bustling crowd, exchanging pleasantries and catching up with familiar faces, Jedidiah eventually stepped into one of the town's general stores. The familiar jingle of the bell above the door announced his arrival.

"Jed, it's good to see you!" Henry Porter greeted him warmly.

"You too," The young entrepreneur replied. "I've been so busy the last few weeks I haven't had much of a chance to stop in for supplies." He paused to glance around at the throng of people shopping in his friend's store. "Looks like you haven't been hurting for business, I see."

"It's been busier than ever!" Henry exclaimed. "And it's all thanks to the railroad. This is going to change everything. I'm glad everything worked out for both you and the town!"

"So am I," Davenport laughed. "I..."

"Oops, sorry, Jed," the store owner suddenly cut him short as he spotted his clerk getting overwhelmed with people trying to pay for their goods. "I've got to go help, but I'll catch up with you later!"

After leaving Henry Porter, Jedidiah encountered Gideon Stewart, who was chatting with a few townsfolk in front of his business. "Jed!" he shouted excitedly. "Isn't this something! Today's just the opening day and already there's more business than Hank and I either one can handle!"

"Sounds like someone needs to open a third general store," Jedidiah said with a smile.

"Well now, let's not get carried away," Gideon almost panicked at the thought of a third business opening and competing with him for customers. After seeing the smile on Davenport's face he relaxed and clapped him on the shoulder. "Very funny, but there's some things we just don't joke about!"

"Understood!" Jedidiah chuckled as he moved down the street. He ran into Luther Caldwell, who was setting up a small stand with refreshments from The Rusty Nail.

"Jedidiah, you should try our new brew. It's been a hit with everyone." Luther held out a glass. "It's made from ginger root."

"Ginger root?" Jedidiah repeated. He then made an odd face as he spotted a woman handing her two young children each a glass.

"It's nonalcoholic!" Luther burst out laughing as he explained to Davenport. "Go ahead, try some."

"Maybe later, Luther. I've got to meet back up with Mr. Harris. He has my train tickets," Jedidiah said, chuckling.

As he continued making his way towards the President of the D.&R.W. Railroad, he found himself speaking with Horace McKinley, who was busy explaining the new telegraph system Jedidiah had invented to an interested group of townsfolk. "Jed, it's good to see you here. The equipment you sent over is all set up and ready for business."

"Good, Horace. I'm glad everyone in the telegraph company accepted my designs," Jedidiah replied, speaking above the bustling activity around him.

"Well you are one of the largest shareholders in the company," McKinley laughed. "I think it was a pretty safe bet they were going to accept your idea."

"I wouldn't have taken advantage of that," Jedidiah replied. "But I do think my invention will revolutionize the telegraph industry as we know it."

"It's already made my job easier!" Horace admitted with a warm smile.

Jedidiah excused himself as he spotted Samuel Harris and Mayor Benjamin Carter engaged in an animated discussion near the station's entrance. As he approached, Harris turned and greeted him with a broad smile.

"Jedidiah, there you are! I was wondering where you disappeared to," Harris said, extending his hand.

"Mr. Harris, Mayor Carter," Jedidiah nodded to both men as he shook Harris' hand.

"Jedidiah, we're truly honored to have you aboard our inaugural journey," the mayor added. "Your presence here is a testament to the progress we've made and will continue to make in the future."

"Thank you, Mayor. It's an honor to be part of this historic event," Jedidiah replied.

Harris handed Davenport an envelope. "Here are your tickets. We've reserved a private sleeping compartment for you and two berths for your friends as a gesture of our appreciation."

"Thank you, Mr. Harris. That's very generous of

you," Jedidiah said as he accepted the envelope.

The mayor then gestured towards the train. "We should get aboard now. We'll be departing soon, and we don't want to be standing on the platform when it does."

"You're going too, Mayor?" Jedidiah seemed surprised.

"Wouldn't miss it for the world!" Mayor Carter laughed heartily as he clapped him on the back.

As the Mayor walked away, Harris continued to speak with Jedidiah. "I wanted to thank you once again for all you've done. If it hadn't been for you, we would have never known the kind of man we had in our employment. Elijah Perkins is a crook and deserves everything he got."

"Thank you, Mr. Harris. It means a lot to hear you say that," Jedidiah replied sincerely.

After boarding the train, Harris guided the young entrepreneur to his compartment. "I hope you find everything to your satisfaction. If there's anything you need, please don't hesitate to let us know."

"I'm sure I'll be just fine," Jedidiah assured him.

Mr. Harris stepped off the train to give one last speech before they began their departure. He climbed onto a small platform near the front of the station, where the mayor and other officials stood.

The train station buzzed with energy and anticipation. Families clustered together, chatting enthusiastically, while children darted between them, their laughter ringing above the murmur of the crowd. The wide, wooden platform that stretched alongside the tracks was a hive of activity, with townsfolk eager to witness the train's historic journey.

The train itself was a magnificent sight. Painted in a rich emerald green with elegant gold accents, it gleamed under the sunlight. The locomotive, a powerful steam engine, was a testament to modern engineering, emitting rhythmic puffs of steam as if eager to start the trip. Behind it, was a series of well-appointed cars, including lavish passenger coaches, sophisticated dining cars, and exclusive compartments for esteemed guests.

After checking in on Tom Miller at the freight office, Matthew Colton joined Phineas B. Hagroves on the platform. The eccentric older man was completely engrossed in the mechanical wonder before them. Despite his earlier grumblings, Phineas couldn't hide his fascination with the intricate workings of the train, closely inspecting the wheels and pistons.

"Ladies and gentlemen," Harris began, his voice carrying over the crowd, "once again I want to thank all of you for being here to celebrate this historic moment. The journey we embark on today symbolizes more than just the completion of a railroad line. It represents the hard work, dedication, and unity of our community. This train will connect us to new opportunities, bring prosperity, and foster growth. We are embarking on a journey that will shape our future for generations to come."

The crowd erupted in applause, cheering, and waving as Harris continued. "Now, without further ado, our adventure begins. Next stop St. Louis!"

Once the applause died down, Harris moved aside as the conductor stepped forward and shouted, "All aboard!"

Phineas and Matthew quickly spotted Jedidiah at the side of the train. He was standing on the steps.

"Quite the send-off," Phineas remarked after they had joined him.

"Indeed," Jedidiah replied as he glanced back at the ground just before they stepped inside and began making their way through the ornately decorated passenger car. The interior was luxurious, with plush seats upholstered in rich fabrics, polished wood paneling, and brass fixtures that gleamed in the light.

As the train prepared to depart, a sharp whistle pierced the air, signaling the conductor's final call. Families and well-wishers waved from the platform, retreating to a safe distance as the train's engine emitted a powerful hiss of steam. The once-bustling boardwalk quickly emptied, leaving only the rhythmic clatter of the locomotive as it began its journey.

As the train began to pull away, Jedidiah handed each of his companions their tickets. Although he had been assigned a private sleeping compartment, he insisted that Phineas take it, assuring him that he would be perfectly fine sleeping in one of the berths.

The eccentric older man accepted it without hesitation and scoffed. "I still think it's absurd to travel by train when an airship could get us there in half the time and twice the style."

Jedidiah smiled. "It'll be a nice change of pace. Besides, we'll only be gone for a few days."

"I think it's exciting, and we could all use a few days away from the ranch and the freight office," Matthew said, his tone full of anticipation for the adventure ahead.

"My dear boy," Phineas B. Hargroves said, turning to Colton with a raised brow, "you do realize it's only been sixteen days since we returned from that two-week air race, don't you?"

"Exactly!" Matthew exclaimed. "We're due for a vacation!" Everyone laughed heartily and then found their way to the passenger car.

The train ride started uneventfully, the rhythmic motion and familiar sounds lulling them into a sense of security. As the evening wore on, they settled in for the night.

The once-bustling boardwalk quickly emptied, leaving only the rhythmic clatter of the locomotive as it began its journey.

The train rocked gently as it sped along the tracks, the rhythmic clatter of wheels against the rails almost hypnotic. Jedidiah lay in his berth, the pocket watch, letter, and torn message resting on the mattress beside him. His mind was racing with so many unanswered questions.

The next morning, the train continued its journey, gliding through picturesque landscapes. Jedidiah, Matthew, and Phineas were already awake and back in the passenger car, each absorbed in their own pursuits.

Matthew sat reading a newspaper. "Did either of you see this article?" he asked, his voice cutting through the quiet hum of the train.

Jedidiah glanced up briefly, his attention drawn to the back page of the paper. An advertisement caught his eye: "Calling All Inventors! A Competition for Steam-Powered Runabouts – Summer 1882, Niagara Falls." He raised a brow and briefly muttered about it sounding like an interesting concept, his focus shifting back to the pocket watch and letter in his hands.

"Not the ad," Matthew said, noticing Jedidiah's distraction. "This." He turned the paper around and tapped a headline that read, "Clockwork Conqueror Strikes Again."

Phineas looked up from the small mechanical device he was adjusting, his eyes narrowing. "Clockwork Conqueror? What sort of absurd moniker is that?"

"Apparently, he's some mastermind suspected to be behind a series of high-profile thefts," Matthew explained. "This article claims he's targeting items with unique designs or historical value. They even think he was behind the robbery at the British Museum."

"That's nice," Jedidiah replied absentmindedly, his thoughts clearly elsewhere.

"The authorities think he's using advanced technology to pull off these heists."

"Probably overblown nonsense," Phineas scoffed, turning his attention back to his own invention resting on his lap.

Matthew shrugged, folding the paper. "I thought it was interesting." He glanced out the window and began watching the scenery.

"Yes, yes." Professor Hargroves mumbled to himself. "Very interesting."

It was at this time that the train suddenly lurched violently. Moments later, the car door burst open, and four men wearing bandanas for masks stormed in, their eerie weapons glowing an unearthly green.

"Hands up, and nobody gets hurt!" the leader of the group of villains barked.

****

There was a collective gasp from the passengers as the notorious outlaws moved down the aisle, collecting valuables from the terrified passengers. When they reached Jedidiah's group, Matthew's eyes narrowed. In a split-second decision, he drew his revolver and trained it on the leader.

Unfortunately, one of the other bandits whirled around, aimed his weapon at the young man, and without hesitation fired!

CHAPTER II

Ray of Trouble

A beam of green light emitted from the strange weapon and struck Matthew Colton. His entire body lit up in the same color as the ray. Suddenly, he froze in his tracks, completely paralyzed and unable to move with his revolver still drawn.

"Matt!" Jedidiah shouted as he instinctively tried to bound to his feet, but the man who had just fired turned the emitter towards him.

The leader stepped closer. "Let's not have any more heroes, shall we?" He reached over and removed the gun from Matthew's hand and stuck it into his own belt loop.

With terror in his eyes, Jedidiah screamed out, "What have you done to him?"

"My dear boy, calm yourself," Professor Hargroves exclaimed as he placed a hand on Davenport's shoulder. "I suspect that the effects are only temporary!" He glanced at the armed men and added, "I suggest we do as they say."

As Phineas tried to calm his young friend, the other two men held up large burlap bags and demanded that everyone empty their belongings into them. Each sack had the name of the D.&R.W. Railroad printed on the side.

Outside the windows, the scenery revealed the train's precarious position. The locomotive had halted on a narrow stretch of track clinging to the side of a steep hillside. Below, a ravine yawned wide, its jagged rocks and tangled underbrush creating a treacherous descent to the winding river far beneath. The train sat perched uneasily on the sloped terrain, its iron wheels barely gripping the rails, as though the entire vehicle were holding its breath.

Jedidiah's eyes darted to the steep incline outside, unease settling in his chest. They were in a vulnerable position. This part of the track was never designed for the train to stop on. Any sudden movement, any shake or tremor, and the train could lose its delicate balance.

The gang leader seemed to realize it too. His eyes flickered briefly to the window before snapping back to Jedidiah, a sly grin spreading across his face.

He turned back and said, "Your friend is fine, but you won't be unless you listen to this old codger's advice!"

The young entrepreneur's mind raced as he calculated the odds. Seeing no other option, he opened his pocketbook and removed the few hundred dollars he was traveling with.

"The watch too!" the fiend demanded as he reached over and snatched the decorative timepiece with the emerald stone from Jedidiah's pocket. He then turned toward Phineas, shouting, "That machine as well, Mr. Twain!"

"Twain?" Phineas seemed slightly confused.

"Come on, old timer," the man laughed. "I know you can afford it, with all the money you've made from your books and newspaper articles."

"Do you by any chance think I'm the author, Mark Twain?" Professor Hargroves asked as he began to catch on.

"You do bear a striking resemblance to him," Jedidiah remarked casually.

"The name happens to be Hargroves! Professor Phineas B. Hargroves to be exact!" Phineas stormed.

"Listen, Gramps," the leader of the hold-up men began losing his patience. "I don't care what you call yourself, just put that contraption into this bag!" He shoved the burlap sack into his face.

"Old codger... old timer... Gramps..." The eccentric older man had just about had enough and started to stand to his feet. Just as he did, he found himself looking down the barrel of another ray gun.

Phineas furrowed his brow and said, "My good man, you have the advantage for now but perhaps we'll meet again at another time in another place." With that said, he reluctantly lifted the device he had been working on and gently let it fall into the open bag.

Glancing over at Matthew Colton, who was still frozen in position, the leader of the gang instructed Jedidiah and Phineas to go through his pockets and empty his valuables into the sack with the others. They exchanged a knowing glance before reluctantly doing as instructed.

After this, the leader turned to one of his men and ordered him to search the baggage car. He then turned to the two men standing closest to him and jerked his thumb toward the front of the train.

"You two, head to the private car," he ordered curtly. "The mayor and that railroad president are up there. Make sure you give them a proper welcome before you clean out the safe."

The two outlaws nodded sharply. "On it, boss," one of them replied with a wicked grin.

They moved through the train, stepping out onto the small platform between cars, then pushed open the door to the next passenger car. Carefully, they made their way forward, stopping just outside the private compartment. One of the men rapped sharply on the door with the butt of his weapon.

"Who's there?" a voice demanded from within.

It was Mayor Carter's unmistakable tone—booming and authoritative, yet with a tinge of unease.

"Railway security," the outlaw replied with a mocking sneer, his eyes glinting maliciously beneath his mask. "There's been a… disturbance. Open up."

Mayor Carter hesitated, his hand hovering over the lock. He glanced at Samuel Harris, who frowned deeply.

"Railway security?" Harris muttered, his tone laced with suspicion. "There's no railway security on this train."

The mayor faltered, his gaze darting between Harris and the door. "Then who—?"

The door suddenly burst open, cutting off the mayor's question. The two outlaws stormed in, their weapons raised and glowing with an eerie green light.

"What is the meaning of this?" Harris demanded, his voice steady but edged with frustration. "Who are you, and what are you doing on my train?"

"Just a little business transaction," the nearest outlaw sneered, ignoring the president's indignation. "Now, empty your pockets and step aside. We know there's a safe in here, and you're going to open it."

Harris' jaw tightened, but he reluctantly moved towards the safe embedded in the wall of the luxurious compartment. His fingers fumbled with the combination lock, the metallic clicks echoing in the otherwise silent car. Mayor Carter clenched his fists, his face flushed with anger as he glared at the intruders.

"Outrageous!" he spat. "You won't get away with this!"

"Oh, I think we will," the outlaw holding one of the paralyzing ray guns replied coolly. "Now, hurry it up, Mr. Harris. We haven't got all day."

With a final click, the safe door swung open, revealing stacks of documents, a few velvet pouches, and a small pile of cash. The outlaw's eyes gleamed as he shoved the contents into a large bag.

"Pleasure doing business with you," he said with a mock bow, backing towards the door. "Enjoy the rest of your trip—what's left of it."

He nodded to his companion, who fired his weapon at the mayor. Mayor Carter froze instantly in his tracks.

Harris' jaw went slack, but he didn't move, his gaze fixed on the petrified politician. "What have you done to him?"

"Don't worry about it," the outlaw replied with a grin. "But I'd suggest you stay put. Wouldn't want you going anywhere now, would we?"

With that, he fired the green ray at him. Harris' body glowed, and then he too froze in his tracks.

Back in the passenger car, the leader turned his back on Davenport and Hargroves as he glanced out at the platform between the cars. That's when Phineas made his move. With a flick of his wrist, he pulled a small, spring-loaded device from his sleeve—a gadget of his own invention. With a soft click, a tiny dart shot out and embedded itself into the back of the leader's neck.

The man grunted as he reached back, feeling for the dart. Suddenly, his body went limp, and his weapon slipped from his grasp as he collapsed to the floor. The ray gun slid beneath Matthew's seat. Jedidiah dove forward, his body hitting the ground with a thud, but Matthew's legs blocked his path, keeping the weapon just out of reach.

"Phineas, get him out of this trance!" Jedidiah ordered as he continued to reach for the weapon with his fingertips.

Phineas moved quickly to Matthew's side, examining the effects of the paralysis. He began by gently patting Matthew's wrists, then slapped his cheeks, gradually increasing the intensity. As time was running out before the other men returned, Phineas resorted to more aggressive slaps, his palm making loud smacks that echoed through the car.

Jedidiah stood and stared incredulously. "Phineas! What are you doing?"

"I'm doing what you asked me to do!" Professor Hargroves huffed, not pausing his flurry of slaps.

"I asked you to work Matt over?" Jedidiah replied, raising an eyebrow.

"I'm trying to bring him around!"

"With your fists?"

"I'm using an open palm, not my fists!" Phineas countered defensively, delivering one final slap for good measure.

"Why don't you just club him with a blackjack while you're at it?"

Phineas paused as if genuinely considering the suggestion. "That's just ridiculous! Besides, my blackjack is back on the Icarus!"

Jedidiah threw up his hands in exasperation. "Can you not try using a more scientific way to bring him around?"

"You'll have to excuse me if I don't carry a full laboratory complete with test tubes in my coat pocket!" The older man snapped.

Jedidiah rubbed his temples. "Fine. Just help me pick him up and lay him across the seats so I can grab that weapon."

Phineas let out a sigh. "You know, I'm a scientist, not a circus strongman!"

"What does that have to do with..." Davenport cut his sentence short as he bent down and wrapped his arms around his friend's legs. "Just lean him back and help me lift!"

Phineas grumbled but complied, muttering, "Remind me next time to bring smelling salts... or maybe a mild electrical charge…"

Just as they began to pick Matthew Colton up and lay him gently across the seats, the rest of the gang came bursting back into the car.

"What's going on!" one of the masked men shouted, his gaze immediately locking onto the prone figure of their leader lying on the floor.

"Boss!" another man cried, rushing over to him. "What happened?"

The gang members crowded around their unconscious leader, confusion and anger flashing in their eyes. One of the men spun on his heel to glare at Jedidiah and Phineas.

"You two!" he barked, raising his ray gun threateningly. "What did you do to him?"

Feigning surrender, Phineas raised one hand with a sheepish smile, nearly dropping Matthew in the process. "Oh, him? He, uh… just needed a little nap, that's all. Too much excitement for one day, I suppose."

"Cut the nonsense!" another thug snarled, his hand trembling as he kept his weapon aimed at him. "He's out cold! What did you use? Is he dead?"

"No, no, of course not!" Phineas assured, shaking his head vigorously. "He'll be back to his charming, villainous self in no time. Just a minor inconvenience, really."

One of the men reached down, feeling his

leader's pulse, and nodded slowly. "He's alive, but…" He frowned, noticing the dart sticking out of his neck. "What's this?"

"Just a little sedative," Phineas explained nonchalantly as if discussing tea. "I'd say he'll be out for, oh, about another hour or so."

The gang members looked at each other, shock giving way to fury.

"You think you can stand there calm as you please after knocking our boss out?" the nearest thug growled, stepping closer.

With his arms still wrapped around Matthew's legs, Jedidiah's eyes darted to the ray gun lying on the floor under the seat. "Now, hold on. Let's all just take a deep breath…"

"I'll show you a deep breath!" The thug aimed the weapon directly at Davenport.

But before he could pull the trigger, the entire train car shuddered violently, a low, piercing hum filling the air. The man's eyes widened as a high-pitched whine, almost like a shriek, reverberated through their bodies. Every person onboard staggered, hands instinctively flying to their ears in an attempt to block out the unbearable noise. Jedidiah and Phineas dropped Matthew onto the seat, and Davenport collapsed into his own chair, clutching the edge as the relentless waves of sound pulsed through his skull. His vision blurred, the air around him vibrating with invisible force, and a wave of nausea hit him like a tidal wave.

"What... what is that?" one of the thugs shouted, his voice drowned out by the overwhelming sound.

Phineas' face twisted in pain as he shouted back, "Ultrasonic disruptor cannon... someone's using an ultrasonic disruptor on us!"

Still grasping his ray gun, the thug doubled over, clutching his head. His fellow outlaws stumbled backward, momentarily disoriented and incapacitated by the unrelenting waves of sound. Around them, the other passengers screamed, clutching their heads as they collapsed into their seats or onto the floor, writhing in agony. Jedidiah gritted his teeth, struggling to stay upright as the car seemed to tilt and sway beneath him.

"Grab the boss! We've got to get out of here!" one of the remaining thugs yelled, his voice strained as he fought through the intense vibrations wracking his body.

They moved with desperation, dragging their unconscious leader off the floor. The sack of loot tumbled from his grasp, but one of the men spotted it and hastily grabbed it. With panicked movements, the remaining gang members fumbled to drag their unconscious leader out of the train car.

Jedidiah tried again to reach for the ray gun, but his vision blurred and his balance faltered under the disruptor's relentless onslaught. All he could do was watch as the outlaws kicked open the door. Their feet tangled as they shoved their way through the exit, barely managing to lift their boss onto a horse before spurring their mounts into a wild, chaotic gallop. They didn't glance back, the disruptor's waves still hammering at their senses, driving them forward in a desperate escape. Their horses thundered down the track, galloping at breakneck speed as if pursued by an unseen force.

Through the haze of pain, Jedidiah managed to witness the sight of them throwing their leader over the saddle of the horse and ride away.

Then, as suddenly as it started, the noise stopped. A silence, almost as oppressive as the sound itself, settled over the train car. Jedidiah, Phineas, and the other passengers took in great, heaving breaths, relief washing over them.

"What just happened?" Jedidiah panted, his gaze turning to Phineas.

Phineas looked just as shaken but managed to straighten up, peering out the window. "I think we're about to find out," he muttered, pointing toward the sky.

Outside, a massive airship loomed, its elegant silhouette a striking contrast against the sky. The airship's sleek, elongated envelope was crafted from a pristine white material, accentuated by delicate blue motifs that swirled along its surface like intricate lacework. The silver bands crisscrossing the envelope gleamed with a polished sheen, reflecting the sunlight in dazzling patterns.

Unlike traditional airships, this one featured a revolutionary propulsion system that combined steam and crystalline energy, allowing it to glide with an elegant grace. Two large, crystal-powered rotors extended from the sides of the gondola, their smooth, quiet hum a testament to the ship's advanced engineering. Beneath the rotors, smaller stabilizer fins adjusted subtly, maintaining perfect balance and control.

The gondola itself was a marvel of modern design—a streamlined, silver structure adorned with the same intricate blue motifs. It featured a row of arched windows along the main deck, each framed in polished brass, allowing a clear view of the airship's interior. A prominent observation deck jutted out from the front, encased in curved glass, providing a commanding view of the world below.

Hanging beneath the gondola was a large emblem—a stylized compass rose intertwined with a crystal coil, symbolizing the ship's mastery over both navigation and energy. Beneath it, the name "Aetherwind" was emblazoned in elegant, sweeping letters, each one outlined in gold.

The entire vessel shimmered with a refined brilliance, exuding an aura of sophistication and power. With a graceful tilt, the Aetherwind began to ascend, its rotors spinning faster as it gained altitude. Even from a distance, the sight of the ship inspired both awe and trepidation, a reminder of the unmatched technology and influence it wielded.

Phineas whispered, his eyes narrowing as he observed the airship in the distance. "Who would use an ultrasonic disruptor cannon on a train? The technology is rare, and not many people have access to it..."

Jedidiah watched as the airship hovered silently for a moment longer, as if surveying the aftermath of its intervention. Then, with a graceful turn, its propellers began to whirr faster.

"Where is it headed?" Jedidiah murmured, unable to tear his eyes away from the magnificent sight.

"Wherever it's going," Phineas replied grimly, "I feel like this won't be the last time we see it."

With that, the Aetherwind soared higher into the sky, disappearing into the distance, leaving behind more questions than answers.

Before either of them could process what had just happened, a sudden thump and a muffled groan snapped their attention back to the train car. Matthew, who had been lying motionless on the seats, jolted awake with a violent start. His body rolled off the seats, crashing to the floor.

"Matt!" Jedidiah exclaimed, rushing over to his friend's side.

Matthew lay there, blinking in confusion as he

The Aetherwind soared higher into the sky,
disappearing into the distance, leaving behind
more questions than answers.

looked around the train car, his eyes wide with disorientation. "What... Where am I?" he muttered, struggling to push himself up.

Phineas hurried over, dropping to one knee beside him. "You're alright, my boy," he assured, his tone a mix of relief and excitement. "Take it easy—don't try to get up too fast."

Matthew grimaced, his muscles aching as if he'd been held in place by iron chains. He rubbed at his arms, feeling the lingering numbness slowly fade away.

"Feels like I was hit by a steam engine..." He paused, glancing around at the disheveled passengers and the empty seats. "What happened? And... where did those men go?" He glanced down at his empty holster. "Where's my six shooter?"

Jedidiah let out a breath he didn't realize he'd been holding. "It's a long story, and one I'm not sure even makes sense. But the important thing is that you're conscious again.'"

Phineas grinned, giving Matthew a gentle pat on the shoulder. "No need to thank me, my dear boy. I just did what was necessary to bring you back around. I'm just glad it didn't take a full laboratory's worth of equipment to rouse you."

Jedidiah gave him a sideways glance and quietly wondered if he had been taking embellishment lessons from Pat Bennington.

Matthew too looked at Phineas skeptically. "Did

what was..." He suddenly felt his bruised cheeks and asked, "You didn't hit me... did you?"

Phineas cleared his throat, standing up abruptly. "One doesn't quibble over the scientific procedures, only in the results they achieve. I assure you, I was quite measured in my application."

Jedidiah couldn't suppress a small smile, shaking his head at Phineas' typical flair for the dramatic. It felt good to have things, at least momentarily, back to normal.

Matthew's brow furrowed, but he shook his head, pushing the question aside. "Fine, fine. So... what now?"

Before either of them could respond, the door at the front of the car burst open. A uniformed conductor staggered in, closely followed by a broad-shouldered man in oil-stained overalls—the train's engineer. The conductor's face was ashen, his chest heaving as if he'd just run a marathon, while the engineer's normally steady hands trembled.

"Everyone, get down! Take cover—now!" the conductor shouted, his voice strained with urgency.

"What's going on?" Jedidiah demanded, his heart pounding as passengers exchanged confused and frightened looks.

"There's no time to explain! Just get down!" the conductor's voice was shrill, bordering on hysteria.

The words had barely left his mouth when a

deafening boom erupted from the front of the train. The entire car rocked violently, sending people sprawling across the floor as the shockwave reverberated through the metal walls. Screams of terror echoed around them as the train was covered in a downpour of dust and debris.

CHAPTER III

Edge of Disaster

"What was that?" Matthew shouted over the chaos, trying to steady himself against a seat.

Phineas' eyes darted toward the shattered windows, his expression sharp with alarm. "Timed charges…" he deduced, the realization dawning on him as he turned to Jedidiah. "They've blown the tracks!"

"He's right!" the conductor announced, gripping the back of a seat for balance. "While we were out checking for signs of sabotage, we spotted some dynamite with a timer already counting down. We barely had time to race back and warn everyone!"

Suddenly a second explosion thundered from the rear of the train—much closer this time—causing the car to lurch violently to one side. The deafening screech of twisting metal filled the air as the floor buckled beneath them. Windows shattered, sending shards of glass flying.

Passengers clung desperately to their seats and to each other, terror etched into their faces. A woman cradled a crying child, shielding it as best she could, while luggage tumbled from the overhead racks. An older man, his face pale and drawn, braced himself between two facing seats, struggling to stay calm amidst the chaos.

Jedidiah shielded his head with his arms, shouting, "Everyone, stay low! Get to the center of the car!"

Through the haze of dust and debris, he caught sight of the conductor now gripping the door frame for support, "We're trapped! They've cut us off from both ends!" He shouted hoarsely. "We can't go forward or back!"

Matthew struggled to his feet, his expression grim as he met Jedidiah's gaze. "What do we do now?"

Jedidiah opened his mouth to respond, but no words came. The car creaked ominously, swaying on the damaged tracks. For a moment, everything seemed to hang in a fragile, breathless pause.

"We need to get everyone off this train and onto solid ground," Phineas said urgently, glancing toward the nearest exit. "Before anything else happens!"

Just then the locomotive began to groan, its wheels straining against the uneven tracks as a faint rumble reverberated through the ground beneath them. Dust and small pebbles began to trickle down the hillside, slipping past the windows like the ticking of an invisible clock counting down. The car lurched again, tilting slightly.

"The explosion triggered a landslide!" Jedidiah shouted as he looked out one of the shattered windows. In one quick motion, he hurled himself to the floor, grabbed the ray gun, and staggered back to his feet. "We need to get everyone out, now!" He emphasized the sense of urgency by waving the weapon in the air.

Suddenly a low, ominous creak echoed through the air as if the very earth beneath them was shifting. The train car began to lean further to one side.

Phineas grabbed the conductor's arm, his voice steady but urgent. "Don't just stand there! You need to make sure everyone gets off now!"

The conductor nodded, wiping sweat from his brow. "I'll do my best, sir. However, the mayor and Mr. Harris are still in the..."

"We'll get them out!" Jedidiah turned back to his companions. "Matthew, Phineas—we need to get to the front of the train before the whole thing goes over the edge!"

"Agreed." Phineas glanced ahead. "We've got to move quickly, or they won't stand a chance."

"I wonder why they didn't come running to the passenger car like the conductor and engineer,"

Matthew pondered, taking up the rear as the three men maneuvered through the swaying car. They dodged falling debris and struggling passengers with practiced agility. Beneath their feet, the ground seemed to shift and crumble, as if the hillside itself was giving way.

"Easy…" Phineas muttered as they reached the door to the Presidential Suite, stepping across from one small platform to the next. He took a deep breath and said, "Let's not make it worse."

Jedidiah glanced over the railing, noticing how its wheels barely clung to the unstable tracks. Every creak and groan seemed to amplify the risk of collapse. Exhaling greatly, he rapped sharply on the door.

"Mr. Harris! Mayor Carter!" he called out, his voice strained over the unsettling sounds of shifting metal and earth.

There was no response.

"They're just standing there, like statues!" Matthew exclaimed as he glanced through the open door.

"They've been hit by the ray gun!" Jedidiah remarked as he held the acquired weapon up as a visual aid.

Inside the private car, the Mayor of Spoon Fork and the President of the D.&R.W. stood frozen in the same positions as when they had been held up.

Their bodies were rigid and unresponsive,

unaffected by the violent rocking caused by the explosions. It quickly became apparent that the safe and the desk had slid over, pinning the two between them and preventing them from toppling over.

"Hang in there, Mayor Carter," Jedidiah murmured as he made his way inside. "We're getting you out of here."

Matthew moved toward the railroad president. "How are we going to get them out? The safe and the desk are blocking the way!"

"Help me move them!" Jedidiah shouted, tugging at the large desk.

"Wait!" Phineas screamed, grabbing the younger man by the shoulder. "You can't do that!"

"Why not?" the young entrepreneur asked confused.

The eccentric older man furrowed his brow, his gaze darting over the two massive objects. "The weight of those, especially the safe, is helping to keep us from tumbling over," he said thoughtfully. "We're already at a tilt, and moving either one could upset the balance, sending this car and the rest of the train plunging into the ravine!"

Jedidiah ran a hand through his hair, assessing the situation. "There's got to be a way to keep the car stabilized and rescue them… We can't just leave them here!"

Phineas' eyes brightened suddenly. "Wait! If we can tilt the furniture just enough to free them without actually moving it, we might be able to lift them both men over it to safety."

Matthew gave him a skeptical look. "And how do we do that?"

Phineas glanced around, his gaze settling on the plush armchairs bolted to the wall and the thick cords securing the car's hanging lamps. "We'll use these as ropes and rig a pulley to lift them."

"How?" Jedidiah nodded slowly as he tried to process the plan. "They're wedged between the desk and the wall."

"My dear boy, I've already told you—we tilt the desk away from them," Phineas explained, already working on his makeshift pulley system. "If one of us braces the desk from behind, we can tilt it just enough to slide them free. The other two can operate the pulley from this side."

Matthew moved to help. "Okay, so we throw the rope over the center beam, and tie it off to one of these armchairs for ballast?"

"Precisely! We just need to hurry, or we're all going over."

Professor Hargroves volunteered to move the desk, wedging himself between it and the wall. As soon as there was enough clearance, he worked quickly, securing the rope around Mayor Carter.

"Jed, you and Matthew pull steadily but don't yank," the eccentric older man instructed.

"Got it," Jedidiah replied, gripping the rope

tightly as he and Matthew positioned themselves.

"All right, on three," Phineas said. "One… two… three!"

They began lifting Mayor Carter's rigid form. The center beam creaked under the strain, but he slowly rose from the floor, clearing the edge of the desk. Phineas braced his legs against the wall, using his back to add more force.

"Steady… keep it steady!" Phineas grunted, releasing pressure on the desk, and letting it settle back down.

Jedidiah held the rope steady, bracing himself as Matthew grabbed the mayor's legs and pulled, inching his rigid body toward him and over the obstacle. With a few more coordinated efforts, they managed to lower him gently on the other side.

"One down," Matthew panted, wiping sweat from his brow. "Now for Mr. Harris."

Using the same technique, Phineas tied the rope around the president of the D.&R.W. Railroad. This time, the professor shifted his position, wedging himself even closer to the safe to get more leverage.

"Ready?" Jedidiah called out, tightening his grip on the rope.

Phineas gave a short nod. "Ready! On three again. One… two… three!"

They repeated the maneuver, lifting Harris inch by inch over the desk. Phineas strained his back against the wall wedged in next to the safe. Matthew braced himself against the armchair, muscles quivering from the tension.

"Almost… there!" Jedidiah said through gritted teeth as they slid Harris over the top of the furniture and lowered him beside Mayor Carter.

"Phew, that's it," Phineas said, exhaling heavily as he pulled himself free from behind the safe. "We did it!"

"Now to get them off the train!" Jedidiah remarked as he felt the car begin to tilt again.

They half-dragged, and half-carried the two men toward the door, their weight making the already treacherous journey even more difficult. Every step seemed to send tremors through the floorboards, the car swaying dangerously.

"We're not going to make it at this rate," Phineas hissed, his gaze flicking nervously to the window, where the ground outside continued to shift and crumble beneath them.

"We have to try," Jedidiah grunted, as they made their way back to the narrow platform between compartments.

Suddenly, the train car jolted violently, the floor tilting sharply. Jedidiah's grip slipped, and Mayor Carter's legs dangled precariously over the edge.

"My dear boy!" Phineas shouted, grabbing the mayor's coat and hauling him back.

Jedidiah tightened his grip, his heart pounding.

"Thanks. Let's keep going."

With each painstaking step, they inched closer to the next car. The wind whipped around them, carrying the scent of smoke and dust as more stones tumbled down the hillside. Finally, they reached the main passenger car, and with a final burst of effort, managed to get both paralyzed men onto the platform. Down the track, they could see the conductor, engineer, baggage handlers, and all the passengers gathered in a safe area beyond the caboose. They were on stable land, unaffected by the explosion.

"All right, let's move. Quickly but carefully," Phineas ordered.

The car creaked ominously, the metal groaning as if the entire train was protesting its precarious position. Phineas kept glancing at the track, the sight of jagged rocks and the churning river below sending chills down his spine. "We've got to be fast," he muttered, swallowing nervously. "This whole thing's about to give way."

Jedidiah nodded, gripping the president's coat tightly. "Matthew, stay with Phineas. I'll lead the way," he shouted over his shoulder. Edging forward cautiously, his boots scraped against the tilting floor as the car groaned beneath him. Together, they exited the passenger car and began their trek to the next compartment.

The train rocked again, more violently this time,

sending a shower of pebbles and dirt cascading down the hillside. Jedidiah gritted his teeth as the floor dipped sharply beneath him. His heart pounded in his chest, each step feeling as though it might be the one to send them all tumbling into the abyss.

"Careful… careful," Phineas murmured, his voice tense as he guided Mayor Carter across the tilting floorboards.

They were almost to the last car when the rear section of the train gave a sudden, jarring lurch. Metal screeched as the back wheels lost their grip on the broken track, and the entire car shifted sideways. Beneath them, the ground slid slowly but steadily, threatening to pull the train further over the edge.

"Go, go, go!" Jedidiah shouted, his voice rising in panic as the train began to tilt dangerously towards the ravine.

Matthew and Phineas scrambled behind him, the mayor's feet dragging limply along the floor. They crossed the platform between cars and entered the baggage car just as the rear of the train tipped further, one side lifting entirely off the tracks.

"We're not going to make it!" Matthew yelled, his voice strained as he fought to keep his footing. The incline made each step feel like an uphill battle against gravity.

"Keep moving!" Jedidiah called over his shoulder. "Don't look back, just—" There was a deafening crack, and the train car jolted violently.

"Jump!" Phineas screamed, his eyes wide with terror.

With one final burst of strength, they heaved the two paralyzed men off the platform, then leaped after them. They hit the ground, landing mere inches apart.

"We made it," Matthew sat up and gasped, his chest heaving. "We actually made it…"

Phineas' eyes were wide, his face pale. "Not yet…" He glanced back at the train. "We still need to get clear."

Jedidiah bolted up, his muscles trembling from the strain. "Don't just lay there! Help me with these two." He ignored the pain shooting through his legs and back.

They moved quickly, hoisting the paralyzed men with a surge of renewed urgency. Staggering under the weight, they climbed the steep hillside, their boots slipping on loose dirt and gravel. At the top, where the passengers and crew had gathered, faces of relief and disbelief greeted them. With care, they laid the mayor and railroad president on the ground, drawing a collective sigh from the onlookers.

"You did it!" the conductor shouted, rushing over. "You saved them!"

Jedidiah waved him off, breathing heavily. "Piece of cake..." he muttered, collapsing to his knees, his chest heaving from exhaustion.

Before they could fully catch their breath, faint groans broke the tense silence. Mayor Carter's lips trembled as his body gave a sudden twitch—the paralysis ray's effects were finally wearing off.

"Mr. Carter? Can you hear me?" Jedidiah leaned close, his voice steady but laced with concern.

The mayor's eyes fluttered open, glassy and confused. He stared up at Jedidiah. "Wh-what… what happened?"

Before Jedidiah could answer, Mr. Harris bolted upright with a gasp, blinking rapidly as his disoriented gaze darted around. "Where… where am I?" he demanded, his voice edged with panic. "What's going on?"

Phineas stepped forward, his tone calm and reassuring. "It's all right, gentlemen. You're safe now. There was an attack on the train, but we managed to get you out in time."

The railroad president's eyes widened as the memory hit him. "An attack? My train—where is my train?"

Jedidiah and Matthew exchanged a knowing glance, their faces somber as they both motioned toward the mangled iron horse, precariously clinging to the fractured track in the distance.

Samuel Harris turned just in time to see the

ground under the train give way completely. With a final groan, the locomotive tipped forward, pulling the train cars with it as they plummeted down the steep cliffside. The iron beast twisted and buckled, its wheels spinning helplessly in the air before crashing into the jagged rocks below. The shattered remnants of the train scattered into the river, its churning waters sweeping away the debris as plumes of dust and smoke billowed upward into the narrow canyon.

Mr. Harris' mouth fell open in shock. He stared, wide-eyed and unblinking, as the twisted wreckage of his once-proud train disappeared into the depths of the ravine. His face went ashen, and he wobbled unsteadily on his feet.

"My... my train..." he whispered, his voice barely audible over the distant crash of debris.

Before anyone could react, the railroad president's eyes rolled back, and he collapsed in a heap on the ground, unconscious.

Jedidiah raised an eyebrow as Harris crumpled. "He took that better than I thought."

With a final groan, the locomotive tipped
forward, pulling the train cars with it as
they plummeted down the steep cliffside.

CHAPTER IV

Return to Automaton Alley

With the president of the D.&R.W. Railroad stretched out on the ground, the faint echo of the train crashing into the ravine still hung in the air. The sheer magnitude of the disaster was too much for Samuel Harris, his body succumbing to the weight of shock.

Jedidiah Davenport exchanged knowing glances with Phineas Hargroves and Matthew Colton before kneeling beside the unconscious man. "We need to get him somewhere he can rest."

"We could all use a rest." Professor Hargroves wiped a smear of dirt from his face, his shoulders sagging as the adrenaline began to fade. Around them, survivors sat in stunned silence, their expressions a mix of relief and quiet horror.

The air was thick with tension, and a gnawing sense of unease crept into Jedidiah's mind. Something about the attack didn't sit right with him, and it wasn't just the explosions. It was something deeper—a feeling he couldn't shake.

The weapons they used to hold up the train... they weren't like anything he'd seen before. They felt out of place, unnatural—almost too futuristic for the time they were living in. He clutched the one left behind by the leader. Where had they come from? Who invented them? The outlaws who wielded them didn't seem the type to be able to create anything so fantastical.

Jedidiah sighed and shook his head as he stuck the weapon in his belt and helped Matthew and Phineas lift the unconscious Harris. Together, they followed the mayor and the other survivors, climbing to higher ground.

****

Three days earlier, on October 2nd, 1881, in a dimly lit workshop on Automaton Alley in Toronto, Ontario, Jonathan Blake and his son Edwin Bancroft had been engrossed in a secret project.

Blake, who only weeks earlier had been consumed by vengeance during the Sky Races, had since discovered a renewed sense of purpose. Alongside Edwin, he had redirected his passion toward scientific innovation and advancing airship travel. The workshop buzzed with the hum of intricate machinery, the rhythmic clank of automatons providing a steady backdrop as father and son worked tirelessly. Sparks flew and gears turned as they crafted their surprise—an ambitious creation intended for their friend and fellow adventurer, Jedidiah Davenport.

"That should do it," Edwin said, stepping back to admire their work. "It's finally ready."

Blake nodded in approval, his eyes scanning the creation one last time. "Perfect timing. We need to be leaving soon."

He stepped back and gestured toward the two automatons standing silently by the entrance to the workshop. The mechanical figures had served him well for quite some time, although their presence still felt uncanny at times.

"Artemis and Apollo, load it into the crate," Blake instructed firmly, his voice carrying over the hum of machinery and clattering tools.

With a faint whirr of gears, the automatons moved forward in perfect synchronization. Their brass-plated hands gripped the creation with care, each movement precise as they lifted it and placed it inside the oversized wooden crate.

Artemis, a towering figure adorned with brass-plated limbs and two glowing eyes, emitted a low hum before speaking. Its voice emanated from a hidden speaker, the words broken by slight pauses and mechanical stutters. "Crate... ready... for trans...port?" it asked, adjusting its top hat with deliberate movements. The mechanical man stood tall, awaiting further instructions, its posture precise and calculated.

Beside it, the other mechanical man, Apollo, equally imposing with a similar brass construction and adorned in matching formal attire—complete with vest, tie, and goggles—communicated in its own distinct way. A series of rhythmic light pulses emanated from its amber eyes, dimming and brightening in patterns akin to Morse code.

This visual language served as Apollo's means of expression, enabling a seamless exchange of information between the two automatons. Artemis responded in the same manner. The intricate system of light signals was a marvel of engineering that only Jonathan Blake, and now his son Edwin, fully understood.

"Load it aboard the Icarus," Blake instructed as he positioned the final wooden panel against the crate and began driving nails into the edges with steady, precise strikes. His voice carried a hint of pride as he admired their work.

The towering automaton responded with a slight whirr as its head turned toward the crate, its glowing amber-colored eyes flickering briefly. "Or...ders...received...loading...now," it stuttered, its brass-plated limbs clanking as it approached.

It turned to its companion and without words, communicated once again through the series of flashing lights. However, as the lights blinked in rapid succession, Blake's brow furrowed. The sequence was slightly off, its rhythm uneven, almost hesitant, as though the automaton was processing something new. A faint pause interrupted the final flash, just enough to unsettle Blake.

He narrowed his eyes, wondering if the programming had shifted or if a glitch had occurred. "Odd... that's a pattern I don't recognize" he murmured under his breath, but he dismissed the thought with a shake of his head.

"Say, that was grand of Professor Hargroves to let us use his airship," Edwin remarked as he watched the two mechanical men grip each side of the crate. The wood creaked and splintered slightly under their grasp, as their brass hands squeezed the sides with more pressure than necessary.

Blake's brow furrowed as he noticed their grip tightening unnaturally. "Careful there," he muttered under his breath, more to himself than to the automatons. He made a mental note to recalibrate their strength.

"I think our mechanical friends might be overdue for a tuneup," he said to Edwin, trying to brush off his growing concern.

The older man watched the automatons head out onto the wooden sidewalk, the crate carried securely between them. The way their hands had crushed part of the wood still gnawed at him as the mechanical men moved with precision.

"I'm sorry, Edwin," Jonathan turned back to his son. "What were you saying?"

"Only that it was really nice of Professor Hargroves to let us use the Icarus," Edwin remarked, watching the automatons as they disappeared down the path. "Especially after... well, after your airship went up in flames when you tried to sabotage everyone else's ships a few weeks ago."

Jonathan's face darkened briefly, the memory of his airship's fiery demise still raw. "Yes. Losing it... wasn't easy. That ship was a symbol of everything I stood for at the time. But maybe it's for the best."

Edwin looked at him curiously. "What do you mean?"

Jonathan sighed, then gave a small shrug. "Take the new airship that Jed is allowing his work crew to build for me. He's only charging the cost of materials and what he paid for those blueprints we stole from him. He didn't have to do that, but it shows how much things have changed. It makes me realize I shouldn't have held on to the past so tightly."

Edwin nodded slowly. "So... guessing you're not going to call the new ship the Retribution II?"

Blake shook his head, a faint, almost wistful smile playing on his lips. "No. The Retribution was built out of vengeance and hate. Every nail, every board—it all represented something dark in me, something I needed to let go of."

Edwin raised an eyebrow. "So what's this new one going to represent?"

Blake nodded. "It's going to be a symbol of hope and progress. A new beginning. We've all been through enough. It's time to build something for the future, not the past."

"Hmm," Edwin pondered for a moment. "How about calling it the Inspiration?"

Jonathan's smile grew wider. "Inspiration? I like that." He clapped a hand on Edwin's shoulder, feeling a surge of pride in his son. "Yes, Inspiration sounds like a perfect name!"

As that was settled, Edwin reached into his pocket and pulled out a folded flyer, holding it up for his father to see. "By the way, thanks for agreeing to let Tom Miller come stay with us next spring. I think he and I will make a great team for this steam-powered runabout competition in Niagara Falls."

Jonathan's eyes flicked to the flyer and back to his son. "The one you and Tom talked about before we left Spoon Fork?"

Edwin nodded enthusiastically. "Exactly! We saw the advertisement in the paper, and we both think we can come up with something extraordinary."

Jonathan smiled faintly, a hint of amusement in

his eyes. "From rivals to partners, huh? It's good to see you two working together."

Edwin grinned. "Yeah, well, we figured it's about time we stopped competing. Besides, it'll be a chance to learn from each other."

Jonathan chuckled. "I'll admit, you both have potential. Just don't expect any unfair advantages from me."

"Thinking about entering the contest yourself?"

"You never know..."

Changing the subject, Edwin reached into his other pocket and pulled out a folded envelope addressed to the two of them. "By the way, we received a letter from Aunt Myra. I picked it up at the post office when I went out earlier. Mind if I read it aloud?"

"Please do!" the older man shouted excitedly as he pulled up a chair, sat down, and began listening intently.

"'Dear Jonathan and Edwin, You wouldn't believe where I am as I write this. I've taken a small detour on my way back to Paris and found myself investigating something rather peculiar...'" Edwin paused, a spark of curiosity in his eyes. "She mentions something about a hidden temple in the Pyrenees Mountains!"

Jonathan raised an eyebrow. "Pyrenees Mountains? How did she get way out there?"

Edwin continued, "'I know it sounds far-fetched, but there's a historian I've met who swears there's something here worth investigating that might possibly be tied to a much larger mystery. I'm planning to follow the trail—don't worry, I'll be safe and I'll keep you posted. This might be my biggest adventure yet.!'"

Edwin folded the letter back up, grinning. "Gosh, sounds like Aunt Myra might be getting in over her head this time."

Jonathan chuckled softly, shaking his head. "Don't worry about your aunt. Myra Wilhelmina Bancroft is the most daring, courageous, adventurous person I've ever met. There's no situation too fierce for her."

"I suppose you're right," Edwin remarked, sliding the letter back into the envelope.

Just then, a faint clatter came from the back of the workshop, catching his attention. His head whipped around toward the sound, and his instincts kicked in.

"Did you hear that?" Edwin whispered, his hand already drifting toward a large wrench lying on the workbench.

Jonathan rose to his feet and moved quickly and quietly toward the door leading into the storage room. "Stay behind me," he murmured. His mind raced, wondering who it could be. He knew his mechanical workers couldn't be back this quickly. It must be some sort of prowler.

The room they were about to enter was dimly lit, shadows casting eerie shapes across the walls as Jonathan opened one of the two large double doors. He threw it open, his heart pounding in his chest, only to find...

Nothing. The place was empty, the shelves stacked neatly with various mechanical parts, tools, and prototypes they had been working on. Yet, something still felt wrong—Jonathan's instincts were rarely wrong.

"Father," Edwin called quietly from behind him, his voice filled with concern. "Look! The open window!"

Jonathan turned sharply just in time to see a shadowy figure peering inside. It spotted the two of them, turned on its heel and raced down the alley.

"After him!" the older man shouted as he raced across the room.

Edwin wasted no time in leaping onto the table and climbing through the open window. His father wasn't far behind him.

The shadowy figure slipped around a corner, his movements hurried but purposeful. "There!" Edwin shouted, at a full run.

Jonathan sprinted behind his son, their boots echoing against the cobblestone streets as they gave chase. The mysterious stranger appeared to be very young and very athletic. He was dressed in a tattered coat, much too large for his frame, and a

Edwin wasted no time in leaping onto the table and climbing through the open window.

cap pulled low over his face. His bare feet slapped against the cold stones, giving him a silent agility that Jonathan couldn't help but notice.

"He's just a boy!" The older man called out, his breath coming in short gasps as they rounded the corner into a narrow alley.

"But what's a kid doing sneaking around our shop?" Edwin replied, his eyes narrowing in suspicion.

The boy darted around a stack of crates, his small frame slipping through gaps that Edwin vaulted over with ease and Jonathan struggled to climb over. The alley was dark and damp, the lingering shadows of the night still clinging to the narrow passageway as the first hints of dawn began to break over Automaton Alley. The sun had yet to rise fully, leaving the streets shrouded in a dim, early morning haze.

They pursued him relentlessly, closing the gap. Jonathan could see the boy glancing over his shoulder, slipping through the narrow streets like someone who knew the alleys well.

"He's fast," Edwin muttered, frustration clear in his voice as they neared a dead-end.

Just as Jonathan thought they had him cornered, the boy—no more than a shadow in the dark—vaulted over a low fence and vanished into the deeper darkness of the city. Jonathan came to a stop.

"Lost him," Edwin huffed, placing his hands on his knees as he caught his breath. "I'm getting too old for this!"

"Yes, at twenty years old you're practically ancient." Jonathan retorted sarcastically, his eyes narrowed as he looked up and down the alley. "Something doesn't feel right."

Reluctantly, father and son had no choice but to turn around and head back to their shop. Instead of climbing back in through the open window, they decided to go around the front of the building. Jonathan's eyes widened as they spotted another figure sneaking out of the entrance. This one was taller and bulkier but moved just as quickly as the first. He headed down the street in the opposite direction and vanished.

"Another one?" The older man gasped.

"The first one was a decoy!" Edwin tensed as if ready to give chase again, but Jonathan put a hand on his arm.

"No point. He's too far ahead and we're both too tired." Jonathan Blake turned towards his shop. "We better go inside and see if anything was stolen."

As they approached the workshop's entrance, Jonathan felt a growing unease settle over him. He pushed open the door cautiously, his eyes scanning the room for any signs of disturbance.

"Anything missing?" Edwin asked, following him inside.

Jonathan moved toward the workbench, his eyes darting across the various tools and mechanical parts scattered about. "Everything seems..."

His voice trailed off as he spotted something out of place on the corner of his desk—an envelope sealed with a wax crest.

"Edwin," Jonathan called softly, lifting the envelope. "This is addressed to Jedidiah Davenport."

Edwin's brow furrowed as he came to stand beside his father. "Who's it from?"

Jonathan carefully studied the seal a look of confusion across his face.

"I'm not sure but I know I've seen this somewhere before..." Jonathan's voice trailed off abruptly as a deafening crash reverberated through the workshop.

Both he and Edwin whirled around just in time to witness the unthinkable: the entire side of the building shuddered violently before a gaping hole burst open in the wall. Bricks crumbled to the ground in a cloud of dust and debris, the force of the impact rattling the remaining windows and sending tools clattering off the workbenches.

For a brief moment, everything was eerily still, the dust swirling in the dim light of the early morning. Then, as the air cleared, an ominous silhouette emerged from the wreckage, barely visible through the rubble.

"Get down!" Jonathan yelled, his heart racing as he instinctively pulled Edwin behind a stack of crates, both of them watching with bated breath, unsure of what—or who—had just torn through their sanctuary.

The mechanical whirr of gears echoed faintly, and a shadow moved across the floor as something large and heavy entered the building.

As the dust began to settle, a hulking form took shape, its edges glinting faintly in the dim light. The whirr of gears grew louder and then came the sound of something inhuman.

CHAPTER V

Rising Tensions

"Holy smokes," Edwin Bancroft muttered, wide-eyed. "What just..."

Before he could finish, one of Jonathan Blake's automatons, Apollo, stepped through the freshly made hole, its brass-plated body rigid amidst the rubble of wood and brick.

"That blasted thing just walked straight through the wall!" Jonathan exclaimed, his voice sharp with both frustration and concern. His eyes darted to the second automaton, Artemis, as it entered through the open door, its glowing eyes flickering rhythmically as it communicated with the other mechanical man.

Artemis turned back towards them, its head twitching as it relayed the information. "Dis...tance...and...depth...percep...tion...mal...funct ion," it said in its stilted, mechanical voice. "Re...calibration...needed."

Jonathan let out a heavy sigh. "I think both of you need a complete system overhaul."

Edwin stepped closer, inspecting the damage. Apollo stood motionless, its brass limbs dusted with debris. "It just walked straight through the wall like it was nothing," he said, incredulous. "Why didn't it use the door like it's supposed to?"

"Like Artemis said, its sensors are off," Jonathan replied, shaking his head. "It must have misread the wall as a doorway."

"But how could it even walk through solid brick?" His eyes shifted from the crumbling facade to the automaton.

"I know they're strong, but the way the wall came down..." Edwin trailed off, studying the machine more closely. His gaze fell to its mechanical hands, noting heavy scuff marks. "It didn't walk through, it punched its way in!"

Jonathan's eyes widened as realization struck. "Apollo must have analyzed the wall as an obstacle that needed to be... removed," he muttered. Without another word, he deactivated the automaton and bolted into the street, locking the door behind him.

"What's wrong?" Edwin called out. "Where are you going?"

"To make sure there's not a hole in the side of Phineas' airship!"

Edwin stepped through the huge hole in the side of the building, glanced at the door his father had just locked, shrugged, and followed.

Jonathan and Edwin sprinted down the cobblestone streets of Automaton Alley, their boots clattering against the pavement as they weaved between early morning vendors and their mechanical men setting up shop. They turned sharply at the edge of the city, heading toward the open farmland just beyond. The soft glow of the rising sun cast long shadows across the fields as they ran, hearts pounding in their chests.

As they neared the Icarus, both men slowed, eyes scanning for any sign of damage. To their relief, the airship stood undisturbed, its wooden frame solid and sturdy under the morning light, anchored securely to the ground.

"Well," Edwin sighed, catching his breath as they reached the base of the airship. "At least it's still in one piece."

Jonathan gave a brief nod, his mind still racing. "All right, we're in the clear here. Let's head back and fix that malfunctioning machine. We'll also need to get the other one started on repairing the wall."

Once they returned to the workshop, Jonathan set to work on the faulty automaton. "We'll need to recalibrate its sensors and adjust the obstacle-recognition protocols," Jonathan muttered, carefully tweaking a series of gears and lenses inside its brass casing. "It obviously misread the wall as something it could push through. If we don't fix its depth perception and route-finding logic, it might end up smashing through every obstacle it encounters."

Meanwhile, as Jonathan Blake began working on Apollo, Edwin gave Artemis its instructions, its glowing eyes flickering as it processed the orders to start repairs on the damaged wall. The machine moved with deliberate precision, clearing the debris and preparing materials to mend the hole.

A few hours later, Jonathan finished his adjustments, he wiped his hands on a cloth and sighed. "That should do it for now."

"Good," Edwin said, watching as Jonathan powered the automaton back on. "Let's run a few quick tests, just to be sure."

Jonathan nodded and issued a few simple commands. The automaton responded smoothly this time, navigating the workshop without incident. It turned to face Jonathan, awaiting further instructions.

"Looks like it's back in working order," Jonathan said with relief. "Alright, have it assist the other one with the repairs."

Without hesitation, the newly recalibrated automaton joined its counterpart, and both machines began working methodically to patch the gaping hole in the wall. Edwin watched them for a moment, then glanced back at Jonathan.

"Hopefully, we won't have any more incidents."

Jonathan gave a small, tired smile. "Let's hope."

Looking over at his father's desk, Edwin suddenly remembered something. "We've got to deliver that letter to Jedidiah. It might be something important!"

"We'll take it with us back to the States." The older man replied. "Instead of sailing straight to Spoon Fork, we'll head to St. Louis. The train they're all traveling on arrives there in a few days, on the 6th. We can leave out first thing Wednesday morning and make it there in plenty of time."

"Wednesday morning!" The young man exclaimed. "I thought we were leaving today!"

"We need to stay here to make sure the repairs to the shop are completed. We also need to run more tests on our mechanical friends to ensure they function within normal parameters."

"What about Mr. Davenport... I mean Jed's gift out in the Icarus?"

"Don't worry about that," the older man chuckled. "It'll be perfectly safe. I've got plenty of traps set up around the landing area to keep any prowlers away."

Edwin Bancroft sighed reluctantly and agreed it would be best to wait until Wednesday morning to leave.

****

Four days later, on Thursday, October 6th, 1881, in the small but bustling town of Spoon Fork, Kansas, the sun had barely begun to rise, casting a soft orange hue across the horizon. The early morning chill clung to the air as Tom Miller, scarcely eighteen and already burdened by the weight of his responsibilities, stood behind the counter at the Davenport Dispatch & Delivery Company. His eyes were fixed on the large wall clock, each tick amplifying the anxiety tightening in his chest.

It had been a long, quiet week, and something about that silence unsettled him. His usual routine of logging shipments, checking inventory for incoming wagons, and tracking the company's airship routes felt like an afterthought compared to the nagging sense that something was wrong.

The bell above the door jingled, breaking his train of thought. Tom looked up to see Henry "Hank" Porter step inside. Hank's older, weathered face, though normally calm, seemed slightly on edge.

"Mornin', Tom," Hank greeted, leaning against the counter. "Any news on my freight shipment?"

"The Eclipse touched down this morning at the Topeka branch. It unloaded your order and left back out for New York."

"New York!" Henry Porter exclaimed. "What in

tarnation is it doing heading to New York?"

"Going to pick up another shipment of goods," Tom replied nervously. "Look, Mr. Porter, the supplies for your store have already been loaded onto a wagon and will be here today by lunch."

The general store owner scoffed in disbelief. "By wagon? What's the point of having a freight company with a fleet of airships if everything's still being delivered by wagon? I've got customers waiting on special orders!"

"I assure you, everything will be here. I..." Something suddenly dawned on the young man, and he stopped mid-sentence. "Mr. Porter, have you always used Mr. Davenport's freight company to deliver your supplies?"

"Never considered using anyone else!"

"Weren't you afraid he'd refuse to deliver to you after you refused to sell to him during his trouble with the railroad?"

"Well... I..." The older man chuckled, shaking his head. "Guess I didn't think that through. Besides, it wasn't exactly my idea. If you remember, I was being forced into it."

"And you also knew that Mr. Davenport wouldn't treat you like that," Tom replied knowingly.

"You're right, he's too nice a fellow to do anyone like that," the older man admitted. "But it doesn't matter now anyway. Besides, I'm sure

Elijah Perkins and his men would've found a way to keep me from using his freight company anyhow."

Hoping to shift the conversation, the older man asked, "Say, have you heard from Jed or any of the others since they left two days ago?"

Tom shook his head, biting the inside of his cheek. "Not yet. I was expecting to hear from them hours ago. They should have arrived in St. Louis early this morning. But, you know Mr. Davenport —he's always getting mixed up in some kind of adventure."

Hank nodded, smiling slightly. "Yeah, ain't that the truth." The older man turned on his heel and started out the door. "Just tell them to deliver the supplies to the back of my store like usual!" He continued down the street without looking back.

Tom glanced up at the clock, his eyes following the second hand as it crawled forward. After what felt like an eternity, he decided to check on the workers loading the wagons out back. Suddenly, the silence of the morning shattered as angry voices erupted in the distance.

His brow furrowed as he hurried toward the back door. Pushing it open, he was met with the sight of two workers, Simon and Charlie, squared off in front of a partially loaded wagon. Their faces were flushed with frustration, and their argument echoed sharply in the cool morning air.

"I told you, that shipment's supposed to go out to Hawthorn Grove! You keep trying to load it on the wrong wagon!" Simon snapped, his arms crossed tightly over his chest.

Charlie, a hot-headed young man known for his quick temper, threw his hands up in exasperation. "And I told you, we got new instructions from Tom. This load's headed to Meadowbank!"

Tom's chest tightened as he quickly stepped forward, raising his hands in an attempt to diffuse the situation. "Hey, what's going on here? What's this argument about?"

Simon jabbed a finger toward the wagon. "Tom, you've got to help me here! Charlie's trying to send out the wrong shipment. This load is marked for Hawthorn Grove—it's been planned for days!"

"Planned or not, we just got new instructions this morning," Charlie shot back, his face flushing. "Are we gonna follow orders or not?"

"Whose orders?"

"Tom's orders!"

Tom's mind raced as he tried to make sense of the situation. Normally, Matthew Colton would handle disputes like this, but with Matthew gone, the responsibility fell squarely on his shoulders. Swallowing hard, he stepped between the two men.

"Alright, let's calm down. Simon, I probably should have shown you this earlier," Tom said, pulling a crumpled piece of paper from his back pocket. "We received a telegram canceling the order for Hawthorn Grove."

Simon snatched the paper and quickly scanned it, his brow furrowing as he read. The cancellation was clear. With a reluctant nod, he handed the paper back.

"Alright, everything's under control now," Tom said, keeping his tone steady. "Let's just focus on getting this wagon ready to head out."

Simon glared at him for a moment longer, then grudgingly agreed. "Fine. But you'd better be right, Tom. I don't want anyone coming back to me later saying it went to the wrong place!"

"I'll take full responsibility," Tom assured him firmly. "Now let's finish loading the shipment. We've already wasted too much time."

Tom exhaled slowly as Simon and Charlie returned to their tasks, the tension between them easing but not fully dissipating. He turned back toward the office, intending to sit down and collect his thoughts.

But before he could take a single step, another commotion erupted nearby.

"You're going to break half of 'em before they even make it to the wagon!" a voice shouted, sharp with irritation.

Tom spun on his heel to find Nathan and William standing over a toppled crate, its corner cracked open. Their voices carried across the yard,

Nathan and William standing over
a toppled crate, its corner cracked open.

loud enough to draw the attention of other workers.

"For the last time, I know what I'm doing!" Nathan shot back, his arms crossed tightly over his chest. "Maybe if you paid attention, we wouldn't be in this mess."

"Attention?" William snapped, throwing his hands up. "You're the one tossing crates like they're made of tin!"

Tom strode toward them, his irritation bubbling over. "Enough!" he barked, cutting between the two men. He gestured to the broken crate. "What is going on here?"

"Nathan here thinks he knows better than me about loading these crates," William snapped, his face red with anger. "But he's gonna break half of 'em before they're even on the wagon!"

Nathan's eyes narrowed, his voice cutting. "I've been doing this for years, William. If you actually knew what you were doing, we would be done by now!"

"Enough!" Tom barked, stepping between them. He gestured toward the fallen crate and fixed both men with a stern glare. "I don't care whose fault this is. Just clean up this mess and load the wagons properly. If there's any damage to that shipment, I'm holding both of you responsible!"

The men exchanged disgruntled grumbles, but instead of getting back to work, they hesitated. Nathan and William shared a glance before turning back to Tom.

"Look, kid," William started, his tone gruff. "No offense, but you've only been in charge for a couple of days. Nathan and I have been loading crates for years. We know what we're doing."

Nathan crossed his arms, nodding in agreement. "Yeah, maybe let the adults handle it, alright?"

Tom immediately resented the challenge to his authority. He knew he was young, but he also knew Jedidiah and Matthew trusted him to be in charge. This wasn't the first time the older workers had undermined him, but it still stung every time.

"I don't care how long you've been loading crates," Tom snapped, his voice sharper than intended. "You don't get to ignore orders just because you've been here longer."

William opened his mouth to argue back when a new voice cut through the tension.

"Tom's right, you know."

Taken by surprise, Tom Miller glanced over his shoulder and spotted Lucas Benson, manager of the Sheffield office, standing a few feet behind him, arms crossed as he surveyed the situation. Both William and Nathan immediately straightened up.

Lucas stepped forward, his voice calm but authoritative. "Is there a problem here?"

"No Sir!" The two men exclaimed in unison.

"In that case, you should get back to work and do as Tom says." He glanced at the damaged crate, his tone hardening. "And next time, let's avoid dropping shipments, shall we?"

The slightly older men exchanged uneasy glances before muttering, "Yes, sir," and shuffling back to their tasks.

Tom Miller let out a breath, a mixture of relief and irritation swirling inside him. The resolve quickly being overshadowed by a growing resentment. He felt as though he was doing fine on his own and didn't need Mr. Benson swooping in and saving the day.

"Sorry, Tom. I could see you had it handled just fine without me," Lucas remarked as he stepped up beside him. His tone was casual, but his presence carried a quiet authority that was hard to ignore. "I was only trying to back you up."

"Thanks," He said, though his tone was tight. Tom appreciated the support but couldn't shake the feeling that the older man had been standing there just waiting for an opportunity to step in.

He tried to keep his voice even, but the resentment was hard to mask. It had only been a few weeks since he'd been passed over for the job of temporarily running the freight office. Lucas Benson had been put in charge instead. The decision still irked him. Now, with Jedidiah and Matthew gone again, it felt as though Lucas had been sent to babysit him—a notion that stung even more.

Lucas, oblivious to Tom's inner turmoil, continued. "Just thought I'd drop by and see if you needed any help."

Tom nodded, though inside, the irritation only grew. "I've got everything handled. I don't need any help."

Lucas seemed to catch on to Tom's mood, offering a small smile. "You're doing a good job, Tom. You don't need to prove anything to anyone. Jed and Matt both trust you. They've told me themselves how much they rely on you."

Tom gave a curt nod. "Yeah, thanks," he muttered, turning to head back inside the office. He could feel his face flush with frustration.

Lucas followed behind him, his footsteps heavy on the wooden floor as Tom took a seat behind the desk. He wanted to collect his thoughts, but the annoyance from earlier still echoed in his mind. He couldn't shake the feeling that Lucas had shown up to keep an eye on him, and the way he stepped in and took control only reinforced that suspicion.

"Look," Lucas said, taking a seat across from him, "I didn't mean to undermine you out there. I know you've got things under control, but sometimes a little backup doesn't hurt."

Tom let out a slow breath, trying to cool off. "I know that," he said, his voice more controlled now. "It's just… I can handle it, you know? I don't need someone looking over my shoulder."

Lucas chuckled lightly, leaning back in his chair. "I get it, Tom. Jed wouldn't have left you in charge if he didn't trust you. Just don't be afraid to let people help out sometimes. Running a place like this isn't easy, and there's no shame in taking a little support when it's offered."

Tom nodded, his irritation easing slightly, though a part of him was still irked at Lucas' words. He appreciated the attempt at reassurance, but he wasn't ready to admit that the older man might have a point.

Before either of them could say more, the door to the freight office burst open with a loud bang, and Horace McKinley, the telegraph operator, stumbled in, breathless and wide-eyed. His cap was askew, and the top button of his shirt was unfastened. His tie was loosened and sideways.

"Tom! Lucas!" Horace gasped, clutching a crumpled piece of paper in his trembling hand. He doubled over, hands on his knees, struggling to catch his breath. "I... I just got this wire... It's urgent!"

Tom bolted out of his chair, his heart pounding. "What is it, Horace?"

"It's... it's the train!" The telegraph operator's voice cracked as he leaned against the doorframe for support. He straightened, thrusting the paper into Tom's hands. "Neither Jedidiah, Mayor Carter nor any of the others ever made it to St. Louis!"

CHAPTER VI

Back at the Ranch

"The train never made it to St. Louis!" Tom Miller shouted in disbelief as he snatched the paper from the telegraph operator's trembling hands. The telegram read:

"TRAIN IS HOURS OVERDUE STOP. MISSED SCHEDULED UPDATES AT STOPS ALONG THE ROUTE STOP. LAST CONTACT WAS LATE TUESDAY NIGHT STOP. NO FURTHER COMMUNICATION RECEIVED STOP. STATUS OF PASSENGERS AND CREW UNKNOWN STOP. IMMEDIATE ASSISTANCE REQUIRED STOP."

"Status of passengers and crew unknown?" Lucas gasped.

"I'm going to show this to Sheriff Thompson," Horace McKinley declared as he took back the paper. Turning on his heel, he raced down the street. "I'm sure he'll want to organize a posse to search for them, especially with the mayor missing!"

"Mr. Benson..." Tom asked with slight hesitation. "Can you take over the freight office while I go see what I can do to help?"

"Of course," the older man quickly agreed. "Are you going to join the posse?"

"Of course not, they'd only slow me down," Tom replied firmly.

He clenched his fists as he hurried toward the door. The thought of Jedidiah, Phineas, and Matthew in danger gnawed at him. This was his moment to act decisively—any hesitation could mean the difference between life and death.

"If I'm going to have any chance of finding them, I have to leave now." He started out the door but quickly turned back and asked, "Can you send a message to Davenport Ranch on the private telegraph line and let them know what's happened?"

"Certainly!"

"Also..." With the confidence of a seasoned leader, the young man gave Lucas Benson a few more instructions regarding the freight office and additional details to include in the telegraph.

"Consider it done!" Benson shouted confidently as he raced toward the unusual machine sitting on

Matthew Colton's desk. His hands trembled slightly as he reached for the keys, the gravity of the situation pressing down on him. "No time to waste," Benson muttered under his breath as he began typing out the message.

This particular telegraph was Jedidiah Davenport's invention—a marvel of modern ingenuity that combined the precision of a typewriter with the automation of a player piano. As the older man typed out the message, the machine punched it into a fresh roll of perforated paper. This roll was then fed into the transmitter, which meticulously read each hole and converted it into a rapid coded signal. On the other end, an identical device at Davenport Ranch would decode the signal and print the message almost instantaneously, ensuring swift and secure communication.

****

An hour earlier, at Davenport Ranch, the morning sun bathed the sprawling land in a warm glow. Inside the stately Victorian manor, Pat Bennington, ever the lively character, was in the midst of persuading Agatha Porter to come outside and watch the demonstration of his latest "genius" idea.

"Another invention?" Agatha scoffed, shaking

her head. "Why do you always wait until Jed is away before you start working on your harebrained schemes?"

"Just fortunate timing, I guess!" Pat tugged at his suspenders proudly. "Now come on, Aggy. I promise you won't be disappointed this time."

The older woman adjusted the bun on top of her head before asking, "If I come out there and your invention fails like it always does, will you promise to give up and leave stuff like this to Jed and Hargroves?"

"I give you my word as a gentleman!" Pat held up one hand in an oath gesture while keeping the other one behind his back.

Agatha raised an eyebrow. "Let me see your other hand!"

Pat quickly moved his hand from behind his back, revealing crossed fingers. "Well now, how'd that happen? Must be my rheumatism acting up!"

Agatha Porter sighed and reluctantly agreed to venture outside. "You won't stop pestering me until I do, will you?"

"Now, Aggy, when have I ever done anything like that to you?"

"Only every day since I've met you!" The older woman sighed. "Fine, but after this, you need to get to that mouse problem in the barn like you promised!"

Pat waved her off dismissively. "Ah, mice can

wait. Science can't!"

Agatha frowned. "That's exactly what you said last week, and now they've chewed holes in two more sacks of grain."

"Priorities, Aggy, priorities!" Pat grinned, clearly not taking her seriously. "Now come on, you're gonna love this!"

Just as the two of them walked outside, the ranch foreman, Jim Davis, came riding up on his horse.

"What's going on?" Jim asked, dismounting his steed with a light-hearted grin.

Agatha smirked. "Pat's up to another one of his crackpot ideas since Jed's away."

"High intellectuals such as myself are never truly appreciated," the older, portly man scoffed, then turned to the newcomer. "Jim, you're just in time to witness my latest breakthrough in scientifical marvels!" As he said this, he began fiddling with the makeshift contraption hidden under a large, heavy cloth.

"Scientifical?" Jim asked, slightly confused.

"Just humor him," Agatha sighed. "Trust me, the fewer interruptions, the faster we can get this over with."

"May I present to you, for the very first time anywhere, The Automatic Rattlesnake Remover!" With that, he removed the cloth with a grand gesture. Laying on a wooden crate was a long, unwieldy pole with a spring-loaded trigger mechanism on one end and a comically oversized claw on the other.

Jim squinted. "What is it?"

Pat gestured grandly. "A marvel of modern science, just like I told you! It keeps you safe from rattlers and other creepy-crawly varmints!"

Jim eyed the device warily. "Looks like it might hurt someone more than the snake."

"Now, you see, Jim Bob," Pat declared with a twinkle in his eye, "this here gizmo will grab hold of any snake before it even thinks about striking!"

"Jim Bob?" The tall, lanky foreman looked confused.

"Humor him!" the older woman reminded him.

"But my name is James Anderson Davis," he protested. "I don't even have anything remotely close to Bob anywhere in my name!"

"Look, I ain't got time to stand here and discuss legalities, Bobby."

"Pat..." Jim took a deep breath and decided to let it drop. "Get on with it!"

"Now, if you've ever dealt with rattlers as often as I have, you know you want to keep your distance." Pat proudly lifted the weapon off the table. "That's why I attached my grabby claw onto this here spear gun." He patted the side of it for emphasis. "That way, I can stand back in what we professionals call the safety zone and grab Mr.

Rattle by the gullet before you can say Jack Robinson."

"That sounds..." Jim frowned, trying to think of the right words. "Dangerous..."

"Sounds idiotic to me!" Agatha Porter exclaimed, leaning over the railing of the porch. She crossed her arms and added, "Pat, you're gonna hurt yourself or someone else!"

"Nonsense!" Pat waved her concern away. "Watch and learn, Aggy!"

With a flourish, Pat swung the pole around, aiming at a suspicious-looking blue jay perched on one of the two wires attached to the telegraph pole.

"Now, since we don't have any actual rattlesnakes around to test it on, we'll have to settle for our fine feathered friend here."

"Pat, I don't know about this..." Jim tried to be a voice of reason, but his words fell on deaf ears.

Pat, still training his contraption on the unsuspecting bird, closed his eyes and pulled the trigger. The pole shot forward and the claw snapped shut on thin air, missing the bird entirely. Not one to be deterred, Pat yanked the gun back with a mighty tug and began reeling in the line.

"Pat, I don't think this is a good idea..." Before Agatha could finish her sentence, the rotund, bearded man closed his eyes again and pulled the trigger once more.

"Whoa!" Pat Bennington yelped, flailing as he

She crossed her arms and added,
"Pat, you're gonna hurt yourself
or someone else!"

lost his balance. The pole flew wildly off course, straight through the open window, the claw clamping down on something inside Jedidiah's study.

"That bird's a lot heavier than I thought!" Pat exclaimed, his face a mix of determination and confusion. The heavy-set man's eyes were still closed, and his hat had fallen over them. "I'll have to give it a good yank before I try to reel it in!"

Before anyone could stop him, Pat gave a mighty pull, jerking the pole violently. A crash echoed from inside Jedidiah's study, followed by the sound of splintering wood and the clatter of metal striking the floor.

Pat had pulled one of the telegraphs off the table, knocking the one beside it over as well. Both delicate machines lay there in a tangle of wires and gears. Sparks flew, and the distinct hum of the telegraph abruptly ceased. In the process, the portly man fell backward to the ground.

Agatha rushed to the window, her face a mask of disbelief. "You clumsy dolt, what have you done now?"

Pat scrambled to his feet, his face red with embarrassment. "I... I was just tryin' to..." His mind raced as the weight of what he'd done sank in. "Jed's gonna skin me alive! What was I thinking?"

"Were you intentionally trying to tear down the whole house?" Agatha snapped, pointing at the damaged machines.

Pat winced, rubbing the back of his neck sheepishly. "Aw, heck, I didn't mean to..." His voice trailed off as the enormity of the situation hit him.

"I'll fix them, I swear. They'll be better than new!" he blurted out, the words coming faster than his brain could process. "Better than new?" he thought to himself. "Who am I kidding? I can't even fix a squeaky door!"

Agatha sighed deeply and looked away from the window. "You'll do no such thing. You'll go inside, clean up the mess, gently place both machines on the table, and walk away while Jed still has a chance of undoing the damage you did."

Pat nodded quickly, swallowing hard. "*Yeah, walking away sounds like a real good idea right about now,*" he thought. Then aloud, he said, "I promise, if you let me work on them, Jed won't even recognize them when I'm finished!"

"I think that's what she's afraid of," Jim chuckled, clapping the older, heavier man on the shoulder.

Pat gave a nervous chuckle as he stared into the open window. "Well, maybe you're right. I might fix 'em so good I'd make Jed feel bad, and he'd get some kind of inferiority complex."

"Uh... yeah..." Jim exchanged a knowing glance with Agatha. "That's exactly what we were thinking!"

Agatha shook her head and turned back to Jim with a softer expression. "Come on, Jim. Let's head to the kitchen. You could probably use a break after all this excitement. How about a cup of Pat's coffee and a slice of one of the apple pies he baked last night?"

Jim's eyes lit up. "Apple pies? Now that's an offer I won't refuse."

"Despite his 'scientifical' methods, Pat does make the best pies in the state," Agatha assured him with a smile, as she led the way. "Just don't tell him I said that, or he'll never let me hear the end of it."

Pat, still staring through the window at the mess on the floor, muttered under his breath, "You could save a slice for me, you know."

Agatha chuckled softly as she glanced back. "Don't count on it!"

As they walked inside the house, Jim grinned. "I gotta admit, I'll never turn down baked goods, no matter who made them."

Agatha opened the door, motioning Jim inside. "I think you can tell by his waistline that Pat's the same way."

The rotund man sighed as he walked into Jedidiah's study and took a long look at the inventions on the floor. "Great. They get pie and I get the hard work." He shook his head, trudging further into the room to start cleaning. "Being a genius is a thankless job."

****

About an hour later, Pat Bennington stepped out of the house, still dusting his hands from cleaning Jedidiah's study. His mind was a mix of regret and stubborn pride as he muttered, "Fixed everything back just fine. Bet Jed won't even notice... unless he tries to send or receive a telegraph..."

Before he could finish his thought, the sound of hooves clattered down the path. A couple of ranch hands came galloping toward him, their faces set with urgency.

"What in tarnation is going on?" Pat asked, confused.

"Jim!" one of them called out, reining his horse sharply. "Have you seen Jim?"

"Yeah, tall lanky fellow," Pat laughed. "Seen him many times."

"I mean recently!" The ranch hand cut his sentence short as he spotted the foreman stepping onto the porch. "Jim! We just came from the north ridge. You won't believe it!"

Jim frowned, stepping forward. "Believe what?"

Levi, still catching his breath, pointed in the general direction of the valley where the airship was stored.

"The roof of the Swift's hangar opened up, and it looks like someone's about to steal it!"

Jim's eyes widened. "Someone's stealing the Swift!"

Without wasting a moment, he barked, "Levi, you and Sam come with me. Pat, you and Agatha stay here. We don't know who we're dealing with."

Pat's usual jovial expression turned serious. "Be careful, Jim."

Jim nodded, mounting his horse. "We'll handle this." He turned to the other ranch hands. "Let's ride. No one's taking the Swift on my watch."

With urgency, Jim and the other two men galloped toward the valley. The morning sun hung high in the sky, bathing the prairie in golden light. As they neared the hangar, its roof ominously open to the sky, a grim determination settled on Jim's face.

The hangar stood silent, a hulking giant. They spread out, circling it like wary predators. The rustling of the prairie wind was the only sound, making every creak of leather saddles and jingle of reins seem unnaturally loud.

Levi and Sam exchanged tense glances, their hands hovering near their holsters. A bead of sweat trickled down Levi's temple as he whispered, "What if it's outlaws, Jim? They could be armed and dangerous."

Jim nodded, his jaw tight. "Stay sharp, but don't shoot unless I give the word. Whoever's in there, we want them alive."

They dismounted, boots crunching softly against the earth as they took up positions around the hangar's entrance. Jim could feel the nervous energy radiating from the others as they held their breath, waiting for the unknown to reveal itself.

With a commanding voice, Jim shouted, "Whoever's in there, come out with your hands up! You're surrounded!"

The prairie seemed to hold its breath as silence enveloped them. For a moment, nothing stirred. Then, the faint echo of slow, deliberate footsteps resonated from within the hangar, each step sending a ripple of tension through the men.

Jim tightened his grip on his revolver, eyes narrowing as he prepared for the worst. Levi's hand trembled slightly on his gun, his face pale but resolute. Sam's knuckles whitened as he gripped the butt of his weapon, muscles coiled like a spring.

The figure emerged from the shadows, stepping into the light with hands raised. Dust swirled around his boots, casting ghostly shapes against the morning sun. As the light revealed his face, Jim's jaw dropped, his grip slackening in sheer disbelief.

CHAPTER VII

Operation Skybound Rescue

"Tom Miller!" Jim Davis' eyes widened as he recognized the young man. His revolver remained drawn, his stance firm. "What are you doing here?"

Tom kept his hands in plain view, his voice trembling with both urgency and caution. "Mr. Davis, I can explain."

Jim's eyes narrowed. "You'd better have a good reason for sneaking in here."

Tom took a deep breath, forcing himself to meet Jim's suspicious gaze. "It's not what it looks like. I got word the train never made it to St. Louis. Jed, Matt, and Professor Hargroves might be in trouble. I was trying to get the Swift ready to go find them."

Jim exchanged a glance with Levi and Sam. The silent communication seemed to weigh Tom's sincerity. Slowly, Jim holstered his revolver, his tension easing but his tone still firm. "Why didn't you let anyone know?"

"I had Mr. Benson send you a telegraph over the private line," Tom insisted, urgency evident in his tone. "Didn't you get it?"

Jim sighed, his stern expression softening slightly. "Well, we might have had a little... accident... with the telegraph machines in Jed's study this morning."

"Accident?" Tom asked, with a look of confusion.

Jim glanced back toward the main house, a faint smirk tugging at the corner of his mouth. "You see, Pat Bennington—"

"That's all the explanation I need!" Tom held up a hand, cutting the tall, lanky foreman off mid-sentence. The mere mention of Pat's name was enough to fill in the blanks. "Say no more."

Jim chuckled, the tension fully dissipated now. "Yeah, it's been one of those mornings." His smile faded as he recalled what Tom had said about the train. "Wait! You mean Jed and the others never made it to St. Louis?"

Tom nodded grimly. "That's why I'm here. And that's why I need the Swift."

Jim's eyes narrowed his voice firm with urgency. "If they're in trouble, we can't waste any time. But if you think I'm letting you take the Swift alone, you've got another thing coming. I'm going with you, and that's not up for debate."

Tom hesitated, recognizing the determination in

the foreman's eyes. He gave a quick nod. "Fine, but we need to move fast."

Before they could head inside, the distant rumble of wheels and the pounding of hooves echoed through the valley. Jim's eyes narrowed as the sound of the approaching wagon grew louder. Dust swirled in the distance, obscuring the figures at the reins. His hand instinctively hovered near his holstered revolver.

"Who in blazes...?" he murmured, squinting into the sunlight.

Jim relaxed only when the familiar shape of a stout rotund frame became visible through the haze. "It's Pat and Agatha," he said, letting out a deep breath.

The supply wagon barreled down the path, the dust cloud behind it growing as it approached. Pat Bennington gripped the reins tightly, his face a mix of determination and excitement. Beside him, Agatha Porter held a shotgun, her usual calm demeanor replaced with fierce resolve.

The wagon screeched to a halt as Pat yanked the reins hard, nearly tipping it over. He grabbed a second shotgun and leaped down, while Agatha calmly climbed over the side.

With his characteristic flair, Pat shouted, "We came to help! Where are the varmints?"

No sooner had the words left his mouth than Pat took a step forward, only to catch his foot on the

The sound of the approaching wagon
grew louder. Dust swirled in the
distance, obscuring the figures at the reins.

edge of the wagon's wheel. He stumbled, arms flailing, and landed flat on his face in the dirt. His hat tumbled a few feet away, coming to rest upside down.

Agatha shook her head, unable to suppress a smirk. "My hero," she said dryly.

Tom and Jim exchanged amused glances, the tension momentarily broken by Pat's antics.

"Well," Jim said, extending a hand to help Pat up, "looks like we've only got one varmint."

Pat dusted himself off, snatching his hat from the ground. "Just one?" he asked, puffing out his chest as he brandished the shotgun. "Where is the scoundrel? I'll handle him all by myself!"

"Let me at the lowlife that planned to steal Jed's airship!" He continued to shout waving his weapon for emphasis.

"Pat," Jim began, his tone steady, "you won't need that gun."

"Unarmed, is he?" Pat glanced toward Tom Miller. He shoved the shotgun into the young man's hands. "Hold this for me. I'll take this cutthroat on bare-knuckled!"

"Pat!" Jim shouted, his voice sharp enough to finally get his attention.

"What?" Pat snapped, spinning around.

Jim gestured toward Tom. "I think he has something to tell you."

Pat turned to the young man, who hesitated

under his gaze.

"Mr. Bennington," Tom began nervously, rubbing the back of his neck, "I'm the one who was trying to steal... er... I mean borrow Mr. Davenport's airship. I..."

"You?" Pat's eyes widened in horror as he stared at the shotgun in Tom's hands. "Ack! I gave you my gun!" he gasped dramatically. "What have I done? I've armed the enemy!"

He dropped to one knee, raising his hands high above his head. "Don't shoot me!"

Agatha rolled her eyes, tossing her own weapon onto the seat of the wagon. She stepped forward with an exasperated sigh. "Oh, for Pete's sake, Pat, he's not going to shoot you." Grabbing the shotgun from Tom, she tossed it next to the other one. "Now, put your arms down, you old fool!"

Pat glanced at her, thoroughly confused, as laughter erupted around him. Jim clapped him on the shoulder, his voice warm with amusement as he began explaining why Tom needed the airship.

Dusting off the last traces of dirt from his trousers, the rotund man straightened up, his expression suddenly resolute. "Well, if you're headed out to save Jed and the others, you're gonna need all the help you can get. I'm coming with you."

"So am I!" Agatha declared her tone firm.

Jim opened his mouth to protest, but Agatha

shot him a steely look that made it clear she wasn't taking no for an answer. "We're not asking, Mr. Davis," she said, determined.

Jim sighed, exchanging a quick glance with Tom. "We don't have time to argue, and let's be honest, telling either of them no is pointless."

Tom gave a reluctant nod. "Alright, but we need to move fast. Time's not on our side."

Turning to Levi and Sam, who had been watching with a mix of amusement and concern, Jim issued instructions. "You two stay behind. Take care of the wagon and the horses. Keep everything ready in case we need you to follow us."

Levi gave a curt nod. "You got it, Jim. Just holler if you need us."

Sam tipped his hat. "Stay safe out there."

With one final glance, Jim motioned to the others. "Let's get to the air. We've wasted enough time already."

Pat was already halfway to the hangar, muttering about "showing those varmints what for," while Agatha followed at a calm, measured pace, a small smile tugging at her lips.

"Pat, we don't know for sure there are any varmints..." Jim called out, but he quickly realized it was a waste of breath.

Tom and Jim exchanged one last look of shared resignation before hurrying after them, the weight of their mission pressing heavily on their shoulders.

Tom grinned despite the urgency in the air. "First, we get the Swift ready. Then, we head out."

Jim gave a final nod to Tom. "Alright, let's move. No time to lose."

The group quickly made their way to the Swift, already gleaming under the open sky, the morning sunlight shining through the open roof highlighting its sleek, polished surface. Even with the urgency of their mission, Jim couldn't help but feel a sense of awe.

"That's a mighty impressive piece of work," he muttered, more to himself than anyone else.

Pat, as usual, was far less restrained. "Gosh, ain't she fine!" he bellowed, practically bouncing on his toes. "Jed really outdid himself on this ship!"

Agatha, ever composed, raised a skeptical eyebrow. "Let's just hope it flies as well as it looks."

Tom approached the Swift's controls, his hands moving with practiced efficiency. "Engines first, then we're airborne."

Jim, Pat, and Agatha climbed aboard, each reacting in their own way. Jim took a deep breath, steadying himself as he gripped the railing. Pat vibrated with uncontainable excitement, already leaning over the side. Agatha found a spot to sit, folding her hands neatly in her lap, though her eyes never left the controls, a hint of curiosity and wariness creeping into her otherwise composed demeanor.

Tom's hands flew over the levers. The engines roared to life, the deep, resonant hum reverberating through the air. The deck beneath their feet began to vibrate as the Swift powered up.

"Here we go," Tom announced as he pulled the lever to detach the mooring lines. The Swift gave a slight jolt before rising smoothly. The sensation of lifting off was unlike anything else—a gentle yet powerful ascent, as though the ship itself was eager to leave the earth behind.

Jim instinctively tightened his grip on the railing, his knuckles turning white. "Steady..." he murmured, his eyes fixed on the horizon.

Pat, meanwhile, was nearly hanging over the side, his eyes wide with wonder. "We're flying! We're actually flying!" His face broke into a grin as bright as the morning sun. "Yahoo!"

Agatha, maintaining her composure, allowed the smallest of smiles to touch her lips. "It's certainly... a unique experience."

As the Swift cleared the immediate area, the landscape unfolded beneath them like a living map. The ranch became a patchwork of greens and browns, dotted with tiny figures of workers who paused to wave at the departing vessel.

Agatha, seated primly at first, appeared the picture of calm. But as the ship climbed higher, she couldn't resist the pull of curiosity. Rising from her seat, she approached the railing. Glancing down at the receding earth, her gaze lingered for a moment. The vastness of the open sky and the shrinking world below seemed to soften her usual reserve.

"What an impressive view..." Her heart skipped a beat, though her face remained impassive. "From way up here..." Agatha murmured as she stepped back and eased into her seat once more. Her voice was steady, but her fingers briefly tightened around the armrest. With practiced grace, she adjusted her posture and smoothed her skirt, as though nothing had happened.

Jim exhaled, at last, his grip on the rail relaxing. Outwardly, he projected calm, but his heart hammered like a blacksmith's forge. Watching the ground shrink beneath them sent an involuntary shiver down his spine.

Fixing his gaze straight ahead, he resolutely avoided looking down. He forced his breathing to steady and spoke with the authority of a seasoned foreman. "Alright, Tom. Where to?" His voice carried a commanding calm that belied the churn of nerves within.

Tom adjusted the controls with precision, setting their course. "We'll head north first, get a good view of the land, and then chart a straight path toward the train's last known location. From there, we'll follow the tracks until we find them."

Pat, still hanging over the side, let out a jubilant

whoop. "This is the best day ever!" Glancing back at the others, he quickly added, "Not counting Jed and everyone else disappearing, of course."

Agatha rose again, making her way to his side. She placed a firm hand on his shoulder. "Pat, if you fall off this ship, I'm not diving over after you."

The rotund man chuckled but shuffled back from the edge. "Aww, Aggy, you wouldn't jump overboard to save me?"

Her lips curled into a sly smile. "Just be glad I don't give you a little push to get started." She chuckled her laughter light but carrying an edge of truth.

Jim shook his head, a grin tugging at his usually stern face. "Alright, folks, enough fooling around. We've got a job to do."

Tom nodded without looking back, his focus locked on the horizon. "Operation Skybound Rescue begins!"

****

Later that same day, over two hundred miles east of Davenport Ranch, Jedidiah Davenport, Matthew Colton, and Professor Phineas Hargroves huddled in a makeshift campsite deep in the woods. They were joined by Mayor Carter and Samuel Harris, the president of the D.&R.W. Railroad, along with the surviving passengers and crew from the train wreck.

The previous twenty-four hours had been a relentless ordeal. The train, swallowed by the ravine, had taken any hope of salvaging supplies with it. Survival now depended on ingenuity and the sparse offerings of the forest. Under the midday sun, the group was scattered about the camp, each person occupied with tasks essential to their survival.

Jedidiah crouched near a small stream, filling makeshift containers with water. His gaze often flickered to the sky, searching for any sign of rescue. "We can't linger here much longer," he said, determined. "If no one comes by nightfall, we'll have to go for help ourselves."

Matthew, busy stripping bark from a tree to create edible rations, nodded in agreement. "You're right, Jed. We can't just sit here waiting for a miracle."

Phineas, hunched over as he fashioned a rudimentary snare from twigs and twine, glanced up. "Personally, I'd prefer not to endure another night in this wretched wilderness. It's getting frightfully cold after sundown."

Jedidiah's jaw tightened as he scanned the weary faces of their companions. "And I don't think these folks can handle many more nights out here. The longer we wait, the worse it'll get."

Matthew paused what he was doing and

surveyed the camp. The fatigue and fear etched into the survivors' faces were impossible to ignore. "We've got to keep spirits up, though. If they lose hope, we're in real trouble."

Mayor Carter, perched on a fallen log, rubbed his hands together for warmth despite the afternoon sun. "I agree. We need to keep everyone busy. Idle minds will only lead to despair. And let's not forget, once the good people of Spoon Fork realize their beloved mayor is missing, the whole town will be out looking for me!"

Samuel Harris, seated awkwardly on a makeshift stool of branches, winced as he shifted his twisted ankle. He let out a dry chuckle. "As comforting as that is, I'd wager the railroad will have a search party out here faster than your townsfolk, Carter. They'd be lost without me keeping the trains running on time."

The mayor arched an eyebrow, a smirk tugging at his lips. "Fearless leader, huh? I didn't realize managing timetables made you a hero, Harris."

Samuel chuckled, adjusting his position to ease the discomfort. "You'd be surprised, Carter. Keeping trains running is no small feat. And let's not forget, it's my railroad that connects Spoon Fork to the outside world. If anyone's coming, it'll be my men leading the way."

Mayor Carter leaned forward, his eyes gleaming with mock challenge. "Oh, really? My constituents are a loyal bunch. They'll be scouring every inch of this forest as we speak. Meanwhile, your railroad men are probably too busy playing cards in the depot to notice you're gone."

Samuel raised an eyebrow, clearly enjoying the back-and-forth. "We'll see who gets here first, Carter. My money's on the railroad. They're efficient, unlike your townsfolk. After all, they won't be able to form a search party until after they've finished their checker game at the general store."

The mayor chuckled, shaking his head. "You underestimate the spirit of Spoon Fork. My people know how to act fast when it matters. Besides, they'll be driven by more than duty. They'll be driven by their love for their mayor."

Samuel smirked, leaning back against a tree trunk. "Well, you can question them about it after my crew gets us back safely."

The banter caught the attention of a few other survivors, who chuckled at the playful rivalry. Jedidiah glanced over with a faint smile. "How about we focus on staying alive? Just a thought."

Both men laughed, their momentary competition easing some of the tension in the camp. "Fair enough, Davenport," Carter said. "But mark my words, it'll be my townsfolk who come to the rescue first."

Samuel leaned forward, wagging a finger. "I'll

take that bet, Carter. And when my men show up first, you owe me a round of drinks in St. Louis."

Carter grinned. "Deal. But when my people get here first, you'll be the one buying in Spoon Fork."

Jedidiah stood, slinging one of the makeshift water containers over his shoulder. "In the meantime, maybe Matthew and I should start walking down the tracks. Maybe we can run into someone along the way."

Phineas, still fiddling with the snare, looked up. "My dear boy, you do realize that St. Louis is still over a hundred miles from here?"

"One hundred and fifty miles, to be exact," the railroad engineer stated as he walked up.

"One hundred and fifty miles?" Jedidiah gulped, then his jaw tightened. "Well, we can't just stay here doing nothing!"

Before anyone could respond, a sudden rustling in the underbrush sent a jolt through the camp. The sound was deliberate and heavy like something large was closing in. Makeshift weapons were gripped tightly, eyes darting nervously. Jedidiah, with steely resolve, seized the paralyzing ray gun from his belt. The air crackled with tension as he stepped forward, the device humming ominously in his hand.

Without a word, he edged toward the source of the noise, every rustle of leaves tightening the knot of fear in his gut. The shadows shifted, and a low, menacing growl broke the silence. Jedidiah's breath hitched. In an instant, the underbrush exploded, and something massive hurtled toward him. His finger clenched on the trigger—

CHAPTER VIII

Through the Wilderness

Jedidiah Davenport's heart raced as the massive figure tore through the underbrush. The ground trembled beneath its heavy steps. A gleaming brass automaton loomed before him, gears whirring and pistons hissing in a relentless advance. Jedidiah's face twisted in shock, the terror momentarily paralyzing him. Then, instincts kicked in.

He squeezed the trigger of his ray gun, the device humming to life as a sizzling beam of green light shot toward the mechanical giant. To his dismay, the charge dissipated harmlessly against its brass plating. Frustration flickered in his eyes as realization struck—the ray gun was designed for living targets, useless against a mechanical giant like this.

The automaton pressed on, each thunderous step reverberating through the ground. Jedidiah's mind raced, searching desperately for a plan. Just

Jedidiah squeezed the trigger of his ray gun, the
device humming to life as a sizzling beam of
green light shot toward the mechanical giant.

as he braced for impact, a sharp voice cut through the tension.

"Cogsworth! Stand down!"

The automaton's movements slowed, its gears grinding to a halt as it loomed over Jedidiah, motionless but imposing. From behind the massive machine, two figures emerged from the underbrush, dirt-streaked and weary, their clothes torn as if they'd trekked through miles of harsh wilderness.

Jedidiah's grip on the ray gun slackened as he recognized the familiar faces: Edwin Bancroft and Jonathan Blake. Though disheveled, both appeared unharmed. A collective sigh of relief swept through the survivors, punctuated by gasps and murmurs of astonishment.

Jedidiah stepped around the mechanical monstrosity, his voice cracking with emotion. "Jonathan? Edwin? Where did you come from?"

Edwin managed a weary smile, brushing twigs and leaves from his coat. "It's a long story," he replied, his voice hoarse but steady. "When we got to St. Louis and heard the train never arrived, we knew something was wrong. So we set out to find you."

****

Earlier that day, over a hundred miles away, the Icarus soared gracefully through the skies, its descent smooth as it glided toward an open field on the outskirts of St. Louis. Edwin Bancroft and Jonathan Blake kept their eyes fixed on the horizon, where the faint outline of the city was slowly coming into focus.

"We arrived a little later than I planned, but I'm sure they're still here," Jonathan murmured, eyeing the nearly empty field. He guided the airship down and hovered it just above the ground, lowering the mooring lines to stabilize the vessel. As they disembarked, their boots crunched on dry grass. They began their trek into town.

Within minutes, the station came into view—a bustling hub of travelers and freight, now overshadowed by a sense of unease. A crowd had gathered near the main platform, their voices a chaotic mix of worry and speculation. Jonathan and Edwin exchanged a knowing glance.

"Something's wrong," Edwin said, his tone uneasy.

As they reached the edge of the gathering, a frazzled station clerk, his hat askew, nearly collided with Edwin in his haste. Edwin caught the man's arm, steadying him.

"Whoa there! What's going on?" he asked.

The clerk's eyes darted nervously. "The train carrying the railroad president and the mayor of Spoon Fork is hours overdue," he blurted, his voice strained. "It should've arrived before dawn."

Jonathan's expression hardened. "When was your last contact with it?"

"Right after it left Spoon Fork, Kansas," the clerk replied, his voice trembling. "Nothing since. It was supposed to check in yesterday morning, then again last night. Folks are sayin' there might've been an accident, but no one knows for sure. Could be anywhere along the hundreds of miles between here and there."

Edwin nodded grimly, letting the man hurry off before turning back to his father. "That's a long stretch of track. If they did run into trouble, it could take some time for word to reach us here."

Jonathan Blake agreed, his mind started racing. "Then we can't wait. We'll have to search for them ourselves. Every minute counts."

Pushing through the crowd, they overheard snippets of anxious conversations:

"No D.&R.W. Railroad train has ever been this late before..."

"...must be some kind of breakdown or worse..."

The tension in the air was suffocating. Many of the gathered onlookers were waiting for loved ones or vital cargo, their faces etched with worry. Jonathan made his way to the telegraph office, where an operator was frantically tapping out messages.

"Any news?" Jonathan asked, his voice low but commanding.

The telegraph operator barely looked up, his fingers moving rapidly across the keys. "Nothing yet," he muttered. "Been trying to reach stations up and down the line, but it's like they vanished into thin air."

Jonathan thanked the man and then turned to his son. "Let's fire up the Icarus and go find them!"

Wasting no time, the two men strode back to the airship with purposeful urgency. Jonathan's mind churned as they walked, picturing the treacherous terrain between St. Louis and Spoon Fork. Despite the new tracks being laid, he knew the region had its dangers. If the train had run afoul of something —or someone—the passengers could be in desperate need of help.

Reaching the Icarus, Jonathan dashed up the loading ramp and headed straight to the helm. His hands moved swiftly over the controls, powering up the engines. The familiar hum filled the air, as steam vents hissed and gears clanked into motion. Edwin followed close behind, securing their supplies and unfolding the maps his father had spread out for their trip.

Jonathan shot Edwin a determined glance. "We'll follow the train's route precisely. If they're out there, we'll find them."

Edwin studied the map, his brow furrowed. "But how long will it take? They could be anywhere between here and Spoon Fork!"

"That's why we haven't a moment to lose," Jonathan said firmly, releasing the mooring lines.

The Icarus lifted smoothly, the St. Louis landscape shrinking below as they gained altitude. Once at cruising height, the airship veered westward, tracing the iron veins of the railway. Each mile brought them closer to the unknown. Edwin stood by the railing, his sharp eyes scanning the landscape below.

For hours, they soared above the terrain, the tracks below snaking through valleys and cutting through dense thickets. Occasionally, Edwin spotted landmarks—a weathered barn, a dried-up riverbed, a crooked tree—and marked them on the map as potential reference points.

The morning crept toward midday, the sun casting sharp shadows across the landscape. Edwin adjusted the telescopic lenses of his goggles to counter the glare and leaned over the edge, his gaze fixed on a distant bend in the tracks. His heart quickened as he scanned the area, hoping for any sign of the missing train.

"There!" Edwin shouted, his voice cracking with urgency as he leaned over the railing and pointed toward the horizon. His heart raced as the faint shimmer of twisted metal caught the sunlight. "The train! Or what's left of it... Down in that ravine!" He adjusted his goggles, his breath quickening. "The tracks... They're blown apart!

And there's a landslide… It's a complete disaster!"

Jonathan immediately glanced in the direction Edwin indicated, his expression grim as he began to slow the Icarus. Edwin, noticing the shift in their trajectory, spun toward his father in disbelief. "What are you doing?" he demanded, his voice sharp with frustration. "You're taking us away from the wreck!"

"There's nowhere to land here," Jonathan said evenly, though his own worry was evident in his furrowed brow. "We'll have to go back to the clearing we passed earlier."

"That's miles away!" Edwin's fists clenched at his sides, his desperation mounting. "We have to check for survivors! We can't waste time!"

Jonathan motioned toward the engine's pressure gauges, their needles quivering dangerously in the red zone. "If we don't land soon, we'll be the ones needing rescue," he said, his tone calm but firm. "We burned through most of what little coal we had flying from Toronto to St. Louis, and we didn't have time to refuel before we left."

Edwin's face fell as the weight of their predicament settled on him. His chest heaved, his frustration boiling over into a single exclamation: "Holy smokes!" His gaze darted back toward the ravine, the sight of the mangled train searing into his mind. The need to act burned in his gut, but the stark reality of their situation tethered him in place.

Jonathan gripped the large wooden wheel, steering the Icarus toward the clearing. As the airship hovered just above the ground, he immediately secured the mooring lines, his movements swift and practiced. The ship might not travel any further, but at least they were safely grounded.

"What are we going to do now?" Edwin asked, pacing as the gravity of the situation sank in.

"We'll head to the wreck and look for survivors," Jonathan said, his voice steady.

"And even if we find them, how will we get everyone out of there?" Edwin shot back.

Jonathan glanced at him with a small smile. "We'll cross that bridge when we get to it."

"A bridge would be nice," Edwin muttered. "We've got to cut through the wilderness just to reach the tracks, and it's only the two of us."

"Only the *three* of us..." Jonathan smiled at his son as he turned on his heel and led the way down into the cargo hold. "Help me open Davenport's present."

They grabbed a couple of crowbars and began prying the crate open. Moments later, the wooden side fell away with a crash, revealing a shadowy interior. Two glowing eyes pierced the dim light as Jonathan spoke with quiet authority: "Cogsworth, activate."

With a soft whirr, the automaton stirred to life.

Gears clicked and pistons hissed as the mechanical figure rose from its crouched position within the crate. Its brass joints gleamed, polished to perfection, while intricate gears churned visibly in its chest with an almost lifelike rhythm. Cogsworth's design was a masterpiece of refinement and strength.

He wore a sleek vest adorned with metallic accents, a top hat perched jauntily on his head, and round goggles resting on its brim. The automaton stood at full height, towering over the two men, its presence both reassuring and formidable.

Jonathan and Edwin stepped back, momentarily awed by the imposing figure towering over them, its glowing eyes casting an eerie light in the confined space.

Edwin watched with a mix of fascination and relief. "He's the most fantastic one you've created yet," he murmured, reaching out to examine the intricate details of Cogsworth's design.

Jonathan chuckled, adjusting a dial on the automaton's control panel. "I always aim to outdo myself. Our mechanical friend here is built for heavy-duty work, and he'll be invaluable in the rough terrain." He turned to the automaton. "Cogsworth, follow us and be ready to assist."

The automaton's gears whirred as it responded in a low, metallic tone. "Command received. Initiating follow mode." Unlike earlier models, this one spoke in complete sentences—a significant upgrade Jonathan had devised during its assembly.

Jonathan and Edwin climbed back to the deck, Cogsworth following with a steady, lumbering gait, each step accompanied by the rhythmic chug of its internal mechanisms. As they disembarked from the Icarus and crossed the open field, Edwin glanced over his shoulder at the hulking figure behind them.

"With any luck," Jonathan said, breaking the silence as they neared the edge of the wilderness, "Cogsworth can help clear the path, and maybe even lend a hand with rescue work."

Edwin nodded, his thoughts fixed on the distant wreckage in the ravine. "Let's just hope we're not too late."

The trio pressed on into the dense underbrush, each footstep crunching on twigs and leaves as they advanced toward the crash site. Cogsworth moved ahead, clearing branches and debris with mechanical precision, his brass hands sweeping obstacles aside. Jonathan and Edwin followed close behind, their attention sharpened on the survivors they hoped to find.

Hours passed as they navigated the rugged terrain, their path winding through uneven ground and thickets. Finally, the ravine came into view, its jagged edges silhouetted against the fading daylight. Jonathan folded his map, pocketed his compass, and turned to Edwin. "We're almost there. If they're still around, we'll find them soon."

Edwin nodded but froze mid-step when a sudden rustling echoed from a nearby thicket. The unmistakable hum of a weapon charging up cut through the silence.

"Hold," Jonathan commanded, raising a hand to signal Cogsworth to stop. But the automaton, either unheeding or unconcerned, kept advancing. Jonathan squinted through the foliage, his heart pounding as he made out a shadowy figure ahead, aiming a weapon directly at the mechanical giant.

Suddenly recognizing the stance and silhouette of the person ahead, Jonathan raised his voice, firm and commanding. "Cogsworth! Stand down!"

The automaton halted instantly, its gears emitting a soft hiss as it froze mid-step. Jonathan and Edwin pushed their way through the dense underbrush, branches clawing at their clothes as they emerged into the clearing.

There, standing with wide eyes and his ray gun still clutched tightly in his hands, was Jedidiah Davenport. His expression flickered between shock and relief as he took in the sight of the two familiar faces.

****

As Jonathan Blake related his story, the other passengers, who had never seen an automaton before, gathered around Cogsworth with wide-eyed fascination. They murmured in awe, tentatively reaching out to touch its gleaming brass casing and intricate gears. The automaton's glowing eyes tracked each movement with a mechanical awareness that left them both captivated and slightly uneasy.

Matthew Colton found himself torn between joining the crowd around the mechanical man and staying close to hear every word of Jonathan's tale.

His gaze darted between the towering machine and the men who had arrived with it, curiosity and excitement battling with his desire for answers. Unable to resist, he reached out, his fingertips brushing Cogsworth's polished arm, marveling at the craftsmanship.

Jonathan's voice pulled him back. "And that's how we happened to find you," he finished with a note of pride.

"Gosh!" Matthew exclaimed, snapping back to attention. "I'm just glad you did. We've been stranded out here far too long. It's about time we were rescued."

"My dear boy," Professor Phineas B. Hargroves commented as he placed a hand on the young man's shoulder. "Perhaps you weren't listening to all the details of the story, considering how much you were ogling that mechanical monster, but the Icarus is out of fuel!"

"Yeah the Icarus is out of..." Matthew whirled around to Jonathan and Edwin. "Wait… That means you're stranded here with us?"

"At least we've got shelter aboard the ship," Jedidiah remarked thoughtfully, then hesitated. "Although, if the airship is that far from the tracks, a rescue party might never find us."

"If I might make a suggestion," Mayor Benjamin Carter spoke up, his tone measured. "Perhaps some of us could go aboard the… what did you call it... the Icarus? Freshen up and get some rest while the rest of you remain here."

He turned to Jonathan and asked, "Does that ship of yours have a sleeping chamber?"

"It's my ship," Phineas cleared his throat, stepping forward. "And, as a matter of fact, it does. But who do you suggest gets the privilege?"

"Well," the Mayor said with a pompous air, "the obvious choice would be the two most important people here—the president of the railroad, Mr. Samuel Harris, and myself. After all, I am your beloved Mayor."

Phineas raised an eyebrow and took another step toward the Mayor. "Perhaps you'd like to hear my opinion of your idea…" He took one final step towards the arrogant man.

Jedidiah and Matthew quickly moved between

the two, diffusing the tension.

"Phineas," Jedidiah said calmly, "I think Mayor Carter has a point."

"Yeah," Matthew added with a grin, "and if the Mayor and Mr. Harris want to hike a few hours through the woods, that's no concern of ours."

"How far is it?" Jedidiah asked Jonathan.

"Oh, I'd say six or seven miles… No more than ten at the most," Jonathan replied.

The Mayor and Mr. Harris exchanged a glance, their confidence quickly deflating. "We'll stay here," they said in unison.

"Wise decision," Phineas muttered.

Jonathan glanced around at the weary faces of the group, the gravity of their predicament evident. "So it's agreed—we stay close to the wreck site if we want the rescue party to find us." Turning to Jedidiah, he added, "I don't suppose you've managed to gather much to eat?"

Jedidiah shrugged. "A little. Mostly berries and tree bark."

Matthew groaned, rubbing his stomach. "I don't know about you all, but I'm so hungry I swear I can smell food cooking."

The others exchanged skeptical looks. Edwin chuckled. "Matt, you've been out here too long. No way you're smelling food."

But then Jedidiah's nose twitched, and his expression shifted from doubt to surprise. "Wait… I think I smell it too."

A murmur of disbelief spread through the group as, one by one, they caught the faint aroma drifting on the breeze. Faces turned toward the wind, bewildered, until Phineas suddenly pointed skyward. "Look there!"

Silhouetted against the afternoon sun, an airship approached. Thick black smoke trailed behind it— not from its engines but from some unknown source onboard. Its course was steady, casting a dark shadow over the trees below.

Jedidiah's breath caught. "It's the Swift."

"And it's on fire!" Matthew shouted.

CHAPTER IX

The Scent of Trouble

"Look!" someone else shouted, pointing toward the sky. The cry shattered the tense silence, followed by a chorus of panicked murmurs. All eyes turned toward the horizon, where the Swift loomed into view, its silhouette framed by a faint trail of black smoke.

"It's on fire!" Jedidiah Davenport echoed the words of his childhood friend, his voice cracking with alarm. "My ship!" He lunged forward, straining against Matthew Colton and Phineas B. Hargroves, who each grabbed one of his arms to hold him back.

"My dear boy," the professor remarked calmly. "Steady yourself. There's nothing you can do about it from here."

Desperation etched across Jedidiah's face as he twisted in their hold, his arm outstretched toward the Swift as if sheer willpower could halt the smoke. "Let me go! I have to—" His voice broke, and he swallowed hard, his breaths coming in short, uneven gasps.

By now, the other passengers had gathered close, their expressions shifting from relief to alarm as a growing sense of dread spread through the group. The ship drew closer, its thin, dark plume curling ominously behind it.

"Everyone, stay back!" Jonathan Blake called, raising a hand to calm the crowd. "If it's ablaze, we don't want anyone too close." Having lost his own vessel to an inferno, the older man was all too familiar with the dangers of a burning airship.

The children in the group huddled closer to their parents, their wide eyes reflecting fear. Mayor Carter muttered nervously, "Heavens, I hope they're alright up there."

As the airship descended, the details of the vessel grew clearer. To Jedidiah's surprise, the smoke wasn't as thick as it had initially seemed, and there were no visible flames licking the hull. Yet something about the scene was strange.

A faint but unmistakable odor began wafting through the air, carried down by the gentle breeze. Jonathan's brow furrowed, his nose twitching slightly. "Is that…?"

"Burnt meat?" Edwin finished, wrinkling his nose in distaste.

As the ship hovered just above the clearing, the

source of the commotion became clear. Standing on the deck, flipping what looked like patties over an ornate portable grill, was Pat Bennington. A plume of black smoke billowed up from his cooking station, accompanied by the unmistakable smell of charred beef.

Pat, oblivious to the alarm he'd caused, focused intently on his task, muttering to himself as he turned one of the patties. Another plume of smoke rose, and he coughed, waving a hand to clear the air. Behind him, Agatha Porter fanned the smoke with a look that balanced irritation and amusement.

As the Swift moved closer, a rope ladder unfurled over the side, swaying gently above the ground since there wasn't enough room for a full landing. Jedidiah, Jonathan, and Edwin rushed forward, laughter bubbling up at the absurdity of the scene.

"The cavalry has arrived!" Edwin declared, raising an imaginary bugle to his lips and mimicking its call.

Moments later, a figure appeared at the edge of the deck, carefully descending the swaying ladder. Tom Miller's face came into view, breaking into a grin as he spotted the familiar faces below.

"Tom!" Jedidiah shouted, waving him down. "What are you doing here? And how did you get my ship?"

Tom landed with a soft thud and straightened,

Standing on the deck, flipping what looked like patties over an ornate portable grill, was Pat Bennington.

his grin widening. "We got a telegraph saying you never arrived in St. Louis, so I rode out to your ranch and... borrowed the Swift to come find you."

"Borrowed it, huh?" Jedidiah smirked, crossing his arms. "Well, what took you so long?"

Tom chuckled, jerking a thumb up toward the deck. "We would've been here sooner if Pat hadn't decided to start his, uh... culinary experiment mid-flight."

Pat leaned over the rail with a broad grin, oblivious to the chuckles below. "What's the big deal? Just cooking up some meat patties for everyone! Figured you'd all appreciate a hot meal!"

Tom rolled his eyes and turned back to Jedidiah. "He found your portable stove in the cargo hold, next to that fancy steam-powered cooler you installed for the airship race."

"Well, I'm glad he did!" Jedidiah laughed, already climbing up the ladder. "We're all starving, and even if they're a little burnt, we'll take 'em!"

"Only a few got burned!" Pat shouted, calling over his shoulder as he flipped another patty. "Still got a ton of 'em that are perfectly fine!"

Jonathan laughed, shaking his head. "Well, you certainly surprised us, Pat. We thought the ship was on fire!"

Pat blinked, genuinely confused. "Fire? Oh, no, just a little well done maybe, but nothing was on fire."

Agatha rolled her eyes, crossing her arms. "Well done, he says. Nearly smoked us all off the deck!"

Pat glanced down at the charred patties, then back at the group, shrugging with a sheepish smile. "Well, I guess I can always toss those few out."

"Nothing of the kind!" Mayor Carter interjected, stepping forward. "I happen to like mine... extra well done!"

"So do I!" Samuel Harris, president of the D.&R.W. Railroad, added, moving to join him.

Everyone else gathered around as Pat began distributing the food. The mood lightened, laughter and gratitude replacing the earlier tension. People eagerly took the patties on rough slices of bread, grateful just for something to eat.

Jedidiah took a bite, chewing thoughtfully despite the burnt edges. He gave Pat a nod of approval. "Not bad, Pat. Not bad at all. I can't believe the three of you set out to rescue us like this."

"Four of us!" Tom corrected, grinning.

"Four?" Jedidiah asked, confused.

Tom motioned toward the helm. Standing there, gripping the wheel with white-knuckled determination, was Jim Davis, foreman of the Davenport ranch.

"I asked him to hold it steady while I climbed down the ladder," Tom explained, his grin widening.

Laughter rippled through the crowd as they bit into their makeshift sandwiches, relief, and gratitude filling the air. But the joy was short-lived.

Without warning, a powerful jolt tugged the Swift downward, sending them stumbling and clutching onto whatever was nearby for balance.

"What in blazes—?" Jim shouted, gripping the wheel as the airship lurched again.

Agatha, who had been leaning over the side, let out a piercing scream. "It's a... It's a monster!" she cried, pointing over the rail with a trembling hand.

All heads turned toward the ground below, where Cogsworth stood, his massive brass frame gleaming in the sunlight. His glowing eyes were fixed on the deck above as his powerful arms gripped the rope ladder. With mechanical precision, he pulled, his incredible strength causing the Swift to jolt downward. The ropes groaned in protest. Its gears whirring and arms churning with mechanical precision as it tried in vain to climb.

"What is that thing?" Pat exclaimed, his face pale. "Jed, is that some kind of otherworldly creature?"

Jedidiah shook his head, his jaw tightening. "No, that's not a creature, Pat. That's an automaton..."

Jonathan quickly stepped forward, his voice firm and commanding. "Cogsworth! Stand down!"

The automaton froze mid-motion, its metal

joints creaking as it clung to the ladder. "Release the Swift and return to the Icarus immediately. Stay there and guard it until we can come for it. Do not attempt to board this ship."

Obediently, Cogsworth loosened its grip on the ladder. The Swift lurched upward a few feet, the ropes swaying as the mechanical man turned in a smooth, precise motion. Without hesitation, it lumbered across the field, heading into the wilderness toward the Icarus.

Everyone on deck stared, their mouths agape as they tried to process what they'd just witnessed.

Agatha clutched her chest, breathing heavily. "I… I thought we were being invaded by some… some monster!"

Jedidiah, still chuckling despite himself, placed a steadying hand on her shoulder. "Believe it or not, that 'monster' happens to belong to our friend Jonathan Blake."

"Doesn't belong to me," the older man replied simply. "That automaton belongs to you!"

"Me?" Jedidiah whirled around in shock. "That —mechanical man belongs to me? How?"

Jonathan folded his arms, a small smile playing on his lips. "It's a gift. To thank you for letting your crew build me a new airship and only charging me for the cost of materials."

Jedidiah blinked. "Well, I appreciate the gratitude, Jonathan, but what exactly am I supposed to do with an automaton?"

Jonathan sighed, scratching the back of his neck. "Cogsworth is worth his weight in gold when it comes to hauling and heavy lifting." He glanced toward Pat Bennington and Agatha Porter, adding with a hint of humor, "And he can also help around the house with cooking and cleaning."

Pat shook his head, still glancing nervously over the edge of the deck. "Well, he's definitely got the strength. He nearly pulled the whole ship out of the sky!"

The group burst into laughter, the tension fading as they regained their composure. Moving toward the deck's edge, they watched the automaton plod dutifully out of sight.

Jonathan gave a reassuring nod. "He'll guard the Icarus until we can come back for it. For now, let's focus on getting everyone here to safety. I think we've had enough surprises for one day."

"Agreed," Jedidiah said, clearing his throat as he addressed the group. "Alright, here's the plan. We'll take the Swift and get everyone to St. Louis as originally planned. Once we've delivered the passengers safely, we'll pick up more coal and return for the Icarus."

Jonathan's expression suddenly shifted, his eyes widening as he patted the inner pocket of his coat. He reached inside, feeling the crinkling of paper, and pulled out a carefully sealed envelope. Its wax seal, bearing the faint impression of an octopus insignia, was still intact.

"Jed," Jonathan said, stepping forward and holding out the envelope. "I almost forgot, I've got something for you. This arrived while Edwin and I were still in Toronto."

Jedidiah raised an eyebrow, taking the envelope with a curious look. His thumb ran over the seal as he examined it. "A letter? Who is it from?"

"That's the thing, we don't know," Jonathan replied, his voice dropping to a murmur, instinctively guarded. "It was left for you by an intruder who broke into my shop while Edwin and I were chasing someone else who'd already broken in earlier."

Jedidiah's brow furrowed as he studied the envelope addressed to him. He nodded slowly, his lips pressing into a thoughtful line. "Well, I can't say I'm entirely surprised," he admitted. Turning it over in his hands, he added, "I'm getting used to receiving strange packages in unusual ways."

As they spoke, the Swift began its ascent, rising gracefully into the sky. Tom Miller manned the helm, his steady hands keeping the ship on course, while Edwin Bancroft, acting as navigator, studied the charts and directed their route toward St. Louis. Jedidiah, Matthew, and Phineas stepped aside, giving the two of them space to focus on their tasks.

In the relative quiet at the ship's edge, Jedidiah looked down at the envelope Jonathan Blake had delivered to him.

With a steady hand, he broke the wax seal and unfolded the letter. His eyes scanned the elegant script before he began to read aloud:

"To Jedidiah Davenport,

It has come to my attention that recent events require an exchange of information. Time is of the utmost importance. I anticipate you will be prepared to accommodate my arrival on the 22nd, at your ranch. Our rendezvous promises to shed light on matters of considerable importance.

I trust you will have the time for me.

Yours,
Lady Seraphina Blackwood."

Matthew raised an eyebrow. "Considerable importance, huh?"

Jedidiah folded the letter neatly and slipped it back into his pocket. "I don't know what most of it's about," he said, his tone thoughtful, "but I've got a feeling all this talk about time has something to do with that pocket watch I was sent from New York."

Suddenly Professor Hargroves darted forward with uncharacteristic speed. Without so much as a word, he reached into Jedidiah's vest and plucked the letter from his pocket. His eyes darting over the elegant script with fervor. His mouth moved as he read silently, his expression shifting from surprise to awe and finally settling on something akin to panic-stricken exhilaration.

"Lady Seraphina Blackwood?" he said, his voice tinged with reverence. "Jedidiah, do you have any idea who that is?" He didn't wait for an answer, his words spilling out like a dam had burst. "She's not just anyone—she's a luminary of society! Patron of the arts, financier of scientific advancements, and rumored to have ties to half the aristocracy in Europe. And she's coming to Davenport Ranch!"

Jedidiah raised an eyebrow at the sudden outburst. "Phineas, I've had visitors to the ranch before. I think you're blowing this out of proportion."

"Out of proportion?" Phineas exclaimed, clutching at his cravat as though the mere thought of inadequacy might suffocate him. "Jed, this is Lady Seraphina Blackwood! We cannot host someone of her caliber in anything less than perfection! There's so much to do—so much to prepare!" He began pacing, muttering a mental checklist aloud. "The drapes will need to be replaced, the crystal and the silver polished. And we'll need to refresh the flowers in the foyer. Why don't we have flowers in the foyer?"

Matthew smirked, crossing his arms. "Since when do we have a foyer?"

"It's the hall." Jedidiah casually explained.

"All of the carpets will need to be cleaned!"

"We don't have any carpets..." Jedidiah tried to speak up.

Phineas waved him off impatiently. "Details, details. The point is, this ranch has to be impeccable. Impeccable, do you hear me?" He turned on his heel, walking away to make plans. "I must oversee everything personally. We'll need to send into town for supplies—no, for experts! Perhaps an entire staff of them! Davenport Ranch must shine like never before!"

Jedidiah sighed, pinching the bridge of his nose. "Phineas, she's coming here for a meeting, not a grand ball."

"Perhaps not," Phineas replied, his tone firm but his eyes alight with determination, "but one never knows what impressions may linger. A lady of her stature deserves no less than our best." He paused dramatically, turning to face the group. "Mark my words, gentlemen, if we do not rise to this occasion, it could reflect poorly on all of us. I will begin the moment we return home!"

****

Two weeks later, on Thursday, October 20, 1881, the late afternoon sun bathed Davenport Ranch in a golden light. Its rays filtered through the open doors of an old barn-turned-hangar, casting a warm glow over the freshly polished brass and iron framework of the Phoenix, Jedidiah's first airship. After weeks of hard work and meticulous care, the ship gleamed, restored to its former glory.

Jedidiah ran a hand along the Phoenix's hull, his expression a mix of pride and nostalgia. Beside him, Matthew Colton stood with arms crossed, his gaze sweeping over the repairs.

"It looks as good as new," Matthew remarked, squinting at the gleaming brass rivets and reinforced panels. "Feels like ages since we had it in working shape."

Jedidiah nodded, a faint smile tugging at his lips. "It's been through a lot, but with these repairs and the upgrades to the engine, it'll be back in the sky, stronger than ever."

Matthew gave a thoughtful nod, glancing around the hangar. "Where's the Professor? Is he on the other side of the ranch overseeing the final touches on Mr. Blake's new ship?"

Jedidiah chuckled softly. "He probably wandered off to the house, fussing over every detail for Lady Seraphina's arrival. That man's got enough plans to keep himself busy for another month."

At the mention of Lady Seraphina, Matthew's eyes lit up with curiosity. "Remind me again what her letter said? She sure knows how to be cryptic."

Jedidiah smirked and reached into his vest pocket, pulling out the now-familiar envelope. With care, he unfolded the letter and read it aloud once more.

Matthew listened intently, nodding as Jedidiah finished. "I trust you will have the time for me... You still think she's talking about the watch you lost during the train robbery?"

"She has to be," Jedidiah replied, his gaze drifting toward the ranch, where preparations for Lady Seraphina's arrival were in full swing. "Either way, we'll find out soon enough. In the meantime, let's check on the others. I'm sure by now Agatha and Pat are both ready to put their hands around Phineas' throat with all the orders he's been giving them."

As Jedidiah and Matthew approached the stately Victorian home, they noticed a group of men from the Davenport Freight Company loading empty crates onto freight wagons near the front porch. The empty boxes were stacked neatly, and the workers moved with practiced efficiency.

Jedidiah's brow furrowed in confusion. "What's going on here?" he muttered to Matthew as they stepped closer to one of the men.

One of the workers paused, tipping his hat respectfully. "Afternoon, Mr. Davenport. We're just finishing up with some deliveries and taking these crates back."

"Deliveries? I didn't order anything," Jedidiah replied, glancing toward the house with growing suspicion.

"No, but Mr. Hargroves did," another man chimed in.

"Mr. Hargroves did?" Jedidiah exchanged a knowing glance with Matthew. "That's... interesting."

Curiosity piqued, Jedidiah strode to the front door and stepped inside, Matthew Colton close on his heels. As they entered the parlor, both men froze, their eyes widening in astonishment.

The room was entirely transformed. Luxurious, Victorian-style furniture had replaced the old, simpler furnishings. Elegant chairs and an upholstered settee flanked a carved wooden table that sat prominently near the window. Ornate wallpaper adorned the walls, complemented by lush red drapery that hung dramatically over the windows. It was a stark contrast to the modest decor the room had previously housed.

In the corner, gleaming in the soft afternoon light, stood a magnificent square grand piano. Its ornate woodwork, intricate carvings, and delicate floral details bespoke exceptional craftsmanship. The sight instantly drew Jedidiah's attention. He approached slowly, running his hand along its polished surface, marveling at how it resembled a piano he'd once seen on a postcard of a grand hotel back East.

Matthew let out a low whistle as he took in the surroundings. "This... this is something else, Jed. It's like we walked into a whole new house."

Jedidiah's hand rested on the piano keys, his fingers pressing down lightly as if to confirm it was real. "But I didn't give him permission to order any of this," he murmured, his tone caught somewhere between confusion and irritation. His eyes swept over the room, taking in the plush upholstery, ornate carvings, and gilded accents. The elegance was undeniable, but it felt out of place—a stranger's vision imposed on his home.

Matthew whistled again, leaning closer to the intricately carved table. "Phineas has certainly outdone himself."

Jedidiah shook his head, disbelief flickering across his face. "Outdone himself? He's turned my home into a museum! What was he thinking?"

Suddenly, a voice called out from the distance, sharp and urgent: "Don't touch that!"

CHAPTER X

Preparations and Perfection

Jedidiah and Matthew spun around to see Phineas B. Hargroves rushing toward them, his face flushed and his tie slightly askew.

"That piano was just tuned and doesn't need to be tinkered with!" he said, hurrying over with an almost protective glance at the instrument.

Jedidiah's brow furrowed as he folded his arms, a mix of bewilderment and irritation crossing his face. "Phineas," he said slowly, the edge in his voice unmistakable, "would you mind explaining what on earth is going on here? Since when do you have the authority to furnish my entire house?"

Phineas straightened, his eyes sparkling with enthusiasm. "Ah, well, you see, Jed, it wasn't the whole house. Just this room and one other to start with." He gestured broadly as if showing off the grandeur. "I thought it was high time you had surroundings that matched the, uh, stature of

Davenport Ranch. And with Lady Seraphina coming, I figured it was the perfect opportunity to… elevate the ambiance, shall we say?"

"Elevate the ambiance?" Jedidiah echoed, incredulous. "And how, exactly, did you pay for this 'elevation'?"

Phineas hesitated, glancing toward the door as though considering escape, but then squared his shoulders. "A minor expenditure from the discretionary fund," he said, attempting a nonchalant wave. "Besides, Lady Seraphina is bound to appreciate the effort."

Jedidiah's eyes narrowed, a twitch of irritation crossing his face. "Phineas, those funds are not for impulse redecorating sprees! And a piano?" He gestured to the gleaming square grand with an exasperated sigh. "Who's supposed to play it?"

Phineas looked absolutely scandalized, his nose wrinkling in visible disgust. "No one! No one is to touch that piano." He straightened, his voice dripping with reverence. "A piano such as this is not meant to be played but to be admired and envied!"

Jedidiah's eyes widened in disbelief, his jaw dropping slightly. "Phineas… You bought a piano that can't be played?" He stared at the ornate instrument, then ran a hand over his face as though trying to make sense of it. "Why would anyone spend money on something so… impractical?"

Matthew stifled a chuckle, glancing at Jedidiah with amusement in his eyes. "Jed, maybe he's right. Lady Seraphina will most likely appreciate the effort."

Jedidiah shook his head, half exasperated and half amused. "I think you're both off your rockers!"

Then his brow furrowed, and he turned to Phineas, a note of suspicion creeping into his voice. "Wait a second... Where's all my old furniture?"

Phineas gave a dismissive wave. "Oh, I had it moved to the barn."

"The barn?!" Jedidiah exclaimed, his voice rising in disbelief. "The barn with all the rats?!"

Professor Hargroves arched a brow. "There may or may not still be a mouse infestation out there."

Jedidiah gaped at him. "Phineas, I won all that furniture at the county fair!"

The eccentric older man allowed himself a sly smirk. "That would explain a few things," he said dryly, before continuing as if nothing had happened.

He suddenly cast a satisfied glance around the room and announced, "Well, I must go check on Agatha Porter and Pat Bennington. They should be getting fitted into their new uniforms about now, and I need to ensure the tailoring is up to standard. I'll be back shortly."

With that, he walked away, leaving Jedidiah and Matthew standing in stunned silence.

Jedidiah blinked, his brow furrowing as Phineas' words replayed in his mind. He suddenly called out, "Wait! What other room?"

Phineas' voice rang out from the hallway, calm and nonchalant. "Oh, don't worry. The new china, china cabinet, and the rest of the dining room furniture will be here tomorrow—long before Lady Seraphina's arrival."

Jedidiah groaned, rubbing his temples as Matthew burst into laughter. "I need to lie down," Jedidiah muttered. He turned toward the settee and began to lower himself, only to hear Phineas' voice call out once again.

"Don't sit down!" the eccentric older man shouted. "No one is to sit on the new furniture until after Lady Seraphina's arrival!"

The tone was so sudden and forceful that Jedidiah froze mid-sit, his eyes wide. Trying to stop himself, he lost his balance and stumbled, landing with an ungraceful thud on the floor. He sat there, blinking up in stunned disbelief.

Matthew burst into laughter, grinning down at Jedidiah. "You alright down there, Jed?"

Jedidiah shot him a half-hearted glare. "Not one word, Matthew Colton. Not one word."

The dark haired young man just laughed harder, while Jedidiah muttered to himself about "elevated ambiances."

While Jedidiah continued to sulk on the floor,

Phineas strode into the kitchen, where Pat was adjusting his freshly tailored uniform in the reflection of a polished brass pot. Agatha stood nearby, stifling a laugh as Pat adjusted his collar with a mix of amusement and indifference.

"Very good!" Professor Hargroves announced as he entered the room. "You both look almost halfway presentable!"

Agatha started to smile, opening her mouth to thank him for the compliment, but froze mid-thought. Her expression shifted, and she placed her hands on her hips, narrowing her eyes at Phineas. "Almost halfway?"

Phineas shrugged, his tone matter-of-fact. "There's only so much I can do, considering what I started with."

Agatha's mouth fell open, a sharp retort already forming, but before she could reply, Pat Bennington grumbled, "Well, I don't see the need for these fancy new getups. I'm perfectly capable of cooking fine meals without needing to look like some high-society butler."

Phineas raised a brow, crossing his arms. "Pat, Lady Seraphina Blackwood is arriving in two days. This is an important event, and appearances matter. We need to make an impression."

Pat snorted, rolling his eyes. "An impression? She's coming to Davenport Ranch, not some ballroom in New York. My regular clothes are good enough, and so is my regular cooking. And speaking of which..." He picked up the menu Phineas had meticulously crafted and scanned it, frowning. "Roasted pheasant under glass? Truffled potatoes? Lavender crème brûlée?" He shook his head. "What's wrong with my stew and biscuits or a nice steak and potatoes? Lady Seraphina probably never had cooking like mine before!"

"And I plan to keep it that way!" Phineas looked horrified. "Stew and biscuits? Steak and potatoes? Pat, this woman is used to the finest cuisine! Her palate deserves more than... well, than basic ranch entrees."

Pat held up a hand, shaking his head. "Well, that is what she'll get here. Besides, Jed has come to expect my cooking, not these high-falutin dishes with ingredients nobody's ever heard of. And don't get me started on those cases of food you had shipped here."

Phineas' brow furrowed, his tone defensive. "What's wrong with the ingredients? I ordered only the best."

Pat crossed his arms, his expression exasperated. "Best? One case was full of snails! Had to throw the whole thing out!"

Phineas looked appalled, his face paling with shock. "You threw them out? Pat, that was the escargot!"

Pat raised an eyebrow, staring at him. "Escar—

what now? Look, all I know is, if it's crawlin' around in a shell, I ain't cooking it!"

Phineas clutched his forehead, looking as though he might faint. "Escargot, Pat. It's a delicacy!"

"Yeah, well, I'll stick with food fit for human consumption," Pat said with finality. "And no amount of fancy words is gonna convince me otherwise."

Phineas was beginning to look exasperated, but he composed himself, lifting his chin with exaggerated dignity. "My good man, allow me to elucidate."

Pat, not missing a beat, replied, "Oh well, go right ahead and elucidate. Just come back when you're done. I'll still be here trying not to soil my new uniform while I get rid of the rest of these gourmet delicacies." He gave a broad smile, his tone so lighthearted it was unclear if he was being earnest or just teasing.

Phineas blinked, momentarily thrown off. "No, you don't understand," he protested, stepping closer. "What I mean is… Let me explain!"

But Pat waved him off with a chuckle. "Look, Hargy, you ain't gotta explain. That's your own personal business. When you gotta elucidate, you gotta elucidate!" He turned and headed toward the countertop, leaving Phineas staring after him in bewilderment.

Agatha Porter, enjoying the exchange and pleased to see someone else being tormented by the rotund man, continued standing in the corner, watching in blissful silence.

Just as Phineas regained his composure, he decided to change the subject. "Ah, Pat, before I forget—have you managed to address the mouse issue in the barn?"

Pat grinned, motioning to a wooden crate set on the kitchen table. Inside were two pairs of gleaming eyes peeking out from the slats. "Consider it handled." He patted the crate, grinning widely. "Meet Dottie and Panther."

Phineas leaned closer, inspecting the occupants of the crate. Two black cats stared back at him. One, a bit plump with a bobbed tail and a white patch on her chest, looked rather bear-like in her stance and eyes. "That's Dottie," Pat explained. "She'll take care of the rodents. The other one's Panther, all sleek and stealthy. He's the baby of the pair, but he'll come in handy when we need him."

Phineas raised an eyebrow, regarding the cats with skepticism. "So… instead of letting me design modern traps, you chose to use these... felines?"

"Better than traps," Pat said, giving the crate an affectionate pat. "These two are naturals. Dottie's a sweetheart, but don't let her size fool you—she's got a good pounce. Panther, on the other hand, will make those mice wish they'd never set foot in the barn."

Phineas leaned in again to look at them. Panther curiously peeked out from behind Dottie, but he leaned in a bit too close. Dottie's eyes narrowed, and with a quick hiss, she swatted him firmly on the nose, making him recoil back into the crate.

Pat chuckled, leaning down to address Dottie. "Now, now, what was all that about?"

Dottie meowed in response, her tone almost indignant.

Pat nodded knowingly. "Oh, I get it. Little brothers can be a handful, can't they?"

Phineas glanced between Pat and Dottie, his expression skeptical. "What exactly are you talking about, Bennington?"

Pat straightened up, grinning. "Simple—Panther here's her little brother, and she didn't appreciate him breathing all over her, so she put him in his place."

Phineas blinked, visibly baffled. "And how, pray tell, do you know that?"

"Because she just told me," Pat replied matter-of-factly, as Dottie let out another series of meows. He chuckled, giving her a reassuring pat on the crate. "Hold on, Dottie. I'll get you and Panther something to eat in a minute."

Phineas threw his hands up in exasperation. "Do you expect me to believe that you're actually communicating with these animals?"

Pat laughed, shaking his head. "And do you expect me to believe you can't understand what they're saying?"

As Phineas opened his mouth to respond, he thought better of it and instead took a deep breath, clearly at a loss for words. He threw a final glance at the cats before turning back to Pat and Agatha, inspecting their uniforms one last time with a scrutinizing gaze.

"Very well, I'll leave you both to your... duties," he muttered, sounding as though he didn't entirely trust them. Just before stepping out, he threw one last comment over his shoulder, his tone firm. "Remember, not a speck of dirt on those uniforms. Lady Seraphina is to be greeted with nothing less than perfection!"

As Phineas' footsteps faded down the hallway, Pat shook his head with a grin. "The man's gonna have us tiptoeing around this place until this is over with," he muttered, sharing a look with Agatha, who rolled her eyes in agreement despite the huge grin on her face.

Pat turned back to the crate, sharing an exasperated but amused look with the cats. "Well, Dottie, Panther," he murmured, glancing into the crate, "looks like you two are our new VIPs in charge of mouse prevention."

In the main room, Jedidiah had finally hauled himself up from the floor, brushing off his trousers with a sigh as Matthew stifled a chuckle. "Maybe I could get some of my money back by charging admission to the Davenport House Museum," Jedidiah grumbled, glancing around at the polished new furniture.

"Well," Matthew replied, amusement dancing in his eyes, "we'll just have to get used to finer living for a while, at least until after Lady Seraphina's arrival."

Jedidiah groaned. "I just hope my old furniture hasn't been chewed up yet by those rats." He turned on his heel and stepped into the hallway to search for Professor Hargroves, gesturing for Matthew to follow.

Outside, the wind picked up, rustling through the trees with an unsettling rhythm. The peaceful buzz of the ranch felt... off, though no one inside seemed to notice. A massive airship loomed, its elegant silhouette a striking contrast against the darkening sky. Its pristine white envelope shimmered faintly, adorned with delicate blue motifs that swirled along its surface like intricate lacework. Polished silver bands crisscrossed the envelope, catching the light in dazzling patterns as the vessel descended.

Painted on the side was the name "Aetherwind" in bold, sweeping letters outlined in gold, leaving no doubt about the ship's identity. The vessel exuded a sense of sophistication and power, its presence both captivating and foreboding as it settled silently into an open clearing near Davenport Ranch.

The airship's hatch opened with a quiet hiss, and four figures emerged, their imposing forms shrouded in long, dark coats that swayed in the breeze. Each one wore a sinister plague doctor mask, the hollow, reflective eyes giving them an eerie, otherworldly appearance. Moving with practiced precision, they dispersed without a sound.

Two of them made their way toward the main door of the house, their masks and long coats blending with the shadows as they advanced. The other two circled to the kitchen entrance, their steps soundless and deliberate.

Inside, the house was calm and peaceful. Pat and Agatha had returned to their work in the kitchen, and Phineas had gone off to make more preparations. But then, in an instant, the calm shattered.

The front door burst open with a force that sent it crashing against the wall, a gust of wind sweeping into the room. Jedidiah and Matthew spun around, their eyes widening in shock as two masked figures pushed inside. Their weapons, large and futuristic, gleamed ominously in the light, their glowing barrels aimed squarely at Jedidiah and Matthew.

At the same moment, the kitchen door crashed

open, startling Pat and Agatha. Two more plague-masked intruders entered, wielding sleek atomic rifles that glinted coldly under the kitchen lights. Pat let out a muffled gasp, instinctively moving behind Agatha, who tried in vain to shove him back in front of her.

The lead intruder raised his weapon, his voice distorted and mechanical as he barked, "Don't move!"

The kitchen door crashed open as
two more masked intruders entered,
wielding sleek atomic blaster rifles.

CHAPTER XI

The Unexpected Arrival

"Don't move!" Jedidiah Davenport echoed the words of the intruder. "What do you mean, breaking into my home and issuing me orders?" The young ranch owner was fuming but kept his hands where the masked men could see them.

Before either of the armed antagonists could respond, a new sound broke the tense silence—the sharp clacking of heels across the wooden slats of his front porch. Suddenly, Lady Seraphina Blackwood made her grand entrance, a faint, captivating scent of lavender and wood smoke preceding her, mingling with the crisp autumn air.

Her presence was commanding, her posture regal as she entered. Dressed in an immaculate ensemble of dark velvet accented with intricate brass detailing and a sweeping cloak that flowed behind her like a shadow, she moved with a grace that seemed almost surreal. Her jet-black hair, streaked with hints of gold, was styled in an elegant updo, and her piercing green eyes scanned the scene with an intensity that made everyone pause.

The masked men immediately lowered their weapons, stepping back in perfect sync, as though retreating from her mere presence.

Lady Seraphina's gaze swept over the room, lingering briefly on Jedidiah before moving to Matthew, then back to Jedidiah. Finally, she spoke, her voice crisp and authoritative, with an accent that hinted at her aristocratic upbringing.

"Stand down," she commanded, addressing the intruders without sparing them a glance.

The distortion in their mechanical voices, as they replied in unison, was unsettling. "Yes, my lady." They filed out of the room, guarding the entrance from the outside. Their movements were silent and efficient.

As the last masked figure disappeared through the doorway, Jedidiah exhaled slowly, lowering his hands. "I assume you're Lady Blackwood," he said, his tone guarded but calm. He immediately recognized her as the same person he had met at the shop in New York during the airship race.

"Care to explain why your men decided to barge into my home unannounced and armed to the teeth?" He demanded.

Lady Seraphina stepped forward, her eyes narrowing slightly as she met his gaze. "My apologies for their abrupt methods, Mr. Davenport," she said smoothly. "Their orders were to secure the premises. You'll have to forgive their... aggressive approach."

"Secure the premises?" Matthew cut in, his tone sharp. "For what exactly?"

She turned her gaze to him, and for a moment, the weight of her stare silenced him. "For matters of great importance," she said, her voice laced with a confidence that allowed no argument.

"Matters of importance that involve pointing guns at me and my friends?" Jedidiah challenged, stepping closer. His expression suddenly shifted, his eyes widening in alarm as a thought struck him.

"Wait—Pat, Agatha, and Phineas!" His voice rose with urgency as he turned sharply toward the kitchen. "What about them? Are they alright?"

Lady Seraphina raised a hand in a calming gesture. "They are unharmed, I assure you." She stepped toward the doorway leading to the kitchen, her voice ringing with authority. "Release whoever is in there and take up positions outside the door."

A muffled response came from the masked men in the kitchen. Moments later, the sound of footsteps echoed as the intruders exited the house and took their positions on the enclosed porch. Almost immediately after, Pat Bennington and Agatha Porter appeared in the hall. Pat was clutching a cast-iron skillet defensively, while

Agatha looked visibly irritated.

Pat's eyes widened when he saw the woman standing before them. "Who's this, Jed? Another one of those troublemakers?"

"Pat, Agatha, this is Lady Seraphina Blackwood," Jedidiah Davenport announced confidently.

Agatha, less interested in pleasantries, pointed her finger at the aristocrat. "You mind explaining why your goons barged in on us like that? I just knew any minute we were going to end up thrown in the corner, stacked up like cordwood!"

Lady Seraphina regarded them with a faint smile, her tone cool but polite. "I understand your frustration, but I must insist you both return to the kitchen. This discussion requires privacy."

"Return to the kitchen?" Agatha's brow furrowed, her arms crossing. "Now see here—"

"Please," Jedidiah interjected, raising a hand. "It's alright, Agatha. You and Pat, please do as she asks." He turned to Pat, his tone slightly worried again. "Where's Phineas? Wasn't he in there with you?"

Pat tugged at the stiff collar of the uniform he had been forced to wear, clearly still disgruntled. "He's off makin' more preparations for this... this person's arrival." He jabbed a thumb toward Lady Seraphina.

"Professor Hargroves can wait," Seraphina said

smoothly, her gaze steady on Jedidiah. "His presence is not necessary for this meeting." Looking around the room, she asked, "Is there somewhere else we can speak?"

Jedidiah hesitated, glancing between Pat and Agatha, who still looked ready to fight. With a nod, he gestured toward the front room he referred to as the parlor. "This way."

Lady Seraphina inclined her head, following Jedidiah inside as Matthew trailed behind them, curiosity flickering in his eyes.

Pat and Agatha returned to the kitchen, exchanging skeptical glances before Pat finally muttered, "So that's the important muckety-muck that Hargy was so all-fired ready to impress." He let out a huff before he and Agatha returned to their work.

In the front room, Lady Seraphina held up a gloved hand, her expression softening slightly. "Mr. Davenport, I assure you, my intentions are not hostile. In fact, I've come to enlist your aid." She paused, glancing briefly around the room before continuing, "And I must also apologize for my early arrival. I realize I was not expected for another two days, but... circumstances demanded I expedite my visit."

"My aid? With what, exactly?" Jedidiah crossed his arms, his brow furrowed. "And what exactly do you mean by circumstances?"

"Never mind that for now." Her lips curved into a faint smile. "As far as your help, it's with something far beyond the petty theft and violence you've encountered up till now. Tell me, Mr. Davenport, are you familiar with the Secret Order of the Clockwork Octopus?"

Jedidiah exchanged a quick glance with Matthew, then shook his head. "Can't say I am. Should I be?"

Seraphina's expression grew grave, her piercing green eyes locking onto his. "The Order exists to protect a series of powerful artifacts—a relic capable of manipulating the very fabric of time and space."

Jedidiah blinked, leaning back slightly as her words settled over the room like a heavy fog.

Matthew frowned, shifting uncomfortably. "Manipulate the fabric of time and space?" he muttered, almost to himself. "Lady, that sounds insane!"

Lady Seraphina Blackwood's expression became more solemn. "I don't expect you to believe me, Mr. Colton. I can understand how that sounds —especially to someone of your limited education. I can only ask you to take my word that the relic must remain under the Order's protection."

Jedidiah glanced at Matthew, who gave a small shrug. Clearing his throat, Jedidiah turned back to Lady Seraphina. "When you say relic, do you mean

Lady Seraphina Blackwood's
expression became more solemn.
"I don't expect you to believe me,
Mr. Colton."

like the artifact that was stolen from the museum in London?"

"Precisely like the one stolen in London," she replied. "Unfortunately, it wasn't the only artifact taken. There are still several more missing, and I need you to secure them, as well as a couple others, before anyone else has the chance to take them."

"You expect me to find them?" Davenport asked in disbelief.

"It shouldn't be too difficult. One of the artifacts is already in your possession. Or rather, the coordinates to it are," she said, her gaze sharpening. "The pocket watch you admired in New York. I sent it to you by mail. It has a location hidden inside the casing. I assume you've been keeping it in a safe place."

At the mention of the watch, Jedidiah stiffened. "It was..." He hesitated for a moment before continuing, "It was stolen from me during the train heist two weeks ago."

"Stolen!" Lady Seraphina exclaimed, disbelief flashing in her eyes. "That watch is one piece of a larger puzzle. Assembling all the pieces will grant the holder unparalleled power. Do you have any idea what you've done?"

She began pacing, throwing her hands up in frustration. "Do you have any idea how critical that watch is? I even intervened during the train holdup! My airship—Aetherwind—fired an ultrasonic disruptor cannon at the train! I was the one who forced the thieves to retreat. All you had to do was make sure they didn't get away with the watch! I guess that was too complicated!" Her tone was sharp, her words cutting.

Matthew stepped forward, his arms crossed. "And I suppose you could have done better?"

"I could, and I have—for the past twenty years!" Lady Seraphina shot back.

"And yet, you just suddenly need our help?" Jedidiah asked skeptically.

"The Order has watched over the relic for centuries, Mr. Davenport. Trust me when I say... you and your companions are not here by mere chance." Lady Seraphina's smile was enigmatic despite the worry etched on her face. "The clock is ticking, and the artifacts must be retrieved before someone else has a chance to fully assemble it. Mr. Davenport, I have no choice but to ask for you help. I believe that you and your team are uniquely equipped to undertake this mission."

Jedidiah's eyes narrowed. "Why us?"

"Because you've already proven yourselves," she said simply, her gaze unwavering. "Your accomplishments speak volumes, Mr. Davenport. Turning a modest one-horse freight company into a thriving empire. Purchasing a few acres and turning it into over ten thousand with a thousand head of steer is no small feat. And when the railroad sought to strong-arm you, you didn't fold—you adapted. Discovering oil, building your own fleet of airships... That kind of ingenuity and determination is exactly what this mission requires."

Jedidiah's brow furrowed as he leaned against the ornate mantle. "Running a ranch and a freight company are worlds away from chasing relics across the globe," he said warily.

"Are they, though?" she countered, her tone sharpening slightly. "You've built your success not on brute force, but on problem-solving, adaptability, and assembling a team you trust implicitly. Look at what you accomplished during the sky race. The skills that brought you here, Mr. Davenport, are precisely the skills needed for this endeavor."

Jedidiah exchanged a glance with Matthew, his skepticism waning. "I suppose you've got it all figured out, then?"

Lady Seraphina smiled faintly. "I wouldn't be here if I didn't."

Davenport studied her for a moment, his instincts warring with his curiosity. Finally, he sighed. "Please, have a seat," he offered with a grand gesture. "We can discuss it under the light of this..." He suddenly cut himself short, his eyes lifting to the ceiling. A large and very expensive gas-light chandelier hung there, its polished brass gleaming under the bright glow.

"Gasolier!" He suddenly exclaimed.

"Where did that come from?" Matthew asked, realizing they had both been too distracted by the new furniture to notice it earlier.

"Care to make a guess?" Jedidiah asked sarcastically.

Lady Seraphina's emerald eyes flicked briefly to the settee, but she shook her head, the golden streaks in her jet-black hair catching the light. "I appreciate the offer, Mr. Davenport, but time is of the essence," she said firmly.

Jedidiah raised an eyebrow but said nothing, respecting her urgency. Matthew, standing near the intricately carved fireplace, looked at the lady curiously. "If this is as important as you're making it sound," he began, "why come to us instead of the authorities? Surely, an operation like this would need—"

"Discretion, Mr. Colton," she interrupted smoothly. Her gaze was sharp as it swept over both men. "What I am entrusting you with cannot fall into the hands of the authorities or anyone else who lacks understanding of what's truly at stake. The Order operates outside of conventional means for a reason."

Jedidiah leaned against the fireplace and took a deep breath. "Alright, Lady Blackwood," he said, his tone steady. "You've made your case for secrecy. Now tell us exactly what you need and how we're supposed to find these relics? Especially if one of them is already stolen."

Lady Seraphina's gaze softened, though her posture remained rigid. "The artifacts have been scattered across continents for centuries, hidden to prevent them from being assembled. Recently, however, certain individuals have come to fully comprehend their true power. This has set events into motion that could..." She hesitated, her voice dropping to a near whisper, "Unravel the very fabric of existence."

Matthew scoffed softly, shaking his head. "Time and space, the fabric of existence... You gotta be putting us on!"

Lady Seraphina fixed him with a cold glare. "I'm not putting you on, Mr. Colton. Furthermore, I suggest you take this seriously before it's too late."

"Let's say we agree to help. Where do we start?" Jedidiah interjected before Matthew could retort.

"First things first!" she replied matter-of-factly. "You start, Mr. Davenport, by retrieving the watch you let get stolen!"

"How do you propose we do that?" Jedidiah asked, astonished. "It's been over two weeks since the train was held up. You might as well be asking us to track down a ghost."

"No disrespect, Lady Blackwood," Matthew Colton spoke up, "but those outlaws could be holed up anywhere."

Lady Seraphina rolled her eyes and sighed. "Start with the weapons they used. Those men are far too crude to have created them on their own. Investigate who invented them," she instructed. "The trail will lead you to the thieves, and ultimately to the watch. Once you've retrieved it, head to Detroit and wait to hear from me."

Jedidiah frowned. "That's a large city. How are we supposed to find you?"

Lady Seraphina's gaze turned mysterious. "When the time is right, the path will present itself."

Jedidiah narrowed his eyes. "Could you at least tell me more about this Order of the Clockwork Octopus?"

Matthew crossed his arms, frowning. "If this Order has been protecting this relic for centuries, why not turn to them for help? Seems like they'd be better equipped than us."

Lady Seraphina's expression darkened, her emerald eyes flashing with a hint of unease. She hesitated briefly before answering, her tone lower and more cautious. "Under ordinary circumstances, I would. However, I have reason to believe one—or possibly more—members of the Order might be involved in this." She paused for a moment before continuing.

"The recent thefts, the sudden disappearances... These are no accidents, Mr. Colton," she said, her voice low and tinged with regret. "The Order is built on trust, but I fear that trust has been compromised."

Jedidiah and Matthew exchanged uneasy glances.

"You believe someone from your own group betrayed the Order?" Jedidiah asked, his voice skeptical.

"Betrayed the world, Mr. Davenport."

"But..."

"Patience," she said, her voice calm but firm. "All will be revealed."

Jedidiah raised an eyebrow. "And what do we get in return for going on this quest for these lost relics?"

"Relic," she corrected sharply. "Singular, not plural."

"But you just said we had to gather..."

"Consider the artifacts as pieces of a larger working mechanism. Each one is meaningless by itself, but together, they form a device capable of unimaginable power. I assure you this is a quest for the lost relic."

Lady Seraphina turned toward the door, her cloak sweeping behind her with regal precision. "You have your instructions, Mr. Davenport. I suggest you begin immediately." Her piercing green eyes lingered on him for a moment before she nodded, as though confirming her choice.

Jedidiah opened his mouth to reply when the faint sound of hurried footsteps echoed from above.

Upstairs, Phineas B. Hargroves stood in his bedroom, carefully selecting a stack of rare, leather-bound books from his private collection. Each one was chosen meticulously, intended to dazzle Lady Seraphina with his intellect and taste.

Still unaware of her early arrival, he glanced out the window, considering the dramatic placement of the volumes in the main room. Instead of admiring his own cleverness, his gaze caught something outside—something that froze him in place.

His eyes widened. "Egads!" he exclaimed.

In a flurry of panic, the eccentric older man bolted for the hallway, his slippered feet slipping and sliding on the freshly polished floor. His urgency, however, outpaced his coordination, and he began to trip.

The first stumble sent the books flying, scattering them across the floor. The second trip left him careening toward the staircase.

"Jedidiah!" Phineas cried out, his voice rising an octave as he tumbled forward, arms flailing in a futile attempt to catch himself. He came rolling down the stairs, landing in a heap at the bottom.

CHAPTER XII

The First Clue

Lady Seraphina Blackwood paused mid-step, her emerald eyes narrowing slightly as Phineas B. Hargroves landed in a heap at the bottom of the stairs, arms and legs sprawled in disarray.

Jedidiah Davenport and Matthew Colton stood frozen, blinking as though unsure whether to laugh or rush to his aid.

"Phineas! Are you alright?" Jedidiah called, his voice tinged with both concern and exasperation.

The professor struggled to his knees, his hair thoroughly disheveled, clutching desperately at a stray book as if it were the last strand of his dignity. He raised a trembling hand, his face pale and his eyes wide with alarm.

"Jed!" he shouted, his voice trembling with urgency. "The airship! The same one that fired the ultrasonic disruptor cannon on the train—it's landed behind the house! We're under attack!"

Phineas B. Hargroves landed in
a heap at the bottom of the stairs.

His panicked words hung in the air for a beat before Phineas looked up and froze. His jaw slackened, and his trembling hand fell to his side. He blinked in stunned disbelief as his gaze met Lady Seraphina's commanding presence.

"Your Majesty!" he blurted, his words colliding in his haste. "I mean—Lady Blackwood!" Groaning in pain but still clutching the book to his chest, he finally stood up. He began brushing off his clothes with exaggerated care, wincing as he straightened his mussed hair.

"You'll have to forgive my entrance," he said, his voice regaining its usual theatrical flair. "I happened to glance out the window and spotted your airship, the Aetherwind. Naturally, I came rushing down to warn everyone... I mean to properly greet you..."

"You shouldn't have bothered," she said, her tone crisp and commanding. "I was just leaving. Time is not on our side." She turned to Jedidiah Davenport and continued, "I have given you all the information you need for now. The rest is up to you. I trust you understand the gravity of this mission."

"Wait!" Phineas said, stepping forward. "Surely you don't intend to leave so soon? I've had an entire menu planned just for you! It won't take more than a few hours to prepare." He chuckled slightly. "After all, we weren't expecting you for another two days."

Lady Seraphina turned to face him, her expression softening only slightly. "Professor Hargroves," she said, her voice firm but polite, "I appreciate your enthusiasm, but I must insist. I've already stayed longer than I intended. The next steps require your focus, not further conversation. The clock is ticking."

"But surely you could—" Phineas started, his words faltering as she raised a gloved hand to silence him.

"My decision is final," she said firmly, pivoting toward the door. Her sweeping cloak followed her movement, the polished brass accents catching the light.

Phineas, undeterred, hurried after her, only to halt abruptly as two of her masked guards stepped into his path. Their mechanical voices issued in unison, "Stand back."

Phineas froze, blinking at the armed figures towering over him. "I... ah..." he stammered, glancing over his shoulder at Jedidiah and Matthew as though for backup.

Jedidiah crossed his arms, arching an eyebrow. "I'd listen to them, Phineas," he said dryly.

Phineas sighed in frustration, his shoulders slumping as the guards turned and followed Lady Seraphina out the door.

The three men moved cautiously onto the front

porch, watching as Lady Seraphina joined the other two guards waiting by the airship. The masked figures stood like statues, their synchronized movements unnerving as they formed a protective perimeter.

Lady Seraphina paused briefly at the foot of the gangway, turning back to cast one last look at Jedidiah, Matthew, and Phineas. "Remember," she said, her voice carrying over the cool evening air, "the fate of this world and more is resting in your hands."

As Lady Seraphina ascended the ramp to the Aetherwind, the faint, captivating scent of lavender and wood smoke lingered in the air—a curious combination that matched her enigmatic persona. It clung to the space where she had stood, weaving itself into the memory of her visit like an indelible signature.

Her guards moved in perfect synchronization. With a sharp, unified pivot, they faced outward, scanning the area as if daring anyone to approach. Their movements were precise, almost mechanical.

The trio on the porch watched in silent unease as the guards stepped in unison, their boots striking the ground with an eerily identical rhythm. One by one, they turned and ascended the ramp, forming a protective line behind Lady Seraphina. Not a single word passed between them, yet their actions were seamless, like a single entity operating multiple bodies.

Moments later, the sleek airship hummed to life, its engines releasing a faint, rhythmic thrum. The cloaked figures disappeared into the ship's shadow, and soon the vessel lifted gracefully into the sky.

The three of them stood in silence, their gazes still fixed on the horizon, where the Aetherwind had vanished moments before. The sky had begun to darken, with streaks of pink and orange fading into deep indigo, casting long shadows across the porch's wooden boards.

"Well," Jedidiah muttered, finally breaking the silence. "That was... something."

Phineas nodded absently, still looking skyward. "Magnificent," he whispered, his voice tinged with admiration. "That's what it was!"

Matthew clapped him on the shoulder, steering him back inside. "Come on, Professor. Let's get you caught up."

Inside, the Victorian home offered a welcome reprieve from the lingering tension. The soft glow of oil lamps illuminated the polished woodwork, their flickering light casting intricate patterns across the walls. A faint trace of lavender still remained in the air. Phineas, however, seemed oblivious to the atmosphere he'd worked so hard to perfect, his focus entirely on the questions swirling in his mind as Jedidiah and Matthew guided him into the main room.

"Did she even sit down?" he asked, realizing everything he had prepared—at Jedidiah's expense —had been for nothing.

"No, but you better take a seat before you fall over, Phineas," Jedidiah muttered, gesturing toward one of the new chairs the eccentric older man had purchased. "That is if it's okay to use them now?"

"Yes, yes, it's quite alright," Phineas said, settling into the seat with a dramatic sigh. "Now, someone catch me up. What just happened? Why didn't anyone let me know she was here? Why did she leave in such a hurry?"

Jedidiah sat down across from him, leaning forward with his elbows on his knees. "Alright, Professor. Here's what we know... First, she wants us to retrieve the pocket watch she sent me from New York. It's apparently the key to... well, stopping the world from falling apart. The fabric of existence or something like that."

Phineas raised an eyebrow. "The fabric of existence?"

"Something like that," Matthew chimed in. "She called it a relic and made it sound like this Order of the Clockwork Octopus is all that stands between us and—"

"Manipulating time and space!" a voice suddenly called out from the hallway, interrupting him.

The three men turned toward the door.

"Sounds like another one of those Jowls Burns novels!" Pat's voice rang cheerfully as he peeked his head into the room. "If you ask me."

"Jules Verne!" Jedidiah barked, his patience fraying as he shot to his feet. "Pat, I thought you were in the kitchen with Agatha?"

"I was," Pat said with an easy grin. "I forgot one thing though."

"What was that?"

"I can't hear from the kitchen..."

"Pat!"

"I'm going, I'm going," Pat said with a laugh, turning on his heel and strolling away, his footsteps fading into the hall.

Phineas B. Hargroves sighed heavily, running a hand through his hair. "My dear boy, why do you even try?"

"Just an eternal optimist, I guess," Jedidiah replied, a small smile tugging at his lips.

"You don't think she was serious, do you, Jed?" Matthew Colton asked skeptically.

"She was serious," Jedidiah muttered, more to himself than anyone else.

"She's gotta be putting us on!" Matthew pressed, his voice laced with disbelief. "Magic pocket watches and unraveling time? Jed, she's off her rocker. You can't seriously be considering any of this."

Jedidiah turned and glared at him. "She didn't seem mad to me, Matt. Determined, yes. Maybe even desperate. But not mad."

Matthew scoffed, throwing up his hands. "Desperate for us to do what? Chase after some mysterious objects like they're the Golden Fleece? We don't even know where to start!"

Jedidiah shook his head, turning to the window and staring out at the horizon. "It's not like we have much of a choice, do we?" he said quietly. "If she's right—and that's a big 'if'—we could be the only ones who can stop whatever's coming."

Matthew opened his mouth to retort but stopped short, his expression softening. Crossing his arms, he leaned against the mantle, his gaze drifting downward before he looked back up to express his opinion.

"Okay, let's throw logic out the window and say we accept this ridiculous assignment. Does she expect us to track down these secret artifacts with nothing but riddles to guide us? If this is so important, maybe she could be a little less mysterious and provide us with a few more facts."

Still thinking about how brief Lady Seraphina Blackwood's visit was, Phineas sighed deeply, sinking back into his chair with an air of defeat.

"All this planning," Phineas muttered, as he ran a hand through his hair. "The books, the redecorating, the perfectly curated menu..." His voice trailed off as his gaze drifted around the room, his expression slowly shifting. Suddenly, he bolted upright, nearly knocking over his chair, his eyes wide and his hands gesturing wildly.

"Wait a moment—hold on!" he exclaimed, his voice rising with each word. "Did she really say the fabric of existence?" He began pacing furiously. "This is preposterous! Utterly preposterous!"

"That's what I've been saying!" Matthew chimed in, throwing his hands up in agreement.

"Manipulating time and space?" Phineas continued, his tone incredulous. "It's ludicrous!"

Jedidiah couldn't help but chuckle, shaking his head. "It does sound a bit far-fetched," he admitted.

Matthew leaned against the mantle again, arms once again crossed. "It's insane. Let's not pretend otherwise."

Phineas paused mid-stride, his expression shifting from disbelief to thoughtfulness. His voice softened. "But... if there's even a grain of truth to it..." He turned to face the others, his gaze steady.

"Truth?" Matthew scoffed. "If there's a grain of truth in it, I'll eat my hat!"

Before Phineas could respond, Jedidiah raised a hand, cutting off any further debate. "Alright, enough for tonight. Let's forget about Lady Blackwood, pocket watches, and unraveling time. Let's get something to eat and talk it over in the morning."

Matthew perked up slightly at the mention of food. "Now," he said, "that's the first sensible thing I've heard all evening."

After a hearty meal, the three of them began to disperse, each lost in their own thoughts about Lady Seraphina's mission. Sleep came, but only reluctantly, as questions lingered in their minds.

****

The next morning, the sun cast a warm glow over the breakfast table, its rays filtering through the curtains in the kitchen. The air smelled of freshly brewed coffee and sizzling bacon, courtesy of Pat Bennington, who was still at the stove, humming a cheerful tune.

At the table, Jedidiah, Matthew, Phineas, and Agatha were seated, their plates already laden with eggs, toast, and sausage. The atmosphere was much lighter than the night before, though the thoughts of Lady Blackwood's visit still lingered.

Just then, the sound of footsteps echoed from the staircase. All heads turned as Jonathan Blake and his son, Edwin Bancroft, entered the room. Jonathan looked every bit the inventor he was, his waistcoat slightly rumpled and his sleeves rolled up, while Edwin, bright-eyed and eager, carried a stack of blueprints under one arm.

"Morning, everyone," Jonathan greeted warmly

as he settled into an empty chair. Edwin followed suit, setting his blueprints on a side table before helping himself to the coffee pot.

"Morning," Jedidiah replied, gesturing toward the spread. "Help yourselves. Pat's been at it all morning."

Edwin grinned. "Don't mind if I do. Thanks, Pat!

"Breakfast is on the house," Pat called over his shoulder, flipping a pancake with a practiced flourish. "But any gratuities you'd like to leave for the chef will be greatly appreciated."

Edwin, already reaching for the bacon, paused with a playful grin and began patting his pockets as if searching for loose change. "Sorry, Pat," he quipped. "I think I left my coins in my other waistcoat."

Jonathan chuckled as he poured himself a cup of coffee. "You'd better hope he doesn't start keeping tabs, Edwin. I imagine the bill for the past two weeks would be quite something."

"Has it really been two weeks?" Agatha asked, her tone laced with disbelief. "Feels like just yesterday Pat and I were rescuing all of you in Missouri."

"Time does move fast." Jonathan settled into his chair, pouring a generous amount of cream into his coffee. After taking a sip, he shifted the conversation to his nearly completed airship. "The

Inspiration is coming along beautifully," he said, a note of pride in his voice. "Another week or so, and it should be ready to take to the skies."

He turned to Jedidiah with a grateful smile. "I can't thank you enough, Jed, for letting your crew of skilled carpenters and mechanics work on it. And for not charging me labor, or for the room and board these past two weeks. You've been more than generous."

Jedidiah waved off the gratitude with a casual motion. "Think nothing of it, Jonathan. Besides, it's not every day we get to host one of the greatest inventors this side of the Atlantic."

Professor Hargroves cleared his throat, a pointed reminder that he had been residing there for months.

"Present company excluded," Jedidiah said with a laugh.

Jonathan chuckled at the compliment, tipping his coffee cup slightly in acknowledgment. "Well, as soon as we're done, I can send Cogsworth in to start helping around the house like I promised. After all, he belongs to you now."

Pat, standing at the stove, stiffened visibly. He turned, spatula still in hand, and cleared his throat. "Uh... that won't be necessary, Mr. Blake," he said carefully, his usual jovial tone tempered. "I think we've got things handled just fine here."

Agatha, who had been sitting quietly at the

table, chimed in, her voice polite but firm. "Pat's right. No need to trouble Cogsworth. He's a... very impressive invention, to be sure, but I don't think he'd be quite comfortable in the house. Too many delicate things about."

Jonathan blinked, a touch surprised by their resistance. "Cogsworth's a marvel of efficiency," he said, his tone reassuring. "He wouldn't touch a thing he wasn't instructed to. I've calibrated him specifically for precision and care."

"Precision or not," Pat muttered under his breath, flipping another pancake, "those clanking gears would drive a man insane."

Agatha nodded, her expression calm but resolute. "It's not just that. A house like this... well, it has a certain... charm. A rhythm. I'm afraid having Cogsworth underfoot might... disrupt that."

Jonathan frowned slightly, setting his coffee cup down. "I don't understand. I thought you'd appreciate the help," he said, his voice carrying a hint of frustration. "Cogsworth's not just a machine. He's a tool, designed to make life easier. Isn't that what you want?"

The tension hung in the air for a moment as Jonathan sighed, leaning back in his chair. Jedidiah, hiding a smirk behind his coffee cup, glanced at him. "You'll have to excuse them, Jonathan. They're both set in their ways. I think it's less about Cogsworth's abilities and more about... unfamiliar territory."

"Unfamiliar territory, my foot!" Pat exclaimed, turning back to the table. "Do you know how terrifying it is cooking breakfast and turning to see a cold, hard face staring at you, void of all expression—not to mention those iridescent eyes? And that's just Agatha. Imagine adding Cogsworth to the mix!"

"Yeah..." Agatha started to agree, then realized she had just been insulted. "Hey!"

"Pat! Agatha!" Jedidiah called out, his tone sharp. "That'll be enough!"

Jonathan's expression softened, though his brow remained furrowed. "Unfamiliar territory or not, I hope you'll reconsider. I wouldn't want Cogsworth's potential to go to waste."

Pat grunted, turning back to his cooking, though he couldn't resist muttering, "Wouldn't hurt to send him out to the garden to scare off the crows."

Finally giving up on the argument, Jonathan leaned back in his chair, a laugh escaping him as he raised his cup in a mock toast. "To Cogsworth, the world's first automaton scarecrow!"

The table broke into chuckles, the tension fading as the conversation turned to lighter topics. Still, the thought of Cogsworth prowling the ranch drew the occasional wary glance from Pat and Agatha.

Jonathan chuckled, shaking his head at the

banter. He took a sip of his coffee before asking, "So, I assume everything's in order for Lady Seraphina's arrival tomorrow?"

The room fell silent. Jedidiah, Matthew, and Phineas exchanged wide-eyed glances, their expressions a mix of shock and realization.

"Wait a second," Matthew began, leaning forward. "You and Edwin don't know, do you?"

"Don't know what?" Jonathan asked, raising an eyebrow.

Phineas straightened in his chair, clearly eager to speak. "Lady Blackwood was here last night!"

"Last night?" Jonathan looked genuinely surprised, setting his coffee cup down. "We were out working on the Inspiration until well after dark. No one mentioned a thing when we came in."

"That's because we'd all gone to bed by the time you came in," Jedidiah said, leaning back in his chair. "She showed up completely unannounced with her guards leading the way. Claimed that circumstances demanded she expedite her visit."

"Guards?" Edwin echoed, his eyes wide. "You're serious?"

"As a steam engine at full throttle," Phineas replied dramatically. "She practically stormed the house, demanding we retrieve the pocket watch she sent Jedidiah from New York. It's apparently the key to... saving the world or some such nonsense."

"She said something about the fabric of

existence unraveling," Jedidiah added, his tone dry but with a hint of lingering disbelief. "Not exactly light breakfast conversation."

Jonathan leaned forward, his brow furrowed. "The fabric of existence? Did she tell you that? And the pocket watch—what happened to it?"

Jedidiah sighed heavily. "It was stolen during the train robbery."

Edwin's jaw dropped. "You mean the train robbery from two weeks ago? She's expecting you to find it now?"

"That's the gist of it," Matthew said with a shrug. "She delivered that shocking news and then left us to figure the rest out on our own."

Jonathan shook his head, clearly absorbing the weight of the situation. "This just keeps getting stranger. But if Lady Blackwood's involved... Whatever it is, it must be serious."

"Serious, yes," Phineas said, waving a hand. "But also utterly preposterous. Coordinates hidden in a watch, unraveling time and space... It sounds like a bad penny dreadful."

"Maybe so," Jedidiah said, his tone firm, "but we'll need to start planning our next steps. If she's right about the stakes, we can't afford to dismiss it."

Jonathan exchanged a glance with Edwin, then nodded. "We'll help in any way we can. Did she give you suggestions on where to start?"

Jedidiah leaned forward, resting his arms on the

table. "She mentioned the weapons used in the train robbery. Said they were far too advanced for common outlaws. If we can trace who supplied them, it might lead us to them and ultimately the watch."

Jonathan rubbed his chin thoughtfully. "Futuristic weapons... That's certainly not something your average gang of train robbers would have access to. What kind did they use?"

"Paralyzing ray guns," Jedidiah said, his tone grim. "One shot and you're frozen in place. No one stood a chance."

Phineas perked up. "We managed to secure one, actually," he said. "The leader dropped it during the scuffle before they fled. It's upstairs in Jedidiah's room. Matthew, would you be so kind as to fetch it?"

Matthew nodded, pushing back his chair. "On it."

As Matthew left the room, Phineas continued, "Our plan is to disassemble and reverse-engineer the device. If we can figure out how it works, we might be able to develop something useful—an antidote, perhaps, or even a countermeasure to use against them."

Jonathan's eyes narrowed slightly, his mind clearly turning over the implications. "The day of the rescue..." he said slowly, almost to himself. "I remember seeing Jed firing something at

Cogsworth. I didn't get a chance to examine it because I was too busy calling off his charge..."

At that moment, Matthew returned, holding the sleek metallic weapon carefully in both hands. The room fell silent as he placed it on the table, the morning sunlight casting a soft glow on the intricate brasswork.

The weapon looked as though it belonged to another world. Its surface gleamed with polished copper and brass, a complex array of gears and dials adorning its frame. A round glass orb mounted underneath glowed faintly, its green liquid swirling as though alive. The barrel, spiraled with dark metal ridges, tapered to a cone-shaped emitter at the end. A single etched plate near the handle read "PARALYZING" in bold, precise lettering.

The weapon seemed too advanced, too refined for the rough-and-tumble world of frontier life. The handle was sculpted with an ergonomic curve, inlaid with strips of polished wood that hinted at its maker's expertise in blending form with function. A small knob on the side appeared to adjust the power setting, while a needle-thin meter ticked faintly, measuring some unseen energy.

Jonathan's breath hitched, his eyes widening in recognition. His usually steady demeanor faltered as he leaned closer to examine the device, his fingertips brushing the surface of the strange metallic casing.

"Good heavens," he murmured, his voice barely above a whisper.

The group exchanged uneasy glances until Jedidiah finally broke the silence. "You know something. Don't you?" he asked cautiously.

Jonathan nodded slowly, his gaze never leaving the weapon. "I know exactly who created this."

CHAPTER XIII

The Hunt Begins

A heavy pause filled the room. Jonathan Blake straightened, his expression grim. "If those outlaws have access to this technology…" He hesitated, his brow furrowing deeply. "Then we may already be in over our heads."

The tension was thick as his words lingered in the air, a weight pressing down on everyone.

"You've seen this gun before, haven't you?" Jedidiah asked, his voice sharp and urgent.

Jonathan shook his head, his tone heavy with regret. "Not in person, but I stole the blueprints for it."

"You stole the blueprints?" Matthew raised an eyebrow. "Why am I not surprised?"

"Yes," Jonathan admitted, his voice low. "Back when I was consumed with revenge and willing to do anything to get ahead. I'd heard whispers about a brilliant yet ruthless inventor. Someone who called himself, The Clockwork Conqueror. He was a ghost, a name whispered in certain circles of inventors and engineers. No one knew where he operated from, but his fantastical creations were unparalleled."

Jonathan hesitated, the memory clearly weighing on him. "When I finally got my hands on a set of his blueprints, I thought I'd hit the jackpot. A weapon, unlike anything the world had ever seen —a paralyzing ray gun. I stole the designs, believing I could make a fortune off of them, but I had no idea the kind of enemy I'd just made."

Jedidiah leaned back, his expression skeptical. "And he just let you walk away with them?"

Jonathan gave a grim laugh. "Not exactly. He wasn't there when I took them, but somehow it didn't take him long to figure out who had. A few days later, he showed up at my shop in Toronto, alone. A prototype of the very design I'd stolen from him strapped to his side.

"He stormed in, demanding his blueprints back. The moment I saw him and what looked like a strange generator strapped to his back, wielding something resembling a lightning rod with an orb on the end crackling with energy. I realized I was completely out of my depth. I didn't stand a chance."

Matthew whistled low. "What did you do?"

Jonathan glanced down, his voice softer now. "I

gave him the blueprints back, of course. What else could I do?"

The older man paused, his expression darkening as he recalled the confrontation. "I tried to stall him, to reason with him, but it was no use. He was calm, methodical. It was like he'd done this kind of thing countless times before. When he demanded to know where the blueprints were, I told him the truth. I kept my rarest designs locked away in a safe in the back of the shop."

He let out a humorless chuckle. "I thought the safe might at least slow him down. It was reinforced steel. After all, it was designed to keep thieves out."

Jonathan's voice dropped lower, his tone grim. "But then he did something I'll never forget. He attached the tesla rod to his side, removed his glove, and rolled up his sleeve, revealing not a hand, but a mechanical arm. It was like nothing I'd ever seen before. Polished brass and steel, with gears and pistons that hissed softly as he flexed his fingers. Before I could even react, he strode to the safe, gripped the door with that mechanical hand, and ripped it completely off its hinges like it was made of paper."

Jonathan's words lingered, the room falling into a heavy silence.

"He ripped the door off with his hand?" Phineas finally asked, wide-eyed. "Egads!"

Jonathan nodded grimly. "Just like that."

Matthew let out a low whistle. "So there's a guy out there with a mechanical arm strong enough to tear through steel? And he's got weapons like that to boot?"

Jedidiah leaned forward, his brow furrowed. "That's when he walked off with the blueprints?"

Jonathan gave him a flat look. "What would you have had me do? Fight him with a wrench? He could've fried me where I stood."

Edwin, looking uneasy, broke his silence. "That must've been terrifying."

Jonathan Blake nodded, his expression heavy. "Obviously, that encounter changed everything for me. I realized I needed protection. Something to defend myself and my work if someone like him ever came back. That's when I decided to build Artemis and Apollo, my two automatons. They were crude at first, but they gave me the peace of mind to keep going."

Phineas, always one for drama, crossed his arms. "And you think he provided the outlaws with these weapons?

Jonathan nodded slowly. "As far as I know, he's the only one with the designs for them. If he's involved, we're dealing with a threat far bigger than we realized."

The group exchanged uneasy glances, the weight of Jonathan's revelation settling over them.

The stakes had just been raised, and the path ahead seemed darker than ever.

Jedidiah frowned. "If this Clockwork Conqueror is as dangerous as you say, how do we track him down? He could be anywhere."

Jonathan shook his head. "Not just anywhere. He has a workshop in St. Louis. Or at least, that's the one I know about. That's where I stole the blueprints."

"You think the gang's hiding there?" Matthew asked.

"No," Jonathan admitted. "But we might be able to find a clue leading us to them."

Phineas crossed his arms. "And what if he's already packed up and moved on? What's to say we're not riding into a ghost town?"

"Because," Jonathan said grimly, "the Clockwork Conqueror doesn't run. I'm confident the workshop is still standing. And if those outlaws are after more of his advanced weaponry, they won't be far from where they can get them."

Jedidiah straightened, turning to the group. "If we're doing this, we need to decide who's going and who's staying. This doesn't sound like it's going to be a walk in the park."

He turned to Professor Phineas B. Hargroves, who was pacing nearby. "I think you should sit this one out."

"Sit this one out?" The older man fumed. "My

dear boy, I'll do nothing of the kind!"

"The fewer people we have on this mission, the less likely we are to get caught," Jedidiah explained. "Besides, we need you here to reverse-engineer that ray gun. Maybe you can come up with that antidote in case we get hit by it again."

Phineas opened his mouth to protest, but his expression softened as the logic sank in. "Well," he huffed, "I suppose I can focus on that, and lend a hand to finish Jonathan's airship."

Jedidiah nodded and turned to Jonathan. "You're the only one who knows where the workshop is. You have to go."

Jonathan gave a small nod. "Agreed. But I insist that Edwin stays behind."

"Wait, what?" Edwin protested, his face falling. "I can help! I'm not a kid anymore."

"I know you're not, and I know you're capable," Jonathan said firmly, placing a hand on his son's shoulder. "But as Jed said, less people mean less risk. And besides Phineas will need your help overseeing the construction of the Inspiration."

Edwin frowned but didn't argue further, though disappointment was clear on his face.

"That settles it," Jedidiah said. "Jonathan, Matthew, and I will take the Swift, and head out immediately for St. Louis."

"Jonathan and who?" Matthew asked, raising a brow.

"You," Jedidiah said with a faint smile. "We didn't discuss it, but I knew you wouldn't want to miss the excitement."

"Well, obviously I don't," Matthew smirked. "But I do like to be asked."

"Don't forget me!" Pat chimed in, shoveling a fork full of bacon into his mouth.

Jedidiah raised a brow. "Pat, you've got no business going on this mission. You're staying here."

Pat crossed his arms, feigning offense. "Come on, Jed! You'll need someone to keep things lively."

"You mean someone to get them into trouble," Agatha quipped.

Before Pat could protest, the older woman raised her teacup and declared, "He's staying!" Her tone left no room for argument, and Pat slumped in defeat.

Jedidiah glanced around the room. "Alright, then. Matthew, Jonathan, and I will prepare the Swift. Everyone else stays here to hold down the fort."

****

After spending a couple of hours preparing Jedidiah's fastest airship, the Swift, the trio set off on their mission. The sleek vessel cut through the crisp morning air with ease, its polished brass exterior gleaming in the sunlight.

Four hours later, they arrived in St. Louis, Missouri. It was now 2:00 PM on October 21, 1881. The bustling city stretched out below them, a patchwork of cobblestone streets, brick buildings, and industrial smokestacks rising into the air.

The Swift hovered gracefully above the city, its propellers humming softly. Jonathan leaned over the railing, scanning the sprawling cityscape with a furrowed brow, his eyes searching for a landmark from his memory.

"There," he said finally, pointing toward a cluster of warehouses near the river. "That's the area. His workshop is hidden among those buildings."

Jedidiah adjusted the ship's course, the Swift gliding smoothly toward the location Jonathan had indicated. Matthew peered over the edge, taking in the city below.

"Not exactly the kind of place you'd expect for a criminal mastermind's lair," Matthew remarked, his tone skeptical.

Jonathan shook his head. "That's the point. The Clockwork Conqueror doesn't just rely on technology. He's a master of staying hidden in plain sight. His workshop looks like any other building from the outside, but inside..." He trailed off, his expression darkening.

Jedidiah glanced at him. "Inside what?"

Jonathan hesitated before answering. "Inside, it's like stepping into another world. You'll see soon enough."

The trio grew quiet for a moment, taking in the view as the Mississippi river glinted below, its vastness a stark reminder of how history and nature intertwined in ways even they, with all their inventions, couldn't fully comprehend.

As the Swift descended, the tension aboard the airship grew. They were flying straight into unknown territory, and none of them could shake the feeling that they were being watched.

The airship touched down gently in a secluded clearing within walking distance of their destination. Its sleek form was hidden behind a grove of trees, masking its presence. Jedidiah cut the engines, and the hum of the propellers faded, leaving an uneasy silence.

"This feels far too quiet," Matthew muttered as they descended the loading ramp.

Jonathan adjusted his coat, checking a small revolver at his hip. "Don't worry—I'm prepared this time."

"Why do you have that?" Jedidiah asked as he realized the older man was armed. "I've just now convinced Matthew to stop carrying his gun."

"Until we have something better to use, we have to defend ourselves somehow," Jonathan countered.

"Fine," Jedidiah said, his tone clipped. "We

don't have time to argue. Let's just go."

Leaves crunching under their feet, the trio made their way across the field. The warehouses loomed ahead, weathered and unassuming. Jonathan led them with purpose, weaving through the narrow alleys between the buildings.

"Here." Blake stopped before an unmarked metal door embedded in the side of a seemingly ordinary warehouse.

Jedidiah examined it skeptically. "Doesn't look like much."

Jonathan smirked faintly. "That's the point." He pressed a hidden latch, and with a faint hiss, the door slid open, revealing a dark passageway leading into the depths of the structure.

Jedediah Davenport and Matthew Colton exchanged a wary glance.

"It's about as inviting as a crypt on a stormy night," Matthew quipped, shrugging off the leather bag he was carrying and setting it on the ground. He opened the bag casually and pulled out a holstered revolver, securing the belt around his waist with practiced ease.

"Matthew!" Jedidiah exclaimed, his voice laced with shock. "Where did you get that? Not only did I think I'd finally talked you out of carrying a gun, but I thought those outlaws made off with yours!"

"They did, and you tried," Matthew said nonchalantly, tightening the holster's strap. "I had a spare in my room back at the ranch."

Jedidiah sighed. "Of course you did."

Matthew shrugged. "Always good to have a backup. You never know when you'll need it."

Jonathan chuckled, despite the tension. "He's got a point."

Jedidiah shook his head in disbelief. "Is anyone in this group ever going to listen to me about non-lethal approaches?"

Matthew gave a lopsided grin, patting the holstered revolver. "I'll make you a deal, Jed. I won't use it unless it's absolutely necessary. Or... unless something really big and scary attacks us first!"

Jedidiah sighed, muttering under his breath. "None of those words are a comfort to me."

Jonathan stepped inside first, striking a match. He lit one of the lanterns on the wall, its soft glow illuminating the narrow hallway. "The workshop is just ahead. But keep your guard up."

The hallway was lined with rusted pipes and wires that snaked along like metallic veins. The faint sound of dripping water echoed through the corridor, and the air grew colder as they ventured deeper inside.

"It's too quiet," Matthew muttered, his voice low as he adjusted the revolver on his hip.

Jedidiah shot him a glare. "Well, you're certainly not. If you don't lower your voice, everyone in Missouri will know we're here!"

Jonathan paused ahead. "This is it," he whispered, motioning to a heavy steel door at the end of the corridor. It bore no markings, blending seamlessly into the grimy surroundings.

He placed a hand on the door's lever, hesitating for a moment. "Be ready. There's no telling what might be beyond this point."

"Or who," Matthew added grimly.

Jonathan pulled the lever, and the door groaned open on creaking hinges. The room beyond was vast and cavernous, its contents hidden in darkness. The faint smell of oil and burned metal hung in the air.

The older man paused, squinting into the gloom. "Hold on," he muttered, his eyes catching on a series of pipes running along the walls and ceiling. His free hand brushed over a nearby valve.

"What's that?" Jedidiah asked, eyeing the pipes suspiciously.

"A little something the Conqueror prepared," Jonathan replied, his tone distracted as he traced the pipes upward. "He hated working in the dark, and he loved theatrics."

Jonathan turned the valve with a sharp motion, and for a moment, nothing happened. Then, with a faint hiss, the sound of gas rushing through the pipes filled the room. Afterward, he turned a knob, which caused a distinct clicking noise. Above them, a massive chandelier—its frame a swirling masterpiece of brass and glass—sputtered to life. One by one, flames ignited along its dozens of globes, bathing the workshop in golden light.

The full scale of the room came into view, and all three froze. The ceiling arched high above, supported by steel girders. Workbenches stretched in every direction, covered in strange, unidentifiable devices. Massive mechanical constructs stood in the corners, their polished surfaces gleaming eerily in the flickering light. Shelves lined the walls, crammed with vials of chemicals, gears, and blueprints. Half-finished gadgets and towering machines loomed like sleeping giants. Cobwebs clung to forgotten inventions, and a thick layer of dust covered the workbenches.

"Well, if this isn't the lair of a mad genius, I don't know what is," Matthew remarked, his voice tinged with unease.

Jedidiah frowned, his eyes scanning the room. "Definitely looks abandoned alright. Like nobody's been here for a long time."

"Oh no, don't let appearances deceive you," Jonathan remarked as he approached a large drafting table at the center of the room. Yellowed parchment, filled with blueprints and schematics, lay scattered across its surface. "This is exactly how the room looked the last time I was here."

The others joined him, their eyes widening at the intricate designs. Strange symbols and detailed diagrams depicted devices that defied imagination —mechanical limbs, energy weapons, and towering automatons.

Jonathan sifted through piles of blueprints, his brow furrowed. "These schematics are all over the place," he muttered. "Half are unfinished, and the other half..." He trailed off, lifting one sheet. "This isn't even practical—it's like he was experimenting with impossibilities."

"You think that's impressive?" Matthew's voice came from the other side of the room, where he stood examining a brass contraption the size of a shoebox. "What about this?" He gave one of the levers a tentative push.

A sharp hiss escaped the device, followed by a burst of steam that sent Matthew stumbling back with a startled yelp. "What was—?"

"Don't touch anything!" Jonathan barked, glaring at him. "This is a workshop, not a carnival."

Jedidiah, meanwhile, ran his fingers along the edge of a massive drafting table. Something about the wood felt out of place—the grain was smoother near one corner. He pressed against it lightly, and with a faint click, a hidden compartment slid open. Inside lay a single folded sheet of parchment.

"Well, well," Jedidiah murmured, extracting the paper. "What do we have here?"

He unfolded the parchment carefully. His brow furrowed as the rough sketch came into view: jagged mountain ranges and a small cave entrance circled in red ink. "This has to be it," he said firmly. "It matches the direction they rode off in after the robbery."

Jonathan took the map, his gaze darkening as he studied it. "The Conqueror always has a purpose. If this is marked, it's not random. Either it's their hideout, or there's something there he wants."

"Or it's a trap," Matthew countered, his tone skeptical. "He's too clever to leave clues lying around without a reason."

"That's why we don't waste time debating," Jedidiah said, folding the map and tucking it into his pocket. "We need to move quickly."

As they turned to leave, the faint sound of metal scraping against stone echoed from deeper within the workshop. The trio froze, their eyes darting to the shadows.

"Tell me that was just the wind," Matthew whispered as he drew his revolver.

"Wind doesn't sound like that," Jonathan replied, his voice steady but quiet, as he too drew his gun.

Jedidiah swallowed hard, his hand brushing the pocket where he'd stashed the map. "Whatever it is, we better not stick around to find out."

They started toward the door at a brisk pace,

boots crunching against the dust-covered floor. The workshop's dim light seemed to cast moving shapes in the shadows, adding to the growing sense of unease.

Then, without warning, a small figure darted across their path. The three men stopped abruptly, their eyes locking on the sleek black shape. For a moment, none of them moved. Jonathan squinted, his mouth opening slightly before snapping shut. Jedidiah tilted his head, his brow furrowed, as though trying to make sense of what he was seeing. Matthew's grip on his lantern tightened, his knuckles whitening as he unconsciously shifted back a step.

It was a cat—jet black save for a white patch on its chest. The creature paused for a moment, its piercing green eyes catching the golden light of the chandelier before it turned and darted down the corridor leading out of the building.

"A cat?" Matthew asked incredulously, lowering his revolver slightly. "That's what we were so worried about?"

Jonathan cleared his throat, his eyes darting back to the spot where the cat had vanished. Jedidiah rubbed the back of his neck, a nervous chuckle escaping his lips. "Well," he said after a pause, his voice forcedly light, "at least it wasn't a rat."

Matthew didn't respond, his gaze fixed on the

corridor where the cat had disappeared, as if waiting for it to reappear.

Jonathan shook his head, his brow furrowed. "What's it doing in here? There's no food or water to draw it in."

Jedidiah's gaze followed the creature as it disappeared into the darkness. "Maybe it's a pet someone left behind?"

"Either way, it knows it's time to leave," Matthew muttered, holstering his revolver. "And I, for one, am inclined to follow its lead."

Jonathan Blake glanced down the corridor, then back at the others. His fingers drummed against the stock of his revolver, a nervous habit he rarely displayed. Jedidiah rubbed his temples, muttering under his breath about the air being stuffy. Matthew shook his head sharply, as though dismissing a thought he didn't want to linger on.

"Let's move—quietly," Jonathan said, his voice lower than before.

The trio exchanged wary looks before following the cat's path, but it was already long gone, disappearing into the shadows as if it had never been there.

As they navigated the dim corridor, Matthew muttered, "Out of curiosity, did anyone else notice...?" He trailed off, his lantern casting jittery light on the walls as his fingers tapped against its handle.

Jedidiah glanced over his shoulder, his tone sharper than usual. "Notice what?"

Matthew hesitated, his gaze lingering on the shadows ahead. "Nothing," he said finally, shaking his head as if trying to convince himself. "Must've been the light playing tricks on me."

When they reached the midway point, the faint outline of the open exit came into view, sunlight streaming in.

Jedidiah froze, his eyes narrowing. "Didn't we close that door behind us?"

"You know we did," Jonathan replied, his voice low and tense.

Matthew's hand instinctively hovered near his holster as his eyes darted around the corridor. "Either someone else—or something else—opened that door."

"Let's not stick around to find out who or what," Jedidiah said, his tone clipped as they quickened their pace, their boots thudding against the worn floorboards.

The unease lingered as they stepped outside, the afternoon sun failing to dispel the chill that had settled over them.

For a moment, nothing stirred inside the villain's lair—only the flickering light of the chandelier cast shadows against the walls. In their haste to leave, they had neglected to turn it off.

Then, with a faint click, one section of a

bookcase near the drafting table shifted. Dust sprinkled down as it swung inward, revealing a narrow, dimly lit passage. From the darkness, a tall figure emerged.

The Clockwork Conqueror stepped forward, tilting his head slightly, the lenses of his ornate brass mask gleaming like eyes in the faint light. He reached into his coat pocket and withdrew a pocket watch. The intricate design on its casing caught the dim glow of the chandelier above—a coiled octopus with outstretched tentacles.

With a practiced motion, he flicked it open, the faint ticking of its mechanism audible in the silence. He gazed at the hands for a moment. His posture shifted slightly as his gaze lifted from the timepiece to the direction the trio had gone.

Snapping the watch shut with a soft click, he slipped it back into his coat. A low, mechanical hum emanated from the gears embedded in his arm as he turned and began to move. His movements were deliberate and fluid, each step echoing faintly in the hollow space of the workshop.

The faint hiss of steam and the rhythmic clink of his mechanical enhancements faded as he disappeared into the hidden passage, leaving only the swinging bookcase and a lingering sense of unease in his wake.

Back in the open field, the Swift was waiting where they had left it, its metal accents gleaming like a lifeline amidst the unease of the workshop.

As they climbed aboard and the airship lifted off, Matthew leaned against the railing, his brow furrowed. "Okay, I have to ask," he said, breaking the silence. "That cat… Did it look... odd to either of you?"

Jedidiah glanced at him, puzzled. "Odd how?"

Matthew rubbed the back of his neck. "Like it was wearing… a vest."

Jonathan stared at him, his mouth opening slightly before closing again. He looked away, muttering, "It was probably just the shadows playing tricks on your eyes."

"Yeah, Matt, that would be ridiculous—for a cat to be wearing a vest and a top hat!" Jedidiah laughed.

"So you didn't see it?" Matthew asked, crossing his arms.

Jedidiah laughed nervously. "Of course not! I'm just saying how silly it would be."

"Then how'd you know it was wearing a top hat?" Matthew shot back, narrowing his eyes. "I only mentioned the vest."

Jonathan suddenly burst out, unable to hold back any longer, "Don't forget the goggles sitting on the brim of the hat!"

Matthew's jaw dropped. "So we all saw it!"

The three men fell into stunned silence, the hum of the Swift's engines the only sound as the workshop faded into the horizon behind them.

Jedidiah finally broke the quiet, shaking his head. "This is obsurd. We've all been breathing in too much oil and gas fumes."

"Right," Jonathan said, though his tone was far from convinced. "Mass hallucination is the only explanation."

The three men exchanged uneasy glances but said nothing more about it.

As the Swift soared over the rolling Missouri landscape, the sunlight began to wane, casting long shadows across the hills and riverbanks below. Jedidiah stood at the helm, his eyes fixed on the map they had found.

Matthew peered over his shoulder, rubbing his chin. "Looks like a whole lot of nothing. You sure we're not on a wild goose chase?"

Jedidiah shrugged. "Only one way to find out."

Jonathan, seated nearby with his revolver disassembled for cleaning, glanced up. "Even if it's a dead end, it's the best lead we have."

An hour and a half after taking off from St. Louis, the Swift descended as they approached the area marked on the map. Rugged hills gave way to a dense forest that stretched out like a patchwork quilt, dotted with jagged rock formations. A faint wisp of smoke caught Matthew's attention.

"There," he said, pointing. "Looks like someone's set up camp."

The mysterious cat wearing the vest, top hat, and goggles as it made its way down the corridor.

Jedidiah adjusted the airship's course, bringing the Swift to a halt in a small clearing just beyond the forest. The airship's brass accents glinted faintly in the dying light as the trio disembarked.

"This feels too easy," Jonathan muttered, checking his revolver and slipping it back into its holster. "If they've got guards posted, they'll know we're here."

Matthew smirked. "Then we'll just have to be extra cautious."

They trudged through the underbrush, following the faint trail of smoke until they came to a steep incline. The forest thinned, and the towering mouth of a cave loomed before them, its dark maw framed by limestone outcroppings. Vines clung to the rocks, and the air grew noticeably cooler.

"This is it," Jedidiah said, his voice low.

"It's definitely a cave—a huge cave," Matthew remarked, slightly impressed. "If they're in there, they could be anywhere."

Jonathan frowned, scanning the entrance. "They're probably deep inside."

As they stepped closer, Matthew paused, his eyes narrowing. Something about the cave seemed... familiar. He shook his head, dismissing the thought. "Must've read too many books," he muttered.

The men each lit a lantern and ventured inside, their footsteps echoing against the stone walls. The musty smell of earth and damp limestone filled the air, clinging to their skin. A faint metallic tang mingled with the scent, and the distant drip of water echoed ominously, adding to the oppressive silence. The flickering lantern light danced across the uneven walls, casting shifting shadows that made the narrow passages feel alive.

"I don't like this," Jonathan said quietly, his hand resting on his revolver. "Too many places for an ambush."

As they pushed deeper into the cave, the passages twisted and turned in a labyrinthine pattern. The walls bore faint etchings, marks left by explorers, or perhaps the outlaws themselves.

"Pay attention to those marks on the walls so we can find our way back out," Jedidiah remarked in a low voice.

Matthew stopped abruptly, his lantern's glow illuminating the weathered symbols etched into the rock. His voice dropped to an urgent whisper. "This... this seems familiar."

Jedidiah glanced at him, impatient. "Familiar how?"

Matthew leaned closer to the wall, his fingers brushing the inscriptions. "I think..." He swallowed hard, his voice a breathless whisper. "This is McDowell Cave. Mark Twain wrote about it in Tom Sawyer. It's the cave where Tom and Becky got lost... and where the treasure was hidden."

Jonathan frowned. "You're telling me the outlaws picked a hideout from a children's book?"

"It's not a children's book!" Matthew hissed. "And if you think about it, it makes sense," he continued. "What better place than a maze of tunnels no one can navigate?"

Jedidiah squinted at the carvings, his lantern casting faint, flickering shadows across the walls. "Do you remember how they found their way out?"

Matthew hesitated, then whispered, "Tom Sawyer followed a thread of light. But that's not going to help us now—not with the sun starting to set."

Jonathan's lips thinned into a grim line. "Well," he murmured, "I doubt the outlaws left us a convenient trail to follow. Let's keep moving."

The deeper they went, the more unnerving the cave became. Their lanterns illuminated strange carvings on the walls—figures and symbols that seemed out of place, as though recently added. The faint sound of water dripping echoed in the distance.

As they rounded a corner, Jedidiah raised his lantern higher, revealing a rough-hewn table piled high with stolen loot. Stacks of paper bills bound with twine, gleaming jewelry, pocket watches, and silverware spilled from open satchels and wooden chests. Scattered across the floor were more bags bulging with pilfered goods, fine silks, polished silver candlesticks, and bundles of bonds marked with bank seals.

Jedidiah's eyes narrowed. "Looks like we've found their base," he said grimly.

"Too bad you won't be getting out to tell anyone about it!" a voice called out from behind them.

CHAPTER XIV

The Recovery

The trio froze, their lanterns casting flickering shadows on the cave walls. Jonathan Blake's hand instinctively dropped to his revolver, his jaw tightening as he turned slightly toward the voice. Jedidiah's eyes darted to Matthew Colton, who was also reaching for his weapon.

The sound of ray guns charging filled the confined space, followed by the crunch of boots on stone. Four outlaws stepped closer, their weapons raised. The faint green glow of the ray guns' energy orbs cast eerie shadows on their masked faces. The leader's eyes glinted coldly beneath the brim of his hat.

"Don't even think about it," he growled.

The cave grew deathly silent, save for the faint hum of the ray guns aimed squarely at the trio. The stolen loot glinted mockingly in the lantern light before them. Among the scattered items was a familiar-looking bag—the same one the leader had carried during the gang's train heist.

"Drop your weapons and turn around slowly," the voice growled. Its owner stepped forward from the shadows—a tall man with his face obscured by a scarf and wide-brimmed hat. The gleam of futuristic weaponry in his hand left no doubt about his dangerous intent. Behind him, three more figures emerged, their faces hidden beneath masks, each holding an identical ray gun.

The trio did as instructed, turning around. Matthew dropped his gun, but Jonathan hesitated, his fingers hovering near his revolver.

"Now, hold on—"

"Don't test me, old man," the outlaw barked. "Drop your weapon!"

Reluctantly, Jonathan complied. Jedidiah raised a calming hand, his voice steady despite the tension. "We're not here to fight. We're just—"

"A group of treasure hunters?" the leader scoffed.

"You might say that," Jedidiah replied. "We're just after a few of the items you took from us. Once we have them, we'll leave, and you can keep the rest." He glanced back at four burlap sacks filled with valuables, each stamped with D.&R.W. Railroad on the side.

The outlaw chuckled darkly. "And what makes you think you're leaving here at all?"

Before Jedidiah could respond, one of the outlaws, noticing where he had just glanced and spoke up. "Hold on! I recognize you! You were on the train a couple of weeks ago!"

The leader glanced at the man, then back at Jedidiah and Matthew. "You're right! How could I have forgotten? You're the ones who knocked me out and stole my ray gun! Which one of you has it?"

"Technically, I wasn't with them on the train, so there's no way I could have it," Jonathan interjected.

"And I was frozen by that blast from your weapon, so I couldn't have..." Matthew's words trailed off as he noticed Jedidiah staring intently at him. "What? He asked!"

The leader's eyes narrowed, his grip tightening on the ray gun. "So, it was you," he growled, pointing the weapon squarely at Jedidiah. "You're the one who humiliated me in front of my own gang."

Matthew stepped forward, raising his hands defensively. He positioned himself between Jedidiah and the armed man.

"He was just trying to survive. You'd have done the same in his boots."

Jedidiah stepped forward, his tone sharp. "Speaking of survival, why did you target us on that train in the first place? Who ordered you to steal my pocket watch?"

The leader's brow furrowed briefly, his expression shifting between confusion and amusement. "A pocket watch?" he repeated, a sneer twisting the corner of his mouth. "What kind of fool do you take me for? I've got no interest in trinkets."

Jedidiah's eyes narrowed, studying him for any sign of deceit. "So, you're saying it was just a coincidence that you held us up and weren't after my watch specifically?"

The leader sneered. "I don't know what you're talking about. We were after gold and whatever valuables we could take. Your watch just happened to be one of them."

"What about the Clockwork Conqueror?" Matthew demanded.

"Who?"

"The man you acquired your ray guns from!" Jonathan Blake added.

"He's just someone we buy weapons from," the outlaw replied, tightening his grip on the ray gun. "Only met him a couple of times. Never even seen his face—he's always wearing a brass-plated mask."

"I've heard enough!" Jedidiah announced his tone firm and commanding. "You're clearly just a bunch of random thieves. We don't have time to waste with you. We're here to retrieve what's ours and nothing more. Let us take it, and we'll leave without anyone getting hurt."

The leader let out a bitter laugh. "You think you're calling the shots? You're outnumbered and unarmed." He gestured at the stolen loot. "Everything here is ours—fair and square."

Jedidiah didn't flinch. "Fair? You call robbing innocent people at gunpoint and leaving them stranded fair?"

The unscrupulous man's eyes flashed with anger, but before he could respond, a low growl rumbled through the cave, drawing his attention away.

"What was that?" one of the others asked nervously.

"Quiet!" the leader barked. "Probably just the wind." But the tension in his voice betrayed his uncertainty.

The growl echoed again, louder this time, reverberating off the stone walls and sending a chill through the air. The outlaws, momentarily startled, turned in unison toward the sound, their weapons raised. The ominous growl grew louder, and closer, the echo distorting it, making it impossible to pinpoint the source. One of the outlaws shifted uneasily, his finger twitching on the trigger.

Jedidiah and Matthew exchanged a knowing glance. Without a word, they dropped to the ground in unison, their movements fluid and purposeful. In a heartbeat, they snatched up the revolvers lying at their feet.

The leader whipped around, fury twisting his face as he raised his ray gun. "You—"

Before he could finish, the cavern erupted with the deafening cracks of revolver fire. Jedidiah and Matthew's aim was precise, each shot shattering the glowing glass orbs on the outlaws' ray guns with violent precision.

A surge of energy burst from the ruptured vials, the strange, glowing liquid crackling, and sparking as it sprayed outward. The outlaws had no time to react. Their bodies stiffened mid-motion, frozen as the charged liquid seeped into their skin. The leader's furious snarl was cut short, his mouth frozen open in silent rage.

The cave fell eerily silent, save for the faint sizzle of dissipating energy from the damaged ray guns. Jedidiah glanced at Matthew, who gave a sharp nod. Together, they swiftly secured the outlaws' weapons while Jonathan scanned the cavern for other threats.

Dusting off his vest, Jedidiah cast a wary eye over the immobilized outlaws. His voice was cool and measured as he said, "That worked out well."

Matthew stood silent for a moment, his revolver still gripped tightly. He glanced at the motionless gang, then back at his childhood friend. "Aren't you glad we brought these along now?"

"I thought you didn't know how to use a revolver," Jonathan remarked, both surprised and confused as Jedidiah handed his weapon back.

"Never said I didn't know how to use one," Davenport replied with a shrug. "Just said I thought there were better options. Now, let's get what we came for!"

Jonathan stepped cautiously closer to one of the outlaws. He waved a hand in front of the man's frozen face, then tapped lightly on the stiffened shoulder. "I can't believe it. They're paralyzed, completely paralyzed," he confirmed, his voice tinged with awe. "How long will they be like this?"

Matthew let out a low whistle, holstering his revolver. "I was out for quite a while when they shot me."

After gathering the four burlap sacks, Jedidiah carefully dropped the four new ray guns into one of them. "These may come in handy later!"

"Yeah," Matthew agreed. "We can't count on whatever that was growling in the cave to save us again."

"I wonder what it was," Jonathan Blake pondered.

Just then, a distant meow echoed through the cave. The men turned to see the dark silhouette of a black cat. The small animal paused briefly in the glow of their lanterns, its green eyes glinting like emeralds. Its top hat, vest, and goggles were now unmistakably visible—it was the same cat from the warehouse. Letting out a faint, throaty rumble—half-growl, half-meow—it vanished into the depths of the cave.

The three men stood frozen, their lanterns casting faint flickers against the cave walls. Jedidiah glanced at Matthew, who raised an eyebrow, then shifted his gaze to Jonathan, who merely shrugged.

Without a word, they exchanged a look—a silent agreement, unspoken yet undeniable. Whatever they had just witnessed, it was something they would keep to themselves.

Jonathan shivered involuntarily, brushing a hand over his coat as though warding off an unseen chill. He was trying not to think too hard about it.

Matthew broke the silence, adjusting his holster. "We should move," he said gruffly. "Before something else decides to show up."

Jonathan nodded, his eyes lingering on the spot where the cat had disappeared. "Agreed."

Jedidiah cleared his throat, straightened his vest, and gestured toward the exit. "This way."

****

A few hours after dark, the Swift touched down at Davenport Ranch. Its brass accents gleamed in the moonlight as it came to rest near Jedidiah's stately Victorian home.

As the loading ramp lowered, Phineas B. Hargroves strode toward them, his coat flapping in the night breeze. He had just returned from his workshop.

"Took you long enough!" he called, his voice tinged with equal parts worry and indignation. "We were starting to think you'd been eaten by a mechanical monstrosity. Or worse, you let Matthew steer!"

"Nice to see you too, Professor," Matthew Colton replied dryly, though a warm smile played on his lips.

From the front door, Pat Bennington leaned out, a wide grin splitting his face. "Agatha told me you'd be back before morning. Guess I owe her a freshly baked rhubarb pie now!"

Jedidiah smirked as he stepped off the ramp, burlap sacks of stolen valuables slung over his shoulder. "We've had quite the adventure. Let's just go inside. There's a lot to discuss."

The group gathered around the large dining table, the comforting aroma of stew and freshly baked bread filling the air. Jonathan Blake carefully laid one of the ray guns onto the table. Phineas' eyes lit up with excitement.

"Fascinating!" the eccentric older man exclaimed, reaching for the weapon. "How many of these did you acquire?"

"We got four this time," Jedidiah replied, nudging a bowl of stew toward Phineas before he could lose himself completely in the technology. "The outlaws had no idea who they were really dealing with. They didn't even realize the man they were buying from was the Clockwork Conqueror."

"That makes five of these now," Phineas said with a satisfied smile. "All we need to do is replace the glass orbs and refill them with the formula." Puffing out his chest with pride, he added casually, "By the way, I cracked the formula while you were gone."

"Gosh!" Matthew exclaimed. "That was fast!"

Phineas' chest puffed out even more. "Of course, it was, my dear boy! You seem to forget that I happen to be a genius."

"So, you also developed an antidote?" Matthew asked quickly, a mischievous glint in his eye.

Professor Hargroves drew himself up, feigning insult. "My dear boy, even geniuses have their limits!"

Everyone burst into hearty laughter before turning their attention to the meal. After finishing, they remained gathered around the table, placing the sacks of recovered goods at the center.

As they sifted through the contents, the clinking of stolen valuables filled the room. Jonathan leaned forward, his brow furrowing. "Do you think it's all still here?"

"It better be," Jedidiah muttered, pulling out a handful of gold coins and setting them aside. "That watch is too important to lose now."

Matthew crossed his arms, his tone tense. "It has to be here. They didn't strike me as the sentimental type."

Finally, Jedidiah's fingers closed around a familiar shape. With a sense of reverence, he pulled out the pocket watch. Its intricate brass design glinted under the chandelier's light, the green stone at its center glowing faintly as if it held a secret of its own. Jedidiah carefully placed it on the table.

"There it is," Matthew said, relief evident in his voice.

Phineas leaned in for a closer look, running a careful finger along the intricate brass designs. "Remarkable craftsmanship," he muttered, his eyes narrowing as he examined it closely. Tilting the watch to catch the light, he paused, the faint green glow of the central stone holding his attention.

Jedidiah turned back to the sack, his movements purposeful. Moments later, he withdrew two folded pieces of paper. One was the mysterious note that read simply: The time has come. The other was a torn scrap of parchment bearing a series of numbers written in a deliberate hand. Both papers bore the emblem of the octopus wearing a top hat and monocle.

Phineas' gaze shifted to the items. His voice was

He pulled out the pocket watch. Its intricate brass design glinted under the chandelier's light, the green stone at its center glowing faintly as if it held a secret of its own.

a mix of awe and determination. "You've found everything—the watch, the letter, the torn paper. Now what?"

"Next, we head to Detroit to rendezvous with Lady Seraphina Blackwood, per her instructions," Jedidiah replied, removing the watch with the gold-embossed train from his pocket and replacing it with the one recovered from the hold-up.

"When do we leave?" Matthew asked, leaning forward, his tone edged with anticipation.

"First thing in the morning," Jedidiah said, his fingers curling around the watch as though its weight was more than physical. His voice dropped, low and resolute. "The clock is ticking—and we're running out of time."

CHAPTER XV

Through Smoke and Silence

Early on the morning of Saturday, October 22nd, 1881, the airship known as the Phoenix soared into the crisp dawn sky, its newly polished brass glinting in the golden sunlight. After careful consideration, Jedidiah decided to take his first airship on the journey to Detroit. This was the perfect opportunity to test its mettle after the extensive repairs and upgrades Phineas had painstakingly implemented.

Though the Swift, the fastest ship in Jedidiah's fleet, could have made the trip in shorter time, he felt it was time to return the Phoenix to service. Where it truly belonged.

The hum of the engines provided a steady, reassuring rhythm as the airship cut effortlessly through the cool morning air. The faint glow of the rising sun painted the horizon in rich shades of gold and crimson, casting warm light across the ship's reinforced hull.

Jedidiah stood near the helm, his hands clasped behind his back, his gaze fixed on the vast expanse ahead. Beside him, Matthew Colton leaned casually against the railing, his hands tucked into his pockets as he watched the world pass by far below.

"The Phoenix feels different," Matthew remarked, tilting his head as he glanced at the intricate network of pipes and gauges along the walls. "Smoother. Faster, even."

Phineas B. Hargroves, perched at a nearby console with a notebook in hand, didn't look up as he replied, "Well, it should. I spent weeks redesigning the system. Thanks to the two of you."

Matthew smirked but didn't take the bait. "Don't give us all the credit, Professor. Those saboteurs deserve most of it. We just handled the landing."

Jedidiah chuckled, shaking his head. "*We* handled the landing? That's one way to put it."

The dark-haired young man raised an eyebrow, grinning. "Well, you may have handled the steering, but I'd like to see how you'd have managed it if I hadn't been working to maintain pressure for the propulsion system."

Davenport laughed, clapping him on the shoulder. "Fair enough. Next time, I'll handle the engine while you take the landing."

"Just be glad it wasn't a total loss," Phineas

interjected, his tone equal parts exasperated and proud. "The Phoenix was never meant to be grounded this long. I'd say it's better than ever now —stronger, more efficient, and—" he gestured to the steam engine gauges near the helm, "—faster. I incorporated ideas from the engine you designed for the Swift, Jed."

Jedidiah nodded appreciatively, his gaze following Phineas' gesture to the gauges. "I can tell, Professor. It's running smoother than ever. You've outdone yourself, as usual."

He paused, a glint of mischief in his eyes, and added, "But still, don't count on it beating the Swift in a race."

The eccentric older man bristled, his chest puffing up defensively. "Hah! That glorified speedster couldn't hold a candle to the Phoenix when it comes to durability and precision. Speed isn't everything, my dear boy."

Jedidiah chuckled, his tone light. "Relax, Phineas. I'm just saying—it's nice to have both ships back in the air again."

Phineas grumbled under his breath, though a faint, begrudging smile tugged at the corners of his mouth. "They are both truly remarkable vessels."

As the ship sailed onward, Phineas disappeared into the sleeping cabin to work on the ray guns. He replaced the glass orbs on each weapon and began carefully refilling them with the liquid used to freeze people. Meanwhile, Jedidiah and Matthew's conversation turned to events earlier that morning.

"Mr. Blake sure seemed eager to take over the construction of his airship," Matthew said, leaning against the helm. "He had that look—like a kid left in charge of a candy store."

Jedidiah nodded, his hands steady on the wheel. "It's going to be his baby once it's completed. Besides, he's anxious to get back to his shop on Automaton Alley."

"And Edwin couldn't wait to ride into town and turn in the rest of the train robbery loot to Sheriff Thompson."

"Someone had to do it," Jedidiah replied. "I think he also wanted to stop by the freight office to see Tom about some secret project they're planning."

Matthew laughed softly. "It's funny how just a month ago they were mortal enemies, and now they're the best of friends."

Jedidiah smiled faintly. "You and I didn't exactly start as close friends either."

"That's not how I remember it," Matthew said with mock indignation. "I recall us being friends from the very beginning."

"You're forgetting the day we met at school."

Matthew's grin turned mischievous. "Ah, the infamous lunch pail incident. I'd almost forgotten about that."

Jedidiah raised an eyebrow, his tone playful. "I'll never forget it. You left yours by the fishing hole that morning and thought I wouldn't notice when you swiped mine."

"Oh, come on now," Matthew protested with a laugh. "I was planning to give it back."

Jedidiah shook his head, chuckling. "After you ate everything inside it?"

"I paid for it with the punch in the nose you gave me!"

"And you gave me a black eye!" Jedidiah laughed. "But after wrestling for five or ten minutes, I seem to recall we ended up sharing everything in my pail anyway."

Matthew tapped his temple, feigning deep thought. "Ah yes, the great compromise. Now that I think about it, that's when we officially became friends."

Jedidiah nodded, his smile widening. "Funny how that works—a black eye and a bloody nose later, and now we're inseparable."

Matthew leaned back, folding his arms with a grin. "Well, I always figured it was better to have you as a friend than an enemy."

The airship hit a brief patch of turbulence, causing a slight jolt underfoot. From the sleeping cabin, Phineas muttered, his voice muffled but clear enough to carry. "I'll need to recalibrate the stabilizers when we land. This should be smoother."

Jedidiah glanced toward the cabin door, raising an eyebrow. "Didn't he just finish adjusting those?"

Matthew shrugged, grinning. "You know him—always chasing perfection."

Before Jedidiah could respond, the Phoenix lurched again, more abruptly this time. From the cabin came a startled yelp, followed by a loud, unmistakable fzzzap!—the sound of the paralyzing ray gun discharging.

"Phineas!" Jedidiah called, his voice sharp with concern.

There was no response.

Matthew was already halfway to the cabin door, his steps quick and sure. Jedidiah followed close behind. They exchanged a worried glance before Matthew pushed the door open.

The cabin was brightly lit, sunlight streaming through the windows and casting warm patches of light across the polished wooden floor. Near a workbench, Phineas stood frozen in an awkward position, the paralyzing ray gun still loosely gripped in his hand.

A faint crackle of dissipating energy hummed in the air, mingling with the steady, peaceful thrum of the Phoenix's engines.

Jedidiah and Matthew exchanged a knowing glance before stepping inside. Matthew approached Phineas, waving a hand in front of his face.

"Phineas? Can you hear me?" He glanced back at Jedidiah and added, "He's out cold... well, frozen."

Jedidiah stepped closer, his eyes scanning the scene. "Looks like he accidentally triggered it... on himself."

"Of course he did," Matthew muttered under his breath. "Guess we should try to wake him up."

A devilish grin spread across Colton's face as he cracked his knuckles. "Oh, I've been waiting for this moment."

Jedidiah raised an eyebrow. "Matt, what are you up to?"

Without answering, the dark-haired young man grabbed a nearby crate, placing it in front of the immobilized Phineas. He stepped onto it so he was at eye level, dramatically rolling up his sleeves. "Turnabout's fair play, isn't it?" Matthew said with a devilish grin. "After all, he didn't hold back when it was me frozen stiff back on the train."

"Oh no, not again..." Davenport groaned as Matthew delivered a playful but firm slap to Phineas' cheek. "Wakey-wakey, Professor!" He paused, waiting for a response, but Phineas remained stiff as a statue.

"He's out deeper than I thought," Matthew said with exaggerated mock distress. "Guess I'll have to keep at it until he comes around." With that, he resumed slapping Phineas' cheeks back and forth with theatrical gusto.

"Matt!" Jedidiah shouted, stepping forward. "Stop! That's not doing anyone any good! We'll just have to wait it out. If it's like the other incidents, the effects will wear off soon enough."

"Are you sure?" Matthew asked, landing a final slap for good measure.

"I'm positive," Jedidiah replied with a chuckle, leaning casually against the doorway. "Besides, you were enjoying that way too much."

Matthew hopped off the crate with a satisfied grin. "Can't say it wasn't therapeutic."

****

Almost thirteen hours after lifting off from Davenport Ranch, the Phoenix began its graceful descent into Detroit. Below, the city sprawled like a patchwork quilt of flickering gas lamps and glowing shop windows. The river carved a silvery path through the darkness, reflecting the shimmering lights of the industrial hub.

The airship hummed softly, gliding toward an area near the docks—a stark contrast to the bustling noise rising from the streets. The clatter of carriage wheels, the distant shouts of dockworkers, and the low whistle of a train wove together in a symphony of urban life, punctuated by the occasional hiss of steam from nearby factories.

Matthew Colton leaned against the railing, his

gaze fixed on the sprawling city below. "It's a far cry from Spoon Fork, that's for sure. Makes you wonder what kind of secrets a city this big might be hiding."

Jedidiah stood at the helm, his eyes sharp as he guided the Phoenix toward the riverfront. "Secrets we're about to uncover, I imagine. Lady Seraphina didn't summon us here for nothing."

Phineas B. Hargroves emerged from the cabin, rubbing his cheeks. He stretched, surveying the scene below with a mock-dramatic sigh. Though he'd recovered from the paralyzing ray hours earlier, the lingering soreness in his jaw served as a reminder of Matthew Colton's "helpful" efforts to revive him.

"Detroit at night," he proclaimed, his tone theatrical. "The perfect setting for cloak-and-dagger affairs. Don't you agree?"

The engines let out a low hiss as the Phoenix floated gracefully down, hovering just above the ground. Its polished brass and sleek lines caught the soft glow of gas lamps lining the dock, gleaming faintly in the night.

Jedidiah secured the mooring lines and stepped away from the helm, adjusting his coat. He lowered the loading ramp with practiced ease. "Alright, gentlemen," he said, his tone firm but light. "Let's not keep our host waiting."

Stepping off the Phoenix, the trio made their

way into the bustling streets of Detroit. The cool night air carried the mingling scents of coal smoke and fresh bread from a nearby bakery. Lanterns flickered along the sidewalks, casting warm pools of light that danced with the shadows of passing pedestrians.

"Well," Matthew began, glancing around at the unfamiliar surroundings, "since we don't know where to find Lady Seraphina, we might as well take in the sights."

Jedidiah nodded. "Agreed. Maybe we'll come across someone who can point us in the right direction."

Phineas eagerly chimed in, his eyes sparkling with curiosity. "An excellent chance to experience the city's nocturnal offerings! After all, Detroit is the beating heart of innovation these days."

They walked along Woodward Avenue, one of the city's main thoroughfares. The street teemed with activity, even at the late hour. Horse-drawn streetcars rattled by, their bells clanging to warn distracted pedestrians. Elegant carriages moved through the streets, carrying well-dressed passengers to evening engagements.

Shop windows displayed a dazzling array of goods—fine clothing, intricate timepieces, and cutting-edge mechanical marvels. A few establishments remained open, their gaslit interiors buzzing with lively patrons.

The trio moved through the city with a mix of curiosity and purpose, their eyes scanning the vibrant streets for clues that might lead them to their enigmatic host.

Further along, they came upon Campus Martius Park, a central gathering place for the city's residents. Even at this hour, vendors were selling roasted chestnuts and newspapers, while couples strolled under the warm glow of lamplight.

Phineas paused to examine a public bulletin board plastered with notices and advertisements. "Say, look at this. They're demonstrating some new steam-powered machinery at the manufacturing hall tomorrow."

Jedidiah glanced over his shoulder. "Tempting, but we're on a mission. Maybe another time."

Just then a newsboy approached, waving the latest edition of the Detroit Free Press. "Evening paper, sirs? Only two cents!"

Jedidiah handed over a nickel and told the boy to keep the change before unfolding the paper. Scanning the pages, his eyes caught an advertisement:

"Grand Masquerade Ball Tonight at 9:00 PM. Detroit Opera House. A Night of Elegance and Mystery. By Invitation Only."

Matthew raised an eyebrow, crossing his arms. "A masquerade ball? Sounds a little too refined for us, doesn't it?"

"My dear boy," Professor Hargroves smirked. "Speak for yourself! Besides, it's exactly the kind of place where someone like Lady Seraphina would make an appearance."

Jedidiah nodded, his expression thoughtful. "It's almost eight o'clock now. We have an hour to find something more suitable to wear and figure out how we're going to get in without an invitation."

Matthew chuckled. "Oh, come on, Jed. When have we ever needed an invitation to get in somewhere?"

Phineas rolled his eyes. "Are you suggesting that I, Professor Phineas B. Hargroves, crash a high-society event like this?"

"You can always stay on the airship and..." Jedidiah's sentence was cut short as the eccentric older man suddenly raised his voice.

"My dear boy, please! I was just making sure I understood the plan!"

Jedidiah smirked. "The first thing we need to do is find a change of clothes." He gestured at their air-travel attire.

"I wonder if Hudson's Department Store is open," Phineas mused. "It's a new establishment, but I've read they have high-quality merchandise. Not to mention, it's on the first floor of the Opera House."

The trio arrived at the stately venue, its grand facade glowing under the gas lamps lining the street. The faint strains of music and laughter spilled into the cool evening air, setting the stage for the night's festivities. Off to the side of the grand staircase, a smaller door bore the words: Hudson's Department Store – Fine Goods for the Discerning Gentleman.

As they approached, the sound of a key turning in a lock drew their attention. Two impeccably dressed clerks, one carrying a lantern and the other locking the door, looked up. Their eyes swept over Jedidiah, Matthew, and Phineas, lingering on their slightly rumpled air-travel attire with thinly veiled disdain.

"You're a bit late, gentlemen," one clerk said with a sneer, snapping the key from the lock. "We're closed for the evening."

"We're looking for formal attire," Jedidiah said evenly, his tone polite but firm. "Surely, you can make an exception."

The second clerk scoffed, adjusting the pristine lapels of his coat. "Even if we were open, I doubt we'd have anything you could afford."

Matthew's eyes narrowed, but Jedidiah placed a calming hand on his shoulder before he could respond. "I see," he said, his voice measured. "Well, thank you for your time."

The clerks exchanged smug glances before turning on their heels and disappearing into the night.

Matthew let out a frustrated sigh. "Of all the pompous, self-important... I ought to—"

"Let it go," Jedidiah interrupted, his voice steady. "We'll find another way. In the meantime, maybe we can buy some invitations to the ball from someone."

Phineas crossed his arms, his expression a mix of irritation and amusement. "Another way? Do tell, Jed, because unless one of us has a trunk full of formalwear stashed in the airship..."

He stopped mid-sentence as a figure emerged from the shadows, cloaked in a stark black plague doctor's outfit. The long beak of the mask gleamed faintly under the gaslight, and the figure moved with an eerie, deliberate grace.

Without a word, the masked individual extended a rolled-up scroll in a gloved hand toward Jedidiah. Instinctively, Jedidiah took it, his fingers brushing against the cold leather of the glove. The figure bowed deeply, the movement fluid yet unnerving, before retreating into a nearby alley. The shadows swallowed him within moments, leaving only the faint rustle of his cloak.

The three men stood frozen, the strange encounter hanging heavily in the air.

"What was that about?" Matthew finally asked, breaking the silence.

Jedidiah unrolled the scroll carefully, his eyes scanning the ornate script. "Your presence is

Without a word, the masked individual
extended a rolled-up scroll in a
gloved hand toward Jedidiah.

requested at tonight's ball, Detroit Opera House, Grand Ballroom. Admission granted upon presentation of this invitation." Two more identical pages were rolled up with it.

Phineas raised an eyebrow, quickly recovering from his earlier surprise. "Well, we have our invitations to the ball, but this does absolutely nothing to solve our clothing dilemma. We still need formal attire."

Before Jedidiah could respond, a faint rustling drew their attention back to the dark alley. The mysterious figure in the plague doctor's outfit had reemerged, standing motionless at the edge of the shadows. Slowly, he raised a gloved hand and beckoned them with a deliberate, almost hypnotic motion.

Matthew narrowed his eyes, his hand instinctively drifting toward the spot where his revolver would normally rest. "I don't like this."

Jedidiah held up a calming hand. "Let's see what he wants. If he meant harm, he could've done it when he handed over the invitations."

The trio exchanged wary glances before stepping cautiously toward the figure. The alley was dimly lit, its brick walls towering on either side. The faint glow of gas lamps from the main street barely pierced the oppressive darkness.

The figure remained perfectly still as they approached, the eerie beak of his mask glinting faintly in the weak light. Without warning, he reached into his cloak and hurled a small metallic orb to the ground at their feet.

The orb struck the cobblestones with a sharp metallic clink that echoed unnaturally in the narrow alley. A split second later, it erupted into a thick, acrid cloud of smoke.

The air filled with the biting stench of sulfur and burnt metal, stinging their noses and throats. Jedidiah coughed violently, his eyes watering as the smoke clung to his skin. The bitter, chemical taste on his tongue made him gag as he stumbled backward, disoriented.

Matthew staggered, raising an arm to shield his face, but it offered little protection. The stinging vapor pricked at his eyes like needles, forcing them shut, and his lungs burned with each gasp of air. "It's… choking," he rasped, his voice hoarse, before his legs buckled and he crumpled to the ground.

Phineas flailed blindly, one hand clawing at the brick wall for support. The smoke thickened around him, a suffocating shroud that smothered his senses. His fingers scraped against the rough surface, leaving faint, desperate streaks before his strength gave out. The acrid fumes filled his nostrils and mouth, sharp and nauseating, as the world tilted and dissolved into darkness.

Jedidiah's vision blurred as the smoke enveloped him, his lungs burning and his thoughts slipping away. The last thing he registered was the faint, retreating sound of footsteps echoing through the alley, disappearing into the shadows. Then there was only silence.

CHAPTER XVI

The Grand Ball

Jedidiah Davenport groaned as he stirred awake, his head pounding like the rhythm of an overworked steam engine. The world around him felt distant and distorted as if he were peering through the warped glass of an old lantern. His fingers brushed against the cool, smooth surface of polished floorboards, the faint scent of lavender and woodsmoke filling his nostrils.

He blinked hard, his vision slowly clearing. The flicker of a gas lamp illuminated the room, casting long shadows across shelves and tables stacked high with bolts of fabric. Rolls of satin, wool, and lace spilled from their places, their vibrant colors dulled by the dim light.

Tailor's dummies lined the room, some draped in half-stitched suits, others bare, their linen padding showing signs of wear.

A worn sign pinned to the wall read: Taylor's

Fine Fashions – Est. 1875.

"Jed…?" A groggy voice broke the eerie stillness.

Matthew Colton was slumped against a pile of fabric rolls, his dark hair disheveled and his shirt streaked with soot. He rubbed his temple as he sat up, wincing. "What… happened?"

"That's what I'd like to know," Jedidiah replied, his voice rough. He pushed himself upright, instinctively reaching for his pocket. The familiar weight of his pocket watch was still there, offering a small comfort.

"Where's Phineas?" Jedidiah scanned the dimly lit room, his eyes narrowing.

"I'm over here, my dear boy," a muffled voice called from behind a curtain separating the backroom from the shop floor. Moments later, Professor Phineas B. Hargroves emerged, clutching his side and looking unusually disheveled. His hair was askew, and his waistcoat was streaked with dust and thread.

"Believe it or not, this isn't the first time I've woken up in the backroom of a haberdashery," he muttered, brushing dust off his sleeves.

Matthew smirked faintly. "How many haberdasheries have you..."

Jedidiah cut him off with a quick motion, holding a finger to his lips. His sharp eyes swept the dimly lit room, his posture tense.

The backroom was cramped but orderly, with patterns pinned to corkboards and scissors hanging neatly on hooks. A sewing machine, its intricate brass mechanisms gleaming faintly, sat on a nearby table.

Jedidiah's voice was low, measured. "How did we get here?"

Phineas stepped closer to the two young men. "I've been attempting to piece that together myself. The last thing I recall was being in that alley, and then—" he gestured vaguely—"darkness."

Jedidiah frowned, his sharp mind already working through the possibilities. "We were ambushed. That smoke... it was just like the bombs Jonathan and Edwin used on us a few weeks ago."

He trailed off, his gaze falling on a small card tucked into the folds of a bolt of fabric. Its edges were gilded, and its surface bore a familiar emblem: an octopus wearing a top hat and monocle. His heart sank as he picked it up.

Phineas plucked the card from Jedidiah's hand, studying it closely. "The Order of the Clockwork Octopus."

Jedidiah's jaw tightened. "Which means Lady Seraphina Blackwood was behind this!"

Before they could speculate further, the faint creak of a door echoed from the shop floor. The three of them froze, hands instinctively moving to their belts—only to remember they weren't carrying weapons. Not even the paralyzing ray guns, which were still aboard the Phoenix.

"Stay sharp," Jedidiah whispered, motioning for the others to stay behind him as he stepped toward the source of the noise.

The door swung open with a soft chime. Two men wearing plague masks stepped inside, each armed with sleek, futuristic rifles. Their dark coats swirled around them as they moved, their presence commanding and ominous. They flanked the doorway like sentinels.

Behind them, a third figure strode in with a markedly different energy.

Dressed in a tailored frock coat and a richly embroidered waistcoat, the older man's silver hair gleamed under the flicker of the gas lamp. A polished cane tapped against the floor with every measured step, and a monocle glinted in his eye. His smile was sharp and enigmatic, his every move exuding confidence and authority.

"Gentlemen," the dapper man said, his voice smooth and urbane, slicing through the tension like a razor. "Let's not be uncivilized. After all, the three of you have a ball to attend—and I am here to adorn you in the latest fashions."

Matthew's brow furrowed, his jaw tightening as he stepped forward, his voice sharp with suspicion. "Not so fast! Nobody adorns me without a fight!"

Phineas B. Hargroves leaned toward him,

whispering with dry exasperation, "My dear boy, he merely means to make clothes for us."

"Oh." Matthew blinked, suddenly looking slightly embarrassed. "Why didn't he just say so?"

"I did!" the well-dressed man retorted, his tone carrying an air of wounded dignity as he placed his cane aside. "Now, I don't have time to craft entirely new ensembles, but I will take your measurements. And while you freshen up down the street, I'll make the necessary alterations to some existing ensembles and have them delivered to you."

A beat of silence followed.

Jedidiah's eyes narrowed. Matthew shifted instinctively, fists clenching slightly. Phineas tilted his head, his expression unreadable.

"Let me get this straight," Jedidiah said flatly. "You basically drugged us and dragged us unconscious to your tailor shop. And now you want to clothe us?"

The tailor sighed, pinching the bridge of his nose as if personally affronted. "Oh, must we dwell on such unpleasantness? It was simply the most efficient way to get you here in a timely manner!"

"Efficient?" Matthew echoed incredulously. "Knocking people out with gas bombs and dragging them off to get dressed is efficient?"

The tailor raised a hand, clearly unimpressed with their resistance. "Time is of the essence, gentlemen. Lady Seraphina has orchestrated a most delicate plan, and you must arrive looking appropriate." His sharp gaze flicked over their travel-worn clothing with thinly veiled distaste. "And frankly, this simply won't do."

The masked men shifted slightly, their weapons still visible beneath their coats.

Jedidiah exhaled through his nose, his gaze flicking from the guards to the tailor. "And if we refuse?"

"Then you attend the ball looking like a trio of wayward chimney sweeps," the tailor said with a dramatic flourish of his hands. "But of course, that would reflect rather poorly on Lady Seraphina."

There was another pause. Then—

Phineas cleared his throat. "Well, I, for one, refuse to enter a grand ball looking as though I've been wrestling wild hogs in the streets."

The tension in the room eased slightly. Matthew shot him a look. "You're taking his side?"

"I am taking the side of fashion, my dear boy." Phineas lifted his chin with an air of dignity. "And if we are to be unwitting pawns in a larger scheme, we may as well look magnificent doing it."

Matthew let out a long sigh, rubbing his temples. "Fine. But I can dress myself!"

The tailor clapped his hands together, beaming. "Now that's the spirit! Let's get to work."

With practiced efficiency, he pulled out a cloth measuring tape and began his task. Once he finished, the tailor signaled to the masked guards. He gestured for them to escort the trio outside.

"Now, gentlemen, just down the street, you'll find a fine establishment where you can refresh yourselves. Everything has been arranged. All you have to do is pay when you get there."

The cool evening air greeted them as they stepped onto the cobblestone street. Gas lamps flickered along the path, casting a warm glow that danced on the wet pavement. As they approached their destination, the sign above the door came into view, painted boldly:

"BATHS." Beneath it, smaller lettering proudly displayed the prices: Cold Water—$1.00. Hot Water—$2.00. Soap—50¢.

Matthew frowned, eyeing the sign. "Two dollars for hot water? They'd better throw in a full meal for that price."

Phineas tilted his head. "I hope they at least provide a towel to dry off with."

Jedidiah groaned, rubbing his temples. "Can we just get this over with?"

The bathhouse owner greeted them with a toothy grin and an outstretched hand. "Welcome, gentlemen! Hot water is ready if you're feeling indulgent—or we can start with a brisk cold plunge!"

"Hot water, if you don't mind!" Phineas spoke up quickly.

"That'll be six dollars for three tubs."

"That's highway robbery!" Davenport exclaimed. "Can't we get a group discount?"

"Only if you don't mind sharing a tub or, ah, slightly *used* water," the owner replied smoothly.

"We'll take three tubs of fresh hot water and three bars of soap." Jedidiah handed over eight silver dollars, expecting change. Instead, the man pocketed the coins with a satisfied nod.

"Glad to see you opted to pay extra for the use of towels!"

The bathhouse owner turned on his heel, leading them through a narrow hallway. The wooden floorboards creaked slightly under their boots. Warm, humid air thick with the scent of lavender and mint wrapped around them, a surprisingly pleasant contrast to the grime of the street outside.

"You'll each have a private room, of course," the owner said, gesturing toward three doors lining the hallway. "These are our deluxe baths. Clean towels, fresh water, and soap are waiting inside. If you're feeling particularly daring, we've even got eucalyptus steam baths in the back. For an extra fee, of course."

"Of course," Jedidiah sighed heavily. "Let's just get this over with. I'd like to regain some semblance of dignity before whatever happens next."

"Enjoy, gentlemen! Take your time, but not too much. The water gets cold fast!"

Once inside his room, Jedidiah eased into the steaming water, letting the warmth soothe his muscles—though his mind remained restless.

In the next room, Matthew grumbled as he tested the water. "I'll say the water cools off fast. It's barely warm now!"

Phineas, on the other hand, was humming a tune as he inspected every corner of his room, seemingly more fascinated by the bathhouse's construction than the bath itself. Unlike the other two, his water was the perfect temperature.

For the moment, all was peaceful and calm—but it didn't last long. Just as they finished their baths, a firm knocking echoed against the wooden doors.

Jedidiah groaned, reluctantly rising from the tub. "So much for peace and quiet." Wrapping a towel around his waist, he cautiously opened the door and peered into the dimly lit hallway.

Hanging neatly on hooks just outside each door were their new clothes, perfectly tailored and pressed. Below them, freshly polished shoes gleamed, reflecting the flickering light of the gas lamps. Atop small tables in front of the garments, carefully chosen top hats rested, adding an air of sophistication to the presentation. Jedidiah reached out, running a hand over the smooth fabric.

Matthew's voice called from across the hall. "That tailor works fast."

Phineas stepped out a moment later, inspecting his own ensemble with a keen eye. "Well, I must admit, the man does have impeccable taste."

Jedidiah sighed as he gathered his clothes. "Let's hope these aren't just costumes for some elaborate trap."

A few minutes later, the trio regrouped in the hallway, looking slightly more polished but still weary.

Phineas adjusted his cuffs. "Well, I must admit, that was somewhat refreshing."

Matthew crossed his arms. "If by refreshing, you mean overpriced."

Jedidiah shook his head. "Let's just hope these new outfits are worth the trouble we've gone through."

As they stepped outside into the night air, the cobblestone streets felt quieter than before, the shadows deeper. Flickering gas lamps cast eerie shapes on the walls, and a faint breeze carried the sound of distant laughter.

Jedidiah scanned the streets, his voice low. "Something doesn't feel right."

Matthew let out a dry chuckle. "We've been knocked out, dragged unconscious into a tailor shop, and forced to take baths. *When* has any of this felt right?"

Jedidiah adjusted his crisp jacket, the fine stitching glinting faintly. Phineas brushed a speck of lint off his lapel, his polished shoes clicking against the cobblestones as he admired his reflection in a nearby shop window. Matthew tugged at his collar, clearly uncomfortable in the formal attire.

"It's like I'm wearing someone else's skin," Matthew muttered.

Phineas smirked. "At least it's the skin of someone with good taste in clothing."

Jedidiah exhaled sharply, eyes fixed on the distant glow of the opera house. "Focus, gentlemen. We've got an invitation to honor and little time to waste."

The streets had fallen eerily still, save for the distant hum of activity from the opera house. Music floated faintly on the breeze, mingling with the sound of their footsteps.

As they approached, the Detroit Opera House loomed before them, a towering testament to the city's burgeoning industrial wealth and culture. Ornate arched windows lined the multi-story facade, framed by intricate moldings and statues gazing down at the bustling street. The street lamps illuminated the richly detailed architecture, casting dramatic shadows over the decorative columns and pilasters. Below, awnings shaded storefronts— including the entrance to J.L. Hudson Clothier.

Above it all, the bold lettering of "Detroit Opera House" gleamed prominently, declaring its cultural significance to all who passed.

The wide marble steps leading to the main entrance were lined with patrons eager to join the festivities. Phineas glanced at his pocket watch and smiled.

"It's twenty after nine. We're slightly late to be on time but too early to be fashionably late."

Matthew rolled his eyes. "I doubt anyone's paying attention to how late or early we are."

Jedidiah reached into his jacket pocket, retrieving the ornate scrolls they'd been handed. "Let's keep this simple—present the invitations, get inside, and find Lady Seraphina."

As they joined the line of guests ascending the wide marble steps, Matthew shifted uncomfortably. "I feel like a bull in a china shop."

Phineas chuckled softly. "Well, try not to break anything valuable, dear boy."

At the entryway, two attendants in immaculate uniforms stood checking invitations. Jedidiah handed over the scrolls, his expression calm but watchful.

The attendant unrolled each one, inspecting them with a discerning eye before nodding. "Welcome, gentlemen. Please enjoy the evening."

As they entered the grand foyer, the sheer opulence of the space momentarily silenced them.

Crystal chandeliers bathed the polished marble floors in dazzling light, while gilded arches framed the room in a breathtaking display of extravagant wealth. The soft hum of a string quartet drifted from the ballroom beyond, mingling with the murmur of well-dressed guests.

Matthew let out a low whistle. "This is... something else."

Jedidiah scanned the crowd, his eyes sharp and searching. "Stay focused. Lady Seraphina has to be here somewhere."

As they wove through the crowd, a few heads turned in their direction. Phineas' eccentricity, Jedidiah's commanding air, and Matthew's rugged edge made them stand out even in a room filled with the elite.

As they approached the ballroom entrance, a young woman in a neatly pressed uniform stood behind a polished counter, her expression polite but disinterested. A small sign beside her read:

Hat Check – Required for Ballroom Entry

Jedidiah sighed, removing his top hat and handing it over. "Of course," he muttered.

Matthew scowled at the sign. "This thing cost more than my horse," he grumbled, reluctantly parting with his own hat.

The hat check girl barely spared him a glance as she accepted it and handed him a numbered token. "It'll still be here when you return, sir."

Phineas, on the other hand, hesitated, adjusting the brim of his hat with exaggerated care.

"Madam," he said solemnly, "I must apologize for my uncouth friend. He is not accustomed to the finer things in life as I am. He's more at home at a barn dance than a grand ball. I, however, will personally keep an eye on him."

The girl stared at the eccentric older man, unimpressed.

"Right," she deadpanned, plucking the hat from his hands and tucking it away without ceremony.

Despite his earlier bravado, Phineas watched in silent horror as his treasured headwear disappeared behind the counter.

"Although, perhaps, if you handled our items with a bit more care, they'd be less likely to be smudged when we return..."

"They won't be," she interrupted flatly, handing him his token.

Jedidiah cleared his throat, nudging Phineas toward the entrance. "Come along, Professor. I'm sure your hat will survive the separation."

"That remains to be seen," Phineas grumbled, pocketing the token as they stepped away from the counter.

The heavy velvet curtains of the grand ballroom parted, revealing a spectacle of unmatched splendor. The room was a whirlwind of color and light, with glittering gowns and sharp suits twirling in time with the orchestra. Masks of every shape and design adorned the faces of the dancers, adding an air of mystery to the lively affair.

As the trio moved deeper into the room, a ripple of whispers spread through the crowd. Glances turned into outright stares, and then came the hushed murmurs:

"Is it him? Could it really be?"

Matthew's brow furrowed. "What's going on? Why is everyone staring?"

Jedidiah, ever alert, scanned the room, noting how the attention seemed to center on Phineas. "I think they're looking at him," he said, tilting his head toward the professor.

Phineas, oblivious to the stares, was engrossed in admiring the room's ornate decorations. "I must say, the craftsmanship on these chandeliers is remarkable," he mused, squinting up at the glittering crystals.

"Phineas," Jedidiah said, lowering his voice. "I think they're talking about you."

The eccentric older man turned, his expression quizzical. "Me? Why on earth would they be talking about me?"

Before anyone could respond, a young woman in an elegant blue gown approached, her face alight with excitement. "Excuse me, sir," she began breathlessly, holding out a leather-bound book and an ornate pen. "I hate to intrude, but would you be so kind as to sign this for me? It would mean the world."

Phineas blinked, taken aback. He took both objects from her grasp. "Sign it? Whatever for?"

The woman laughed as if his question were part of some clever jest. "Oh, Mr. Clemens, you're as witty in person as you are in your books!"

Matthew choked back a laugh, clapping a hand over his mouth, while Jedidiah's lips twitched in a barely suppressed smirk.

"Mr. Clemens?" Phineas echoed, confused.

The woman's eyes widened in surprise. "Why, yes! Samuel Clemens—Mark Twain! Everyone here is positively thrilled that you've graced us with your presence tonight."

Jedidiah and Matthew simultaneously burst into laughter.

"Well, 'Mr. Clemens,' it looks like you've been recognized."

Phineas sputtered, still gripping the book and pen. "I am not Mark Twain! Though I do appreciate the man's wit and literary contributions, I assure you, young lady, you are mistaken."

But the woman didn't seem to hear him. She had already turned to wave at her companions across the room, beckoning them over.

"It is him! Samuel Clemens is here!"

Within moments, a small crowd began to form around the trio, their excited whispers blending into

Phineas sputtered, still gripping the
book and pen. "I am not Mark Twain!"

an unintelligible hum.

"Sign this, Mr. Clemens!"

"My father's a great admirer of yours!"

"Can we get a photograph, sir? They have one of those new-style cameras set up. It will only take a few seconds instead of a few minutes."

Phineas raised his hands in protest, his cheeks flushing as he tried to assert himself. "Now, now, I am not Samuel Clemens!"

Jedidiah, once again trying to hold back his laughter, leaned in. "You might as well give them what they want, Professor. Otherwise, we'll be stuck here all night."

Matthew snorted. "I wouldn't mind. This is the most fun we've had in weeks!"

Phineas shot them each a glare. "Very well," he grumbled. "But I'm signing it as myself, not as Mark Twain."

The woman beamed as Phineas scrawled his name in neat, looping script:

Professor Phineas B. Hargroves.

When she glanced at the signature, confusion flickered across her face. "Who's Phineas B. Hargroves?"

Phineas' voice dripped with dry humor. "Why, madam, the very man you've just accosted for an autograph."

"Must be another one of his pen names," she mused to a friend.

The crowd hesitated, the buzz of excitement dimming as confusion spread.

Jedidiah seized the moment, guiding Phineas out of the circle and motioning for Matthew to follow. "Let's move before someone else decides you're Mark Twain—or Charles Dickens."

"My dear boy, Charles Dickens has been dead for over ten years."

"What's your point?" Matthew smirked.

"Do I look like I've been dead for ten years?"

"Matt!" Jedidiah warned. "Don't answer that!"

As they slipped away, Matthew couldn't resist one last jab. "You know, Professor, you really do have a Twain vibe about you. Maybe you should take up writing in your spare time."

Phineas sniffed, adjusting his tie. "If I did, I assure you, my work would be far superior."

Jedidiah chuckled, shaking his head. "Let's just hope this doesn't happen again. We've had enough complications for one day."

"If this does happen again, I'm charging a fee," Phineas muttered, slipping the pen he kept from the young woman into his pocket with mock dignity.

The trio continued through the opulent ballroom, their earlier amusement fading as their focus sharpened on the task ahead. The soft strains of the orchestra filled the space, but beneath the harmonious melody, something else caught Jedidiah's attention.

The faint aroma of lavender and wood smoke wafted through the air, subtle at first but growing stronger.

Jedidiah's stride faltered. A prickle of awareness crept up his spine. His brow furrowed as he exchanged a glance with Phineas, who had also stopped mid-step, his nose twitching as he turned toward the source.

"Do you smell that?" Jedidiah murmured, his voice low and wary.

Matthew took a slow breath, his expression shifting from curiosity to alertness. "Lavender… and smoke. Just like at the ranch. And earlier at the tailor shop."

Silence.

Around them, conversations faltered, laughter faded, and glasses were slowly lowered. A ripple of stillness passed through the ballroom as if an unseen force had just entered the room.

Jedidiah's jaw tightened.

The orchestra's melody swelled—yet the shift in energy was unmistakable. A murmur swept through the guests, a rising wave of whispers crackling with hushed urgency.

Then, as if responding to an unseen cue, the entire ballroom turned toward the grand staircase.

And then she appeared.

Lady Seraphina Blackwood descended the staircase with a commanding presence.

Her tailored black attire exuded power, with structured shoulders and intricate brass details that caught the glint of the chandeliers. The fitted jacket flared slightly at the waist, paired seamlessly with slim, practical trousers tucked into polished boots. A brooch in the shape of a clockwork octopus adorned her high collar, its delicate gears subtly turning.

Her gloved hands gripped the banister with an air of quiet control, and her piercing emerald eyes scanned the room, sharp and calculating.

CHAPTER XVII

Beyond the Mask and the Map

The orchestra played a lively waltz as Lady Seraphina Blackwood moved through the crowd, her steps measured and deliberate. Though her presence commanded attention, it wasn't met with gasps or a hush—she was simply a striking figure in an already distinguished room.

A sleek black mask adorned her face, its edges glittering faintly under the chandelier's glow, accentuating the intensity of her gaze.

Jedidiah straightened, nodding to Phineas and Matthew. "Here we go."

Matthew tilted his head. "You sound thrilled."

"Should I really sound more excited?" Jedidiah muttered under his breath. "Her requests haven't exactly been the most pleasant."

Phineas adjusted his tie nervously, his gaze locked on Lady Seraphina as she approached. He fidgeted trying to hide the faint flush on his cheeks.

"Well, I for one think her presence is a breath of fresh air," he murmured, smoothing a stray hair from his brow.

Matthew shot him an amused smirk. "You're practically glowing, Professor. Should we leave the two of you alone?"

Phineas sniffed, feigning indignation. "Don't be absurd. I'm simply appreciating her… remarkable poise and unparalleled intellect."

As Lady Seraphina strode toward them, her emerald green eyes flicked across the ballroom, sharp and assessing. But as she drew closer, an expression of irritation crossed her face.

She stopped before them, lips pressed into a thin line.

"Tell me, gentlemen," she began, her voice edged with impatience, "is there a particular reason you're choosing to make yourselves conspicuous?"

Jedidiah blinked. "Excuse me?"

Seraphina's gaze was pointed as she gestured toward their faces.

"Your masks," she said tersely. "Or rather, your lack of them."

Matthew exchanged a glance with Phineas, then Jedidiah. "We weren't given—"

Seraphina sighed sharply and gestured to their coat pockets.

"Check again."

Davenport reached into his jacket, his fingers

Lady Seraphina Blackwood strode
toward them, her emerald green eyes flicked
across the ballroom, sharp and assessing.

brushing against a smooth piece of lacquered material. Pulling it out, he found a simple, understated mask—black with silver trim.

Matthew did the same, producing one in deep bronze, its color shifting subtly in the light.

Phineas, ever the meticulous one, retrieved an elaborate gold-trimmed mask, its intricate filigree catching the chandelier's glow.

Seraphina folded her arms, watching as they examined their forgotten disguises.

"This is a masquerade ball, gentlemen. I chose it for a reason. Your identities were meant to be protected."

Jedidiah exhaled, slipping his mask on without further argument. "Duly noted."

Matthew sighed, fastening his mask into place with a muttered, "I feel like a highwayman with this on."

Phineas, on the other hand, beamed as he carefully positioned his mask. "Ah! Much better. You see, gentlemen, a proper ensemble isn't complete without—"

"Yes, yes, you're very stylish, Professor," Matthew cut in.

Seraphina ignored their banter, though her gaze lingered on Phineas for a second longer before shifting back to Jedidiah. Her irritation softened, replaced with something more calculating.

"Gentlemen," she said smoothly, her tone now

lighter. "I trust you didn't have any issues finding me?"

Jedidiah dipped his head slightly. "Lady Seraphina. Did you give us much choice?"

She smiled faintly. "Mr. Davenport, given the circumstances, I felt my methods were... necessary."

Her gaze swept over Phineas and Matthew once more, now visibly more satisfied. "Much better," she murmured, then added lightly, "Your masks suit you well."

Her emerald eyes lingered on Phineas a moment longer than necessary before she turned back to Jedidiah.

"Would you two excuse us for a moment?" she asked—though it was clearly more of a command than a request. "I need a word with Mr. Davenport."

Phineas hesitated, looking as though he might protest, but Matthew clapped him on the shoulder, steering him toward the refreshments.

"Come on, Professor. Let's give them a moment before you start reciting her poetry."

Phineas cast a wistful glance over his shoulder as they walked away. "Her choice of mask is impeccable—so elegant, yet commanding."

Matthew snorted. "You're hopeless."

Jedidiah sighed. "What's going on? And please, don't give me another vague response about the existence of reality being at risk."

Lady Seraphina gestured toward the dance floor, where couples swirled gracefully in time with the music.

"Dance with me. It's less conspicuous."

Resisting a groan, Jedidiah hesitated before taking her offered hand. He was better at dodging bullets than leading a waltz.

Reluctantly, he followed her onto the floor, their steps falling into the measured rhythm of the dance.

"Do you have the watch?" she asked immediately.

"I think you know I do, or you wouldn't have gone through the trouble of having us knocked out, forced into these clothes, and brought here."

"I mailed that watch to you for a reason, you know," she said, her voice low. "I couldn't risk bringing it myself—I was being watched. Possibly followed. Now, I can finally tell you more about the relic."

Jedidiah kept his tone even. "Our part in this mission isn't over, is it?"

"Far from it," she replied.

She guided him through a slow turn, her voice dropping lower. "First, let me tell you more about the Order of the Clockwork Octopus. It was created to safeguard a device capable of altering reality itself. Each of the current members was entrusted with a fragment of the relic. But the Order has fractured—three of the five members have been captured. One is temporarily out of commission. And I am the last."

Jedidiah's brow furrowed. "Current members?"

She guided him through a slow turn, her voice dropping lower.

"The Order was founded centuries ago," she continued. "Five individuals, each a master in their field, recognized the danger of the relic. Its origins remain a mystery—some claim it was technology from another world, and others believe it predates any recorded history. The original members safeguarded it in its entirety, passing it from generation to generation."

"So why was it dismantled?"

"To lower the risk." Her expression darkened. "Trust eroded over the years as successor after successor replaced the original guardians. Greed, ambition… betrayal. It was decided that dividing the relic into five pieces was the only way to keep it from falling into the wrong hands. Each guardian hid their fragment in a location known only to them. Even if one fell, the others could preserve the balance."

Jedidiah's jaw tightened. "What happened to the others?"

"Lord Ignatius Gearsoul, Doctor Leopold Van der Meer, and the Baroness Evelina Frost," she listed, her voice steady. "Each taken, one by one. Their fragments of the relic are unaccounted for."

She exhaled slowly. "Lord Ignatius' artifact was the first to vanish. It was stolen from the British Museum weeks ago—despite layers of security and secrecy."

Jedidiah held her gaze. "Who is the fifth member of the Order?"

"Professor Thaddeus Montgomery."

Jedidiah's grip tightened slightly on hers. "Wait a moment—did you say Professor Thaddeus Montgomery?" His steps faltered.

"I did."

"That can't be right. He's in prison!" His fingers curled more firmly around her hand. "He sabotaged the airship race! I left him, his gang, and his airship stranded in the middle of nowhere just outside of Wichita. He was picked up and arrested shortly after the race ended."

Lady Seraphina's expression darkened. "And you think a prison can keep him safe from whoever is behind this? Even behind bars, he's in danger. He and I were the last two active members of the Order before I went into hiding."

Her voice tinged with bitterness. "I suspect he has more information about the relic than even I do. Which is why you must visit him in prison. But first—"

She leaned closer, her voice dropping to a near whisper. "As I told you before, inside the watch are coordinates. Follow them to the artifact I was charged with protecting. It won't be easy to reach. It's hidden far from prying eyes."

Jedidiah frowned. "Why not go yourself?"

Her gaze swept the room. "I've already told you. I'm being watched—even now," she said softly. "The masks may hide faces, but they don't hide intent. My presence here is risky enough. I'll need to leave shortly, and you must act quickly. After retrieving my piece, you must go to Professor Montgomery. He may have the information we desperately need."

The music swelled as the dance ended, and they stepped apart. Lady Seraphina inclined her head slightly.

"Good luck, Mr. Davenport. I hope you're as resourceful as your reputation suggests."

Jedidiah hesitated, a frown forming on his lips. "Wait!" he called after her. "You didn't tell me what I'm looking for!"

She paused, turning her head just enough for her emerald eyes to catch the light. A faint, enigmatic smile curved her lips.

"You'll know it when you see it," she said, her voice low and deliberate, before disappearing into the crowd.

Phineas and Matthew rejoined him moments later, the former looking flushed and uncharacteristically quiet.

"Well?" Matthew asked. "What have you gotten

us into now?"

Jedidiah's jaw tightened. "Trouble—just as we suspected."

Phineas adjusted his tie again, his voice unsteady. "She looked magnificent, didn't she? That jacket—functional yet elegant."

Matthew groaned. "Focus, Professor. We're here to save reality not to admire her wardrobe."

Jedidiah nodded in agreement. "We need to find her piece of the relic—and fast. If Seraphina's right, it's the only way to stay ahead of whoever's after it."

He glanced toward the exit, a determined glint in his eye.

"And after that," he said, his voice firm with resolve, "we pay a visit to an old friend behind bars."

****

Around midnight, the hum of the Phoenix's engines filled the cabin, a low, steady thrum that mirrored the tension in the air.

Jedidiah stood over the navigation table, his brow furrowed as he studied the maps spread before him. Phineas hovered nearby, muttering to himself, while Matthew leaned against the wall, arms crossed as he watched the scene unfold. After a moment, he stretched his shoulders, tugging at the familiar fabric of his shirt.

"Feels good to be back in my own clothes," he muttered, rubbing his temples.

Phineas chimed in from across the room. "Speak for yourself. I rather enjoyed those tailored outfits—functional and fashionable."

Jedidiah glanced up from the maps, a faint smirk tugging at his lips. "Look at the bright side. We got brand-new tailored clothes, and they didn't cost us anything."

"Nothing but a pounding headache from those smoke bombs!" Matthew groaned.

"Well," Jedidiah quipped, "some people pay a lot of money for custom fittings. We just had to endure a little inconvenience."

Matthew arched a brow. "Little inconvenience? I'd call what we went through more than a little inconvenience!"

Phineas picked up the mask he'd worn at the ball, turning it over in his hands with a wistful expression. "You'll never know when these might come in handy again. Besides, just look at the elegant quality that went into the craftsmanship."

Jedidiah rolled his eyes and gestured to the maps. "Focus, gentlemen. We've got work to do."

With a dramatic flourish, Phineas gestured toward the pocket watch lying on the table, as though it were a priceless artifact. "The moment of truth," he murmured, retrieving a fine-tipped tool from his vest pocket.

Leaning over the table, he pressed the tool against a nearly invisible notch on the back of the watch.

A soft click broke the silence as the back popped open, revealing intricate brass mechanisms within. Nestled over the spinning gears and delicate springs was a thin, polished metal disk, no larger in diameter than a coin, etched with finely engraved numbers.

"Ah-ha! Here it is!" Phineas declared, holding the gleaming fragment up to the light. The coordinates were unmistakable:

Latitude: 44.3611° N, Longitude: 79.3464° W.

Matthew leaned in his brow furrowing. "And where exactly does that point to?"

Phineas traced his finger along the nearby map interface, his eyes gleaming with curiosity as the location was revealed.

"Lake Simcoe," he announced, his voice tinged with both excitement and apprehension. "Just north of Toronto, in Ontario."

Jedidiah leaned over the map, studying the area. "That spot is underwater," he muttered. "That explains why she couldn't—or wouldn't—retrieve it herself."

Matthew crossed his arms. "So what's the plan? We're gonna skinny dip in freezing water to fetch it?"

"Not quite," Phineas shook his head, a glimmer of excitement in his eyes. "This will be a challenge, but nothing we can't handle—especially with the right equipment."

Jedidiah frowned. "If you're talking about that diving suit you've been working on, it's still in your workshop back at the ranch. We don't have to go for it. We could send a telegraph, but the ones in my study haven't been repaired yet."

Phineas adjusted the goggles on top of his head thoughtfully. "My dear boy, you're forgetting—we can still telegraph Spoon Fork. We can get in touch with young Tom Miller and…"

Matthew raised an eyebrow. "And he can toss it over his saddle and bring it to us?"

Jedidiah shook his head. "He can ride out to the ranch and have Jonathan Blake and Edwin Bancroft bring it to us in the Swift. It's the fastest airship I've got. We'll tell them to meet us off the coast of Georgina Island, on Lake Simcoe. That'll give us plenty of time to find and rent a boat to dive from."

Phineas nodded, already scribbling on a piece of paper. "I'll draft the message and include detailed instructions. The suit and pump for breathing should be in the workshop near the forge—Jonathan should be able to find it with no problems."

Matthew smirked, leaning back in his chair. "Sounds simple enough. Let's hope they're fast, or we'll be waiting a while."

Phineas grinned, his eyes lighting up. "Fast or not, it'll be worth it. You underestimate the ingenuity of my design, my dear boy. With that marvel, not only will Jedidiah survive the frigid waters, but he'll look rather heroic while doing so."

Matthew rolled his eyes. "Heroic? In that clunky thing? Sure, Professor."

Jedidiah tapped the map, his tone sharp. "Enough joking around. Once we reach Lake Simcoe, we'll rent the boat and wait off Georgina Island until the Swift arrives."

CHAPTER XVIII

Inspiration Comes Suddenly

Early Sunday morning, October 23rd, 1881, the Phoenix descended toward the outskirts of Toronto, its brass accents gleaming in the pale light of dawn. Below, the city slowly stirred awake, its streets dotted with horse-drawn carriages and early risers beginning their routines. A thin veil of mist clung over the rooftops, catching the golden hues of the rising sun.

Inside the airship, Jedidiah stood at the helm, scanning the horizon. Behind him, Phineas hunched over a workstation, muttering to himself as he fiddled with a mechanical contraption, while Matthew paced the cabin, his boots echoing softly against the polished floor.

"Toronto," Matthew muttered, glancing over the railing. "Didn't think I'd be back here so soon."

Jedidiah adjusted the controls, his gaze fixed on the approaching city. "We're not here to sightsee.

We need to send that telegraph as soon as the office opens."

Matthew stopped mid-stride. "And then what? Twiddle our thumbs while we wait for Jonathan and Edwin?"

"We head straight to Lake Simcoe," Jedidiah replied without hesitation. "We've got plenty to do in the meantime."

Phineas looked up from his workstation, his magnified goggles making his eyes appear comically large. "Plenty indeed! This device alone will keep me occupied the entire journey!"

He gestured toward the object on the table—a small brass cylinder fitted with several intricate mechanisms, its gears humming faintly. A soft hiss of steam escaped from one of the valves as he made an adjustment.

Matthew eyed it warily. "And what exactly is that supposed to be?"

Phineas puffed up with pride. "A subcutaneous medication delivery device! You might call it a syringe without a needle—if you're unimaginative. But this—" he lifted the device reverently, "—this is the future! It delivers medicine directly through the skin using compressed air and a burst of steam pressure. Bloodless, efficient, and elegant."

Matthew frowned. "And this is supposed to counteract the effects of the paralyzing ray gun?"

Phineas nodded eagerly. "Precisely! Once I

create the formula for the antidote. That's the tricky part, but I have a few promising leads. The delivery system, however, is nearly complete."

Jedidiah cut in, his tone firm. "Focus on getting it ready. We might need it sooner than we think."

The Phoenix touched down in an open field on the outskirts of Toronto, hovering just above the ground. Jedidiah and Matthew disembarked, making their way toward the telegraph office as the city slowly stirred to life around them.

Brick buildings lined the streets, their windows glowing faintly in the morning light. The rhythmic clatter of hooves on cobblestones mixed with the murmur of early risers, and the crisp air carried the scent of fresh bread from a nearby bakery.

Inside the telegraph office, a bleary-eyed young operator glanced up from his desk as they entered.

Jedidiah wasted no time, drafting a message to Tom Miller back in Spoon Fork:

"TO TOM MILLER STOP.
URGENT STOP RIDE TO DAVENPORT RANCH STOP. LOCATE DIVING SUIT AND PUMP NEAR FORGE IN HARGROVE'S WORKSHOP STOP. INSTRUCT JONATHAN BLAKE AND EDWIN BANCROFT TO BRING THEM ABOARD THE SWIFT STOP. MEET US OFF GEORGINA ISLAND LAKE SIMCOE STOP. TIMING IS CRITICAL STOP. SAFE

TRAVELS STOP.
    JEDIDIAH STOP."

The operator nodded, his fingers flying over the telegraph machine. The rhythmic clatter of the keys filled the small office, each tap sending its message across the miles.

Jedidiah paid the fee and turned to Matthew. "That's done. Let's move."

****

By the time the Phoenix reached Lake Simcoe, the crew had settled into a steady rhythm of preparation.

Jedidiah and Matthew wasted no time securing a sturdy boat from a local fisherman, ensuring it was large enough to accommodate the bulky pump required for the diving suit.

"This thing's built to last," Matthew remarked, running a hand along the boat's wooden railing. "Should do the trick, nicely."

With Phineas still aboard the Phoenix, hunched over his latest invention, Jedidiah and Matthew loaded the boat with supplies.

A heavy silence settled over them as the weight of their task loomed. The relic was within reach but so were the dangers that came with it.

****

Later that same day, the sun hung high over the sprawling expanse of Davenport Ranch, casting long shadows over the stately Victorian mansion and the surrounding outbuildings.

Tom Miller rode hard, pushing his horse to its limits, the urgency of Jedidiah's message burning in his mind. Dust billowed behind him as he raced past the main house, his heart hammering almost as hard as his horse's pounding hooves.

If he didn't deliver the message fast, Jedidiah might be diving into those freezing waters with nothing but his own breath to rely on.

With a sharp pull on the reins, Tom brought his horse skidding to a halt outside the hangar, where the newest airship was under construction. He swung down with practiced ease, striding toward the open double doors as the rhythmic clank of hammers and hiss of steam echoed from within.

Inside, Jonathan Blake, his sleeves rolled up and his face streaked with soot, glanced up from his work on a gleaming brass mechanism.

"Tom!" Jonathan called over the din. "What brings you out here?"

Tom held up the telegraph. "Message from Jedidiah. It's urgent."

Jonathan wiped his hands on a nearby rag, took the paper, and sat down to read it. From the

Tom Miller rode hard, pushing his horse to its limits, the urgency of Jedidiah's message burning in his mind.

shadows of the workshop, Edwin Bancroft emerged, curiosity flickering in his young features.

"What's it say?" Edwin asked, leaning over his father's shoulder.

Jonathan's expression hardened as he handed the message to Edwin. "We need to deliver the diving suit and pump to Lake Simcoe, off Georgina Island. They're waiting for us."

Edwin's brow furrowed. "I'll ready the Swift!"

Jonathan shook his head, a glimmer of pride in his eyes. "We're taking the Inspiration. It's finally ready for its maiden flight."

Edwin blinked, turning toward the airship in question.

Sleek and imposing, the Inspiration stood gleaming in the filtered sunlight. Its polished hull glinted like burnished gold, twin propellers poised for action. The brass steam engine at the rear sat proudly, its intricate pipes and gears hissing softly, eager for flight. Etched into the prow in elegant script was its name:

Inspiration.

"It's finally finished?" Tom asked, crossing his arms skeptically. He glanced around—the usual crew of engineers was nowhere to be seen.

"Jed said to take the Swift. Do you think the Inspiration will hold together?"

Jonathan grinned, the confidence in his expression unmistakable. "It'll do more than hold together. With the modifications I've made to the engines, I'd say it could give either the Swift or the Phoenix a run for its money!"

Suddenly, Jonathan whistled sharply. A moment later, the faint hum of gears signaled the arrival of Cogsworth. The automaton's mechanical legs whirred rhythmically as it strode into view, its glowing eyes fixed expectantly on its creator.

Jonathan instructed, gesturing toward the hangar housing the Icarus, "fetch the diving suit and pump from Phineas' workshop next to the forge. Handle them with care."

"Affirmative," the automaton acknowledged, its articulated limbs moving with surprising precision. It turned smoothly, steam hissing softly from its joints, and began its task. Edwin stepped in to assist, guiding the automaton as they loaded the equipment into the Inspiration's cargo bay.

Jonathan climbed aboard, calling back over his shoulder. "Edwin, check the steam pressure and make sure the boiler is topped off. We'll need to leave as quickly as possible."

Tom watched the preparations, his arms crossed, expression caught between awe and unease. "Hope this thing lives up to its name."

Jonathan smirked, adjusting a lever near the helm. "Trust me, Tom. The Inspiration is going to make history."

Outside, the low hiss of steam and the rhythmic

chug of the engine built steadily—a pulse of energy and promise. The Inspiration seemed to vibrate with anticipation, eager to take to the skies and deliver its precious cargo to the waiting team at Lake Simcoe.

With the diving suit and pump secured, Jonathan settled into the pilot's chair, his movements fluid and confident. The brass controls gleamed under the midday sunlight streaming through the hangar doors. Steam hissed from the valves as the airship's powerful engines rumbled to life.

Edwin took his place at his father's right hand, his excitement barely contained as he adjusted gauges and monitored the steam pressure.

"Boiler's topped off, and the pressure's holding steady," he reported eagerly. "We're ready to fly."

Tom hesitated at the base of the boarding ramp, skepticism etched across his face. "I still think Jed would've preferred you took the Swift," he muttered. "But since I'm here, I might as well make sure this thing doesn't fall apart mid-air."

Jonathan shot him a grin full of confidence. "You can doubt all you want, Tom, but by the time we get to Lake Simcoe, you'll be singing the Inspiration's praises."

He gestured toward the navigator's seat. "Now get aboard. We've got work to do."

With a grumble, Tom climbed the ramp.

"Relax," Jonathan said, his hands steady on the controls. "I've got it under control."

Suddenly, Cogsworth boarded the ship, its mechanical legs clanking against the ramp as it descended into the cargo bay. The automaton's glowing eyes scanned the interior, its gears whirring softly.

"All items secured, sir," it reported in a steady, metallic voice before moving to a corner of the cabin, bracing itself for takeoff.

Jonathan nodded approvingly. "Good work. Take a seat and hold on. This'll be a smooth ride, but I don't want anything—or anyone—tumbling around."

His hand tightened on the throttle lever as he turned toward his son. "Edwin, release the mooring lines."

"On it!" He replied, flipping a switch on the control panel.

A sharp jolt rocked the Inspiration as the last restraints clattered away, freeing the airship to ascend.

"Engines at full steam," Jonathan announced, pushing the throttle forward.

The Inspiration lifted gracefully, its polished hull gleaming in the sunlight as it rose through the already open hangar roof.

Higher and higher it climbed, the thrum of its engines steady and confident, carrying them away from Davenport Ranch and toward the distant horizon.

Edwin leaned forward, eyes scanning the controls with keen excitement. "It's handling beautifully, Dad."

Jonathan's lips curled into a proud grin. "Of course it is. The Inspiration was built to take on anything."

Tom, arms crossed, stepped to the railing, glancing over the side. Below, the sprawling prairie shrank, morphing into a patchwork of green and brown, the ranch fading into the distance.

"I'll admit," he muttered grudgingly, "it's a smooth ride."

Jonathan chuckled, throwing him a knowing look. "Told you."

The Inspiration cut through the air like a bird of prey, its gleaming brass accents catching the sunlight as it climbed higher. Ahead, the vast expanse of blue stretched endlessly, a silent reminder of the urgency of their mission.

With Jonathan at the helm, Edwin at his right hand, and Tom at his left, the Inspiration soared toward Canada—toward the unknown dangers that awaited them beneath the waters of Lake Simcoe.

****

Early the next morning, the first light of dawn crept over the still waters of Lake Simcoe, casting a pale golden glow across the rippling surface. The air was crisp and bracing, carrying the faint scent of damp earth and pine. Gentle waves lapped against the wooden hull of the rented fishing boat, moored near the rocky shoreline.

Jedidiah stood at the edge of the dock, his hands tucked into the pockets of his overcoat. His breath fogged in the cool morning air as he scanned the horizon. Behind him, Matthew secured the last of their equipment, ensuring everything was ready for the impending dive.

"Are you sure you want to do this, Jed?" Matthew asked, tightening a strap on one of the supply crates. His voice carried a hint of concern. "The temperature dropped below freezing last night, and it hasn't warmed up a whole lot."

"I have to," Davenport replied calmly. "The suit is conveniently too small for Phineas. He made it for someone my height... or yours..." He turned to look directly at his childhood friend. "If you're that concerned about my safety, perhaps you'd like to go down instead?"

Matthew grimaced, rubbing the back of his neck. "How long do you think it'll take Edwin and Mr. Blake to get here?" He changed the subject smoothly, knowing full well he wouldn't be the one diving into freezing waters.

Jedidiah glanced skyward, where streaks of pink and orange stretched across the horizon, signaling the sun's slow rise. "If they left when they were supposed to, they should be here soon. The Swift will get them here faster than any airship out there."

****

On the Phoenix, Phineas continued tinkering with the small device, as he muttered to himself. A faint hiss of steam escaped from the contraption, followed by a soft click. He straightened with a look of triumph.

"It's finished!" Phineas declared, holding up his latest invention—a sleek, compact antidote delivery device. "Now all I have to do is finish the formula and this will be ready for field use. No needles, no blood—just pure, elegant science."

****

Above the fishing boat, the faint hum of an approaching airship broke the stillness. Jedidiah's attention snapped upward as the whirr of its engines grew louder. Shielding his eyes against the rising sun, he squinted at the silhouette emerging over the treetops. The brass hull gleamed as it descended, its engines chugging steadily.

Then he frowned.

"That's not the Swift," he muttered, a flicker of alarm tightening his chest. Suddenly he began to calm as read the name on the side. "Inspiration..."

Slightly annoyed but still glad to see them, he remarked, "I specifically told them to come in the Swift!"

As the airship descended gracefully toward the shoreline, the hiss of steam and the rhythmic chug of its engines grew louder. Jonathan Blake's confident voice called out from the helm as the Inspiration hovered just above the waterline.

"Blake & Sons Cargo Delivery!" he called out with a wide grin.

"Sons?" Tom Miller asked, confused.

"You act surprised!" Jonathan laughed. "You've become like a brother to Edwin, and any brother of my son is naturally a son to me!"

Still slightly confused but pleased that Jonathan considered him family, Tom smiled and said, "Sounds good to me... Pop!"

Edwin Bancroft leaned over the railing, waving enthusiastically. "Everything's here and ready to go!"

Behind them, Cogsworth ascended from the cargo bay, its mechanical frame glinting in the sunlight. "All items ready for departure," the automaton reported in its steady, metallic voice.

Matthew gave a low whistle of appreciation.

"I'll give him credit. That's one fine-looking airship."

As the Inspiration's gangplank extended to the dock, its brass joints gleaming in the early morning light, Cogsworth sprang into action. With the soft hum of its servos, the automaton began unloading the diving suit and pump with ease, each movement guided by precise internal calculations.

Meanwhile, Jedidiah Davenport and Matthew Colton worked nearby, their breath still visible in the cold air as they hauled planks of lumber from a stack on the dock. Frost glittered along the wooden edges, the chill biting through their gloves as they laid the planks carefully across the gap between the dock and their rented boat. The makeshift bridge creaked slightly under its own weight, but held firm as they secured it.

"That should do it," Jedidiah said, straightening and wiping his brow. "Cogsworth, start loading the equipment onto the boat."

"Affirmative," the automaton replied. It hefted the diving suit with ease, its mechanical arms adjusting effortlessly to the bulky weight. The pump followed, Cogsworth's whirring legs navigating the narrow plank with the precision of a well-calibrated machine.

Matthew tightened the mooring lines, securing the boat against the gentle pull of the current. "Any colder, and we'd have to chip a hole in the ice for you to dive through," he muttered, his breath curling into small clouds in the frosty morning air.

As Cogsworth loaded the last of the equipment, Tom Miller and Edwin Bancroft stepped down from the Inspiration, their boots echoing on the wooden dock. Matthew Colton, noticing their approach, gestured toward the Phoenix, nestled nearby.

"Phineas is aboard, perfecting his latest invention," Matthew said. "I need the two of you to go get him. He'll have to walk us through setting everything up."

Without hesitation, Tom and Edwin rushed off to do as they were instructed. They raced up the loading ramp to the Phoenix. Inside, they found Professor Phineas B. Hargroves hunched over his workstation, muttering to himself as he worked with chemicals, fine-tuning the formula for the antidote.

The eccentric older man looked up as they entered. "Ah, gentlemen! Come to witness a genius in action, have you?" He gestured toward a set of vials filled with blue liquid. "I haven't tested these yet, but I've completed my first attempt at the formula for the antidote."

"That's great, Professor," Edwin said, leaning against the doorframe. "But we're actually here because Jed's ready to go down in the suit, and he needs—"

"Ah, yes! The suit!" Phineas exclaimed, cutting him off. He set down his tools, grabbed a notebook filled with schematics, and gestured for them to follow. "No time to waste!"

The trio exited the Phoenix, making their way back to the dock, where Jedidiah was overseeing the final preparations. Phineas approached the diving suit, flipping through his notebook with barely contained excitement.

"Jedidiah, my dear boy, allow me to introduce you to a true marvel of engineering!" He patted the suit's heavy outer shell with a flourish.

Jedidiah crossed his arms, eyeing the bulky contraption. "Looks heavier than I expected."

Phineas beamed. "Ah, that's the beauty of it! The weight is necessary to counteract buoyancy. Without it, you'd float like a cork."

Tom raised an eyebrow. "Sounds really encouraging."

Phineas waved a hand dismissively. "Nonsense! Jed will be perfectly safe." He gestured to the interior lining. "Now, this—this is critical. Beneath the outer shell is an insulated lining made from a special composite fabric I designed. It traps heat while wicking away moisture. You'll feel like you're in a warm cocoon, even with the water pressing in from all sides."

Matthew shot Jedidiah a look. "That's assuming it works."

Jedidiah smirked. "Wouldn't be the first time we tested one of Phineas' 'perfectly safe' inventions under questionable circumstances."

Phineas huffed. "You wound me, gentlemen. Do I not have a sterling reputation for reliability?"

Tom and Matthew exchanged a knowing glance but remained silent.

Phineas ignored them and moved to the helmet. "This locks into place here." He pointed to the thick brass collar ring. "Once secured, it creates a watertight seal. The glass panel is reinforced for clarity and durability. It's resistant to pressure up to —well, far more than the depth you'll be going."

Jedidiah tapped the glass experimentally. "So I'll be able to see just fine?"

Phineas nodded proudly. "Crystal clear. Now, let's talk about air." He gestured to the coiled hose beside the suit. "This connects directly to the pump on the boat. It's reinforced to withstand pressure and movement, ensuring a steady flow of oxygen."

Jedidiah's brow furrowed. "And if something happens to the hose?"

Phineas grinned, tapping a small brass tank on the back of the suit. "I anticipated that! This emergency air supply will give you about three minutes of breathable oxygen."

"Three minutes?" Tom asked skeptically. "That's it?"

Phineas lifted a finger confidently. "Ah, but

three minutes is ample time—provided one doesn't panic."

Matthew scoffed. "So the key to survival is 'don't panic'?"

Phineas tilted his head. "My dear boy, that is always the key to survival."

Jedidiah exhaled, running a hand through his hair. "Fine. Let's get this thing on and test it before I freeze to death."

Phineas clapped his hands, his enthusiasm bubbling over. "That's the spirit! Edwin, Tom— help him into the suit. Matthew, ensure the pump is operational. And Cogsworth—stand by for final adjustments."

As the team sprang into action, Phineas stood back, watching with a mix of pride and nervous energy. The suit was a masterpiece, and soon, it would face its ultimate test in the depths of Lake Simcoe.

CHAPTER XIX

Dangers Above and Below

Jedidiah Davenport stood on the deck of the rented fishing boat, encased in the bulky diving suit. The morning sunlight glinted off the polished brass fittings of the helmet, its multiple glass windows reflecting the rippling surface of Lake Simcoe. The intricate yet functional design bore a series of rivets that secured its reinforced plates, giving it the look of both a protective shell and a marvel of engineering.

The suit itself was thick and heavy, its rubberized fabric reinforced with tightly woven layers designed to withstand the immense pressure of the depths. Thick metal cuffs secured the gloves and boots, the latter clanging softly against the wooden deck with each step he took. The weighted boots, meant for stability underwater, made movement on the surface cumbersome, each step heavy and deliberate.

Jedidiah Davenport stood on the deck
of the rented fishing boat, encased
in the bulky diving suit.

The brass collar ring connecting the helmet to the suit gleamed in the early light, its locking mechanism carefully fastened by Phineas moments earlier. A coiled air hose ran from the back of the helmet to the pump aboard the boat, its durable construction promising a steady flow of air—so long as the crew above remained vigilant.

Jedidiah shifted slightly, testing his range of motion within the suit. The insulated layers beneath, designed to protect him from the freezing waters, pressed snugly against his body, offering both warmth and an unavoidable sense of confinement. A small emergency air tank sat securely on his back, its brass valve polished and primed for use should the worst happen. The steady hiss of air flowing through the hose was a constant reminder of the fragile balance of the operation.

Matthew stood nearby, watching with a mix of admiration and concern.

"You certainly look like something from a Jules Verne novel now," he remarked, his voice light despite the tension in his eyes.

"Jowls Burns... I mean... argh..." Jedidiah frowned under the heavy helmet, momentarily tripping over his words. He had grown so used to correcting Pat Bennington that he confused himself.

Phineas, still adjusting the pump and inspecting the connections, called over with enthusiasm.

"This, my dear boy, is cutting-edge technology! A triumph of both form and function!"

Jedidiah raised a gloved hand in a small wave, his voice muffled yet steady as it echoed through the helmet.

"Let's hope your triumph holds up down there."

Turning towards the dock, the adventurous young man gave his final instructions.

"Jonathan, Tom, Edwin—stay here with Cogsworth and guard the airships. If anything happens, I don't want all of us caught out in the open."

Jonathan nodded, his hands resting on his hips as he glanced toward his sleek vessel anchored nearby.

"Understood. We'll make sure everything here is secure."

Tom hesitated his youthful eagerness to help barely contained.

"You sure you don't need me to—"

"We're sure," Jedidiah interrupted gently but firmly. "You've done your part getting us here. Now it's up to us to finish this."

Edwin crossed his arms, leaned against a post, and said, "They'll be fine out there, Miller. Stop worrying!"

Matthew untied the mooring lines while Phineas stood by, his hands clutching both his notebook and toolkit. The vessel rocked gently as the final preparations were made. Jedidiah took a deep breath, the weight of his suit pressing down on him—like the responsibility of the task ahead.

The small steam-powered engine sputtered to life, and with a faint hum, the boat began cutting a path across the calm surface of Lake Simcoe. The water, crystal clear, reflected the soft gradient of pale blue and orange in the morning sky. A serene sight... but an unshakable feeling of foreboding hung in the air.

As the boat reached the coordinates marked on Phineas' map, the trio slowed to a stop. The water here was deep, its depth obscuring whatever lay beneath. The beauty of the scene was tempered by the silence—a quiet so profound that it seemed to press against their ears.

Phineas leaned over the side, peering into the depths.

"Incredible," he murmured. "The clarity is remarkable to a certain depth... but it also means you'll have no cover if anything—or anyone—is down there."

Jedidiah glanced down. The suit was doing its job—he didn't even feel the cold air whipping past him.

Matthew steadied the boat as Jedidiah stepped toward the edge, his weighted boots clanging softly against the wooden planks.

"You sure about this, Jed?" Matthew asked, his

voice low.

Jedidiah gave a short nod. "We didn't come all this way to turn back now."

Phineas adjusted the pump's connections and checked the air hose one final time.

"Remember—keep an eye on the depth gauge inside your helmet. If you feel anything unusual—pressure changes, a snag in the hose—signal us immediately."

"Got it," Jedidiah's voice echoed through the helmet.

Phineas hesitated, his fingers hovering over the pressure gauge.

"Your oxygen supply is stable, and the emergency reserve will buy you time if needed. But keep it simple, Jed. No unnecessary movements. Less exertion means more air."

Matthew gave Phineas a skeptical look. "That your way of telling him to hurry?"

Phineas sniffed. "My way of telling him to be efficient."

The water lapped against the boat as Jedidiah positioned himself at the edge, gripping the railing with his gloved hands. He paused for a moment, the weight of the suit anchoring him both physically and mentally.

With a final glance at Matthew and Phineas, Jedidiah stepped off the edge and into the depths.

The water swallowed him in an instant, the

surface rippling outward in perfect circles. For a moment, all was still—except for the steady hiss of the air pump and the faint creak of the boat.

Matthew leaned over the edge, watching as Jedidiah's figure descended.

"There he goes," he muttered. "Let's hope he finds whatever we're looking for—and gets back in one piece."

Phineas adjusted a valve on the pump, his eyes fixed on the gauge.

"He'll be fine. The suit is designed to handle conditions far worse than this. Besides, Jedidiah Davenport isn't the type to let a little water stop him."

****

The world grew colder and quieter as Jedidiah descended into the lake's depths. The sunlight above dimmed, filtering through the layers of water, yet the clarity allowed him to see the rocky terrain below with startling detail.

The silence was absolute, punctuated only by the soft rush of air through his helmet. It was a world untouched and indifferent, beautiful yet forbidding—a reminder of how small he was in the vastness of nature.

As he continued his descent, the weight of the diving suit pressed against him, a constant reminder of the fragile balance between safety and the immense pressure of the lake. His gloved hands gripped the guide rope trailing down from the boat, his lifeline anchoring him to the surface.

The underwater world unfolded around him, a surreal expanse of shimmering blues and greens. Sunlight filtered through the water, casting fleeting patterns that danced across the rocky lakebed below, now coming into sharper focus. Smooth stones and patches of sand dotted the terrain, interspersed with wisps of aquatic plants swaying gently in the current. Occasionally, a small fish darted into view, its iridescent scales catching the dim light before vanishing into the shadows below.

Jedidiah checked the depth gauge inside his helmet, noting that he was nearing the target depth. His breath remained steady, the rhythmic hiss of air from the hose filling his ears. Each exhalation sent a stream of tiny bubbles spiraling upward, marking his path back to the surface.

His eyes scanned the lakebed below, searching for any sign of the relic Lady Seraphina had spoken of. The coordinates had led them here, and the area appeared undisturbed—a forgotten corner of the world where time seemed to stand still.

Then—something caught his eye. A faint glint in the distance. Subtle. Almost imperceptible. But distinct against the muted tones of the underwater world.

Jedidiah adjusted his trajectory, using the guide rope to angle himself toward the anomaly. His movements were deliberate, each step weighted by the suit, his body suspended in the cold, clear water.

The glint grew brighter as he closed the distance, revealing the unmistakable shine of metal. Half-buried in the sediment was an ornate chest, its surface encrusted with barnacles and veiled beneath a thin layer of algae.

Even beneath the grime of time, the craftsmanship stood out—intricate gears and cogs etched into its sides, a signature of clockwork origins. A faint golden hue radiated from its edges, as though it defied the corrosion of time itself.

Jedidiah crouched carefully, the suit creaking softly with the movement, and began to clear away the sediment with his gloved hands. The chest was heavier than expected, resisting his efforts to lift it fully. A large brass lock secured the lid, its metal dulled but unyielding.

He studied it for a moment, realizing he'd need assistance to bring it to the surface.

Reaching for the tethered cable running from his suit to the boat, he felt the tension in the line— the unspoken link to the world above. Unclipping a small metal tool from his belt, he gripped it firmly and tapped a rhythmic sequence against the cable, the vibrations traveling upward through the water.

The sequence was deliberate and precise, each tap spelling out the Morse code they had agreed upon earlier.

"F-O-U-N-D."

A brief pause.

Then another sequence—"P-U-L-L M-E U-P."

Jedidiah steadied his breath, his eyes fixed on the metallic object partially embedded in the rocky lakebed. The relic's edges shimmered faintly, intricate patterns hinting at its mysterious significance. The weight of the suit pressed against him was a constant reminder of the depth and the danger.

The urgency of his message was clear—he needed to surface now.

As he waited for a response, his gaze lingered on the chest.

This was it. The relic Lady Seraphina had entrusted him to find.

But what secrets did it hold?

And more importantly—what dangers might it bring to light?

****

Aboard the small fishing boat, Matthew Colton paced anxiously along the narrow deck, his boots thudding against the wooden planks. His eyes locked onto the taut air hose running from the pump to the depths below, its subtle vibrations the only sign of Jedidiah's movements in the water.

Phineas B. Hargroves sat beside the pump, fingers drumming against the brass housing. A small steam gauge hissed softly, its needle wavering within the acceptable range. He adjusted a valve, his goggles perched awkwardly on his forehead.

"He's been down there almost twenty minutes," Phineas muttered, his voice tight with worry. "It's not good for him to stay at that depth this long."

Matthew held up a hand, jaw tight. "He knows what he's doing, Professor. Let's not panic until we have to."

The lake stretched endlessly before them, silent and unmoving.

Then—

A sound.

A faint creak.

Something brushing against the boat.

Matthew stiffened. "Did you hear that?"

Phineas frowned. "Hear what?"

Then—silence again.

Just the steam engine powering the pump and the rhythmic bubbling of Jedidiah's air hose.

Phineas exhaled, shaking his head. "Nothing. Just nerves, my dear boy."

They both turned their attention back to the water's surface. Tiny bubbles rose steadily, a reassuring sign that Jedidiah was still okay.

Neither noticed the faint creak of oars in the water behind them, nor the quiet splash as a small rowboat glided silently toward the fishing vessel.

And then—they struck.

The four outlaws from earlier moved swiftly, their faces still hidden beneath scarves, their footsteps silent against the deck. Each one clutched a sleek, futuristic ray gun, identical to the ones our heroes had confiscated earlier.

The first outlaw was already aboard when Matthew turned—

A blast of green light lit up the deck.

Matthew barely had time to react before the energy beam slammed into his chest. His body locked up instantly, frozen mid-turn, his face stuck in an expression of shock. His arms rigid at his sides, every muscle seized by the paralyzing force of the ray.

Phineas opened his mouth—

The second shot fired.

The impact hit like a lightning bolt, a sharp jolt of unnatural stillness locking his joints in place. His raised hands froze mid-air, and his breath caught in his throat.

His goggles slid down over his eyes, a comically misplaced final movement as he stood there, motionless, his body twisted in a way no human should be.

Suddenly, the cable hanging over the side of the boat vibrated—an urgent tapping, the distinct rhythm of Morse code. The outlaws whipped around, their attention immediately drawn to the edge of the boat.

"What about the one still underwater?" one of them asked, gripping Jedidiah's air hose and giving it a hard yank. "He's trying to signal the others."

"Not for long." The leader smirked as he stepped forward. He pulled a knife from his belt, its edge glinting in the morning light. His voice was calm—but cruel.

"Cut it."

CHAPTER XX

The Depths of Treachery

While the fishing boat was under attack, some distance away on the dock, Jonathan Blake stood with his arms crossed, his sharp eyes scanning the horizon. Beside him, Edwin Bancroft adjusted a telescopic spyglass, the weight of anticipation thick in the crisp air.

Tom Miller leaned against a wooden post, his unease growing by the second. He glanced at Cogsworth, the automaton standing motionless, its glowing eyes fixed on the water where the fishing boat floated in the distance. The steady pulse of the pump carried on the breeze—a rhythmic reassurance that Jedidiah was still safe below.

Tom exhaled sharply. "I don't like this." His fingers drummed against the post as he shifted uneasily. "They've been out there too long."

Jonathan turned, his expression calm—but firm. "Phineas knows what he's doing, and Jedidiah wouldn't take unnecessary risks. They'll signal if something goes wrong."

Edwin squinted through the spyglass—and suddenly, he froze.

His voice came out tight. "Uh, Dad? I think something's wrong."

Jonathan snatched the telescope from Edwin's hands and raised it to his eyes. The scene aboard the fishing boat came into sharp focus. His stomach tightened as he took in the sight of masked figures creeping aboard. The faint glint of their ray guns was unmistakable—as was the sudden, unnatural stillness of Matthew and Phineas.

Jonathan's jaw clenched. "They've been boarded." His voice was grim. "Same outlaws from before. And they've got new ray guns."

Tom straightened, his alarm spiking. "What do we do?"

Jonathan lowered the spyglass, his mind already racing. "Maybe we should have taken the Swift after all. It's the only airship fitted with an ultrasonic disruptor cannon."

He turned sharply. "Edwin—prepare the Inspiration for take off!"

Before Edwin could respond, Tom whirled toward Cogsworth. "Don't just stand there you mechanical monster—do something to save them!"

The automaton's gears whirred to life. It nodded, then stepped toward the edge of the dock.

"Acknowledged."

Then—without hesitation—Cogsworth stepped off the edge and plunged headfirst into the icy water below.

"Cogsworth!" Jonathan shouted, his eyes widening as he watched his creation sink like a rock. Its top hat still floating on the surface of the water.

For a brief moment, he hesitated—his mind reeling over what had just happened. But there was no time to dwell.

He turned sharply, racing toward the Inspiration with the others at his heels. The older man turned to his son. "Edwin—man the helm. I'll handle the weapons."

Tom skidded to a stop. "The Inspiration has weapons?"

Jonathan shot him a tight smile as he passed him the spyglass. "Of course it does. You think I'd build an airship without a way to defend it?"

Tom barely had time to react before he raised the glass back toward the fishing boat—and his blood ran cold.

"They're cutting the air hose!" he shouted, voice cracking with urgency. "Mr. Davenport's still down there!"

Jonathan's stomach twisted into a cold knot. "No, no, no—" he started, but before he could finish, the outlaws tossed the severed hose overboard.

The limp line unraveled like a dead snake, floating uselessly on the surface.

Jonathan's grip tightened around the controls, his knuckles white.

"Edwin, get us down there—NOW."

His voice was sharp, commanding. There was no room for hesitation.

He turned to the other young man and said, "Arm yourself with something." Back to his son, he added, "Steer us in close enough to draw their attention, but not so close they can board us."

Tom's voice was tight with worry. "What about Mr. Davenport?"

Jonathan's jaw clenched. "We'll distract them long enough for him to get back to the surface. If we can disable their weapons, he might have a fighting chance."

The Inspiration's engines roared to life, steam billowing as the sleek airship lurched forward. Jonathan clambered aboard, boots pounding against the polished deck. Edwin was already at the controls, his hands steady despite the tension in the air. Tom followed close behind.

Jonathan pointed toward the fishing boat. "Edwin, take us low and fast. I don't want them to know we're coming."

The hum of the engines built into a thundering roar, the Inspiration cutting through the morning sky like a blade.

Below, the outlaws laughed as they watched both the cable and air hose disappear beneath the surface.

Jonathan's hands curled into fists.

"Hold on." He muttered under his breath. "We're coming."

Jonathan gripped the controls of a Gatling gun mounted on the Inspiration's starboard side, his jaw set with grim determination. The airship hovered low over the lake, its engines humming steadily, its shadow stretching ominously over the outlaws' rowboat below.

"Steady, Edwin," he called out as the Inspiration drew closer. "I've got this."

With a thunderous whirr, the Gatling gun roared to life, unleashing a barrage of bullets. Wood splintered, the rowboat shuddered under the assault, jagged planks bursting apart as water surged through gaping holes. A warning shot. A message—surrender or sink.

"They're going to retaliate!" Tom shouted from his vantage point.

Sure enough, the outlaw leader snapped his sleek ray gun upward and fired. A streak of green light lanced through the air— but the shot glanced harmlessly off the Inspiration's reinforced hull.

Jonathan smirked. "A paralyzing ray? Against a steam-powered airship? Amateur move." He swiveled the Gatling gun toward the fishing boat, aiming to put an end to their fight.

Below, chaos erupted. The outlaws scrambled, barking orders, their plan crumbling.

Then—Jonathan's stomach dropped.

Two of the masked men suddenly grabbed Phineas and Matthew.

"NO!" Jonathan shouted—just as the outlaws shoved them overboard.

The freezing lake swallowed them instantly. Their buoyant vests kept them afloat—but they were paralyzed. Helpless. Trapped.

Jonathan's hands clenched around the controls. Every instinct screamed to gun the outlaws down where they stood.

Below, the fishing boat's steam engine sputtered —then roared to life. The propeller churned the water into a frothy wake as the outlaws sped away, escaping into the mist.

"They're getting away!" Tom yelled.

Jonathan cursed under his breath, his hands tightening on the Gatling gun. "We can't go after them. Phineas and Matt will drown if we do!"

"Dad!" Edwin's voice cut through the chaos. "I'm taking us down—close to the surface!"

The Inspiration descended swiftly, its hull skimming the waterline, steam hissing from its vents.

Edwin called out over the hum of the engines.

"Take the helm, Dad! Tom and I will get them!"

"Edwin, wait—" Jonathan began, but his son was already moving.

Edwin kicked off his shoes and tore off his jacket. Tom followed suit, his expression grim as he cast a quick glance at the water below.

"Throw the rope ladder over the side for us to climb back up!" Tom shouted just before the two of them dove off the Inspiration.

Jonathan moved quickly to the port side, releasing the latch that secured the coiled rope ladder. With a sharp tug, it unfurled, its weighted ends sinking beneath the surface.

The water hit Edwin and Tom like a wall of ice. Edwin gasped as the cold stole his breath, but he powered through, swimming toward Phineas, whose goggles gleamed faintly in the water. Tom angled toward Matthew, whose rigid form bobbed nearby, paralyzed but still afloat.

"I've got you, Professor!" Edwin said through chattering teeth as he reached Phineas. He wrapped an arm around the older man's shoulders and began paddling back toward the Inspiration.

Tom gritted his teeth, struggling with Matthew's dead weight. His muscles burned as he fought against the water's drag. "Come on, Matt," he grunted. "You're not going down on my watch."

Above, Jonathan steadied the airship, maneuvering it as close to the water's surface as possible. The rope ladder dangled just low enough for Edwin and Tom to pull Phineas and Matthew aboard.

"Careful!" Jonathan called as the two young men emerged from the lake, soaked and shivering but determined.

Edwin hauled Phineas over the side while Tom pushed Matthew upward, both of them straining under the effort.

"We've got them!" Edwin yelled.

As the Inspiration stabilized, Jonathan's focus snapped to the fleeing fishing boat. His grip tightened on the controls, jaw clenched.

"This isn't over."

****

Meanwhile, far below the surface, Jedidiah was just beginning to feel the repercussions of the battle raging above.

The rhythmic hiss of air through his helmet— the sound that had been his only companion—was suddenly gone.

The silence was sudden and deafening.

Jedidiah froze, his gloved hand hovering over the chest. The cable that had been taut with pressure only moments ago now dangled loosely, curling lifelessly in the water.

Slowly, he turned his head. The weight of his

helmet shifted as his gaze followed the line upward.

Nothing.

The air hose floated limply, a clear and terrifying sign.

The realization hit him like a ton of bricks. His air supply had been cut.

Fighting the surge of panic threatening to overtake him, Jedidiah reached behind him with deliberate, measured movements. His gloved fingers found the valve of the emergency tank strapped to his back. A quick twist released a faint hiss, and the reassuring flow of breathable air filled his helmet once more.

It wasn't much—barely three minutes' worth—but it was enough to buy him precious time.

He exhaled slowly, forcing himself to focus. Stay calm. Think. The surface isn't too far.

But as he shifted to take a step upward, the weighted boots resisted, anchoring him in place. Each movement was a struggle, the lakebed pulling at him like an unyielding chain.

As he strained against the weight, something caught his eye in the distance. A dark shape descended slowly from the shimmering surface far above. Squinting through the reinforced glass of his helmet, he recognized it—a small rowboat, sinking at an angle, one oar still attached and trailing like a broken limb.

Jedidiah's chest tightened. What's happening up there?

The rowboat drifted lower, settling on the lakebed hundreds of feet away. It lay eerily still, its shadow stretching across the murky depths like a ghostly specter.

He glanced upward again. The faint bubbles from his exhalations spiraled toward the surface.

No movement.

No signal.

Just the oppressive silence of the underwater world.

Panic threatened to creep back in. The minutes on his emergency air supply were ticking away, and his attempts to climb upward were futile. The cumbersome suit and its weighted boots kept him firmly anchored.

Then—he saw them.

Two faintly glowing orbs pierced through the darkened blue, moving steadily toward him.

Jedidiah's breath caught. At first, he thought it might be some underwater predator. The lights grew closer, revealing the distinct shape of legs… mechanical legs.

Relief washed over him as recognition set in.

Cogsworth.

The automaton moved with purpose, each step sending up small puffs of sediment from the lake bed. Its glowing eyes locked onto Jedidiah, and it raised one metallic hand in a gesture of reassurance.

Jedidiah waved back, pointing to the chest half-buried on the lake floor. He mimed lifting it, his movements deliberate and exaggerated to ensure Cogsworth understood.

The automaton raised one hand in acknowledgment before turning its attention to the chest embedded in the lakebed. Its mechanical arms gripped the edges with surprising precision. With a sharp tug, it pulled the chest free from its sedimentary prison, holding it aloft like a prize.

Next, Cogsworth examined the tethering cable. With a single sharp motion, it tore the line in half, securing a short section around the ornate chest. Its powerful hands worked quickly, knotting the cable to hold the chest tightly against its torso.

Jedidiah tapped his helmet, signaling his dwindling air supply. Cogsworth turned back to him, its glowing eyes assessing the situation. The automaton slipped an arm under Jedidiah's shoulder, gripping him securely. With its free hand, it adjusted a vent hidden along its metallic leg.

A burst of steam erupted, propelling them forward.

The sudden movement jolted Jedidiah, and he instinctively braced against the lakebed. Cogsworth adjusted its grip, pushing Jedidiah ahead while maintaining its balance against the rocky terrain.

The lakebed shifted beneath them, transforming from smooth sediment to jagged outcroppings and uneven ground. The automaton paused briefly, recalibrating its approach. With another calculated burst of steam, it propelled them over the first obstacle.

Jedidiah's breathing grew shallower. The rhythmic hiss of his emergency air tank was fading, each exhalation a reminder of how little time he had left. He tapped Cogsworth's arm in Morse code: "Hurry."

The automaton's glowing eyes flickered once in acknowledgment. It adjusted its vents, sending bursts of steam in rapid succession. The force propelled them forward, though the terrain grew more treacherous.

They reached a steep incline, the rocky wall looming before them. Cogsworth braced Jedidiah against the edge, anchoring him in place with one arm. The automaton's free hand gripped the rocky outcropping, and with a powerful motion, it hauled them both upward.

For a brief moment, Jedidiah felt weightless as they crested the incline. Cogsworth landed with a metallic clang, its legs absorbing the impact. Its glowing eyes scanned the path ahead—now clear and sloping gently toward the faint outline of Georgina Island.

The automaton quickened its pace, each step

sending small plumes of silt spiraling behind them. Jedidiah's vision blurred slightly as the last traces of air in his emergency tank dwindled.

The surface of the water shimmered above them, fractured rays of sunlight piercing through. Cogsworth adjusted its grip, positioning Jedidiah upright. With a final, calculated burst of steam, the automaton propelled them both upward.

They broke through the surface in a cascade of bubbles and spray. The chest remained secure against Cogsworth's torso, the improvised cable holding firm.

Cogsworth's mechanical limbs sank into the wet sand as it finally reached the shoreline of Georgina Island. Jedidiah hung limp in its grasp, his weighted suit making even the faintest movement impossible. The automaton placed the chest down carefully, removing the cable before turning its full attention to Jedidiah.

Its glowing eyes scanned the figure in the suit, detecting no visible motion. Steam hissed softly from its vents as it worked swiftly, its mechanical hands locating the latches securing the diving helmet. With a sharp twist and a metallic click, the helmet was removed, revealing Jedidiah's pale face.

His features were unnerving. No breath fogged the chilly air, and his lips had taken on a faint bluish hue.

Cogsworth tilted its head, its glowing eyes

Jedidiah's features were unnerving.
No breath fogged the chilly air, and
his lips had taken on a faint bluish hue.

dimming slightly as if assessing the situation. The automaton emitted a series of rapid beeps—an alert signal to any who might hear it—before gently lowering Jedidiah onto the rocky shore. Its hands hovered momentarily over his chest, mimicking the motions of a human in uncertainty, before it paused, awaiting his next command.

Silence.

CHAPTER XXI

Rising from the Deep

The Inspiration hovered low over the shimmering surface of Lake Simcoe, its engines humming steadily as it maintained position above the still waters. Tom Miller's knuckles whitened as he gripped the deck railing, his sharp eyes scanning the lake for any sign of his employer, Jedidiah Davenport. Beside him, Edwin Bancroft leaned forward, his own gaze locked on the water below.

"Wait—there!" Edwin's voice rang out, cutting through the tension. He pointed to a trail of air bubbles rising to the surface, a faint line carving its way toward the dock.

Jonathan Blake raced to the helm, adjusting the throttle slightly to angle the Inspiration toward the movement. His expression was grim but focused. "It's got to be him," he said. "No other explanation for that kind of movement underwater."

Tom's excitement flared. "You think Mr.

Davenport's somehow making his way back on his own?"

"Not on his own. Those bubbles are too steady, too directed. Something—or someone—is helping him." Jonathan's eyes flickered with recognition, and a small smile tugged at his lips. "I have a feeling what that something is. We'll find out in a moment. Hold on, I'm taking us back to the dock."

The Inspiration surged forward, its engines roaring as it sped toward the shoreline. The faint trail of bubbles grew clearer as they neared the dock, then suddenly began to fade. The water, however, still rippled faintly in the wake of unseen movement.

Tom's grip tightened on the railing. "Come on, Jed. Hang in there."

With a final burst of steam, the Inspiration touched down near the shore of Georgina Island, a hiss of pressure escaping from its engines as they idled. Despite being the oldest among them, Jonathan Blake was the first down the loading ramp, his boots striking the damp earth with a solid thud. Edwin and Tom followed close behind, their strides urgent as they raced toward the shoreline.

They skidded to a stop at the sight before them —Cogsworth crouched beside Jedidiah's still form.

The automaton had just removed Jedidiah's helmet, revealing his pale, unmoving face. Its glowing eyes flickered as it emitted a series of rapid beeps, a distress signal ringing out in the quiet morning air.

Jonathan dropped to his knees, placing a hand on Jedidiah's chest.

No movement.

No rise and fall of breath.

"He's not breathing!" Jonathan shouted, his voice tight with urgency. He pressed two fingers against Jedidiah's neck, his expression grim—until he felt it.

"But he has a faint pulse!"

He exhaled sharply, tilting Jedidiah's head back slightly, recalling the basic principles of clearing an airway.

"I read about a method," he muttered. "The Sylvester Method. It's crude, but it's all we've got."

Tom Miller nodded quickly. "The arms! Yes, I've read about that too. We need to simulate breathing."

Without hesitation, the older man shifted Jedidiah into position, lying him flat on his back. Tom knelt near his shoulders while Jonathan positioned himself closer to his chest.

Tom took hold of Jedidiah's arms, extending them outward and lifting them above his head in a smooth, rhythmic motion. "This should draw air into the lungs," he explained, his voice tight with focus.

Jonathan nodded, counting under his breath to

keep the rhythm. After a few seconds, Tom brought Jedidiah's arms back down, pressing them gently but firmly against his chest to force air out.

"Again," Jonathan instructed. "Slow and steady."

They worked in unison, moving Jedidiah's arms methodically, mimicking the natural rise and fall of breath. Edwin hovered nearby, fists clenched, his helpless expression betraying his fear.

Seconds stretched into what felt like hours. The only sound was the rhythmic movement of Jedidiah's arms.

Then—

Jedidiah's body jerked suddenly, a strangled gasp escaping his lips. His fingers twitched.

"Come on, Jed," Tom urged, shaking his shoulder slightly.

Another cough. Then—his chest rose sharply.

His eyes fluttered open, glassy and unfocused. He coughed weakly.

"He's breathing!" Tom shouted, his voice cracking with relief.

Jonathan leaned closer, pressing two fingers gently against Jedidiah's neck. "His pulse is getting stronger."

Jedidiah's eyes flickered open briefly, dazed but alive. His coughs were harsh and raw. Jonathan quickly rolled him onto his side, helping him breathe more freely.

"You're safe now," Jonathan said softly, gripping Jedidiah's shoulder. "We've got you."

Jedidiah coughed again, his voice faint but audible. "Took you... long enough," he rasped.

Jonathan chuckled, the sound laced with both relief and exhaustion. "Better late than never, as they say."

Tom slumped back onto his heels, exhaling a shaky breath. "I never want to go through that again!"

"Yes, I can imagine it was a rough experience for *you*..." Jedidiah muttered sarcastically.

"I just meant..." Tom's sentence was cut short as Jedidiah forced a weak laugh and waved his hand dismissively. His gaze drifted to the automaton standing nearby, its glowing eyes flickering with mechanical precision.

"That thing... I mean... Cogsworth saved my life," he murmured, offering a faint nod of gratitude.

Jonathan raised a brow. "I think Tom and I helped a little too." He rested a firm hand on Jedidiah's shoulder, helping him sit up.

"Oh yes," Jedidiah said. "I didn't mean that. I just meant I'd still be under the lake right now if it weren't for him."

The older man laughed, shaking his head. "I knew what you meant. My creation came in pretty useful, didn't it?"

Jedidiah exhaled, still catching his breath. "It certainly did. It even brought up the chest I was looking for... where is it?"

Tom gestured to the ornate box resting beside Cogsworth, its intricate gears and brass inlays glinting in the sunlight. "Safe and sound, next to our mechanical friend."

Jedidiah's gaze lingered on the chest for a moment before his brow furrowed with sudden concern. He turned back to Jonathan. "Where's Matt and Phineas?"

Jonathan hesitated, his expression tightening. "They're aboard the Inspiration," he said, his voice low. "But... they were hit with the paralyzing ray gun."

Jedidiah's breath hitched, and he instinctively tried to stand, only for Jonathan to place a firm hand on his arm.

"Easy, Jed," Jonathan warned. "You were underwater for quite some time. You might have a mild case of the bends."

"I don't care. Take me to them," Jedidiah insisted, his voice gaining strength despite the exhaustion weighing on his body.

As he tried again to push himself up, his limbs refused to cooperate. His head spun. It felt like trying to stand with lead weights strapped to his bones.

Jonathan continued to press a steadying hand

against his shoulder. "Easy."

Jedidiah gritted his teeth. "I'm fine."

"Do you know how close you came to being dead just a few minutes ago?" Jonathan shot back. "Humor me."

"I've got to get to them!"

Jonathan exhaled sharply before relenting. "Alright. But you'll need help getting there."

Tom moved to Jedidiah's side, supporting one arm, while Edwin took the other. Together, they helped him to his feet. His legs felt like lead, each step slow and unsteady, but his jaw was set with determination.

Jonathan retrieved the diving helmet and turned to Cogsworth. "Pick up the chest and bring it with us. We don't dare leave it behind."

The automaton stood motionless for a brief moment, its glowing eyes flickering faintly. Then, with a sudden jerk, its mechanical limbs creaked into motion. It bent stiffly, joints groaning as if water had seeped into its intricate mechanisms. With both hands, Cogsworth lifted the ornate chest from the ground.

"Com...mand ac...cep...ted," the automaton intoned, its voice no longer smooth but stilted and halting. The mechanical stutter was jarring, as though it were struggling to process its own words. "Chest will... be trans...port...ed."

Jonathan's brow furrowed. "That's not good," he

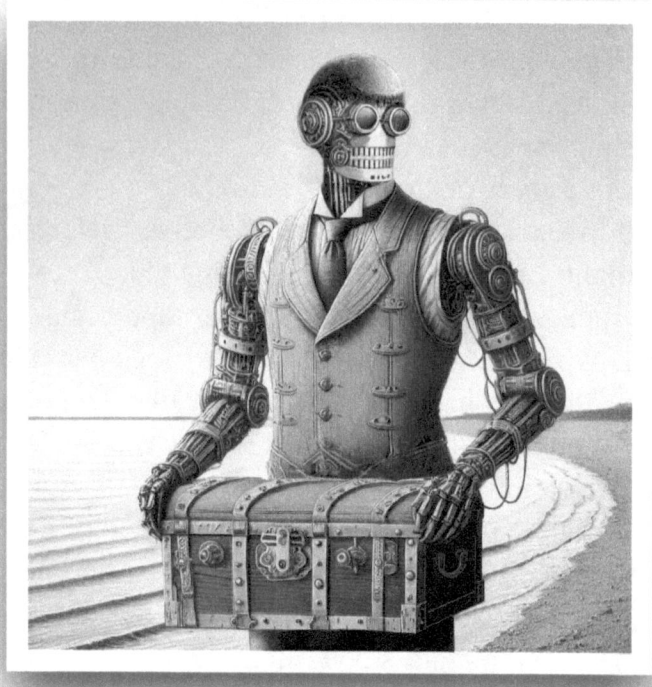

With both hands, Cogsworth lifted
the ornate chest from the ground.

muttered under his breath, stepping closer. "Cogsworth, status report."

The automaton's head twitched slightly, as if struggling to process the request. Its voice, more distorted now, crackled from the embedded speaker behind it's grille.

"Sys...tem in...teg...ri...ty... com...pro...mised. Ex...ten...sive wa...ter ex...po...sure de...tect...ed."

Jedidiah glanced back, his face pale but alert. "Jonathan, what's wrong with him?"

The older man sighed heavily, watching as the mechanical man staggered slightly under the weight of the chest. "I was afraid of this. The water's obviously caused some damage. It's affecting his motor functions and speech systems."

As if to confirm Jonathan's assessment, Cogsworth paused mid-step, its arms trembling as it adjusted its grip on the chest.

"The hu...man who or...ders me to car...ry this ob...ject will... re...ceive—" It faltered. A pause, then—"Full co...op...era...tion."

Jonathan's jaw tightened. "We've got to get you dried out and run some tests." He exchanged a worried glance with Jedidiah. "In the meantime, let's hope it doesn't get worse."

Cogsworth resumed its march toward the airship, its movements jerky and labored. The chest gleamed in its grasp, the intricate patterns etched into its surface catching the sunlight.

"Keep moving," Jonathan ordered, his voice firm. "And don't drop that chest."

As they stepped aboard the airship, Jedidiah's gaze immediately sought out his two friends. Matthew and Phineas lay side by side on cots in the sleeper cabin, their bodies unnaturally still. Phineas' goggles sat askew on his face, and Matthew's hat rested on his chest—somehow, it had stayed on his head even after being pushed overboard.

Jonathan stepped forward, hands on his hips. "As usual, the ray gun left them completely immobilized. I guess we just wait for the effects to wear off."

"Dad," Edwin spoke up, "should we get them out of these wet clothes? They might catch pneumonia if we leave them like this."

"Impossible." His father shook his head. "In their current state, we can't even budge them let alone redress them. We'll just have to wait until they come around."

"We don't have time!" Jedidiah turned to Jonathan. "These effects have lasted anywhere from twenty minutes to over an hour, depending on how large of a dose they were hit with. We need to bring them around now. What about Phineas' antidote? He was working on it before we left."

Edwin nodded quickly. "He said he'd made some progress, but he didn't have time to test it."

"Well, here's the perfect chance to see if it works!" Jedidiah's gaze shifted to Tom. "The two of you—race to the Phoenix and bring back whatever he has."

Jonathan Blake frowned, hesitation evident. "It could work... or it could make things worse. Are you sure?"

Jedidiah's jaw tightened, his eyes locked on his friends. "I trust Phineas' work. Experimental or not, he's the most brilliant mind I know."

Jonathan exhaled but nodded in agreement. "Alright. Let's get to work." He turned to Edwin. "Go with Tom. We'll follow Phineas' notes and hope for the best."

As the two young men rushed to retrieve the antidote, Jedidiah shifted uncomfortably, the weight of the soaked diving suit pressing against him. The heavy layers were stiff with grime and water, clinging to his frame like a second skin.

He started working the clasps with stiff fingers. The outer layers resisted, stiffened by the cold, but determination drove him forward.

"Jonathan," he called, his voice still hoarse. "A little help here?"

Jonathan stepped over without hesitation. "Of course. Let's get you out of this contraption."

Together, they worked to remove the bulky suit, starting with the weighted boots that had anchored Jedidiah so firmly to the lakebed. Each piece landed on the wooden floor of the Inspiration with a muffled thud, leaving faint damp patches in its wake.

Jedidiah exhaled deeply as the last layer peeled away, finally free of the suit's confining grasp. He flexed his fingers and rolled his shoulders, relishing the sensation of warmth and mobility returning to his chilled limbs.

"Thanks," Jedidiah muttered, offering Jonathan a faint smile.

Jonathan gave a curt nod, tossing the last piece of the suit aside. "You're welcome. But take it easy, Jed. You've been through enough for one day."

Before he could respond, the sound of two young men racing aboard the airship interrupted their conversation. Tom and Edwin burst into the cabin, one clutching a polished metal device with intricate brass and copper fittings, while the other carried two small vials of shimmering blue liquid.

"We've got it!" Tom announced, holding up the device triumphantly, his face flushed from the run.

Jonathan stepped forward, his eyes narrowing as he inspected the device. "Phineas never ceases to amaze me. A syringe without a needle... but it looks like a miniature steam engine."

Edwin handed over the vials. "Here's the formula. Phineas wasn't entirely confident in it, but it's all we have."

Jedidiah sat down nearby on a crate and

wrapped a blanket over his shoulders. He looked up —pale but resolute. "No time for second-guessing. If it works, it works. If it doesn't, we wait for the effects to wear off naturally."

Jonathan carefully loaded one of the vials into the delivery device, his fingers steady but his expression somber. The chamber sealed with a soft click, and a faint hiss of steam escaped as the system activated.

"Who first?" Jonathan asked, looking from Jedidiah to the two unconscious men.

"Phineas," Jedidiah said without hesitation. "He'd never forgive us if we used his invention on Matt before him."

Jonathan nodded and moved to Phineas' side. Gently, he rolled up the inventor's sleeve, exposing his forearm. "Let's hope this works," he muttered, pressing the device against the skin.

With a soft hiss and a puff of steam, the device delivered the formula through Phineas' skin. The inventor's body twitched slightly. Moments later, his chest rose with a sharp intake of breath, and his eyes flickered open.

"Egads!" Phineas exclaimed, sitting bolt upright and clutching his arm where the device had been used. His goggles still askew, he reached up and adjusted them. "What—what happened?"

Jonathan let out a relieved laugh. "Welcome back, old friend. You were out cold thanks to that gang of outlaws and their paralyzing ray guns. But your formula worked."

Phineas blinked rapidly, his gaze darting around. "It worked? Of course, it worked! I never doubted it for a moment." Then, his expression turned serious as his eyes landed on Matthew. "And now we use it on him."

Jonathan quickly reloaded the device with the second vial and moved to Matthew's side. He repeated the process, pressing the device against Matthew's forearm and activating it. Another hiss. Another puff of steam.

Everyone watched anxiously.

After a tense moment, Matthew's body jerked slightly. His fingers twitched. His eyes opened slowly, and he let out a low groan.

"Where am I?" he murmured, looking around groggily.

"You're alright," Jedidiah said, his voice thick with relief. "We all are."

Matthew blinked, his gaze focusing on his childhood friend. "Jed? What happened? Last thing I remember, we were on the fishing boat and you were at the bottom of the lake."

"You got hit by a paralyzing ray," Jedidiah explained. "But thanks to Phineas' brilliance, you're back with us."

Phineas grinned, his energy already returning. "Don't mention it, my dear boy. Just another day in the life of a brilliant professor, scientist, and inventor!"

As he said this, a chuckle rippled through the group.

Everyone laughed heartily, except for Jedidiah, who was already thinking ahead. He pushed himself to his feet, still pale but determined. "Jonathan, I think you, Edwin, Tom, and Cogsworth should take the Inspiration and follow those men who attacked us."

Jonathan raised an eyebrow, his weathered face etched with concern. "What about the rest of you?"

"We'll head back to Toronto in the Phoenix," Jedidiah replied. "I need to wire Sheriff Thompson about Professor Thaddeus Montgomery. If anyone can pull strings to get us in to see him, it's Sheriff Thompson."

Jonathan's gaze lingered on Jedidiah, noting the stiffness in his movements and the sheen of sweat on his brow. "You're not looking great, Jed. Maybe you should rest."

Jedidiah waved him off. "I'm fine. Just a little tired. We've all been through worse."

Tom stepped forward, glancing at Edwin. "We'll catch those outlaws, Mr. Davenport. You just focus on getting some rest"

Jedidiah nodded. "Be careful out there. I have a feeling, those men won't go down without a fight."

As the Inspiration's engines roared to life,

Jedidiah and his team descended the ramp. The Phoenix waited nearby, its sleek frame gleaming in the sunlight.

Jedidiah took a deep breath as they approached, and stumbled slightly.

Matthew frowned, catching his arm. "You alright?"

"Fine," Jedidiah muttered, though his voice lacked conviction. His joints ached, and the world seemed to tilt slightly. He shook his head, trying to clear the dizziness. "Let's get aboard."

Phineas cast a worried glance at Matthew but said nothing as they helped Jedidiah up the gangplank. Once inside, the familiar hum of the Phoenix's engines surrounded them—a comforting sound despite the tension in the air.

As they prepared for departure, Matthew and Phineas moved to change into dry clothes. Jedidiah leaned heavily against the cabin wall, his fatigue becoming more apparent. When Phineas returned, his gaze narrowed as he realized how pale Jedidiah had become.

"Sit," Phineas ordered, his tone leaving no room for argument. "Actually, no—lie down. Now."

"I'm fine—"

"No, you're not," Matthew cut in, rejoining them. "You've been pushing yourself since that mechanical monster pulled you out of the lake. You need rest."

Jedidiah opened his mouth to argue but was silenced by the combined force of their stern expressions. With a sigh of resignation, he allowed them to guide him to his bed.

"Cogsworth," he remarked casually as he sank into the feather mattress, his body protesting every movement.

"What?" Matthew asked, confused.

"His name is Cogsworth!"

A faint smile tugged at Jedidiah's lips as exhaustion finally took hold. He had a whole new respect for the mechanical man who had saved his life.

****

A short time later, as the Phoenix descended into a field just outside Toronto, Professor Phineas B. Hargroves and Matthew Colton reentered the cabin to let Jedidiah know they had arrived.

"Stay here," Phineas said, pulling a blanket over him. "We'll handle the telegraph office. We can't risk you collapsing on us."

Jedidiah smirked faintly, realizing there was no use in protesting.

"Bossy as ever," he remarked.

Phineas rolled his eyes but said nothing, ushering Matthew out of the cabin. The two men made their way to the telegraph office, leaving the

Phoenix in a tense but quiet calm.

Jedidiah lay still. His body ached, and his mind raced with worry. Eventually, exhaustion won out, and he managed to doze off.

An hour later, the sound of footsteps roused him.

Phineas and Matthew were walking across the deck, their boots thudding softly as they approached his sleeping cabin. One glance at their faces told him something was wrong.

"What is it?" Jedidiah asked, sitting up slowly.

Phineas responded by handing him the handwritten telegram, his fingers tightening around the edge for a moment before letting go.

Jedidiah's eyes scanned the text, his stomach twisting as he read:

"JEDIDIAH STOP. MARSHAL CROMWELL REPORTS THADDEUS MONTGOMERY AND GANG ESCAPED FROM CUSTODY STOP. AIRSHIP KNOWN AS THE DAUNTLESS STOLEN FROM SECURED LOCATION STOP. SHERIFF THOMPSON STOP."

Jedidiah's grip on the paper tightened.
"Sizzling steam pipes!"

CHAPTER XXII

Infiltrating the Museum

Jedidiah reread the telegram, his eyes scanning the words again and again.

His grip tightened.

The Dauntless—stolen.

Thaddeus Montgomery—escaped.

A tightness settled in his chest like he'd taken a punch to the ribs.

He exhaled sharply. "He's on the loose."

Phineas stepped forward, his face pale but alert. "If Montgomery's free, it means—"

"It means we're all in trouble," Jedidiah interrupted, his jaw clenching as the implications sank in. "If he's not behind this, he's been taken by someone who is. If what Lady Blackwood said about that relic is even half true..."

Matthew Colton shifted uneasily, arms crossed. "What now?"

A heavy silence settled over the cabin, each of

them lost in thought, processing the weight of the telegram.

Then—BOOM.

Heavy boots thundered up the loading ramp.

The eccentric older man and Matthew sprang into action. Without hesitation, Phineas grabbed one of the four Ray guns stored nearby, tossing one to Matthew Colton. He caught it in midair, his movements swift and instinctive. Phineas picked up another and pressed it into Jedidiah's hand.

"This time, we're ready for whoever's out there," Matthew muttered, narrowing his eyes as he leveled the ray gun toward the door.

Jedidiah raised a hand, signaling for him to wait. "Let's see who it is first."

The door creaked open, revealing the imposing figures of Lady Seraphina Blackwood's guards.

Dressed in dark, heavy coats and their signature plague doctor masks, they stepped inside with unnerving silence. Their boots struck the wooden floor with sharp, deliberate thuds, each step resonating like a harbinger of dread.

Once inside, they stopped abruptly, standing as still as statues. Their masks—hollow, unblinking eyes behind hooked beaks—tilted slightly as they surveyed the room with silent, oppressive scrutiny.

Not one of them moved. No fidgeting. No shifting of weight. Just eerie, disciplined stillness, thickening the already heavy air in the cabin.

Phineas tightened his grip on his ray gun.

Jedidiah's eyes narrowed on the lead guard as they stepped forward. From the folds of their coat, the figure produced a sealed parchment, the wax bearing Lady Seraphina's unmistakable insignia.

The silence stretched unbearably as the guard extended the letter. Finally, Jedidiah lowered his ray gun slightly and accepted it, breaking the seal with deliberate care. He read the letter aloud:

"Mr. Davenport,

Time is against us. Thaddeus Montgomery and his gang are no longer in custody. I suspect they may be seeking to reclaim his piece of the relic. You must reach the British Museum before they do and secure Montgomery's artifact.

There is a room beneath the third basement. Take the old entrance. It hasn't been used in decades. You will have no issues recognizing the concealed stairway. It leads to the Order's hidden headquarters. My intel confirms Montgomery hid his piece there before the airship races. Move quickly. Failure is not an option!"

"So Montgomery might actually be behind all this?" Matthew asked doubtfully. "He's been behind bars for weeks now!"

"Doesn't matter if he is or not," Jedidiah replied. "If he's headed to retrieve—"

"And there's no proof that he is!" the dark-haired young man scoffed.

"But, if he is," Jedidiah continued, "he's far too dangerous a man to be wielding that much power."

Matthew tightened his grip on his ray gun. "So once again, we're supposed to blindly follow her request?"

Jedidiah glanced back at the guards, who remained impassive. "I don't think she's asking."

The lead guard stepped forward again, unfurling a small, detailed map. It depicted blueprints of the British Museum.

"She just happens to have a map of the museum?" Matthew raised an eyebrow. "Rather convenient, isn't it?"

"Well, it is the location of one of the Order's secret headquarters," Jedidiah replied matter-of-factly.

Professor Phineas B. Hargroves gave a small shake of his head, a faint, wistful smile tugging at his lips. "Dramatic and thorough. Precisely her style. She's... remarkable..."

Matthew shot him a skeptical glance. "Remarkable?"

"Skilled." Phineas cleared his throat, fumbling slightly with his ray gun. "Remarkably skilled. You didn't let me finish..."

Matthew smirked, his tone dripping with mock sincerity. "Of course. Remarkably skilled. Nothing at all to do with how remarkable you find her personally, eh?"

Phineas' blush deepened as he mumbled something incoherent, suddenly very interested in inspecting the ray gun.

Jedidiah folded the letter and map, tucking them into his pocket. He looked at his companions, his voice steady despite the mounting tension. "We're going."

As the guards turned to leave, the lead figure paused at the threshold, its masked face tilting slightly toward Jedidiah. For a fleeting moment, it felt as though the unblinking eyes bore into him, searching for something unspoken. Then, with deliberate precision, the guard exited, the echo of their boots fading into the hum of the Phoenix.

Phineas finally relaxed his stance. "Well, that was a relatively pleasant visit."

"It was?" Matthew asked sarcastically.

The eccentric older man clapped him on the shoulder. "They didn't shoot us or hit us with knockout gas this time, did they?"

Matthew smirked faintly, lowering his ray gun. "That's what you call a pleasant visit?"

Jedidiah ignored the banter, already focused on their next move. "Matt, raise the loading ramp. We need to leave for London right away!" He tried to climb out of bed but fell back, still too weak to stand.

"Just let me know when we arrive!"

As Phineas headed toward the helm, Matthew did as he was asked and raised the ramp. Afterward, he returned to the cabin and glanced at the chest Jedidiah had risked his life to retrieve.

"Aren't we even going to open it and see what's inside?" he asked.

"We should at least find out what all this trouble is about," Jedidiah agreed, gesturing to the massive box. "See if you can lift it up and place it on the bed beside me. I'll try to pick the lock—"

Before Jedidiah could finish his sentence, Matthew grunted and hefted the chest with both hands.

He hesitated.

Then—

With a resounding CRASH, Matthew slammed the chest down onto the floor. The lid splintered with a loud crack, breaking it open.

Jedidiah blinked. "Well, that's one way to do it."

Inside the shattered chest, nestled within a waterproof container, lay a peculiar object: a green circular device with copper coils radiating outward and a radiant amber gemstone at its core. It shimmered with a brilliance, unlike anything they had ever seen, casting flickering reflections across the cabin.

It was no bigger than the palm of his hand.

Such a small object for such a huge chest.

Upon hearing the crash, Professor Hargroves raced back into the room, his eyes wide. "Remarkable... What on earth is it?"

Jedidiah reached out for it, and Matthew placed it in his hand. "I'm not sure," he murmured. "But something tells me we'll find out soon enough."

****

The Phoenix soared through the skies, its engines humming steadily as it cut through the Atlantic air. Below, the vast, unbroken expanse of ocean glimmered faintly under the midday sun. The journey was marked only by the rhythmic churn of steam and the occasional adjustment of the controls.

Despite the calm, tension brewed within the cabin. Jedidiah lay in his quarters, his body still aching from his ordeal at Lake Simcoe. Hours stretched into days, the hum of the engines and the ever-present ticking of the ship's mechanisms became a quiet backdrop to the crew's growing unease.

Professor Phineas B. Hargroves stood near the helm, staring at the navigation table. He pored over Lady Blackwood's blueprint once more, his fingers tracing the intricate layout of the British Museum.

"It's like a fortress," he muttered, noting the layers leading deeper and deeper beneath the structure. "Three basements, concealed stairways... It's no wonder the relic and their headquarters had been kept a secret for so long."

Across the deck, Matthew cleaned one of the ray guns. He was determined to be ready for anything.

"You'd think she could've given us more details about what we're looking for," he said, his voice laced with frustration. "An artifact is a pretty vague description, don't you think?"

Phineas glanced up, his expression distracted. "Lady Seraphina's instructions are vague. But that's just part of her... charm, I suppose."

Matthew smirked, setting the ray gun aside. He glanced out at the unchanging horizon, a hint of impatience flashing in his eyes. "Charm? You mean her infuriating habit of keeping secrets?"

"Remarkably skilled habit," Phineas corrected with a sheepish grin, earning an exasperated shake of the head from Matthew.

The conversation trailed off, leaving the cabin in silence once more. As the hours ticked by, Phineas occupied himself with his tools, Matthew alternated between rest and keeping watch, and Jedidiah remained mostly confined to his quarters.

****

The gas lamps along the city streets flickered to

life, casting a warm, golden glow across the sprawling metropolis. The distant clatter of carriages and the faint smell of coal smoke rose to meet them, enveloping the Phoenix as it descended.

It was just past 7:30 PM on October 27th, 1881, when the familiar silhouette of the British Museum came into view—its imposing structure standing out even under the night sky.

Phineas guided the Phoenix toward a secluded field a short distance from the historic landmark. The area was shielded by a tree line, providing enough cover to keep the airship hidden from prying eyes. The open space was close enough to make the walk manageable but far enough to avoid drawing attention.

Jedidiah emerged from his quarters, looking like a whole new person. He no longer needed to steady himself against the wall, his voice strong despite his previous exhaustion.

"Did we make it?" He asked.

Phineas nodded, glancing up from the navigation controls as the Phoenix gently touched down. "We've arrived. The British Museum awaits."

Matthew adjusted the goggles on the brim of his cap, his expression grim. "Let's just hope we're not too late."

Jedidiah marched forward, determined. "We won't be. Let's move!" He paused long enough to grab a lantern and a ray gun.

Phineas quickly secured the mooring lines, grabbed a weapon for himself, and followed the other two.

****

About twenty minutes later, the British Museum loomed before them, its Greco-Roman façade bathed in the warm glow of gas lamps. The sprawling building seemed more like a fortress than an institution, its imposing columns casting long shadows over the cobblestone street.

Jedidiah Davenport, Phineas B. Hargroves, and Matthew Colton stood in silence, the weight of their mission pressing down like a physical burden.

"Guards at the main entrance," Matthew whispered, nodding toward the two uniformed watchmen standing by the massive double doors. Each carried an oil lantern, their conversation faint but discernible in the quiet night.

"Too obvious," Jedidiah muttered. His sharp eyes scanned the perimeter before landing on a side door tucked away in the shadows. "There. That's our way in."

They moved quickly but quietly, sticking to the shadows as they approached the staff entrance. The door was locked, as expected. Jedidiah pulled a slim leather case from his jacket pocket, flipping it open to reveal an assortment of lock-picking tools.

"You carry lock picks?" Matthew asked, raising an eyebrow.

"A birthday present from Phineas," Jedidiah replied with a smirk, crouching before the lock.

"Never can be too prepared!" the eccentric older man said with a grin.

Jedidiah's hands worked deftly, the faint clicks of tumblers the only sound as Phineas and Matthew kept watch. Moments later, the lock yielded with a soft click, and the door creaked open. Jedidiah gestured for them to enter.

Inside, the air was cool and stale, carrying the faint scent of old paper and polished wood. The corridor was dimly lit, the gas lamps casting uneven light across the marble floors and ornate paneling. Phineas adjusted the hood of his lantern, narrowing the beam to a soft glow.

"Stick to the map," Jedidiah whispered, unfolding Lady Blackwood's blueprints. His finger traced their route to the basement levels.

The trio moved cautiously, their footsteps muffled against the well-worn runner stretching along the corridor. The occasional echo of a guard's patrol kept them on edge, forcing them to duck behind exhibits or into alcoves.

As they crept through the dimly lit halls, Matthew suddenly tensed.

Footsteps. Getting closer.

They ducked behind an ornate display case, pressing themselves into the shadows as a uniformed museum guard rounded the corner.

The guard stopped. His lantern swung in their direction.

His eyes landed on Phineas' face.

He squinted. His brow furrowed.

"Wait a minute," the guard muttered.

Phineas stiffened.

"Holy smokes," Matthew whispered. "Here we go."

The guard tilted his lantern higher, illuminating Phineas' wild silver hair, thick mustache, and formal suit. His eyes widened.

"Well, I'll be… ain't you—"

Phineas groaned.

"Not this again," he muttered.

"I just reread *Roughing It*, and I'm about to start on your newest book!"

"My good man, I am not—"

Jedidiah stepped forward smoothly, cutting him off before the professor could finish his sentence.

"Ah! Yes, sir, you are very astute," Jedidiah said with an easygoing smile. "You are indeed in the presence of none other than the illustrious Mark Twain himself."

The guard gasped, nearly dropping his lantern. "I knew it was you!"

Phineas sighed. "It most certainly is not—"

"Mr. Twain!" Jedidiah interrupted loudly, jabbing Phineas playfully in the side. "I told you your disguise wasn't going to fool anyone!"

Matthew stifled a laugh.

"Oh, my stars," the guard gushed. "I've been an admirer of your writing for years! It's an honor to meet you, sir! What are you doing here?"

Thinking fast, Jedidiah adopted a confident tone.

"Mr. Twain is considering a generous donation of artifacts to the museum," he explained. "And as his personal assistants, Mr. Colton and I have accompanied him for an after-hours walkthrough of the facilities. We were assured that a man of his stature would be granted access without the usual red tape."

The guard frowned. "Huh. I haven't received any orders about that…"

"Oh, well, of course not," Jedidiah continued smoothly, adjusting his vest. "Arrangements were made at the highest level. Discretion is key, you see. Imagine the chaos if the public knew the great Mark Twain was considering such a philanthropic gesture!"

The guard hesitated, clearly torn between duty and hero worship.

Jedidiah leaned in conspiratorially. "Tell you what. You seem like a fine, upstanding gentleman. I can trust you, can't I?"

The guard straightened immediately. "Of course, sir!"

"Splendid," Jedidiah said. "Then I shall personally ensure that museum leadership is made aware of your cooperation tonight. In the meantime, I need you to do me a huge favor."

"Anything, sir!" The guard practically vibrated with excitement.

"This visit must remain strictly confidential." Jedidiah's voice dropped to a hush. "If word got out, Mr. Twain's generosity might be taken advantage of. Do you understand?"

The guard nodded solemnly. "Say no more, sir. Mum's the word."

Phineas sighed, rubbing his temple. "This is absurd."

The guard beamed. "Oh, I always knew you had that sharp wit, Mr. Twain! Just like in your books!"

Matthew clapped a hand over his mouth to keep from laughing.

"Yes, yes, brilliant wit," Jedidiah said, ushering them forward. "Now, if you'll excuse us, we have a very important tour to complete."

The guard stepped aside immediately, giving a deep bow. "Of course! Please, take all the time you need, sir."

As they hurried past, Phineas muttered under his breath, "I despise you both."

"That's the spirit, Mr. Twain," Matthew teased.

Jedidiah smirked, adjusting his hat as they disappeared into the museum's lower halls. "Don't complain—after all, we're giving you plenty of inspiration for your next book."

"I'm not—" Professor Hargroves cut himself off, realizing how loud he was getting. Instead, he shook his head and gestured for them to keep moving.

Minutes later, they reached a heavy wooden door marked "Archives" on a brass plaque. Phineas tried the knob, but it didn't budge.

The older man crouched in front of the door, running his fingers over the keyhole. "Standard issue. Not even reinforced," he muttered, almost disappointed.

"Now's not the time to criticize its design," Matthew groaned. "Can you open it?"

Phineas grinned as he pulled out a small leather pouch of his own. "This is child's play. I'll need... about three seconds."

Matthew shook his head, turning to keep watch down the dimly lit corridor. "Just don't start monologuing about the art of lock-picking."

"My dear boy," Phineas said as he inserted his tools into the keyhole, his hands moving with deft precision, "a proper lock should offer resistance, make you sweat a little. This? It's practically inviting me in."

A click echoed through the hall almost

immediately. Phineas stood, pocketing his tools with a flourish. "There. Simple and efficient."

Jedidiah gave a nod of approval as he pushed the door open. "Let's hope the rest of this is just as open and inviting."

'Matthew smirked as they stepped inside. "I don't know what's more concerning—how fast you picked that or how much you enjoyed it."

Phineas gave a sheepish grin. "I, my dear boy, am a professional."

Just beyond the doorway was a narrow staircase that descended into more darkness. Jedidiah led the way, lantern in hand, its flickering glow casting shifting shadows against rough-hewn stone walls. Faint scratches marked the edges—evidence of time and history. With each step, the air grew cooler and heavier, carrying the damp, earthy scent of stone and mildew.

After descending several flights, their footsteps echoed into a vast, dimly lit expanse—the lowest level of the museum's underground chambers. The space stretched wider than they had anticipated, its corners swallowed in darkness, filled with forgotten relics and the weight of centuries.

Phineas glanced over his shoulder. "It's astonishing... Think about how many layers of history we're walking under. You think they even realize all the secrets buried here?"

Matthew tightened his grip on his ray gun, his

sharp gaze sweeping the shadows. "I'm more concerned about not becoming one of those secrets buried here."

As they entered, the oppressive silence was broken only by the distant drip... drip... of water echoing through the cavernous corridor. Dust motes swirled lazily in the lantern's glow, disturbed by their movement. Wooden crates lined the walls, some marked with faded shipping labels, others with no markings at all. Ancient sculptures and relics rested haphazardly, their forms partially obscured by cobwebs.

"Oil lamps," Jedidiah murmured, pointing to a series of sconces affixed to the walls. "Phineas, help me light them."

Jedidiah passed his lantern to Matthew as he and Phineas worked methodically, striking matches to bring the lamps to life. One by one, the flames flickered, casting a warm, golden glow. The room stretched further than they had initially realized.

Matthew stood near the center, his sharp gaze sweeping the gloom. Suddenly, his voice cut through the quiet. "Jed! Professor Hargroves! Over here! Quickly!"

The urgency in his tone made both men freeze for a moment before rushing toward him. Matthew's lantern illuminated a towering shape, most of it hidden beneath a heavy, dust-covered cloth. The faint outline beneath hinted at something massive, intricate... and intentional.

Matthew hesitated, his fingers curling around the edge of the fabric.

The dust beneath his touch felt like the weight of time itself—a relic undisturbed for who knew how long. He exhaled, steadying himself as a sense of anticipation and reverence settled over them.

With a sharp pull, the cloth slid away.

The sound of it falling to the ground barely registered as his gaze locked on the massive statue before them.

An imposing twelve-foot-tall octopus on a giant pedestal loomed before them, its presence both commanding and surreal. Each tentacle curled with lifelike precision, as though frozen mid-motion. A brass top hat gleamed atop its head, perfectly polished despite the years spent in concealment. A monocle rested over one unblinking eye, the glass catching a flicker of reflected light.

And in front of it, perched with regal poise on a polished metal pole—a falcon.

It, too, wore a brass top hat and monocle, its gaze sharp and piercing.

The three men stood motionless, the weight of history pressing down on them.

Jedidiah exhaled sharply, breaking the silence. His voice was barely above a whisper.

"The symbol of the Secret Order of the Clockwork Octopus."

Matthew pulled the cloth away
revealing an imposing twelve-foot-tall
octopus on a giant pedestal.

CHAPTER XXIII

The Guardians of the Relic

Phineas B. Hargroves' jaw dropped, his gaze locked onto the ornate metal sculpture.

"Incredible... absolutely magnificent!"

Matthew Colton's brow furrowed as he stepped closer, studying the intricate details. "Look at that octopus—it's the same one from Lady Seraphina's letterhead. And the falcon..." He pointed to the polished metal bird perched on the pole in front of the octopus. "It's a lot like the statue you received when you won the Sky Race, Jed. Don't tell me that's a coincidence."

Jedidiah Davenport took a cautious step forward, his lantern casting shifting shadows over the gleaming surface of the sculpture. "This is definitely a sign. The entrance must be nearby." His lips pressed into a thin line as his gaze moved between the octopus and the falcon.

Phineas leaned closer, examining one of the

curling tentacles. His voice brimmed with excitement. "Perhaps one of these opens a secret passage." Without hesitation, he began tugging on the nearest one.

The other two quickly joined in, each testing a different tentacle. But no matter how hard they pulled or twisted, none of them budged.

Frustrated, Jedidiah turned away from the statue, letting his eyes wander. The golden glow of the oil lamps illuminated more of the room now, revealing details that had been hidden in shadow.

Then—he noticed the floor.

"Wait a second..." Jedidiah muttered, crouching down.

The area surrounding the statue wasn't solid stone like the rest of the room. Instead, it was divided into a grid of square panels, each one bearing faintly etched numbers.

Matthew said, stepping closer. "What do they mean?"

Jedidiah reached into his shirt pocket and pulled out a familiar scrap of paper. His heart quickened as he unfolded it—the torn note with the mysterious sequence that had been dropped during the party at the ranch. At the time, the numbers had seemed random, meaningless.

But now... they suddenly felt important.

"Phineas, take a look at this," Jedidiah said, handing over the paper.

The eccentric older man examined the note, his brow furrowing in concentration. His gaze flicked between the paper and the numbered panels on the floor.

His voice was quiet but certain.

"These numbers aren't random... they're a sequence. It's a puzzle."

"A puzzle?" Matthew asked, incredulous.

Phineas' expression brightened, his enthusiasm returning. "Yes! These panels must be pressure plates, and we have to step on them in the correct order to activate something—likely the entrance!"

Matthew's eyes narrowed as he studied the floor. "Wait, what if we get the sequence wrong...?"

Phineas' grin faltered slightly. "Well, it's probably best not to find out."

Matthew rolled his eyes. "Because it's obviously booby-trapped, isn't it?"

Phineas ignored the remark and knelt by the first numbered panel indicated on the note. "It starts here." He gestured for Jedidiah and Matthew to stay back. "If I'm right, the first person must stand on the first tile until after the second tile is locked into place—then that person can move to the third tile. However, one misstep could... complicate things."

"Well, that's encouraging..." Matthew groaned.

Phineas' gaze darted between the paper and the

numbered panels, his excitement growing as he stood and took charge. "Jed, start here," he instructed, pointing to the first tile.

Jedidiah hesitated for a moment, then stepped onto the indicated tile. The panel sank slightly with a muted click. He glanced back at Phineas, his brow furrowed.

"Good, good," Phineas said, his voice brimming with enthusiasm. "Now, Matthew, the next one is yours." He pointed to a panel diagonally to the left.

Matthew stepped forward, his boot landing carefully on the tile. Click. The floor beneath him dipped ever so slightly.

"Excellent!" Phineas said, scanning the numbers again. "Now, Jedidiah, move to this one—"

Before he could finish, Matthew shifted his weight slightly, his foot sliding an inch off the tile, pressing down on the one next to it.

A low, distant rumble vibrated beneath their feet.

Phineas let out a startled yelp, scrambling back instinctively. "STOP MOVING!"

Matthew froze, wide-eyed. The rumbling faded as he readjusted his position.

A beat of silence.

Phineas shot him a look of pure exasperation, his face pale. "Please be careful! Do you want to bring this whole place down on our heads?"

Matthew exhaled sharply, making sure not to

move at all. "Right. No pressure, then."

Jedidiah shot him a warning look. "Just don't move unless Phineas says to."

Matthew lifted both hands. "Noted."

Phineas took a breath, returning his focus to the sequence. His voice remained steady despite the tension. "As I was saying… Jed, the next step is yours—there."

Jedidiah nodded and shifted to the next tile as instructed. Click. Another faint sound echoed through the room.

"Matthew, over there." Phineas pointed to another tile.

The dark-haired young man followed the instruction, his movements precise. Again, the panel sank with a reassuring click.

The process repeated several times, with Phineas directing Jedidiah and Matthew to alternate stepping on the numbered panels. Each click brought a new wave of anticipation, the silence amplifying every sound.

Finally, only one tile remained. Phineas set the note aside. "Well, gentlemen, this is it."

He stepped forward, planting his foot on the final panel.

For a moment, nothing happened.

Then—a series of loud clicks echoed through the room, followed by the unmistakable sound of gears turning beneath them. The floor trembled slightly.

The massive statue began to move.

Slowly and with a metallic groan, it slid backward along hidden tracks, revealing a narrow staircase spiraling down into darkness.

Phineas' eyes widened, his voice barely above a whisper. "A staircase... leading even further down."

Jedidiah picked up his lantern and peered into the revealed passage. "This has to be the entrance to the hidden headquarters."

Matthew exhaled sharply, his grip tightening on the ray gun strapped to his side. "Let's hope we're not too late."

The staircase spiraled downward, the air growing colder with every step. Phineas noticed a few torches along the walls and lit them as they went, their flickering flames casting eerie shadows on the rough stone.

"This just keeps getting better," Matthew muttered. "There's no telling where this is gonna lead us."

At the base of the stairs, they found themselves in a long, narrow hallway. The walls were lined with intricate engravings of mechanical tentacles and gears, their designs so detailed they seemed almost alive in the dim light.

At the end of the corridor stood a solid wooden door, its dark surface framed by the aged stone archway. The door featured eight recessed panels, their edges softened by time and wear. At its center, a striking octopus-shaped brass knocker gleamed, its sculpted tentacles curling around a heavy ring, giving it an almost lifelike presence. Just below, a brass tentacle-shaped handle twisted elegantly, as if frozen mid-motion, its polished surface catching the dim light. The craftsmanship mirrored the eerie precision of the statue they had encountered earlier, evoking a sense of something both ancient and unnervingly sentient.

Phineas was the first to speak. "Well, my dear boys," he gestured toward the knocker, "shall we announce ourselves?"

Matthew rolled his eyes. "Because knocking on the door at the end of a dark tunnel, multiple floors underground, sounds like a great idea."

Jedidiah stepped forward, placing a firm hand on the brass tentacle handle. "We're not knocking," he said flatly, his voice carrying a weight of authority. His expression remained tense as he added, "We don't know what—or who—might be on the other side."

He tested the handle, twisting it gently. It turned with a soft creak, the sound echoing faintly in the otherwise silent hallway.

"It's unlocked," Jedidiah whispered, glancing back at the others.

Phineas grinned nervously. "And blindly

At the end of the corridor stood a
solid wooden door, its dark surface
framed by the aged stone archway.

marching through unlocked doors is such a better plan."

"Maybe we can at least surprise whoever's in there," Matthew said, adjusting the goggles perched on the brim of his hat. "Or we can just hope that nobody is."

Jedidiah pushed the door open slowly, the hinges groaning slightly. The light from his lantern spilled into the space beyond, revealing what lay ahead.

A massive underground sanctuary that seemed to hum with an invisible energy.

Jedidiah stepped inside cautiously, his lantern casting flickering light across walls of polished brass and dark wood. The chamber stretched far beyond their initial expectations, its arched ceiling supported by ornate metal beams engraved with mechanical tentacles.

"This..." Phineas' voice trailed off as he stepped past Jedidiah, his gaze roaming the space. His excitement was momentarily eclipsed by awe. "This is extraordinary."

The room was a masterpiece of both design and purpose. Along the walls, rows of brass shelving units held leather-bound tomes, rolled-up schematics, and peculiar devices whose functions were as enigmatic as their construction. Glass display cases housed artifacts—ancient tools, gleaming gear mechanisms, and what appeared to be fragments of clockwork automatons.

At the center of the room stood a circular brass table, its surface inlaid with a detailed map of the world. Tiny gears embedded in the map clicked faintly, suggesting the table wasn't merely decorative—it was functional. A series of levers and dials surrounded its edge, awaiting activation.

Above the table, a massive chandelier hung— shaped like the octopus motif they had seen repeatedly. Its brass tentacles stretched outward, each one ending in a glass globe that glowed faintly, casting warm light throughout the space.

"Look at this," Matthew said, nodding toward a row of lockers built into the far wall. Each bore a different symbol—an octopus, a falcon, a gear, a key, and a clock—but they were locked with intricate mechanisms. "These must belong to members of the Order."

Phineas approached a nearby desk, its surface cluttered with handwritten notes, faded blueprints, and diagrams drawn with meticulous precision. He picked up one of the papers, holding it close to the lantern. His expression shifted from curiosity to alarm.

"Schematics for more mechanical men..." he murmured, turning the page to reveal another intricately detailed diagram. His eyes widened as he scanned the annotations. "No, wait—these aren't simple service automatons. These are heavily weaponized!"

Matthew stepped closer, peering over Phineas' shoulder. "Weaponized?"

Jedidiah frowned, his gaze moving from the diagram to the rest of the room. "Why would the Order need to build anything like that?"

"Perhaps to help safeguard the relic," Phineas suggested.

He set the blueprints back on the desk, his fascination giving way to unease. "Either way, I don't like the idea of machines having built-in weaponry."

Matthew, who had started scanning the room for anything suspicious, stopped abruptly.

"Hey… over there," he said, gesturing toward the far end of the chamber.

Jedidiah raised his lantern, revealing a plain, unassuming door set into the wall. Unlike the ornate surroundings, this door was utilitarian, almost forgotten amidst the grandeur. He exchanged a look with the others before stepping forward.

"Let's see what's behind it."

The door creaked open, revealing a long, narrow hallway lit by faint, flickering gas lamps.

As they ventured deeper, the hallway opened into a space lined with iron-barred holding cells.

"Prison cells?" Phineas muttered, his voice barely above a whisper.

The first cell held a gaunt, sharp-featured man sitting upright on the floor. His disheveled clothing hinted at a once-proud demeanor, but now his gaze was hollow and tired.

Jedidiah's lantern fell fully on him, and the man stirred, squinting against the light.

"Davenport?" The voice was weak but unmistakable.

"Montgomery?" Jedidiah stepped closer, gripping the bars. "What are you doing here?"

Professor Thaddeus Montgomery pushed himself upright with some effort, his normally commanding presence diminished but not extinguished. "It's a long story," he said hoarsely. "And for once, I'm actually glad to see you."

"Who locked you up?" Matthew asked warily, his hand hovering near his ray gun.

Montgomery merely shrugged. "I haven't the foggiest clue," he said darkly. "One minute, I was sitting behind bars in prison, the next, I woke up here in one of the Order's holding cells."

Jedidiah's brow furrowed as he absorbed Montgomery's words. "And you have no idea how you got here?"

Montgomery nodded weakly. "I've been a member for years, but I never thought I'd end up a prisoner here."

Jedidiah lifted his lantern higher, casting its glow down the row of cells. "We need more answers than that."

As Jedidiah moved, the lantern's glow spilled into the second cell. A figure stepped forward, his silhouette cast long against the stone wall. He moved with calculated precision as if even his captivity was on his own terms.

Then, he chuckled softly, his voice smooth and reassuring. His calm, piercing eyes studied them with measured intensity, though his expression remained warm and inviting.

Matthew muttered under his breath, his grip tightening around the handle of his ray gun.

The captive's face was now fully visible in the flickering light. He smiled faintly, his voice carrying an air of effortless charm.

"I assure you, I'm not as intimidating as I might appear. Please, there's no need for hostility."

Phineas stepped forward, his curiosity evident. "And who might you be?" he asked, his tone tentative but open.

The man smiled faintly, nodding in acknowledgment. "Lord Ignatius Gearsoul. A pleasure to meet you, though I wish it were under better circumstances."

Jedidiah's lantern moved again, revealing the next cell. Inside stood a woman with sharp, calculating eyes. She leaned casually against the bars, her posture exuding both grace and defiance. Though her clothing was slightly worn, the cut and fabric spoke of refined taste.

When the light caught her face, a sly smile curved her lips.

"Well, well," she said smoothly, her voice dripping with charm. "Visitors. How unexpected— and delightful."

Matthew instinctively took a step back, his instincts screaming caution. "Who are you?" he demanded.

She tilted her head, studying him with a mix of amusement and intrigue. "Names are such powerful things. Best not to give them away too freely."

Phineas frowned, his keen eyes narrowing. "You're hiding something," he said, his tone measured but firm.

The woman chuckled softly, a sound both disarming and unsettling. "Oh, darling," she purred, her voice like silk. "Aren't we all?"

Jedidiah stepped forward, his expression unreadable as he held her gaze. "All secrets eventually come to light."

Then, turning to his friends, he said, "Let's leave the Baroness to her thoughts for now."

"Evelina Frost!" Phineas B. Hargroves suddenly shouted in recognition.

The sly smile faltered for just a moment before she recovered, her eyes narrowing slightly. "You're even more clever than I thought."

Jedidiah shook his head and moved the lantern

to the fourth cell. A man with a gaunt face and sharp eyes stood there, his hands clasped behind his back. He regarded them with detached curiosity, as though they were specimens under his examination.

"Another one," Matthew muttered, his grip on the ray gun tightening. "And he's just as unsettling as the others."

The man gave a faint smile, but it didn't reach his eyes. "Unsettling?" he repeated, his voice soft but carrying a calculated precision. "I suppose that is one way to describe a man of science."

Phineas stepped slightly closer. "A man of science, you say? And what, pray tell, is your field of expertise?"

The prisoner inclined his head slightly, as though pleased by the question. "Doctor Leopold Van der Meer," he introduced himself with a calm, measured tone. "My work involves the integration of mechanical precision with biological imperfection—cybernetics if you will."

Jedidiah frowned. "Cybernetics? That sounds... advanced."

Van der Meer's smile widened just slightly. "The human body is a remarkable machine, Mr. Davenport. My work merely aims to improve it. Weaknesses can be eliminated. Limitations transcended."

"By turning people into machines?" Matthew asked sharply, his distrust evident.

The doctor tilted his head, his gaze sliding to Matthew. "Not machines, young man. Perfection. Flesh and blood, enhanced and made stronger by the wonders of engineering. It's a dream come true for most!"

"Sounds like a nightmare to me," Matthew retorted.

Van der Meer chuckled, a low, unsettling sound. "To the uninitiated, perhaps. But progress often frightens those who do not understand it. Besides, some—like the Clockwork Conqueror—have already benefited from some of my scientific breakthroughs."

"His mechanical arm!" Jedidiah exclaimed. "You're the one who built it?"

Van der Meer's smirk deepened. "Ah, so you've encountered him?"

"Only by reputation," Professor Hargroves interjected, stepping forward.

Jedidiah's voice cut through the growing tension. "Do any of you know how you got here?"

"None of us do," Van der Meer replied, his faint smile faltering for just a moment before returning. "However, we obviously know why."

Montgomery interjected, his tone heavy with frustration. "One by one, we were taken."

"And now we're all here," Baroness Evelina Frost added, her voice laced with a mix of sarcasm and unease. Her sharp eyes darted toward Jedidiah as if weighing his role in their predicament.

Lord Ignatius Gearsoul stepped into the faint light spilling from Jedidiah's lantern, his voice deliberate and calm. "All of us... except Lady Seraphina Blackwood."

Jedidiah Davenport stood lost in thought. The reminder of Lady Seraphina's absence gnawed at him.

"So you think she's the one behind this?" Matthew asked, confusion evident in his voice. "That would explain why she's so vague and mysterious."

Phineas frowned, his tone laced with irritation. "Lady Seraphina would do no such thing! She's been on the run this entire time, keeping one step ahead of the real scoundrel!"

Doctor Leopold Van der Meer chuckled darkly, his voice cutting through the heated exchange like a scalpel. "I, for one, don't suspect her. The true mastermind behind this is obviously the Clockwork Conqueror," he said with cold certainty. "Wouldn't you agree, Ignatius?"

Gearsoul scoffed. "I think you give that petty thief more credit than he deserves."

Before anyone else could respond, a familiar scent wafted through the hall—lavender and wood smoke.

Jedidiah crinkled his nose, sniffing the air. His instincts flared. Immediately, he whirled around, raising his lantern.

Leaning casually against the iron bars of an empty cell stood Lady Seraphina Blackwood—her usual composure intact, her piercing gaze scanning the room as she suddenly made her presence known.

A voice, smooth and unbothered, echoed through the chamber.

"Someone call my name?"

CHAPTER XXIV

The Final Piece

The unmistakable fragrance of lavender and wood smoke was now stronger than ever.

Phineas and Matthew froze, their eyes widening as the familiar figure stepped into the light—her usual calm demeanor intact, yet her piercing gaze swept over the room with quiet authority.

A heavy silence filled the chamber.

Phineas was the first to recover, his mouth opening—then closing again—as if debating whether to demand an explanation or simply gasp. Instead, he blurted out, "How—?! When—?! We didn't even hear you come in!"

Matthew took an instinctive step back. "You weren't here a minute ago."

Jedidiah narrowed his eyes. "How long have you been standing there?"

Seraphina's lips curved slightly, her posture relaxed, yet her eyes glinted with something unreadable.

"Long enough."

Montgomery let out an exasperated sigh, shaking his head. "Typical. The woman vanishes when it's convenient, then materializes just in time to keep us all guessing."

Van der Meer gave a thoughtful hum. "Fascinating... You were the only one of us to remain uncaptured. Which begs the question—how did you achieve this?"

Lord Ignatius Gearsoul, standing eerily still in his cell, regarded her with measured interest. His expression betrayed nothing, but his eyes flickered with calculation.

Seraphina ignored them all and turned to Jedidiah, Phineas, and Matthew.

"The three of you looked like you could use some help."

Jedidiah crossed his arms, his voice steady but wary. "And what exactly are you helping with?"

Seraphina arched a single brow. "Isn't it obvious? Whoever orchestrated this little gathering is close to obtaining the relic. That means time is about to run out."

The Baroness' melodic voice chimed in from her cell, cutting through the tension.

"Fascinating as this debate is, the fact remains —we're all in here, and the four of you are out there."

The other prisoners, as if on cue, turned their collective gaze to the quartet.

"You need to release us. Immediately," Montgomery declared.

"Absolutely not," Lady Seraphina Blackwood interjected sharply, stepping forward. "Leaving them locked up is the only way to ensure they don't interfere. We don't know who can be trusted, and we don't have time to find out."

Montgomery scoffed. "How convenient. You waltz in at the last second, and now you're calling the shots?"

Van der Meer's eyes narrowed. "She was the only one who didn't get locked up. That alone should make you question her loyalties."

"If I were working against you," Seraphina said coolly, "I wouldn't be standing here now. I would have the relic in my hands and be somewhere else... anywhere else in space and time!"

She turned to Jedidiah, her expression unwavering. "If we release them, we lose our advantage. You know that."

Jedidiah hesitated, scanning the faces of the prisoners. Van der Meer looked ready to lunge at the bars. The Baroness simply smiled, as if she were enjoying the exchange. Even Montgomery, normally composed, seemed tense.

Phineas nodded quickly. "She's right. We can't risk it. We've got enough trouble on our hands already."

Jedidiah crossed his arms, studying each prisoner in turn. "Releasing any of you isn't high on my priority list. I don't trust anyone here—especially not you, Professor Montgomery."

Van der Meer's eyes glinted dangerously. "You can't just leave us like this!"

Jedidiah exchanged a glance with Matthew and Phineas, the weight of their unspoken decision clear in their expressions.

Lady Blackwood broke the silence, her voice calm and steady. "We need to secure Montgomery's piece of the relic and stow it with mine."

She paused, looking directly at Jedidiah. "You do have my part of the device with you, don't you?"

The young entrepreneur reached inside his coat and lifted the item in question. A chain hung around his neck, the metal object glinting in the lantern light.

"We need to get both of these pieces far away from here. Once that's done, we'll send someone back to deal with the rest of you."

Phineas, still standing a little too close to Seraphina, shot her a quick glance before turning to Jedidiah. "See? She's been trying to help us from the start! Honestly, I don't know why any of you would ever doubt her."

Montgomery's face twisted in frustration. "You think you can handle this without us? The relic is far too powerful. Whoever is behind this already has three of the five artifacts."

His sharp gaze flicked to Seraphina. "And yet, somehow, you managed to stay out of harm's way while the rest of us were imprisoned here. How convenient."

"Because unlike you," Seraphina said smoothly, "I don't make a habit of getting caught."

"Or maybe," Montgomery countered, "you were never meant to be a prisoner at all."

Jedidiah ignored the protests from the cells and stepped toward the doorway. "That's why we're making sure they don't get their hands on the remaining two."

He reached for the artifact hanging from the chain around his neck, its amber-colored stone shimmering against the green metal wheel wrapped in copper.

"Professor Montgomery," he added, "would you be so kind as to tell us the location of your part of the relic?"

Montgomery leaned against the bars, a smirk tugging at his lips. "It's hidden in my private chamber, through a secret passage that only I know exists. It's secured inside a Porcupine Vault."

"A what?" Matthew asked, crossing his arms.

"A clever little trap," Montgomery explained. "The spikes appear harmless, but try to withdraw your hand without disarming it, and they'll latch on and dig deep. The glyphs engraved along the base contain instructions on how to disarm it. But good luck deciphering them without me."

Phineas' expression tightened. "And you've kept this here the entire time?"

Montgomery shrugged. "Better than keeping it on display upstairs in the museum where anyone could steal it." He leaned against the bars and shot a glance toward Lord Ignatius Gearsoul.

Jedidiah stepped closer, his voice firm. "We're retrieving it."

The Baroness chuckled from her cell. "You think you'll succeed without us? Bold."

"We'll manage," Jedidiah said, already moving toward the door.

"Good," Seraphina said, stepping beside him. "I'll stay here and keep an eye on the others."

Matthew frowned. "You enjoy being one step ahead of everyone, don't you?"

"Believe what you want," Seraphina replied. "But I'm not the one you should be worried about right now."

As they walked away, Montgomery called after them, his voice laced with warning.

"That vault isn't a toy, Davenport. You'll need me if you don't want blood on your hands."

Jedidiah glanced back briefly. "Then let's hope we're as clever as you think you are."

Matthew smirked over his shoulder. "Don't go

anywhere."

As the trio made their way back through the hallway of cells, Jedidiah's lantern flickered against the iron bars of another cell. Inside stood three men, their postures tense and watchful.

A low whistle cut through the silence, drawing their attention.

"Well, well," came a familiar, mocking voice. A man stepped into the lantern's glow, his face twisting into a sly grin. "If it isn't the famous airship captains. Been a while, hasn't it?"

Phineas froze mid-step, his eyes narrowing as he processed the voice. Matthew's hand instinctively moved to the ray gun at his side.

The man leaned casually against the bars, his gaze flicking from Jedidiah to Matthew and then to Phineas. "You look good, Professor. Still sore about that little hotel misunderstanding?"

"Dawson!" Phineas' glare darkened. "You're the one that ambushed me not once but twice!"

"And you lived to tell the tale," the hardened criminal retorted with a shrug. "I'd say that's a win."

Briggs, the lean, sharp-eyed man standing behind him, stepped forward. "Careful, Dawson. You don't want to scare these good folks who had us put behind bars," he said dryly, though his calculating gaze lingered on Jedidiah.

"You two again?" Matthew asked, his tone

sharp. "Can't we ever get rid of you?"

Briggs smiled his tone even. "We're never going to be completely out of your story. Not even prison can hold us."

"You do realize you're behind bars right now, don't you?" Phineas asked ironically.

Jedidiah shifted his lantern to reveal the third man standing slightly apart from the others. Unlike Dawson's bravado and Briggs' quiet menace, this one exuded an unsettling calm. He inclined his head slightly, his voice smooth and deliberate.

"Carter's the name." He introduced himself. "I'm sure you remember my handiwork sabotaging the airships in the race."

Jedidiah's jaw tightened. "How could I ever forget?"

Carter smirked faintly. "Now, how about letting the three of us out—for old time's sake?"

"Enough," Jedidiah cut in, his tone firm. "Whatever history we have, it ends here. You're staying put."

Dawson grinned, his expression daring. "You think locking us up solves your problems? Don't forget, Davenport—things have a way of turning around."

Phineas scoffed, giving Dawson a scathing glare before turning to leave.

The trio moved down the hallway, the gang's murmured arguments fading into the distance.

Jedidiah's lantern swung gently in his hand, its light casting flickering shadows on the stone walls as the three exchanged tense glances.

****

The trio emerged from the hallway of cells into the expansive main room. The flickering lantern light caught on the intricate brass details of the walls and the towering chandelier above, giving the space an eerie sense of life.

Phineas, his usual bravado somewhat subdued, scanned the room. His gaze settled on a series of doors set into the far wall, each bearing a polished brass plate etched with a name.

Jedidiah stepped closer, lifting the lantern to get a better look. "Montgomery," he read aloud, his voice echoing in the quiet chamber. "Looks like this is where we start."

Phineas glanced at the other plates, noting the names of the other prisoners. "Each of them has their own private room. Must've been a perk of membership."

Matthew folded his arms, his tone dry. "Fancy prison cells and private rooms. This Order really knew how to do things in style."

Jedidiah ignored the remark and pushed the door to Montgomery's chamber open. The hinges groaned slightly, and the air inside was cool and stale. The room was exactly what they'd expect from the eccentric professor—an organized chaos of books, schematics, and tools strewn across a heavy wooden desk. A large, imposing wardrobe sat against one wall, while a brass bed frame with neatly folded blankets occupied the other.

Matthew moved toward the far corner, where a tall bookshelf loomed, its contents spilling onto the floor. "If there's a hidden passage, it's got to be behind something like this."

Jedidiah knelt near the floor, inspecting the baseboards for anything unusual. His fingers traced along the wood until they caught on something—a faint seam where two panels met.

"Here," he said, beckoning the others over. "There's a hidden panel."

Phineas crouched beside him, his eyes lighting up with excitement. "Clever. Let's see if it opens."

Jedidiah pressed along the seam, feeling for a mechanism. After a moment, there was a soft click, and the panel slid inward, revealing a narrow tunnel carved into the stone.

"There it is," Matthew said, his voice tense but impressed. "Montgomery's secret passage."

Jedidiah held the lantern aloft, the light casting long shadows down the dark corridor. "Let's move. The relic won't wait forever."

****

The passage was tight, the walls damp and rough-hewn. It sloped downward slightly, the air growing colder with every step. Phineas trailed his fingers along the wall, murmuring softly about the ingenuity of such a hidden design.

After a few minutes, the passage opened into a small chamber. The walls were bare stone, save for one section where a large, unique vault was embedded. Its bronze spikes gleamed ominously in the lantern light.

"Montgomery wasn't kidding about this thing," Matthew muttered, eyeing the prongs. "That doesn't look inviting in the least."

Jedidiah approached cautiously, his gaze settling on the faint etchings at the base of the vault. "These must be the instructions for disarming it."

Phineas squinted at the symbols, muttering under his breath. "Ancient glyphs… not exactly my area of expertise."

Matthew crossed his arms. "Montgomery said we'd need to follow these instructions. Think he was bluffing?"

Jedidiah shook his head. "Not likely. But we're not going back to get him."

Phineas studied the engravings, his expression shifting from uncertainty to determination. "Give me a moment. I might not speak 'ancient rock-scratch,' but I can figure out any mechanism I run across."

Matthew Colton wasn't known for his patience. While Phineas muttered over the drawings, his brows furrowed in concentration as he stepped closer to the vault.

"We don't have time for this," Matthew whispered, eyeing the spikes. With a quick glance at Phineas to ensure he wasn't looking, he slipped his hand between the sharp bronze points. His fingers brushed against something solid—a small chest.

At first, the spikes didn't interfere with his movements. But as he began to pull back—

Pain shot through his arm.

The spikes dug into the back of his hand.

"Holy smokes!" Matthew hissed under his breath, freezing in place.

His breath caught as he felt the sharp points press deeper.

Gritting his teeth, he assessed the situation. Carefully sliding his trapped hand forward, he felt the spikes loosen their grip. With his other hand, he pressed them inward from a higher angle. His fingers closed around the chest, and with a sharp tug, he yanked it free from the vault.

Matthew stumbled back, cradling the chest triumphantly. "Got it!"

Phineas turned abruptly, startled. "Got what?" He narrowed his eyes. "Do you mind keeping it down while I attempt to decipher this?"

"No need," Matthew interrupted with a grin, cradling the small chest in his arms. "I've already got it."

Phineas' face turned a shade paler, then deepened to red. "You reckless fool!" he snapped. "Do you realize what could've happened? You could've lost your hand—or worse!"

"Lost my hand?" Matthew gulped. "Or worse?"

Jedidiah stepped closer, his expression a mix of exasperation and relief. "This is it. Montgomery's piece of the relic."

Phineas, still fuming, inspected the chest and immediately noticed the polished brass dial on its face. His irritation gave way to fresh exasperation.

"And of course, it has a combination lock," he said, throwing his arms up.

Jedidiah sighed, taking the chest from Matthew. The brass dial was adorned with engraved numbers, each meticulously etched.

"We're not getting anything out of this without the combination," he said flatly.

"Which means…" Phineas trailed off, his tone dripping with annoyance.

Jedidiah nodded grimly. "We're going back to Montgomery."

****

The trio retraced their steps through the secret passage and into Montgomery's chamber. As they exited back into the main room, the lantern now in Matthew's hands swung in rhythmic arcs, its light bouncing off the brass plates of each door.

As they emerged back into the hall, Lady Seraphina was already waiting, arms crossed, watching their return with a keen, expectant gaze.

"That took longer than expected," she remarked, her tone neutral but edged with curiosity. "I assume you found what you were looking for?"

Jedidiah held up the chest, his expression grim. "We have it."

"Good," she replied smoothly. Then, noticing Matthew nursing his hand, she arched a brow. "I see someone couldn't resist the challenge."

Matthew scowled but said nothing as he flexed his fingers.

Seraphina turned toward the cells, her gaze settling on Montgomery with the faintest trace of amusement. "Let me guess. The professor locked it behind an ancient trap, expecting to use it to negotiate his way out."

Montgomery smirked. "You wound me, Lady Blackwood. But you're not wrong."

Jedidiah sighed, holding the chest up. "The combination. Now."

Montgomery leaned casually against the bars, his smirk widening. "I could give it to you, but where's the fun in that? Let me out, and I'll open it for you."

"Not a chance," Jedidiah said firmly.

Seraphina stepped forward, her voice crisp. "Enough games, Montgomery. Do you think stalling will somehow give you the upper hand? The only thing it's doing is wasting our time."

Montgomery's smirk faltered slightly.

She continued, her eyes narrowing. "If you truly understood what was at stake, you'd be helping— not playing your usual self-serving tricks."

Montgomery sighed, eyeing the others. "Fine, fine. I guess you can just figure out the combination yourselves."

Jedidiah scoffed. "We'll just open it the same way we did the last chest!" He lifted it above his head before slamming it onto the stone floor. The chest skidded across the hall, completely unharmed.

Shocked, Matthew picked it up and hurled it down again. The result was the same.

Several more attempts ended in failure.

Then—

A slow, deliberate voice cut through the air.

"Perhaps I can assist."

The group turned sharply toward Lord Ignatius Gearsoul, standing eerily still behind the bars of his cell. His piercing eyes glinted in the dim lantern light.

Phineas shot him a skeptical look. "And why, pray tell, would you help us?"

Gearsoul's tone remained even, almost soothing. "Because the relic belongs to the Order. Whatever quarrels you have with the professor or anyone else here, my concern lies solely in ensuring it is protected."

Jedidiah lifted the chest once more but hesitated, weighing the sincerity in Gearsoul's voice. "And you'd just help us out of the goodness of your heart?"

"Not entirely," Gearsoul admitted with a faint smile. "But I am the only hope you have."

Phineas stepped forward, his hand hovering protectively over the chest. "Nice try, but we're not that gullible."

Gearsoul spread his hands, palms open in a gesture of peace. "You're wasting time debating with Montgomery. Bring the chest closer, and I'll show you what to do."

Jedidiah glanced at Phineas and Matthew, then slowly stepped toward Gearsoul's cell. "If you try anything—"

Before he could finish, the cell door swung open with an ominous creak.

In an instant, Gearsoul's mechanical arm shot out, its polished brass plating gleaming as it wrapped around Jedidiah's wrist with unyielding strength.

"Jed!" Phineas shouted, moving to intervene, but Gearsoul was faster.

With a forceful tug, Gearsoul yanked Jedidiah into the cell and slammed the door shut behind him. The lock clicked into place, sealing them inside together.

Jedidiah stumbled but managed to stay on his feet, his free hand gripping the chest tightly.

Matthew reached for his ray gun, but Gearsoul raised his other hand in a warning gesture. "I wouldn't do that if I were you," he said calmly. "Not unless you want me to harm your friend." His mechanical hand pressed firmly against the back of Jedidiah's neck.

Seraphina shot out a hand, her voice sharp. "Wait!"

The urgency in her tone made him hesitate for half a second—but then he tightened his grip more.

Seraphina's gaze flicked between Gearsoul, Jedidiah, and the chest. "You're making a mistake," she said smoothly. "You're letting your arrogance blind you to forces beyond even your comprehension."

Gearsoul scoffed. "I think I'll be just fine. After all, I orchestrated this entire thing."

Phineas staggered back, his face turning pale as realization dawned. "You're the Clockwork Conqueror!"

Matthew's jaw clenched. "You're the one behind

all this!"

The revelation seemed to unsettle everyone except Van der Meer, who leaned casually against the bars of his cell.

"Well, well," the doctor mused. "I was wondering when you'd reveal yourself, Ignatius."

"Thaddeus," Gearsoul turned his gaze toward the other cell. "The combination. Now!"

Montgomery's smirk returned. "What makes you think I'll give it to you?"

Gearsoul's grip on Jedidiah tightened. "Simple. If you force me to end their friend, I'm sure Professor Hargroves and the other one won't take too kindly to it."

Montgomery sighed, eyeing the others. "Fine, fine. I'll give you the combination." He rattled off the numbers, and Jedidiah quickly turned the brass dial.

With a soft click, the chest unlocked.

The lid creaked open, revealing a gleaming brass piece inside—its delicate etchings shimmering in the dim light.

Phineas inhaled sharply, his voice filled with awe. "It's… remarkable." He took a step closer, transfixed.

Before anyone else could react, Gearsoul's mechanical arm tightened even more around Jedidiah's neck.

The metallic plates hummed faintly, a subtle

reminder of the technology coursing through his augmented body.

"That piece belongs to me," Gearsoul hissed. His voice, now colder and more commanding, sent a chill through the chamber. "As does the one you're wearing," he added coldly.

With his free, flesh-and-blood hand, Gearsoul reached out and seized the chain dangling from Jedidiah's neck.

The sharp snap of breaking links echoed through the chamber as the artifact was ripped away.

"Stop!" Matthew shouted, raising his ray gun— but before he could fire, Gearsoul's mechanical grip tightened.

The artifact gleamed ominously in the dim light —the circular, green metal magneto, its copper wiring coiled around each spindle, and the amber-colored stone at its center reflecting the flickering glow of the lanterns.

Gearsoul held it aloft, his piercing gaze glinting with triumph.

"This," he said, his voice thick with satisfaction, "is what will bring the Chronomechanism to its full potential. With this and the stabilizer both in place, the power of time and space will be mine to command."

From his cell, Van der Meer chuckled, utterly unfazed by the tension.

"A grand performance, Ignatius. Always the dramatist."

Gearsoul ignored him, his attention fixed solely on the relic pieces.

Montgomery stepped forward, slamming his fists against the metal bars. "You don't understand what you're tampering with, Gearsoul! The Chronomechanism isn't just a machine—it's a force beyond comprehension!"

"Exactly," Gearsoul murmured, his tone almost reverent. "And in the right hands, it will reshape the fabric of existence as we know it!"

From another cell, Baroness Evelina Frost grasped the bars, her knuckles white.

"You… can't control it… You'll destroy the world!" She screamed.

"Spare me the warnings," Gearsoul sneered.

With a casual flick of his wrist, he tossed the green metal magneto onto the cot behind him, alongside the artifact retrieved from Montgomery's chest.

Then, his hand moved swiftly to his pillow. With a triumphant smirk, he pulled out the bulk of the Chronomechanism—the intricate brass machine, its surface engraved with gears, dials, and crystalline elements.

Matthew froze, his breath catching. "You had it in there the entire time…"

Phineas' face paled as realization struck. "You

planned everything," he whispered.

Gearsoul's mechanical grip tightened on Jedidiah to the point he was forced to drop to his knees in agony.

With deliberate precision, his other hand slotted the magneto piece into the machine.

The Chronomechanism hummed faintly, gears turning as the stabilizer core was placed into its central slot.

A pulse of energy rippled outward, making the air feel suddenly heavier.

The device glowed brighter, gears whirling faster, their metallic whirr clicking in perfect synchrony.

Behind the clear crystal lens on the front, a silhouette of something resembling an octopus seemed to swirl and shift, as though dancing between dimensions.

Tiny sparks of light flickered between the copper spindles, their glow intensifying.

From his cell, Van der Meer's voice wavered, his earlier smugness gone. "You don't know what you're unleashing, Ignatius! You can't control it!"

Gearsoul's lips curled into a sneer. "Control is for the unimaginative. This is destiny."

The Chronomechanism whirred louder, the glow swelling to an almost blinding brilliance.

The very air in the chamber seemed to distort, warping unnaturally as if the fabric of reality itself was straining against the power surging through the machine.

Then—

With a violent shove, Gearsoul hurled Jedidiah aside.

The young entrepreneur rolled across the stone floor.

"Jed!" Matthew and Phineas shouted in unison, rushing toward the cell door.

The Chronomechanism emitted a deafening crack as reality itself seemed to fracture. The air around Gearsoul shimmered, bending unnaturally as though the very fabric of existence struggled to hold its shape. A low, electric hum filled the chamber, growing into a sharp, ear-piercing whine.

A burst of crackling distortion erupted around him, rippling outward like heat waves rising from a furnace. Gearsoul's silhouette flickered, wavering between moments—there, and yet not there, his form frozen in a ghostly afterimage that lingered unnaturally.

The high-pitched whine of the machine reached an unbearable peak—

And then—

Gearsoul was gone.

A burst of crackling distortion erupted
around him, rippling outward like
heat waves rising from a furnace.

CHAPTER XXV

The Battle for Time and Space

"He vanished!" Matthew Colton shouted, his voice tinged with stunned disbelief.

An unnatural silence followed, broken only by the faint smell of ozone and the lingering hum of the machine as it faded into nothingness. The space where Lord Ignatius had stood pulsed as if reality itself was struggling to adjust to his absence.

Jedidiah stumbled to his feet, his breath hitching as he grasped at empty air—where, just moments before, Gearsoul had been.

The relic—and their only chance to stop him—was gone.

"You let him get away!" Lady Blackwood snapped, her voice sharp with fury. "How could you be so foolish?"

Jedidiah's jaw tightened, but his tone remained even, refusing to rise to Seraphina's accusation.

"We didn't let him do anything. Gearsoul

planned this from the start—he manipulated all of us, including you. If you'd been more forthcoming, perhaps we would've uncovered his identity as the Clockwork Conqueror sooner—and had a real chance to stop him."

"What's done is done." His voice carried a rare, commanding edge. "Standing here pointing fingers won't fix anything."

Jedidiah turned to Lady Blackwood, his patience wearing thin. "Then perhaps it's time you explain exactly what this device—this relic—is truly capable of."

Seraphina's expression faltered just for a moment before she straightened, her voice clipped but clear.

"It should be obvious to you by now." She met Jedidiah's gaze head-on. "The Chronomechanism allows movement not just through time and space, but between parallel universes. It was meant as a tool, but in the wrong hands, it can be used as a weapon—one capable of reshaping reality itself."

Silence.

Matthew blinked, glancing between her and Phineas as if waiting for someone to tell him she was joking.

When no one did, he exhaled sharply.

"Parallel universes?" His voice held a mix of skepticism and unease.

Seraphina nodded, unwavering.

"Yes. Imagine time as a great river. Every choice, every possibility, is like a stream branching off into a new direction. Some are nearly identical to our own, while others could be vastly different—worlds where history took another path, where events played out another way."

She took a step closer, her voice steady but urgent.

"The Chronomechanism doesn't just allow someone to move forward or backward in time—it allows them to step sideways, into a reality where circumstances may be entirely different."

Seraphina turned toward Jedidiah, her voice measured. "For example, imagine a world where you never discovered the oil hidden on your land. Or one where you never met Professor Hargroves, who helped you build your first airship. Maybe, in that reality, you had no choice but to sell your ranch to Elijah Perkins—losing everything in the process. In that world, you're not an airship captain or an inventor. You're just another man, forced out by the changing times. That version of you exists somewhere, just as there are other versions of all of us, shaped by different choices and circumstances."

Jedidiah frowned, arms crossing as he processed her words. "If that's true, wouldn't that mean every possible outcome already exists somewhere? Even ones we haven't considered?"

Seraphina gave a slow nod. "Precisely. The

Chronomechanism doesn't create new realities—it taps into ones that already exist. If someone were to manipulate it recklessly, they could bring knowledge, technology, or even people from those worlds into ours… or worse, erase what was meant to be."

Matthew rubbed the back of his neck, his voice uneasy. "So you're saying there's more than just one world? Other versions of us, living on each of them?"

Jedidiah, normally composed, took a half-step back, his brows furrowing in disbelief. "This is ridiculous. Time travel is already absurd enough, but now you're saying there are alternate realities?"

Phineas adjusted the goggles sitting on top of his head and crossed his arms, his expression shifting from shock to deep thought. "Actually, my dear boy, the concept isn't entirely without merit. Some scientists theorize that every decision creates a branching path, leading to an infinite number of possible realities. But no one has ever been able to prove it."

Matthew stared at him. "And you're just… fine with this? Like it's some minor footnote in a science book?"

Phineas shrugged. "I wouldn't say *fine*—more like *fascinated*."

Jedidiah exhaled, his mind racing. "If this thing can reach other worlds, that means… Gearsoul could have escaped into any one of them... at any point in time." His voice grew grim as the weight of it sank in.

Seraphina gave a sharp nod. "Yes. And if we don't stop him, he may return with forces beyond our imagination."

Professor Hargroves frowned. "I don't mean to question your reasoning, but why are you just now telling us this?"

Seraphina's eyes flashed. "I thought someone of your intellect would be able to figure that out on your own. I certainly didn't think any of you would be reckless enough to let it fall into the hands of the Clockwork Conqueror!"

She pulled out a small handheld device and tapped out a Morse code signal, transmitting wirelessly to her armed guards aboard her ship. "We must get ahead of Ignatius before it's too late."

Jedidiah's voice remained steady. "If this device truly moves through time, space, and alternate universes, how will we ever find him?"

Lady Seraphina's sharp gaze softened slightly, though her frustration was still evident. However, before she could respond, Phineas spoke up, his tone thoughtful.

"If the Chronomechanism is as powerful as you claim, any disruption to the timeline must leave ripples—distortions that could be traced, right?"

Seraphina hesitated, considering his words.

"Theoretically, yes. Such ripples could be detected with the right equipment. But we don't have time to construct such a device."

Jedidiah frowned. "Then how do we find him?"

"We don't. We wait for him to come to us!" Seraphina's lips curved into a faint, grim smile. "I have a feeling I know exactly where he'll return."

Matthew raised an eyebrow. "Where?"

"Where it all began," Seraphina said, her voice laced with certainty. "Octopus Island—a remote place off the coast of Ireland. It was the birthplace of the Order of the Clockwork Octopus and the site where the Chronomechanism was first discovered by its original guardians."

Jedidiah frowned. "Why would Gearsoul go there?"

"Because the island is more than symbolic," Seraphina explained. "It holds the largest known supply of Luminaris Crystals—the rare element that powers the Chronomechanism. Without it, the relic's energy is limited. But with a fresh supply, Gearsoul could extend its capabilities indefinitely."

Phineas' expression darkened. "You're saying he's going there to stockpile the crystals?"

"Exactly," Seraphina confirmed. "The island's mines were sealed decades ago when the Order dismantled the relic, but Gearsoul has the means to reopen them. If he succeeds, he'll have enough crystals to manipulate time and space on a scale we can't begin to comprehend."

A heavy silence followed as the implications sank in.

Jedidiah's gaze sharpened. "So, you're proposing we take the fight to him?"

Lady Blackwood nodded. "Yes. But we can't do it alone. We'll need everyone—Doctor Leopold Van der Meer, Baroness Evelina Frost, Professor Thaddeus Montgomery, and even the three outlaws who aided him. They're all skilled in their own ways, and we'll need every resource available to complete this mission."

Matthew Colton raised an eyebrow. "You want us to trust them? Montgomery sabotaged us in the Sky Race. Van der Meer knew that Gearsoul was the Clockwork Conqueror and said nothing Also, what do we really know about the Baroness?"

Lady Seraphina's gaze hardened. "Trust them? Mr. Colton, I don't expect you to trust any of them. But we need them. Montgomery's intellect, Frost's cunning, Van der Meer's expertise—they're assets, whether we like it or not. As for the three outlaws, we'll keep them in a holding cell aboard my ship until we need them."

Professor Hargroves spoke up, his voice calm but resolute. "Jed, you and Matt are right to question this, but Seraphina's right too. We're out of options, and Gearsoul holds all the cards. If we're going to stop him, we need every advantage we can get."

Matthew muttered under his breath but eventually nodded. "Fine. If Jed says we go, I'll go. But if any of them so much as thinks about double-crossing us—"

"They won't get the chance," Seraphina interjected sharply. "We'll keep them in line."

Matthew Colton turned to his childhood friend, his expression serious. "What do you say, Jed?"

Jedidiah Davenport exhaled, glancing at Phineas B. Hargroves before meeting Matthew's gaze. "I say... we go!"

Matthew scoffed, shaking his head. "I say next time, I don't leave the decision up to you."

Jedidiah smirked. "We'd better start preparing. Let's get everyone aboard the airships and head for Octopus Island!"

****

At ten o'clock, two airships—Davenport's Phoenix and Lady Seraphina's Aetherwind—soared through the skies, their courses set for the Atlantic. Aboard the Aetherwind, the freed Order members were kept under close watch, guarded by two of Seraphina's masked men. Meanwhile, Briggs, Dawson, and Carter remained securely confined in a reinforced cargo hold, two more guards ensuring they stayed put.

Through the darkness, the airships pressed on, engines humming steadily as they crossed the Channel.

By seven o'clock the next morning, Friday, October 28, 1881, the rugged silhouette of Octopus Island emerged from the mist. Jagged cliffs and a shadowy tower loomed ominously above the churning waves.

"Land ho!" Jedidiah called from the helm of the Phoenix.

Matthew Colton, standing beside him, narrowed his eyes at the foreboding sight. "So that's it? That's the birthplace of the Order?"

The airships descended cautiously, their pilots navigating treacherous winds to a small clearing near the island's center. The Phoenix touched down first, followed closely by the Aetherwind. Crews disembarked into the salt-laden air, weapons drawn, scanning the terrain. They met in the middle.

Lady Seraphina Blackwood's sharp voice cut through the roar of the waves. "Take Montgomery below and secure him with his gang. I don't want him causing any trouble."

Her guards nodded and escorted him away. His muffled protests were quickly swallowed by the wind.

Jedidiah frowned. "I thought you said we needed everyone's help to take down the

Clockwork Conqueror?"

Seraphina didn't hesitate. "I've changed my mind about Thaddeus." She turned to another guard. "You—stay with Van der Meer. Make sure he doesn't wander off."

The doctor scowled but didn't protest as a guard stepped closer, weapon ready.

Seraphina's gaze flicked to Baroness Frost. "And you—" she nodded toward another masked man, "watch her closely."

"You don't trust me either?" The Baroness' lips curved into a faint smirk. "Oh, Seraphina. I wouldn't dream of betraying you. But I suppose a little company won't hurt."

Lady Blackwood's stony expression didn't change. "Everyone else—follow me. We need to find Ignatius before he secures the crystals." She picked up a large brown leather satchel that stood out against her solid black outfit and strapped it to her back.

Jedidiah exchanged a knowing glance with Matthew and Phineas, who nodded in silent agreement. Together, they followed Seraphina toward the heart of the island, their boots crunching over uneven terrain. The air was thick with the scent of salt and earth, and the distant cawing of seabirds echoed over the cliffs.

"Strange place for a secret society to originate," Matthew muttered, his hand lingering near his holstered ray gun.

"Secrecy thrives in isolation," Phineas replied, his voice tinged with unease. "And nothing says isolation like an island surrounded by rocky cliffs and icy waters."

Ahead, the jagged cliffs gave way to a dense thicket of twisted trees. Gnarled branches cast eerie shadows, and rusted remnants of ancient mining equipment peeked through the undergrowth.

"These rocks you mentioned..." Jedidiah began to speak but was immediately corrected by Lady Blackwood.

"Luminaris Crystals."

"Yes... those..." Jedidiah shrugged. "Why have I never heard of them?"

"Well, they wouldn't be a secret if everyone knew about them, now would they?"

"I suppose not, but is this the only source of them in the whole world?"

"As far as I know, yes."

Phineas suddenly cleared his throat and spoke up. "I beg your pardon, Lady Blackwood. What about the discovery I read about in the paper near Lake Ontario? Some eccentric professor recently unearthed a peculiar mineral beneath his estate— one with rather unusual properties. If the reports are to be believed, it reacts strangely in the presence of certain metals and emits an energy unlike anything previously documented."

"While similar, they are not the same as—"

Seraphina suddenly halted, raising a hand for silence. She crouched near a fresh set of tracks, her keen eyes narrowing.

"Footprints," she muttered. "Recent. He's already here."

Jedidiah knelt beside her, inspecting the prints. "He's not alone." He pointed to a few larger, heavier tracks.

"Holy smokes!" Matthew frowned. "They look huge!"

Phineas lowered his goggles, inspecting the indentations. "Looks like the ones Cogsworth leaves behind."

Tension thickened as they pressed on. The path opened into a clearing, dominated by the remnants of an old Order outpost—crumbling stone walls and rusted gears, long abandoned. In the center stood a massive, blackened tree, its bark scarred as if scorched by fire.

Seraphina motioned for the group to fan out. "Search the area. If Gearsoul is here, he won't be far."

Jedidiah approached the tree cautiously. The ground beneath his boots felt warm—unnaturally warm. He exchanged a glance with Matthew, who raised his ray gun, poised to fire.

Then—

A low hum emanated from behind another tree,

breaking the silence.

The air rippled as the sound grew louder, resonating deep within their chests.

Jedidiah instinctively tightened his grip on his weapon.

The hum intensified—and from the shadowed mouth of the mine entrance, three massive figures emerged. Three enormous mechanical men.

Each automaton towered over the group, their hulking frames gleaming with polished brass and reinforced steel. Their movements were fluid yet mechanical, their joints whirring with the precision of finely tuned clockwork.

For a moment, no one moved.

Then Matthew exhaled sharply. "Something tells me we've found him."

"My dear boy," Phineas muttered, eyes widening. "I believe you are correct!"

Suddenly, from behind the tree, a figure emerged.

The man who had once pledged himself to protect the relic as a member of the Order was gone. In his place stood the Clockwork Conqueror —his brass mask gleaming. In both hands, he proudly held the fully assembled relic.

As the group closed in, Gearsoul turned two dials on the rear of the Chronomechanism. A low hum filled the air. The ground beneath the tree rippled unnaturally.

Lord Ignatius placed the device gently on the ground. He stood back up and placed both hands inside his long leather coat. Then—from behind the trunk, two more figures emerged.

Each one was nearly identical to Ignatius Gearsoul in every way.

They both wielded strange and devastating weapons, their movements eerily synchronized.

Matthew's voice broke the stunned silence. "Lord Gearsoul has twin brothers?"

"Egads!" Professor Hargroves exclaimed. "My dear boy, those aren't his twin brothers."

"They're alternate versions of himself," Lady Seraphina quickly added, her voice tense. "From parallel Earths."

One of them casually handed over his Tesla rod, while strapping an attached power source to his back. A stunned silence followed, the weight of realization sinking in.

Then—lightning flashed.

The Clockwork Conqueror raised his modified lightning rod, electricity crackling along its length before he unleashed a bolt of searing energy. The battlefield lit up in a blinding flash, the sound echoing through their chests.

Lady Blackwood's armed guards, still clad in their ominous plague doctor attire, stepped forward and shielded her with their bodies.

The lightning struck them directly. Sparks

Then—from behind the trunk,
two more figures emerged.

erupted as they convulsed, electricity coursing through them. Their masks cracked, smoke rising from their scorched uniforms as they collapsed with a heavy thud.

"My word!" Phineas gasped. "Those poor souls!"

Before anyone could react, one of Gearsoul's alternates slammed a spiked mace into the ground.

A shockwave rippled outward.

The ground trembled as the team struggled to regain their footing.

Then came the sound of whirring machinery.

The three towering automatons lurched forward, flanking the three versions of Gearsoul. Their massive brass frames gleamed ominously, their mechanical limbs pumping as they marched ahead —unstoppable, relentless.

Suddenly, Van der Meer hurled a smoke bomb, the explosion shrouding them in a swirling gray mist.

"Spread out!" he barked.

Matthew darted to the side, raised his paralyzing ray gun, and fired at the third Gearsoul.

The beam struck his gear-powered shield— which absorbed the blast with a flicker of deflective energy.

"That's not fair!" Matthew shouted, watching in frustration as his attack had no effect.

Another automaton swung its hammer-like arm

toward him—he barely dodged, rolling out of the way just in time.

Seraphina removed her leather satchel and placed it on the ground next to a large stone. She drew her dual atomic-powered pistols and began firing, forcing the first alternate Gearsoul into a momentary retreat.

Jedidiah aimed his paralyzing ray gun at one of the automatons—only to watch in horror as the beam bounced harmlessly off its reinforced plating.

One of the automatons unleashed a barrage of cannon fire, forcing the team to scatter.

A second well-timed smoke bomb, this time thrown by Baroness Frost, gave them more cover.

Matthew and Phineas coordinated an attack on another automaton, targeting its exposed gears. Their combined efforts sent a jolt of electricity coursing through its system, causing it to stagger.

"We need backup!" Jedidiah shouted, his voice barely audible over the chaos.

Then—

As if in answer to his call, the roar of airship engines filled the sky.

The Inspiration descended rapidly, its sleek form cutting through the clouds.

At the helm stood Jonathan Blake, his expression grim and determined.

Edwin Bancroft leaned out from the side, directing Cogsworth, who stood ready to deploy, while Tom Miller manned the ship's Gatling guns.

The Inspiration fired a volley of precisely aimed shots, striking the automatons—yet the blasts merely bounced off their thick armor.

However, the attack created an opening for the team. Jonathan expertly guided the airship to a clearing before leaping down, Edwin, Cogsworth, and Tom close behind.

"Hope we're not too late to join the party!" Jonathan called out, brandishing a large wrench, ready for action.

Cogsworth, his brass frame repaired and polished, rushed toward an automaton, his mechanical limbs moving with startling agility.

One of the villainous automatons swung at him, but Cogsworth blocked the strike and retaliated with a blow that dislodged one of its armored plates.

"About time you showed up!" Phineas exhaled sharply, wiping soot from his goggles.

Tom, armed with a ray gun, fired at the second alternate Gearsoul, aiming for his chest. Even with the power turned as high as it would go, the blast wasn't strong enough to penetrate the thick leather vest. However, it sent him staggering backward—colliding into one of the towering automatons.

In the confusion, the villainous doppelgänger dropped his spiked mace.

The heavy weapon slammed into the ground.

A shockwave tore through the battlefield.

The force ripped through the terrain, sending jagged debris flying. His long coat snagged on a piece of shattered metal, tearing as he stumbled to regain his footing. The rip went straight through his vest and shirt, leaving his side vulnerable. He quickly adjusted his stance, but the momentary exposure did not go unnoticed.

Edwin, quick to read the battlefield, shouted, "Matthew! His side is exposed—take the shot!"

Colton didn't hesitate. Darting from cover, he leveled his paralyzing ray gun and fired. The beam struck true, hitting the unprotected flesh of the second alternate Gearsoul. The tall man immediately froze in place.

This left the Chronomechanism, momentarily unguarded, lay on the ground where the original Gearsoul had placed it.

Seraphina's sharp gaze zeroed in on the relic. Without hesitation, she dashed forward, her coat billowing behind her, and snatched it up. Holding it aloft, she turned toward the others, her expression a mix of triumph and cold calculation.

Lady Blackwood skillfully turned knobs on the device, causing a vortex to open directly behind the alternate Gearsoul.

"Push him back into the portal!" Seraphina commanded, her voice cutting through the chaos.

Tom and Edwin exchanged a knowing glance—

No words needed.

They ran.

The second alternate Gearsoul, still locked in paralysis, couldn't react.

Tom leaped first, legs coiling beneath him before shooting out in a flying double-footed kick.

Edwin followed half a second later, his timing flawless, mirroring the move.

Their combined force slammed into the alternate Gearsoul's chest—

The impact launched him backward.

He was sucked into the portal, disappearing in a burst of light and a rush of displaced air.

"One down!" Matthew shouted, his voice cutting through the lingering tension. He turned to Jedidiah, his eyes darting toward the fallen guards. "We need those rifles!"

The young entrepreneur nodded sharply and immediately broke into a run. Matthew followed close behind, the two of them sprinting toward the crumpled bodies of the masked guards. The ground trembled beneath their feet as one of the towering automatons lumbered toward them, its massive gears grinding ominously.

Matthew reached the first guard and yanked the atomic rifle from his slackened grip. The weapon was unfamiliar, but his fingers instinctively found the trigger and power mechanism. He barely spared the fallen figure a glance—until something odd caught his eye.

The sleeve of the guard's coat had torn during the fall, exposing not flesh—but polished brass plating.

Matthew's stomach dropped. "Jed—" he started.

Jedidiah had already pried the second rifle from the other fallen guard, his expression set with grim determination. But as he moved, something cold and metallic brushed his fingers. He hesitated, then pulled back the mask covering the man's face— only to reveal an unmoving, mechanical visage beneath.

Davenport's breath hitched. "They're—"

"Automatons," Matthew finished, his voice tight with shock.

For a fraction of a second, neither of them moved. The realization shifted everything. These weren't just guards—they were machines masquerading as men.

How could they not know?

Were the other two back on the Aetherwind mechanical as well?

But there was no time for questions now.

Jedidiah clenched his jaw, forcing himself to focus. "We'll deal with that later. Right now—" He hoisted the rifle and spun to face the advancing automaton. "We have bigger problems."

Matthew exhaled sharply and adjusted his grip on his own weapon. "Yeah. Let's take down the

Clockwork Conqueror first."

The two men took up defensive stances, standing side by side as they aimed their newly acquired weapons at the hulking mechanical construct bearing down on them.

Phineas' voice rang out from across the battlefield. "Aim for the joints! That'll slow it down!"

Matthew adjusted his aim, targeting the automaton's exposed knee joint. He pulled the trigger, and a brilliant beam of energy erupted from the rifle, striking the metal with pinpoint accuracy. The joint warped and sparked from the concentrated blast. The automaton stumbled, its balance momentarily compromised.

Jedidiah wasted no time, aiming for the creature's shoulder joint. Another crackling beam of energy shot forth, severing one of its massive arms. The automaton let out a mechanical roar, its stability faltering as it struggled to stay upright.

"Keep firing!" Matthew urged, his voice laced with adrenaline.

Together, he and Jedidiah unleashed a relentless barrage. Each shot chipped away at the automaton's structural integrity until, at last, with a thunderous crash, it collapsed onto the ground, its gears grinding to a halt.

The second automaton, its armor scorched and battered, lashed out in desperation, its massive limbs swinging wildly. But Jonathan and Cogsworth, working in perfect tandem, moved in to disable it. The towering mechanical warrior swung at them once again, but Cogsworth dodged with startling agility. Jonathan used his wrench to pry loose an essential power conduit, and within seconds, the massive automaton shuddered and collapsed, its systems sparking and groaning as it shut down for good.

"Only one automaton and two Gearsouls left!" Seraphina called out, her sharp voice rallying the group.

"Hold your ground!"

Phineas adjusted his goggles and glanced toward the spiked mace that had been left behind by the alternate Gearsoul. He gave an approving nod as he strode toward it, muttering under his breath, "Not quite my usual instrument, but it'll do."

Lady Blackwood twisted the dials on the Chronomechanism, intensifying the swirling vortex behind the first alternate Gearsoul. The fabric of space seemed to shudder as the portal's energy surged. Her voice rang out over the battlefield, unwavering and commanding. "The portal's ready —send him through!"

With a determined glint in his eye, Phineas sprinted forward, gripping the spiked mace tightly. He lifted it high above his head.

"My good man, let's see how you like this!" he bellowed before bringing the weapon down with all his might.

The ground trembled from the force of the impact, sending a powerful shockwave rippling through the dirt. The alternate Gearsoul, already struggling to regain his footing, staggered backward, arms flailing. The vortex behind him surged, its gravitational pull intensifying, dragging him toward its churning depths.

The doppelgänger let out a distorted, furious cry as he lost his balance. His body twisted violently in the air before the portal swallowed him whole.

With a final whoosh, the portal collapsed in on itself, leaving behind only silence and the faint scent of ozone.

Phineas, still leaning on the mace for support, let out a triumphant huff. "Two Clockwork Conquerors down!" He straightened, brushing dust from his coat. "I must admit, that was exhilarating. Perhaps I've missed my calling as a gladiator."

Jedidiah and Matthew exchanged a glance, shaking their heads. But despite the tension of the battle, small, appreciative grins tugged at their lips.

However, there was no time for celebration.

Lady Blackwood's voice cut through the fading noise of battle. "Only the original Ignatius left! Don't let him escape!"

All eyes snapped toward the Clockwork

Conqueror, who now stood alone on the battlefield. His imposing form remained rigid, his brass mask obscuring whatever emotions lurked beneath. Beside him, the final automaton, its towering frame gleaming in the pale light, took a protective stance beside its master.

Realizing he was now outnumbered, Gearsoul clenched his fists, his voice a furious growl. "Attack!"

The automaton lurched forward, its internal servos whining as it gained momentum. With each heavy stomp, the ground trembled beneath its weight. Its massive brass fists clenched, and the faint hum of its core energy vibrated through the clearing.

Phineas tightened his grip on the spiked mace, his eyes darting between Jedidiah and Matthew. "I hope you lads are ready!"

Jedidiah and Matthew nodded in unison, gripping their atomic rifles. On Phineas' signal, they opened fire. Twin beams of concentrated energy lashed out, striking the automaton's chest and shoulder. Sparks erupted as metal warped and cracked, but the hulking machine pressed forward, its optic sensors burning red.

"Not so fast!" Phineas shouted. He lifted the mace and brought it down with force, sending a shockwave rippling through the battlefield. The tremor disrupted the automaton's balance, causing it to stagger.

Jonathan, seizing the opportunity, called out to his mechanical companion. "Cogsworth, now!"

The mechanical man responded instantly, his bronze-plated frame a blur of movement as he charged forward. With astonishing speed and force, Cogsworth slammed into the automaton's side, his metal body colliding with a resounding crash.

The rogue automaton reeled, its internal gears grinding in protest. It swayed violently before its left knee buckled, sending it crashing down with a deafening metallic groan.

Cogsworth didn't hesitate. He followed up with a devastating shove, forcing the automaton's massive frame to topple backward. Its glowing optics flickered, its mechanical limbs twitching before finally falling still.

Phineas, still gripping the mace, let out a breath. "Well, that takes care of that."

With the automatons defeated, all focus turned to Ignatius Gearsoul.

Jedidiah stepped forward, holding his atomic rifle steady. His voice was calm but resolute. "Your forces are gone. It's over."

Gearsoul's brass mask tilted slightly, as if in defiance. His gloved hand tightened around his lightning rod. "You think this is over?" he snarled. Electricity crackled along the length of the weapon, the power growing dangerously unstable. "You've merely delayed the inevitable!"

Tom and Edwin exchanged a sharp glance. Without hesitation, they motioned to Jedidiah and Matthew, signaling them to toss their rifles.

Jedidiah and Matthew threw the weapons, and Tom and Edwin caught them mid-air before sprinting to flank Gearsoul.

Meanwhile, Van der Meer and Baroness Frost used smoke bombs and ray gun blasts to keep Gearsoul distracted. The battlefield became a haze of shifting shadows and electric arcs, the air thick with tension.

Edwin spotted the glowing energy core strapped to Gearsoul's back. "There it is!" he shouted.

Tom, already moving into position, nodded. "On my mark!"

They aimed together—then fired.

Twin beams of atomic energy sliced through the smoke and struck the power source for the Clockwork Conqueror's tesla rod. The core shattered, sending a cascade of sparks and energy discharges bursting from his back.

Gearsoul let out a strangled gasp, his body jerking violently as his weapon shorted out. His knees buckled, his coat smoking, and with a final shuddering step, he collapsed.

Jedidiah stepped forward, his paralyzing ray gun trained at Ignatius' unmasked face. "Now it's over."

The defeated Clockwork Conqueror lay still, his breath ragged. Cogsworth moved in and secured his arms, ensuring he couldn't escape.

Gearsoul let out a breathless chuckle, his metallic fingers twitching weakly. "You think you've won?" he sneered. "This is only the beginning."

Seraphina, ignoring him, carefully set the Chronomechanism onto a large stone. Her voice was clipped. "Save your speeches. You've lost."

The battlefield fell into silence, broken only by the faint hum of residual energy.

Phineas, still catching his breath, brushed soot from his vest and gently set the mace down. "Egads," he murmured. "We did it. We actually did it."

But Jedidiah's gaze remained fixed on the Chronomechanism.

"It's not over yet." His voice was quiet but firm. "That thing is too dangerous to leave intact."

Doctor Leopold Van der Meer and Baroness Evelina Frost wholeheartedly agreed.

Seraphina, however, stepped between them and the relic. Her usual commanding presence now carried something heavier—almost ominous.

"Dangerous? Yes." She placed her hands on her hips. "But also powerful. More powerful than any of you realize."

Matthew frowned, his instincts kicking in.

"What are you getting at, Lady Blackwood?"

Seraphina turned to face them, her eyes alight with something unfamiliar—ambition. "This device is the key to reshaping the world. To fixing the mistakes of the past. To securing my future... the future! Imagine what could be accomplished with its power."

Jedidiah's jaw tightened. "Accomplished by whom? And at what cost?"

Seraphina's tone sharpened, her eyes flashing with unchecked ambition. "By someone with the vision to wield it properly. Someone who understands its potential and won't squander it on petty fears of what *might* go wrong. Did you really think, after all I've gone through to reassemble this device, that I'm going to let you take it apart again?"

Phineas stepped forward, his expression darkening as the truth finally sank in. His voice was laced with disillusionment—the weight of betrayal evident. "You never wanted to protect the relic, did you?" he said, shaking his head. "You were after it the whole time—for your own selfish desires!"

Seraphina's smirk was unwavering. "Ignatius was a fool," she shot back. "He was never meant to wield such a powerful device. A weapon of this magnitude should only be in the hands of someone truly worthy of it."

Jedidiah crossed his arms, his jaw tightening. "And that person would happen to be you?" He already knew the answer.

Her gaze met his, unapologetic. "I knew Lord Gearsoul was the Clockwork Conqueror and behind the kidnappings," she continued smoothly. "I also knew he had confiscated almost all the pieces. I planned to steal the Chronomechanism for myself the moment it was assembled!"

"No one should have that kind of power," Jedidiah said, his voice calm but firm. "You said so yourself."

Her smirk returned, colder now, more calculating. "Ah, but you see, Mr. Davenport, I don't plan to wield this power alone."

She paused, her gaze dropping briefly to the Chronomechanism. A dangerous gleam flickered in her eyes.

Before anyone could react, Seraphina lunged forward.

Her fingers closed around the relic, gripping it tightly as she yanked it off the stone. Energy pulsed beneath her fingertips, the intricate gears and glowing core whirring to life.

Jedidiah realized the danger a second too late. "Lady Blackwood—!"

Seraphina turned to face him, a smirk tugging at her lips.

"Egads," Phineas muttered, taking a cautious

step forward. "You can't be serious!"

Her hand shot to her belt, drawing a sleek weapon—a compact energy pistol, its barrel glowing faintly. The air crackled around it, charged with power. She leveled the weapon at them, her expression unreadable but her intent unmistakable.

"Stand down."

Before anyone could stop her, she activated the Chronomechanism. Without warning, time suddenly seemed to pause, the world bathed in an eerie stillness. Only Jedidiah, Matthew, Phineas, and Seraphina remained unaffected.

Matthew's breath hitched as he took in the surreal scene, his voice tight with disbelief. "You've frozen everyone but us!"

Phineas, his scientific mind racing, adjusted his goggles with a grim expression. His keen eyes flicked between the relic and their surroundings, analyzing the anomaly as quickly as his mind could process it.

"She didn't freeze them," he corrected, his tone measured yet urgent. "She's frozen time!"

Jedidiah's brow furrowed, confusion evident in his voice. "How come we're unaffected?"

Phineas exhaled, rubbing his temple as he formulated an explanation. "We must have been close enough to the device when she activated it. That means we're trapped with her in this... pocket of time."

Matthew blinked, trying to grasp the enormity of the situation. "What?"

Phineas gestured around them. "Think of it like being inside a bubble."

"Enough!" Seraphina shouted, gripping the whirring relic as its intricate gears shifted and pulsed with a faint, ethereal light. Her voice echoed unnaturally, layered over itself from multiple points in time.

"This is only a sample of what it can do," she said smoothly. Her piercing gaze moved over them, weighing their reactions. "I'm offering the three of you a chance to join me."

Phineas' sharp eyes flicked to the relic, studying its mechanisms with both fascination and a trace of dread. He exhaled slowly, then exchanged a knowing glance with Jedidiah and Matthew.

The young entrepreneur nodded slightly, stepping forward, his voice steady. "You think we would ever join you in whatever plan you have to take over the world?"

Seraphina arched a brow, tilting her head ever so slightly. "It's better than the alternative."

Matthew folded his arms, his stance defiant. "Which is?"

She gave a mocking shrug, her voice coolly indifferent. "Oh, I don't know… perhaps I'll use it to travel back in time and prevent each of you from ever being born."

Jedidiah's expression didn't waver. "That won't work."

Seraphina narrowed her eyes. "And why not?"

He took another step forward, his words deliberate. "Because if you succeed in doing that, we wouldn't have been here to help you secure the pieces to assemble the Chronomechanism in the first place."

A brief flicker of hesitation crossed her face. It lasted only a second, but it was enough to distract her.

As she began to speak again, Matthew moved subtly, circling toward her flank, while Phineas' hands inched closer to the Chronomechanism.

"That's enough!" she shouted. "You're all coming with me!"

She adjusted a few knobs, and the device began to hum louder, gears grinding, dials shifting as energy surged through its core. Suddenly, a swirling vortex opened behind her. The air around them picked up, pulling anything close to it inside.

Lady Blackwood glanced down toward the leather backpack resting at her feet—one she had placed there earlier, now partially unbuckled. She couldn't reach it without lowering her weapon, so instead, her cold eyes landed on Jedidiah.

"Pick up the bag," she ordered. "Now!"

Jedidiah's jaw clenched, but he knew better than to hesitate. Slowly, he stepped forward, hands steady as he bent to grab the pack.

The moment he lifted it off the ground, the flap flew back—

A blur of black fur exploded from the bag.

The same black cat from earlier shot out like a cannonball, her small frame twisting midair as she latched onto Seraphina's arm with her claws.

"WHAT—?!" Seraphina's voice broke in startled disbelief.

The cat's sharp green eyes gleamed as she hissed and bit down on Lady Blackwood's cloth sleeve just above her gloves. With a yelp, Seraphina flinched—just long enough for her ray gun to slip from her grip and clatter to the ground.

Matthew tensed, his muscles coiling in preparation. Jedidiah reached out instinctively, grabbing at Matthew's arm, but he was already moving. In a blur of motion, he leaped forward and tackled her around the legs, the force dislodging the relic from her grasp. She stumbled backward, her cry of rage quickly swallowed by the vortex.

Professor Hargroves instinctively dove for the device and managed to snatch it before it hit the ground.

Jedidiah reached out to grab the black cat before she could be pulled in with Lady Blackwood, but it had other plans. She leaped onto his shoulder and ran down his back, her claws digging in as she slid off, landing gracefully on the ground.

With a quick turn of a knob, the vortex suddenly closed. The last words heard were Seraphina shouting, "We'll meet again, at some other place in time!"

Suddenly, time resumed with a shudder. The world, once eerily silent, became alive with the sounds of everyone talking at once. The team gathered around, asking what had happened to Lady Blackwood.

"We'll explain later..." Jedidiah remarked as he turned to look for the black cat who had just saved their lives. But she was gone.

"What do we do with this?" Matthew asked, placing a hand on top of the Chronomechanism, his voice heavy with exhaustion.

Jedidiah took it from Professor Hargroves, his grip firm. "We dismantle it, like I said before!"

Phineas nodded solemnly. "Agreed."

As they turned toward the airships, a faint echo of Seraphina's voice whispered through the air. "We'll meet again... some other place in time."

The team exchanged uneasy glances. As they walked away from the battle-scarred field, the weight of what had just transpired settled over them—heavy, uncertain, and far from over.

The Aftermath

A few days later, the group of adventurers gathered at Davenport Ranch. They stood in the recently redecorated main room, where Phineas' flair for Victorian elegance shone brightly. Rich mahogany furnishings, vibrant patterned rugs, and golden accents adorned the space. The fire crackled in the ornate hearth, casting flickering shadows across the faces of Jedidiah Davenport, Matthew Colton, Phineas B. Hargroves, Jonathan Blake, and Baroness Evelina Frost.

Tom Miller and Edwin Bancroft were absent, having volunteered to pilot the Aetherwind and escort Gearsoul, along with Montgomery and his gang, into custody. Their grumbling protests had been quickly muffled by the hum of the airship's engines as it lifted off, carrying them away under the close guard of the two remaining masked automatons. For now, at least, that threat was contained.

Doctor Leopold Van der Meer lingered near the window, his posture stiff as he gazed out over the sprawling Kansas landscape. Earlier that evening, he had formally announced his decision to step down from the Order of the Clockwork Octopus. His voice had carried both regret and resolve—a clear indication that he believed it was the right course of action.

"Say, Jonathan," Phineas spoke up. "Now that all the excitement is over, how about telling us what happened after you left us at Lake Simcoe and how you happened to find us on Octopus Island?"

"Well, now, that's an interesting story—one that could probably make an exciting book." Jonathan took a sip of coffee, exhaling as he leaned against the fireplace. "The outlaws we were chasing got a good head start, and we almost gave up on finding them," he muttered.

"But you were in an airship, and they were in a steamboat," Matthew reminded him.

"That's true, but by the time we caught up with the boat, they had already abandoned it. It was drifting free just off the shoreline."

"Well, at least we'll be able to return it to its owner, and I won't have to—" Jedidiah said thankfully but was cut off mid-sentence by Blake.

"About that..." Jonathan took another sip of coffee and sheepishly added, "We didn't know it was abandoned until after I unloaded a whole round from the Gatling gun on it."

"Let me guess..." Davenport began.

"It's at the bottom of the lake..." Blake finished.

"Guess I've bought myself a fishing boat." Jedidiah laughed despite himself.

"So how did you find them?" Phineas asked impatiently.

"I've still got a few connections in the underworld from when I was dealing in stolen goods."

"Wasn't that just around a month ago?" Matthew asked with a smirk.

Jonathan chose to ignore that remark and continued. "I paid a few people I've worked with in the past for some information and discovered the men we were after had been spotted less than three miles away."

"They were holed up in an old logging camp. They'd barricaded themselves in pretty well too— figured they could hold out." Jonathan paused a moment to smirk. "They didn't count on Cogsworth, though."

Matthew leaned forward. "Let me guess—he walked right through the barricade?"

The older man chuckled. "Close enough. I told him to knock, and he just punched the entire door in."

Phineas nearly choked on his tea. "Not one for

subtleties, is he?"

"While they were busy blasting Cogsworth in vain with their paralyzing ray guns, Tom, Edwin, and I managed to get the drop on them! They didn't last long—especially after our mechanical friend got his hands on them."

"Gosh!" Matthew exclaimed, hanging on every word.

Jonathan shook his head with a grin, then turned serious. "The real surprise came after we rounded them up. We had thought they were lying about working with Gearsoul."

Jedidiah frowned. "They weren't?"

Jonathan set his mug down with a soft clink. "They were telling the truth about not knowing he was the Clockwork Conqueror. At least they stuck to their story about only buying those futuristic weapons from him."

"Let me guess." Jedidiah's eyes narrowed. "After we relieved them of their ray guns, they went back to him for more."

Jonathan nodded. "After our run-in with them in the cave, they were desperate. They found their way back to Gearsoul and begged him for more. Only this time, he didn't sell them outright."

Matthew's expression darkened. "Let me guess. He made them do something in exchange."

"Exactly." Jonathan crossed his arms. "Told them they could have all the weapons they wanted

—if they did him a favor first."

Jedidiah exhaled sharply. "Lake Simcoe!"

Jonathan nodded. "He ordered them to attack you, Matt, and Phineas. They were supposed to get Seraphina's piece of the relic and deliver it to him on Octopus Island."

Silence settled over the room.

Phineas took a sip of tea. "Egads. The man's been playing chess this whole time, and we didn't even know we were on the board."

Matthew scowled. "So where are they now?"

The older man smirked. "Locked up tight. The Canadian Mounties were happy to take them off our hands. Turns out they were wanted in Canada as well as the States. They've been crossing the border and committing all sorts of heinous crimes in our northern neighbors' territory."

Jonathan took another sip of coffee and then shot Jedidiah a pointed look. "They truly had no idea what they had gotten themselves into."

Jedidiah nodded, his mind turning. "Gearsoul was using them as disposable pawns."

Jonathan leaned forward. "And from what they told us... they weren't the only ones."

A heavy silence filled the room.

Phineas sighed, shaking his head. "Well, isn't that comforting?"

Moments later, Baroness Frost stood up and walked to the center of the room, her commanding presence drawing every eye. She cleared her throat, her piercing gaze sweeping over the gathered group. It was clear that something significant was about to be said.

"I have an announcement to make," she began. "The Order of the Clockwork Octopus has endured a great upheaval. Betrayal, loss, and failure have left it fractured. But it is not broken." She paused for effect, letting her words settle before continuing. "As the sole remaining steward of the Order, I have resolved to rebuild it—with individuals who have proven their worth. In fact, there is one individual here I wish to invite as one of the Order's newest members."

Phineas straightened his waistcoat and nudged Jedidiah with a sly grin. "Well, I suppose I should prepare myself for the honor."

"You think it's you?" Matthew Colton asked, raising an eyebrow.

"My dear boy," Phineas replied, clapping a hand on Matthew's shoulder, "who else could it be? The Baroness clearly recognizes genius when she sees it."

With exaggerated confidence, he stepped forward, smoothing his waistcoat as he prepared to accept his new title.

Baroness Frost, however, took a step to the side and walked right past him.

The eccentric older man froze mid-stride, his

jaw dropping as he turned to watch her approach Jedidiah Davenport.

"Egads!" he exclaimed. "The Baroness is clearly suffering from trauma-induced impaired vision. She missed me entirely!"

Matthew clapped him on the back with a laugh. "Or maybe she has perfect vision and—"

"My dear boy, if you don't stop talking, I'm going to make you honor your wager and eat your hat." Professor Hargroves spoke to his young friend directly while continuing to watch the Baroness approach Jedidiah.

Matthew Colton immediately stopped talking.

"Mr. Davenport," Baroness Frost spoke again, her voice firm yet warm, "your courage, ingenuity, and unwavering commitment to justice make you the ideal candidate to help guide the Order into a new era."

She stepped forward and presented him with the pocket watch she had taken from Lord Ignatius Gearsoul. Its intricate octopus design gleamed in the firelight.

Jedidiah stared at it in surprise. "Me? But I'm no aristocrat or social giant like you and the others. I'm just a plain, simple ranch owner."

"You also own and operate one of the largest freight companies around," Matthew chimed in, his tone full of pride.

The Baroness smiled. "The Order needs a

steady hand—someone with vision and practicality. It needs you."

The group erupted into thunderous applause as Jedidiah accepted the pocket watch and the position, his expression a mix of humility and pride.

"If you believe I'm the right man for the task," he said solemnly, "I'll do my best to live up to the honor."

The Baroness inclined her head. "Together, we will ensure the Order rises stronger than ever."

Just as everyone began to congratulate Jed, a panicked voice suddenly rang out from the other side of the house.

"Help! Somebody stop this monster!"

Jonathan Blake turned toward the commotion, his expression shifting from satisfaction to mild concern. "Uh-oh. It sounds like Cogsworth is still malfunctioning from that stroll he took across the bottom of the lake." He pulled a large wrench from his hip pocket and rushed toward the kitchen.

Inside, he found Pat Bennington standing in the middle of what looked like a war zone—covered head to toe in flour, his shirt now a patchwork of stains from various sauces. Broken dishes littered the floor, dough stuck to the ceiling, and a pot clanged ominously as it rolled to a stop near the door.

"Somebody stop this overgrown tin can!" Pat

shouted, dodging a flying ladle that narrowly missed his head.

Jonathan froze, his eyes widening at the sight. "What in blazes is happening?"

At the counter, the automaton's mechanical hands moved in a blur, alternating between tossing ingredients into the air and smashing them down with unnecessary force. A trail of batter splattered against the wall behind him as he hummed a cheerful yet disjointed tune.

Pat wiped some of the flour dust off his face. "If this is your idea of help, I'd hate to see what sabotage looks like!"

Jonathan sighed. "It's the water damage from Lake Simcoe for sure." He rolled up his sleeves and approached Cogsworth cautiously.

The automaton didn't stop throwing food, even as it tilted its head in a jerky, unnatural manner.

"Do... do... do you re... require assistance, Mister Blake?" it asked, its voice warbling slightly, punctuated by mechanical sputters.

"More like I require a bath," Jonathan muttered as an egg was smashed into his face. "Hold still!"

He tightened a bolt on Cogsworth's shoulder and gave a quick twist to one of the dials on its chest panel. The automaton jerked once, then straightened, its movements suddenly smooth and precise.

Jonathan wiped his hands on a rag. "That should

hold him for now. I'll get my tools and do a full tuneup after dinner."

"What dinner?" Pat gestured wildly around the room. "I know I've always bragged that my floors were clean enough to eat off, but this is ridiculous!"

Jonathan chuckled as he shook his head. "Well, I'm sure you'll figure something out." Glancing back at the automaton, he added, "If he gets rowdy again, just offer him some tea. That always calms him down."

Pat's expression darkened. "Oh sure, I'll offer him some tea. Maybe whip up a batch of crumpets to go with it..." He paused as he heard laughter from the other room. "I should just sweep all this mess up, put it on plates, and feed it to them hooraying out there."

Just as he was about to clean up, a faint pawing at the kitchen door caught his attention.

Frowning, Pat wiped the flour from his hands and walked over. When he opened it, his face immediately lit up.

Sitting on the threshold, cool as you please, was a black cat wearing a top hat, goggles, and a vest. She blinked up at him with those sharp green eyes, her tail curling lazily around her paws.

"Velvet!" Pat chuckled, crouching down. "I was wondering if you managed to get back aboard the Phoenix without anyone seeing you."

The cat let out a soft, amused trill—as if to say,

of course, I did.

Pat stood, shaking his head. "Sneaky as ever. Hang on." He moved to the pantry and pulled out a small tin. After a moment of rummaging, he found what he was looking for—a small feeding bowl with a looped handle.

Setting it down in front of her, he grinned. "Be sure to share that with Dottie and Panther in the barn, you hear?"

Velvet picked up the bowl with her teeth, turned, and trotted off into the night—her tail flicking in that distinctly smug way of hers.

Pat called after her, shaking his head. "Be sure to tell me all about how you helped Jed and the others out later!"

Still grinning to himself, he closed the door and reached for a broom. Just as he did, he heard a faint whirring sound behind him. Slowly, he turned to find the mechanical man standing perfectly still, its glowing red eyes locked on him.

"Uh… nice Cogsworth," Pat said nervously, backing away as the automaton took a single, deliberate step forward.

The whirring grew louder, punctuated by the soft clank of shifting gears.

Then, with a metallic screech, its arm began to raise—a spatula still clutched in its mechanical hand.

Pat gulped audibly. "Jed... Jed... Jed!!!!"

Velvet picked up the bowl with her teeth,
turned, and trotted off into the night—her tail
flicking in that distinctly smug way of hers.

****

The adventures of Jedidiah Davenport have only just begun. Prepare for an epic clash in The Mechanical Rebellion: A Jedidiah Davenport Adventure. As humanity stands on the brink of a war like no other, Jedidiah must rally his allies to face the rising tide of automatons gone rogue. Can they restore peace before it's too late? What truths lie hidden within the gears of rebellion? Join us for the next thrilling chapter of Jedidiah's saga and find out!

And for those of you curious about the mysterious top-hat-wearing black cat, don't miss Steampunk Velvet: A Victorian Cat and her Amazing Adventures. Velvet embarks on her own escapades full of clever schemes, curious discoveries, and a few surprising ties to Jedidiah's world. Dive into a whimsical steampunk tale from a whole new perspective!

Current titles in the
Jedidiah Davenport Adventure Series

Coming in 2025